ALL OUR
BEAUTIFUL
GOODBYES

HISTORICAL ROMANCE

The American Heiress Series

To Marry the Duke
An Affair Most Wicked
My Own Private Hero
Love According to Lily
Portrait of a Lover
Surrender to a Scoundrel

The Pembroke Palace Series

In My Wildest Fantasies
The Mistress Diaries
When a Stranger Loves Me
Married By Midnight
A Kiss Before the Wedding—A Pembroke Palace Short Story
Seduced at Sunset

The Highlander Series

Captured by the Highlander
Claimed by the Highlander
Seduced by the Highlander
Return of the Highlander
Taken by the Highlander
The Rebel—A Highland Short Story

The Royal Trilogy

Be My Prince
Princess in Love
The Prince's Bride

Dodge City Brides Trilogy

Mail Order Prairie Bride
Tempting the Marshal
Taken by the Cowboy

STAND-ALONE HISTORICAL ROMANCE

Adam's Promise

ALL OUR BEAUTIFUL GOODBYES

A NOVEL

JULIANNE MACLEAN

LAKE UNION
PUBLISHING

Text copyright © 2025 by Julianne MacLean Publishing Inc.
All rights reserved.

Published by Lake Union Publishing, Seattle

www.apub.com

Amazon, the Amazon logo, and Lake Union Publishing are trademarks of Amazon.com, Inc., or its affiliates.

ISBN-13: 9781662519116 (paperback)
ISBN-13: 9781662519109 (digital)

Cover design by Caroline Teagle Johnson
Cover image: © Abigail Miles / Arcangel; © Mael Vincent / Getty;
© Karl Hendon / Getty; © Jane Khomi / Getty; © Agencia / Stocksy

Printed in the United States of America

For my mother, Noel

PROLOGUE

On the night of May 8, 1946, a wild and terrible gale whipped up fifty-foot waves and swept a British merchant ship off course, thrusting her hard and fast toward the dangerous shores of Sable Island.

Crescent shaped, like a narrow sliver of the moon, Sable is remote and desolate—a burial ground for hundreds of wrecked ships, their wave-battered remains concealed beneath the ever-shifting shoals. From time to time—after a storm that leaves the island's landscape forever changed—a long-forgotten vessel emerges like a skeleton from a shallow grave.

Yet Sable is also a place of rare beauty, an island of sand and grass where wild horses run free and a small, close-knit community of residents maintains two lighthouses, a telegraph station, and a lifesaving establishment to rescue shipwreck survivors from the Atlantic.

The British ship that fought those giant swells on the evening of May 8 was no stranger to turmoil at sea. She and her captain had served heroically in World War II. They'd patrolled trade routes in search of German U-boats and provided rescue support during one of the largest convoy battles of the war.

Why—exactly one year after VE Day celebrations—would wind and water thrust her so cruelly and undeservedly upon such treacherous shores? It's a question that has no answer—because nature answers to no one. She simply does what she wants.

On the island, however, people fight for some semblance of order amid the chaos of their surroundings. To preserve life and provide an oasis of calm, they willingly go to battle with the waves.

PART ONE

THE ISLAND

CHAPTER 1

The storm had been raging all night, violently, without mercy. At dawn, the wind continued to howl. Waves thundered and pounded onto the beaches.

Emma Clarkson, the superintendent's daughter, sat on a stool in front of the mirror at her vanity. Feet flat on the floor, knees pressed tightly together, she held a letter on her lap and ran the pad of her thumb over her name on the envelope. She felt a mixture of pride and dread, the emotions alternating, taking brief turns. It had been three days since the letter arrived on the supply ship *Argyle*, but she'd told no one of its contents. Not even her father.

Emma, an only child, was now a woman of twenty-one and fully cognizant of the fact that she'd always been doted upon. She and her father were a close pair because her mother had died in childbirth a year into the marriage, which had begun with the adventure of moving to Sable Island during her final trimester. They'd intended to stay five years and save enough money to return to Halifax on the mainland, where their children would receive a proper education. But the death of Emma's mother had been a terrible blow to her father, who had lost all interest in starting over in a new home. Instead, he chose to raise his precious daughter on the island.

Emma could count on one hand the number of times she'd visited the mainland. Three, to be precise. Everything about those trips was imprinted on her brain—the blaring car horns and engines, the crowds that gathered in the Public Gardens for concerts at the bandstand, and the mouthwatering aromas from downtown restaurants. For Emma, it was like traveling into the future or to another planet.

This was why she knew that she needed to cease stalling, go straight downstairs, and tell her father about the letter.

Wouldn't it be wonderful if he could be happy for her?

The windowpanes trembled in a furious gust of wind, and the roof timbers creaked.

Oh, what a dreamer she was.

~

The wind was still thrashing around the house when Emma finally entered her father's study. He was seated behind his desk under the light of a single lamp, focused on some documents in front of him. She waited until he turned a page before she cleared her throat.

His eyes lifted. "Emma. Sweetheart. What are you doing awake? The sun's barely up."

"Who could sleep in this storm?" she asked.

He removed his glasses, laid them on top of his papers, and sat back in his chair. "At least it's rain and not snow. Summer can't come soon enough."

"Agreed." She moved to the window and drew back the curtain to look out at the ashen sky, the driving rain, and the marram grass on the high dune, whipping wildly in the wind. All of it together mirrored the storm of dread in her belly. For a moment she wanted to slink back upstairs and return to bed, but she'd been putting this off long enough, so she turned and faced her father. "I need to talk to you about something."

He gazed up at her with uncertainty, then stood and switched off the desk lamp. "All right. Let's go sit in the great room."

Emma led the way and chose a spot on the sofa directly across from her father, who took a seat in his big brown leather armchair. She gave him a moment to settle in, then willed herself to speak assertively, because she knew what she wanted. It was time that he knew it too.

"A few months ago," she told him, "I sent an application to Dalhousie University for the psychology program, and I was accepted."

With a sudden look of confusion, he frowned. "I'm sorry?"

Emma pushed on. "I've been accepted to Dalhousie, and I want to go. It starts in September." She paused uneasily. "I'm hoping you'll help me with the tuition."

The wind gusted through the gutters, and the whole house shuddered. Glancing briefly at the ceiling, Emma worried that the roof might blow off at any second.

Meanwhile, her father was tapping his forefinger on the armrest of his chair and quietly mulling over the news she'd just delivered. Emma suspected he was most troubled by the fact that she had taken such action without discussing it with him first and had followed through behind his back. She felt an urgent need to explain.

"I didn't tell you because I knew you wouldn't like the idea and you'd worry about me leaving the island. You'd lose sleep for months about something that might not even happen if I wasn't accepted." She sat up a little straighter and raised her chin. "Besides that, you'd spend the whole time trying to talk me out of it, and I just wanted to see what would happen if I applied."

He spoke with dismay. "You've never said anything about wanting to go to university. Why wouldn't you share that with me?"

"I just told you why."

His expression grew strained. "But I thought you were happy here. This is your home. And you've had a better education than most."

"I am happy," she maintained. "I've loved growing up here, and you've been the best teacher I could ever ask for. But you know how much I enjoy learning . . . and you know that I've always been interested in animal behavior." She'd been studying the wild horses of Sable Island since she was ten years old. "I feel the same way about human behavior, but how can I learn about that when my world is so small? There are never more than forty people living here at a time, and we're spread out across miles. I'm tired of learning everything from books."

Her father scrutinized her expression. "How long have you been thinking about this?"

"About a year, I suppose," she confessed. "But with the war on, it seemed like a pipe dream. I couldn't possibly fathom leaving the island then. But the war is over now, and I want to get away."

Her father exhaled harshly, as if she had sucker punched him in the gut.

"Not from *you*," she quickly amended. "That's the hardest part of this, the one thing that holds me back because . . ."

Emma paused. How could she tell him that she feared he might become lonely or depressed?

"Because you mean everything to me," she said tactfully.

"I'd never want to hold you back," he insisted. "But I don't want you to make a mistake either."

"How would it be a mistake?"

All at once, she felt contentious. It was no surprise that her father was against the idea—she knew he would be—and this was exactly what she'd been dreading since the letter arrived: An argument that would require her to stand up to him, to disregard his wishes, and to disobey him if he laid down the law. And ultimately to disappoint and hurt him.

He pointed at the window. "You have no idea about the world out there, Emma. It's a dangerous place, even during peacetime. Especially for a young woman alone. You've lived a sheltered life here among good people, and you don't know what evils exist beyond these shores." His tone was growing increasingly intense.

Emma swallowed hard. "Now you're just trying to scare me."

"I'm trying to educate you," he said, "as I've always done—and to help you appreciate the life you have here."

"I do appreciate it," she argued, "which is why this decision has been so difficult. And I won't pretend that I'm not nervous about going away, because I am. What if I get there and I hate living in the city, or I fail in the program? I've never gone to a real school before."

"You're intelligent and disciplined," he said. "You won't fail in the classroom. That's not what concerns me."

"What is it, then?" she asked, feeling her confidence wane.

His cheeks reddened. "Like I said, it's a scary world out there. I don't want anything bad to happen to you. If you were hurt somehow, in any way, I'd never forgive myself for letting you go."

There it was. The truth at last.

Emma's heart softened, and she moved to kneel on the floor in front of him. She took both his hands in hers. "Nothing bad will happen, and I'll write every day. When the *Argyle* arrives, you'll have enough letters to keep you reading for a month."

He looked down at their linked hands. "I don't want to lose you."

"I know," she gently replied, "but I can't stay here forever. I need to live my own life."

"But you could have a good life *here*," he persisted pleadingly. "I don't know why you won't consider Frank O'Reilly. He's obviously in love with you."

Frank was the chief wireless operator, who had taken up residence on Sable in '44. He was young and handsome, and every woman of every age on the island had developed a crush on him the day he'd leaped out of the surfboat. Even Emma had felt exhilarated at the sight of him. But after a few evenings in his presence during her father's Saturday socials, the infatuation had been short lived.

"I don't like his arrogance," she said.

"He's not arrogant," her father explained. "He only appears that way because he wants to impress you. And you said yourself that you're happy here. Wouldn't you like to start a family and raise your children on this little slice of heaven?"

Emma didn't want to get into an argument with her father about the so-called virtues of Sable Island. It was like banging her head against a wall.

She rose to her feet and returned to the sofa. "Please, Papa. I want to go to university. It's important to me."

Another powerful blast of wind from the north lashed against the house, and when her father offered no reply, Emma sighed in defeat.

"Maybe we should talk about this another time," she said, "after you've had a chance to think about it."

He took a breath to respond when the telephone rang in the kitchen. They were both startled by the interruption, and her father rose to answer it.

"Main Station," he said. He listened for a few seconds and frowned. "Where did you say? The west bar. How far out? I see." He glanced briefly at Emma. "Sound the alarm at all stations, and get the crews out there with the lifeboats. Every minute counts. I'll meet you at the boathouse."

He hung up the phone and crossed the kitchen toward his yellow slicker on the coat-tree by the door.

"There's a ship grounded on the west bar," he said.

"Oh, dear Lord." Emma was instantly engulfed by a sense of panic. "I'll get dressed and help Mrs. McKenna load the cart. We'll bring blankets and hot tea."

With a rush of adrenaline, she dashed up the stairs, leaving all thoughts of her own future behind.

CHAPTER 2

Leaning into the fierce wind, Emma trudged across the sandy station yard toward the McKennas' house, where Abigail, the meteorologist's wife, was hitching the horse to the broad-wheeled wagon.

"I'm here to help!" Emma shouted over the roar of the surf beyond the dunes.

Abigail peered up from beneath the hood of her raincoat. A gust of wind blew the hood back, and her brown hair went wild in all directions. "It took you long enough! Go inside and get my first aid kit and the large thermos on the kitchen table. I've already loaded the blankets." She returned to the task of hooking the leather pull straps to the harness while the horse tossed its head in the driving wind.

Emma quickly went inside and found the items on the table. She picked up the thermos and first aid kit but noticed a full bottle of whiskey on a shelf over the refrigerator. Deciding it might come in handy, she fetched it and stuffed it into the first aid bag, then hurried out the door.

Abigail was seated on the wagon bench, gathering up the reins.

Emma placed the items in the back and shouted, "That's everything! I'll saddle Willow and follow you!" She watched the wagon drive off, then ran to the barn.

~

Beneath the broody, gray sky, Emma rode Willow out of the station yard, across the heath, and eventually onto North Beach, where giant foaming breakers crashed and roared. The horizon had been swallowed whole by dense, dark clouds that rolled and curled in fury. The wind was most ferocious on the beach, but it was the fastest route, so Emma kicked in her heels and urged Willow into a flying gallop toward the western tip of the island. She overtook Abigail on the way.

When at last she reached the rescue operations, she slowed Willow to a halt and took in the situation.

Her father's Jeep—the only motorized vehicle on the island—was parked at the edge of the high dune. Two horse-drawn boat wagons had been unloaded and the surfboats successfully launched.

Emma's father stood at the water's edge with his binoculars, his slicker whipping in the wind as he observed the stranded ship in the distance. It was at least a mile offshore, lying on its side, half-submerged, while violent breakers battered its hull and washed over the bridge. The crews in both lifeboats were rowing hard to reach it, riding up and down massive twenty-foot swells.

Emma dismounted and led Willow across the sand to her father. "Abigail is on her way," she told him. "She has blankets, hot tea, and her first aid kit. I threw in a bottle of whiskey at the last minute."

"Good thinking." He handed the binoculars to her, and she raised them to look.

"Any idea how many souls on board?" she asked.

"Not yet. I only spotted one member of the crew waving at us from the portside rail when we first arrived, but I haven't seen anyone since. They must be inside, taking shelter."

Emma refocused the lenses and examined the wreck, which appeared to be a commercial cargo ship. She searched from bow to stern and back again. "I don't see anyone now." She swung the binoculars' field of view to locate the two lifeboat crews still making their way to the wreck. They rode up a giant swell, disappeared over the other side, and reappeared seconds later, ascending the steep slope of another.

Emma handed the binoculars back to her father. "Why didn't the captain order the launch of their own lifeboats?"

"I believe they tried. A boat washed ashore around Station Number Two with no one in it. That's what alerted the patrols to a wreck."

"I hope no one perished trying to make it," Emma said.

"We'll find out when we bring the others in, but we've seen no bodies yet."

It was a macabre conversation, but Emma understood the dark realities of life on Sable Island. Since childhood, she'd witnessed more than her share of old bones rising out of the dunes. And there was a disturbing collection of skulls on display in the boat shed. When she was young, she'd had nightmares about such things, but she was over that now.

"Can I look again?" she asked.

Her father offered the binoculars, and she zoned in on the wreck. "It's British. Probably three thousand tons."

"That was about my estimate," he said. "Two hundred and fifty feet. Steam engine."

Philip McKenna, the weather station chief, came running to join them. He panted heavily as he spoke. "Frank finally got through to the coast guard. He's waiting for more information, but I doubt they can send help anytime soon. They'll have to wait for the storm to let up."

"I expected as much," Emma's father replied. "For now, we'll just have to rely on ourselves."

Philip looked through his own set of binoculars. "They're almost there."

Abigail finally arrived with the blankets and supplies. Emma hoped they'd be able to put them to good use.

"They've made it!" her father shouted, still watching. "There's a crewman on the deck, and he's thrown a rope down. I see others climbing out of the bridge. They're clinging to the rails."

"Thank goodness." Emma laid a hand over her heart and said a silent prayer that every soul on board would make it safely to shore.

~

Watching the ordeal from the beach became a nightmare with no end. The two lifeboats had been lashed to the steamship, but with every powerful swell, they were thrust mercilessly against the steel hull. The men attempting to abandon ship held on to the ropes and rails for dear life as they were knocked about by the waves. One man, about to leap into a lifeboat, slipped from the deck and plunged into the sea, but by God's grace, he was pulled to safety by a crewman in the second lifeboat.

At last, the two boats began the treacherous journey back to shore. The trip seemed to take forever, while the thunder of the foaming waves on the beach made it difficult to think, talk, or breathe.

When the lifeboats finally approached, Philip waded into the surf and helped drag the first vessel onto the beach. The second followed close behind, and all the men spilled out. Those who had come from the wreck fell to their knees in gratitude, some digging their fingers into the wet sand. A few wept, others laughed, but all were thankful to have been rescued from the frigid water of the North Atlantic.

Emma and Abigail moved quickly and covered each man with a dry woolen blanket. One stood up and grabbed hold of Emma. He hugged her and sobbed. "Thank you, miss! Thank you!"

Her father approached and spoke in her ear. "You should fetch that bottle of whiskey."

"Right away." She hurried to Abigail's wagon.

Her father helped one man to his feet. "What's your name, son?"

"Billy Perkins." He was tall and lanky with a space between his two front teeth and spoke with a cockney accent. "I'm just a cook."

"That's fine, Billy. My name is John Clarkson, and I'm superintendent of this island. Can you tell me . . . Is this all of you?"

Billy pulled the gray blanket more snugly about his shoulders and regarded John warily. "I'm not sure, sir."

By now Abigail was beginning to serve hot tea to the survivors. Emma returned from the wagon and followed behind her, adding a splash of whiskey to each cup.

Her father addressed the whole group. "Who else is out there?"

No one spoke.

Emma turned toward the wrecked ship. Surely, it couldn't withstand the punishing forces of those waves much longer. If there was anyone else on board, they'd be done for.

Billy's teeth were chattering, and panic filled his eyes, as if he were about to face harsh discipline.

"Someone speak!" her father shouted.

One man finally volunteered. "Captain Harris refused to abandon his ship, sir."

Her father stared at the man incredulously. "And you left him behind?"

"Those were his orders."

Emma looked to her father. "Why in the world would anyone want to stay on that doomed ship?"

Her father pointed at another man. "You, sir. What's your name?"

He quickly rose to his feet. "Davey Parker."

"What's your ship's cargo?"

Emma understood her father's reasoning. Perhaps there was something valuable on board.

"It ain't the cargo," Davey replied. "A crewman was swept overboard, and the captain stayed behind to keep searchin' for him."

"But we all knew there was no hope," another said. "We saw him go overboard three hours ago."

Emma approached Davey. "But your captain believed there was a chance?"

"I doubt it. I think it was his sense of duty. He's a proud man, determined to go down with his ship."

Emma locked eyes with her father. "We can't just leave him out there."

Her father glanced back at the rescue crew, who sat exhausted on the beach. "I don't know if they're up to it."

One of the boat-wagon horses whinnied and shook himself in the harness, rattling the chains and buckles.

"We can't just let him die," Emma argued.

"We tried to talk him into coming with us," Billy insisted. "But he wouldn't hear of it. And I'll tell you right now . . ." He pointed at the ocean. "Going back out there would be a fool's errand. More good men will end up dead!"

"It's not a fool's errand," Emma replied. "It's our sole purpose here. We're a rescue station." She turned to her father again. "We have to try."

He turned to the water and raised his binoculars again. For a full minute he studied the swells and breakers as they struck the ship. At last, thankfully, he nodded in agreement and strode to the lifesaving crew, who had been watching and listening to the exchange. Emma followed.

"It's a lot to ask," her father said, "but are any of you willing to go out there again and bring the captain back?"

They sat in silence, knees hugged to chests, shivering.

Joseph, the crew captain, got to his feet. "If we go, and he still refuses to get off . . ."

"Then I suggest you remove him by force!" Emma shouted over the roar of the ocean. "God knows what he's been through! He might not be in his right mind!"

Her father nodded. "I need four volunteers."

No one stepped up, so Emma raised her hand. "I'll go."

There was a sudden communal shout of protest as six men leaped to their feet.

"Now we're talking," Joseph said. "Larry, you're the biggest. I could use your muscle."

~

While Philip and Abigail drove the shipwreck survivors back to Main Station to be fed and housed, Emma remained on the beach with her father to watch the second rescue attempt.

When, at last, the crew reached the ship and lashed the boat to the south side of the bow, they found some shelter from the breakers.

"What's happening?" Emma asked, her breath coming short, her heart pounding against her rib cage.

"Joseph just climbed aboard," her father replied. "He's entering the bridge."

Emma waited with bated breath for more information. Seconds ticked by like minutes, minutes like hours. The salty spray blew relentlessly off the water, and Emma gathered her coat collar tighter about her neck and sniffled from the cold.

"They have him!" her father shouted. "He's getting into the lifeboat!"

"He's not resisting?" Emma asked.

Her father watched for a few more seconds. "He appears compliant."

"Is there anyone else? The missing crewman?"

"It doesn't appear so."

He handed the binoculars to Emma while the men on the beach cheered. She focused on the lifeboat, which was no easy task as it crested steep swells like mountaintops and descended into the troughs, out of view. Where was the captain? At last, she spotted him seated at the stern, hunched over, his head bowed, hugging himself, probably chilled to the bone.

She and her father waited anxiously, in grim silence, for the lifeboat to reach shore. Again, minutes felt like hours.

"Damn!" Her father lowered his binoculars. "They've capsized!"

Emma strode forward, desperately scanning the waves. When she finally caught sight of the surfboat, it was overturned and sliding up a giant swell. Then it plunged forward while crewmen bobbed about in the waves. They were less than two hundred feet away. The men on the beach quickly pushed the second lifeboat into the surf and rowed frantically to their rescue.

Two men were pulled from the sea, but where were the others? Emma covered her mouth with both hands to stifle a sob.

Just then, a third man was hauled into the boat. Emma's keen gaze searched the ocean for the last two, still unaccounted for.

"There!" She pointed. "Twenty yards to the left!"

A man was floating on the swells and dragging another. Suddenly, the lifeboat was thrust onto the beach by a massive breaker. Joshua and Larry jumped out and dragged it farther onto the sand, while three others dashed into the surf to meet the swimmer, who was washed onto the shore only to be dragged back out by the undertow. Thankfully, on the next wave, he was tossed onto the beach again.

It was the ship's captain. He crawled on all fours until two men hooked their arms under his and dragged him on his knees.

The second man, unconscious, was also dragged clear of the breakers. It was Ezra, the oldest member of the rescue crew.

The world went silent in Emma's ears. She ran to where the men had laid Ezra on his back. They all crowded around.

Emma's father dropped to his knees and put his ear close to Ezra's nose. "He's breathing." He slapped him lightly on the cheeks until Ezra opened his eyes, coughed, and sputtered.

"Thank goodness." Emma then turned to the captain, who had collapsed onto his back, his forearm resting across his eyes. While the others tended to Ezra, she hurried to the captain with a blanket, dropped to her knees beside him, and covered him with it. "Are you all right, sir? Can I do anything for you?"

He gave no answer.

"You're safe now," she told him. "We took your crew to the rescue station, where we have food and shelter."

He shook his head as if he didn't want to share in any of that. He merely lay with his arm over his face. For a moment, Emma feared he was in a state of shock or mental paralysis, but then he sat up abruptly, tossed the blanket aside, and stared at her, unseeing, as if he were staring into an abyss. His clothes—black trousers and a black wool turtleneck—were sopping wet. His jet-black hair dripped onto his broad shoulders, and suddenly he began to shiver uncontrollably.

He turned a piercing gaze to Ezra, who, with help from the men, was rising unsteadily to his feet.

"Your man's alive," the captain said shakily.

"Yes," Emma replied. "Thanks to you."

Her father came striding across the sand just then. "Good morning, sir. I'm John Clarkson, superintendent of Sable Island." He offered his hand to the captain, who allowed her father to pull him to his feet.

Emma quickly snatched the discarded blanket off the sand.

"Oliver Harris. Captain of the *Belvedere* out of Britain."

"Thank you for what you did out there," her father said. "You saved a life."

Captain Harris bit back a response, then staggered slightly as if he were about to collapse. Emma grabbed hold of his arm.

"I don't deserve gratitude," he tersely replied. "I bear full responsibility for what happened here."

"It was a bad storm," her father assured him. "The worst we've seen in years. And you're not the first to run aground on these shoals."

The captain wiped a hand down his face. "It's a first for me."

He gazed out at the wreck, which was starting to break apart in the battering waves. He shook his head, then pressed the heels of both hands to his forehead. "You should have left me out there."

Emma's lips parted. "No, Captain. You can't mean that."

His angry eyes shot to hers. "I mean every word I speak."

Feeling as if she'd been slapped by his tone, Emma couldn't make her tongue work. All she could do was blink up at him.

"Forgive my daughter," her father said uneasily. "She's young." He held an arm out to gesture toward the Jeep. "If you'll come this way, Captain Harris, I'll take you to Main Station, where you can have a hot meal and a brandy. Then we can discuss arrangements to get you and your crew safely transported to the mainland."

Without glancing back at Emma, Captain Harris walked with her father to the Jeep, where he climbed into the passenger seat.

Emma remained on the beach, feeling suddenly weak in the knees and woozy as she watched them drive off. It must have been the adrenaline wearing off, she thought.

Slowly, she made her way back to her horse, Willow, who was waiting patiently at the base of the dune. Emma reached Willow, placed her foot in the stirrup, and swung a leg up and over the saddle, but it took a moment for her to regain any semblance of calm. She took a few deep breaths, closed her eyes, and waited for her racing heart to decelerate.

When she opened her eyes, Willow's head was turned. She was waiting for Emma to decide which way to go.

As Emma gathered up the reins, she welcomed the return of her composure.

"Did you see all that?" she said to Willow. "Quite an ordeal, I agree. And just now, I was only trying to be helpful with the captain, but Papa told him that I was young—as if I didn't know the first thing about how to talk to people and he had to apologize for me." She stroked Willow's neck. "It was humiliating, to say the least. And that's why I need to leave this island. I need to get educated. Although I'll miss you terribly."

Willow began to trot, and the ocean raged behind them as the rescue crew heaved lifeboat number one back onto the boat wagon.

~

By the time Emma returned to the house, Captain Harris was seated in the great room, in her father's heavy leather armchair. He held a snifter of brandy in his hand, just as her father had promised. When she shut the door behind her, silencing the wind, her father rose from his chair to greet her.

"Where have you been?" he asked quietly, with a touch of annoyance.

"I had to take Willow back to the barn," Emma explained as she lowered the hood on her rain slicker.

"Abigail needs your help preparing extra food," he said. "She's called twice now. But before you go over there, I need your help here. We have to feed Captain Harris."

Emma peered into the great room, where the captain was taking a lavish swig of his brandy. "I can warm up the beef soup from last night," she suggested.

"Good. He'll need some bread and butter," her father added, speaking in low tones. "The man must be famished. They were out there all night fighting the waves."

Emma spoke softly as well while she removed her slicker and hung it on the coat-tree. "I can't imagine what they went through."

She followed her father into the kitchen, where he fetched the half-empty brandy bottle, then returned to the great room.

"Would you care for another?" he asked the captain.

Emma moved to the sink to wash her hands. She was just reaching for the towel to dry them when she heard a heavy thump that shook the floor under her feet.

"Emma! Come quickly!" her father shouted.

She dropped the towel and ran to the great room, where Captain Harris was on his back on the rug, thrashing about. She came to an abrupt stop, panting in terror. "He's having a seizure!"

She'd read about such things but never witnessed them. All she could do was stare in shock.

"Call Abigail!" her father shouted.

In her younger days, Abigail had been a nurse during the First World War, and she was a great asset to Sable Island, which had no hospital or doctor.

Emma ran to the phone and rang the McKennas' house.

"Hello," Abigail answered snappishly.

21

"Hello, Abigail. It's Emma."

"Finally. I'm up to my elbows in egg salad. You need to come over."

"I'm sorry, but we need you here right away. Captain Harris is having a seizure, and we don't know what to do."

"Don't do anything," she calmly replied. "Don't try to restrain him. I'll be right there."

The line went dead, and Emma ran back to the great room. "She's coming, but she said not to restrain him."

Her father let go of the captain's shoulders and sat back on his heels. Sheer black fright rooted Emma to the spot as she watched the captain convulse on the floor, his eyes rolling back in his head. He didn't even seem present in his body. It was as if he'd gone somewhere else.

After a moment or two, the convulsions slowed, and he went still, eventually slipping into unconsciousness.

Emma was breathless and terror struck. "Is he okay?"

The kitchen door flew open, and Abigail swept inside from the storm. She ripped off her coat, tossed it over the back of a chair, and strode purposefully toward them.

"Move back." She knelt down beside the captain.

"The seizure stopped a few seconds ago," Emma told her.

Abigail pressed two fingers to the pulse at his neck.

"Is he alive?" Emma's father asked.

"Yes." Abigail pulled the captain's eyelids back, checked both pupils, and looked up at them. "Was he complaining of any pain before it started?"

"In the Jeep, he told me he'd been knocked in the head when the lifeboat capsized. He thought he might have lost consciousness in the water for a few seconds."

Abigail ran her fingers through the captain's thick black hair and felt around his scalp. "Yes, yes, here we are. He's got quite a goose egg. That must have hurt like the dickens. I'm surprised there's no bleeding." She leaned directly over his face and tapped his cheeks. "Captain Harris, can you hear me?"

He failed to respond, so she tried again, slapping harder and speaking firmly. "Captain Harris. Can you open your eyes?"

He managed to open them briefly, but it seemed to take great effort, and his eyes rolled back and he fell into a state of unconsciousness again.

Emma, frantic with fear, laid her hand over her heart. She didn't know this man. He was a stranger to her, but the thought of him dying, after everything he'd been through over the past twelve hours, was horrendous, too dreadful to contemplate. He must have people somewhere who loved him and would mourn for him. He was someone's son, or perhaps a child's father. The idea of his death in her home, the finality of it, cut her to the quick.

"This is unbearable," she said. "Will he be all right?"

"I'm not sure," Abigail replied. "It depends what happens in the next few hours. It could just be a concussion. There might be some swelling under the skull that caused the seizure, and once that swelling goes down, he'll recover." She rose awkwardly to her feet and turned to Emma's father. "But it could be worse than that. He should go to a hospital. Can we get him to the mainland tonight?"

"It's unlikely," her father said. "The storm hasn't let up, and Frank said it'll be at least a day or two before the coast guard can get here." He looked down at Captain Harris. "Why isn't he waking up?"

Abigail cupped her forehead in her hand. Her stress was evident in the set of her jaw. "It could just be a postictal state after the seizure. If he wakes up and starts to regain strength over the next few hours, that'll be a good sign."

"So, there's still some hope," Emma said, aching and yearning for it to be so.

"Yes, but I'll need to keep a close eye on him." Abigail directed her next question to Emma's father. "Can we get a few staff men over here to bring the stretcher and move him to the sickroom at my house?"

"I'll call Joseph right away." He hastened to the phone in the kitchen.

"Emma," Abigail said. "I'll need you to finish the sandwiches and deliver them to the men at the staff house. Everything is on my kitchen table."

"I can do that." But something held her in a tight grip. She couldn't seem to pull herself away from the captain before he woke up. She needed to know that he was going to be all right.

"Go *now*," Abigail snapped, wrenching Emma out of her stupor.

She moved quickly to don her slicker and venture outside to brave the storm again.

CHAPTER 3

Wind was a constant on Sable Island, but storms like this reminded Emma that she and her fellow residents were merely guests in this place, at the mercy of Mother Nature. Those cruel, immortal waves would continue to break upon these shores long after they were gone.

After returning from sandwich duty, she sat on the sofa in the great room at home, staring numbly at the window and listening to the house creak in the mighty gusts from the north, like an old ship at sail. She thought of the countless lives that had been lost in the wrecks that surrounded the island. They were all buried in the sandbars, not far beneath the ocean floor. The *Belvedere* was the most recent, but it would not be the last.

She wondered how the captain was faring and wished Abigail would call.

A sudden loud rapping at the back door caused Emma to jump. She rose from the sofa and hurried to the kitchen, where her father was already pulling the door open.

"Philip," he said. "Come inside. How are the men holding up?"

Philip entered the house, wiped his boots on the welcome mat, and lowered the hood of his coat. "They're in good spirits, surprisingly. They have exciting stories to tell, and the staff men are gobbling them up."

Emma could smell whiskey on his breath from halfway across the kitchen. "How's the captain?" she asked.

Philip removed his glasses, reached into his shirt pocket for a hand-kerchief, and wiped the salty film from the lenses. "I haven't been home yet. I thought I'd stop in here first."

Her father turned to her. "Put the kettle on, will you, darling?"

Emma moved to the stove, picked up the kettle, and filled it at the sink.

"Frank has been keeping in touch with the mainland," Philip said, "and they still can't predict when it'll be safe to reach us. They're aware of the situation with the captain and want to be kept informed of any changes in his condition."

"When can we call Abigail?" Emma asked.

"Be patient," her father replied testily, and she rubbed at her brow, resenting the reprimand.

"The men are concerned about him," Philip added. "But some seem more worried about their own welfare if he doesn't make it—worried they'll be blamed for leaving him behind when the first rescue boat came."

Her father invited Philip to sit down at the table. "They said it was his choice and they were just following orders."

"So they say."

The telephone rang, and Emma rushed to answer it. "Superintendent's residence."

"Hello, Emma. It's Abigail. Put your father on."

"One moment." Her pulse accelerated as she handed the phone to him.

"John Clarkson speaking. Hello, Abigail." He listened and nodded while Emma fiddled with her locket, impatient for news.

"That sounds promising," he finally said.

Emma felt a great release of tension in her muscles and bones.

Her father listened for a few more seconds. "Yes, Philip just arrived. He'll stay for a while. Emma is making tea." He paused. "Thank you, Abigail. I appreciate the call." He hung up the telephone and turned to face them. "He's awake."

Emma pressed both her open hands to her chest. "Thank God."

"He's drowsy and confused," her father continued, "and having some memory problems, but Abigail says that's normal after a seizure. She still needs to keep an eye on him, but she feels any life-threatening danger isn't as imminent as we thought."

The kettle hissed, and Emma removed it from the burner. "Can I go over there and see if she needs any help?"

But even as she asked the question, she knew she wouldn't be welcome. Abigail was not a sociable person. She preferred to do most things on her own.

Philip gave her a sidelong glance that suggested he had the same opinion about his wife.

"I don't see why not," her father replied, oblivious as usual to the complexities of the female mind. "But don't make a nuisance of yourself. By the sounds of things, the captain probably doesn't have the strength for visitors."

"I'll just help in the kitchen," Emma replied, recalling the mess she'd left after preparing the sandwiches.

She filled the teapot with hot water from the kettle, went to the fridge for a can of Carnation milk, and set it on the table, leaving the men to discuss the situation further. She then hurried upstairs to her room to select a few books for the patient—who would no doubt need plenty of rest in bed over the coming days. Some good books might help him pass the time.

~

Oliver Harris, restless and agitated, confused about where he was, tried to sit up in the strange bed, but his body refused to cooperate, so he collapsed against the pillow.

The nurse in the kitchen hung up the telephone and returned to his bedside. "How are you feeling now?" She laid the back of her hand on his forehead.

"Knackered," he replied. "But thank you for . . ."

What was the word? He couldn't seem to articulate his thoughts. The nurse—Abigail was her name—had explained that he was in a weary state after a seizure but that he would feel normal again soon.

He'd never had a seizure before. What in God's name had happened? He remembered the shipwreck, but the details were muddled. A short while ago, Abigail had fed him some warm broth and asked to remove his shirt because he was having some pain on his left side. She'd found some severe bruising and diagnosed him with a fractured rib. He didn't doubt Abigail, but he had no recollection of how that could have happened. He barely remembered the wreck, much less how he got to shore. Everything over the past twelve hours was broken and splintered in his brain. Only fragments were accessible.

"Just doing my job," she replied as she sat down in the chair beside the bed. "Although I'm not employed as a nurse here. It's Philip who works for the government, taking care of the weather station."

Oliver spoke slowly, grasping clumsily at words. "So, it's my good luck that you have nursing skills?"

"Good luck indeed," she cooly replied without smiling, without looking him in the eye. "We don't get many shipwrecks these days. I suspect this lifesaving establishment is running on borrowed time. It'll soon be a thing of the past."

The seizure had drained him. He felt nothing but darkness in the depths of his core. He turned his head on the pillow, away from her. "We all become relics sooner or later."

He felt Abigail studying his profile. Not wanting to appear weak, he forced himself to meet her gaze.

"Where did you learn to be a nurse?" he asked with fatigue.

She raised her chin. "I served in the Great War," she told him haughtily. Or perhaps she was just proud. "I spent time in France and saw more head wounds than I care to remember."

He shifted on the bed and felt a sudden agonizing wrench in his side. "Oh, God . . ."

"Is it your rib?" Abigail rose quickly and leaned over him.

He tried to change his position, but the room began to spin. "Whoa."

She touched his arm. "You might experience some vertigo over the next few days, and nausea. Difficulty concentrating. But it's all normal with a concussion. You'll need to get plenty of rest."

"I'm not accustomed to being at rest," he told her, feeling sick and wretched.

Three aggressive knocks sounded at the door. Abigail's gaze swung away from him, irritably. "Will you excuse me for a moment?"

She stood and walked out of the room. Oliver lay sleepily, eyes closed, listening to the storm still raging outside. Despair pressed down on him, along with a terrible sense of defeat.

Faintly, he heard Abigail open the door. "What are you doing here?"

A woman's voice replied, or perhaps it was the voice of a child. It was difficult to make sense of things after the seizure and through the noise of the storm.

"I brought some books for the patient," the lady said, "and I wanted to help you tidy the kitchen. I'm sorry I left you with such a mess earlier."

Abigail spoke in a clipped tone. "I took care of the mess already."

Oliver opened his eyes in time to see a gust of wind blow violently into the kitchen. A few papers flew off the table.

"But I have these books I'd like to lend to the captain," the young lady persisted, more firmly this time, standing her ground.

"Fine," Abigail replied. "Come in, then. But you can't stay long. He tires easily."

Oliver closed his eyes again.

~

Emma removed her boots on the McKennas' rubber mat and hung her coat on the hook. Abigail had already disappeared into the room off the kitchen where the captain was resting, so Emma tentatively followed in that direction, where she paused in the open doorway.

Her gaze fell upon Captain Harris. He was sitting up against the pillows. "Good afternoon," she said.

"This is Emma." Abigail punched and fluffed the pillows behind him. "She's the superintendent's daughter, and she's brought you some books."

Emma met the captain's gaze. With a furrowed brow, he studied her for a moment, as if he were struggling to recognize a familiar face. "We've met," he finally said, appearing almost relieved as he spoke the words.

"I'm pleased to see you're feeling better," Emma replied.

"Not by much."

An awkward silence ensued. Emma remained in the doorway while Abigail tucked the blanket tightly around the captain's feet.

Eventually, he glanced down at the sack of books Emma had carried from home. "What did you bring?"

Taking the question as an invitation, she crossed the threshold and approached the chair beside the bed. She set the white canvas sack on the seat and reached in to withdraw one book at a time. "I wasn't sure what you might like, so I brought a broad selection. This is one of my favorites." She handed him a dog-eared copy of *The Toilers of the Sea*, by Victor Hugo.

He took hold of it and frowned at the title. "I read this when I was young. Now, under the circumstances, I wish I hadn't." He dropped it onto the mattress beside him. "What else have you got?"

Aware of Abigail observing from the doorway, Emma reached into the bag again. "This is about the biology and behavior of wild horses. I'm not sure if you're aware, but we have wild herds here. You might see them when you're up and about, when you feel ready to go for a walk."

"If the weather ever clears," Abigail said sourly.

"The sun will come out again. It always does." Emma reached into the bag for more books and presented each one to the captain, giving him time to peruse a cover or a table of contents.

When the bag was empty, she folded it and placed it on the lower shelf of the bedside table.

No one spoke, and Emma glanced uneasily at Abigail, who was still standing in the doorway, watching with eyes like a malevolent cat's.

Emma wasn't normally a judgmental person, but there was no question that Abigail was bitter. That had become clear mere days after she'd arrived three years ago with her husband, Philip, who had replaced Howard Montgomery, the previous chief of the weather station. Howard had lived on Sable with his wife, Ruth, for fourteen years. They'd taken up residence when Emma was four years old, and Ruth had become a cherished mother figure to her. Emma still missed Ruth terribly, but they kept in touch through letters on the supply ship each month.

"Could I bother you, Abigail, for some more broth?" the captain asked.

"Of course."

As soon as Abigail moved out of the doorway, a cold shadow seemed to depart. With relief, Emma sat primly on the edge of the chair. She clasped her hands together on her lap. It was not until she heard the loud clanking of a pot on the stove that she was able to place her full attention on the captain, who chose that moment to speak directly to her.

"I owe you an apology," he said quietly but gruffly.

"For what?"

"I was rude to you on the beach, when I first came ashore. I'm only just remembering that now."

Surprised by his open acknowledgment of their first encounter, Emma felt a little unraveled. "No need to apologize."

"You're too forgiving."

"I can't help it. No one's perfect, and you'd been through a terrible ordeal, not to mention a head injury."

He ran his fingers gently over the bump at the back of his head. "I know I fell out of the boat, but I have no memory of being struck. I only remember coming to under the water and swimming to the surface. Then talking to you on the beach. Then waking up in this bed."

"I'm sorry that happened to you," she replied. "But you didn't fall out of the boat. It capsized." She frowned. "Are you in much pain?"

"The headache has no mercy."

Emma glanced at the pile of books on the bed. "You probably won't feel much like reading, I suppose."

"I don't think so. At least not today." He closed his eyes, tipped his head back, and neither of them spoke.

Discreetly, while the wind howled around the house, Emma scanned the room and took in the small metal cabinet with glass doors. It was full of pill bottles and other supplies—a jar of tongue depressors, a box of latex gloves, and a blood pressure cuff.

"You don't need to stay," the captain said, his eyes still closed, his brow rutted from discomfort. Whether it was physical or emotional, Emma had no idea, and she wished there was something she could do for him.

"I could read to you if you'd like," she suggested.

"No, thank you."

"Or I could return tomorrow," she said, undeterred, "after the storm passes. Fresh air might do you good. I could take you to see the wild horses."

At that, he opened his eyes, lifted his head, and stared at her rigidly. There was a sheen of sweat on his forehead. "If you're trying to cheer me up, you might be wasting your time."

Abigail walked into the room just then, carrying a food tray. "I have your broth." Again, she did not make eye contact with Emma.

Captain Harris sat up straighter against the pillows, and Abigail placed the tray on his lap.

Emma slowly rose from her chair. "I should be going. But perhaps I'll stop by again tomorrow."

"Captain Harris needs to rest," Abigail frostily replied.

The captain's eyes lifted, and he watched Abigail's face as she bent over him, arranging the cutlery on his tray.

Feeling defeated, Emma backed away from the bed and headed for the door, but the sound of the captain's voice arrested her on the spot.

"Thank you for the books, Emma. It was very kind of you."

She swung around. "You're welcome."

Abigail tucked a large napkin into the captain's shirt collar and handed him a spoon, so Emma turned and left. She crossed the kitchen, donned her coat and boots. But before she walked out into the storm, she turned to look back at the sickroom. The captain was sitting up in bed, contemplating the broth.

Suddenly and unexpectedly, Abigail filled the open doorway, glowered at Emma, and promptly slammed the door shut between them.

~

For the next five hours, the nor'easter continued to blow, unrelenting. After dinner, in the superintendent's great room, Emma's father poured himself a second glass of brandy.

"You were helpful today," he said to Emma, who sat across from him on the sofa, reading. "Abigail couldn't have managed without you."

Emma lowered her book. "I was happy to help. I only wish I could have done more, especially for the captain. His wounds aren't just physical, you know."

Her father slowly swirled his drink around in the snifter. "I know where you're going with this, Emma, and I wish you wouldn't, because it's been a long and difficult day."

It had indeed been grueling and exhausting, but also illuminating for Emma. She felt more inspired and motivated than ever and couldn't resist the compulsion to assert herself. "I only want you to understand what I want to do with my life. Psychology is an important form of medical therapy. The captain experienced severe trauma, and it's not going to be easy for him to forget about that or forgive himself for what happened. He might recover quickly from the effects of the concussion and the cracked rib, but other internal wounds, like guilt or terror, could cause permanent damage to his psyche and affect his future career and livelihood."

Her father scoffed. "Please. Don't use what happened today as ammunition."

"Ammunition?" Emma replied. "Papa, I don't want to *fight* you. I only want you to try and see that psychotherapy is a noble profession, and I want you to understand how passionate I am about it."

Her father frowned, and she felt like she was talking to the wall.

"What happened when you went over to visit the captain today?" he asked. "I hope you didn't try and practice any sort of psychoanalysis on him. You're not a doctor, and you shouldn't play at that."

"Of course I didn't," she replied, feeling offended by the suggestion that this was a game to her. "I only offered to read to him."

Her father sipped his brandy. "Good. Because he's not your guinea pig."

Emma returned her attention to her book, though she was seething inside. How much longer would she have to endure being treated like a child?

After a moment, however, she began to wonder if there might be some truth to her father's words.

CHAPTER 4

Oliver woke to the hush of solitude and shadows. The house was no longer groaning in the brutal gale, and the windowpanes were clean and dry of rain. Miraculously, outside of Abigail McKenna's sickroom, the whole world seemed to be at peace—or perhaps just sleeping.

Either way, it mattered not, because inside was the menacing silence that Oliver had been dreading. It was an open door to his dark thoughts, which crept stealthily into his head and dug a deep hole there. He saw his crewman going overboard and flailing in the waves. He threw a life preserver, but it was tossed about in the wind, utterly useless. The storm roared like a beast. The deck was slippery, and the spray was as cold as ice on his flesh. He grabbed at the rail . . .

Oliver heard the sudden clang of a ship's bell. He squeezed his eyes shut and pressed the heels of his hands to his forehead. *Stop thinking. Look around you, dammit.*

His eyes flew open. He was in a bedroom. It was quiet. Warm and dry.

As his heart rate began to slow, he ran a finger over the tender lump on his skull that had not yet diminished in size. At least he was no longer nauseated. He felt rested, along with a noticeable improvement in his cognitive abilities.

He sat up in bed. With pupils well adjusted to the gloom, he tossed the covers aside, swung his feet to the floor, and stood up—rising carefully in case the dizziness returned. *Bloody hell.* Every muscle in his body ached.

He took a moment to gain confidence in his sense of balance before he padded stiffly to the window and looked out at the night sky. A rose pink light over the rooftops of Main Station glowed on the horizon. It was the light of a new dawn.

He returned to the bed, sat down on the edge of the mattress, and asked God why he'd been spared. It was the young crewman who should have been saved.

But who was Oliver to question the decisions of God? Because Oliver certainly hadn't made the best decisions in his own life.

~

A short while later, Oliver walked out of the house and descended the porch steps to the yard. The salty pang of the sea filled his nostrils. Mixed with a plethora of other unfamiliar fragrances, it created an extravagant perfume. He stopped to inhale deeply and listen to the roar of the waves beyond the dunes.

Clearly, the ocean was still angry after the storm.

Turning toward the thunder of the breakers, he slid his hands into his pockets and strode across the yard, his boots grinding strangely on the sand. The grains sang like crystal, like nothing he'd ever experienced, and fleetingly he wondered if he'd passed away during the night and was now walking on a different plane or heavenly dimension.

It was a ridiculous thought, he knew, but nothing seemed normal that morning. He'd slept like the dead after narrowly skirting death, and he felt an unsettling urge to glance over his shoulder to check for the grim reaper—to make sure he wasn't following, eager to launch a second attempt.

Eventually, Oliver reached the top of a high dune. He stopped and gazed down at the beach below and the raging ocean beyond. The sky was growing brighter. His eyes scanned the incoming waves, searching for a body washed ashore, but saw nothing.

With a raw mix of sadness, shame, and despair, he looked toward his ship, wrecked off the western tip of the island. She lay on her side while the constant cruel whip of the waves rained down on her.

Suddenly in need of a closer look, Oliver skidded down the steep slope of the dune to the beach and walked briskly. Perhaps she was not yet done for. Perhaps her hull had not been damaged. Perhaps it might still be possible to float her when the tide came in . . .

Suddenly, his desperate thoughts were wrenched away from the *Belvedere*. Thunderous galloping hoofbeats on the beach reached his ears. With a hot rush of doom in his blood, he turned, but it was not the grim reaper, here to collect another soul. It was Emma, the superintendent's daughter.

For some inexplicable reason, Oliver was embarrassed to be out on the beach at dawn, marching toward his half-sunken ship. What could he possibly do about the situation?

She slowed her horse to a trot, then a walk, and drew up beside him. He stopped and noticed the color of her long hair matched her chestnut mare almost exactly.

She regarded Oliver jauntily. "Good morning, Captain. You must be feeling better."

Her cheeks were flushed from exertion and the chill of the cool morning air, and he found himself judging her as a woman immensely confident for one so young. Or perhaps it was because of her position, high in the saddle, looking down at him.

"Somewhat better," he replied dully.

The mare blew a forceful breath from flaring nostrils and tossed its head. Emma patted the horse on the neck, and when Oliver resumed his trek toward the West Spit, she dismounted. Within seconds, she caught up with him. "May I walk with you?"

"Of course," he replied, though clearly she'd already taken it as a given.

Emma led her horse behind her, and they fell into a matched pace.

"It was nice to wake up to a clear sky," she said, and Oliver wondered if she'd ever known a truly dark day in her entire young life. "But that's the thing about storms, isn't it? They always blow over."

"Do they?" he replied pessimistically, feeling her gaze lingering on his profile as he walked.

"Yes, but I'm just talking about the weather," she said.

He stopped and faced her. "I suppose I wasn't."

She stopped as well. "I gathered that."

They stared at each other for a few seconds, then started walking again at a slower pace, a significant distance from the waves that crashed and rolled, foaming onto the beach.

"I don't suppose you've heard anything about when we can leave the island," Oliver said.

"The last thing I heard before I went to bed last night," she replied, "was a plan to wait for the supply ship next week."

Oliver stopped abruptly. "Next week?"

Emma's horse nickered and tossed its head again.

"Yes. I'm so sorry. It's not easy to come and go from here, especially after a storm."

"But the skies are clear now." He gestured angrily with a hand.

"Yes," she argued, "but the beaches aren't safe to land a plane. After a storm, the sand shifts, and it takes a while for everyone to get a handle on things."

Oliver realized his headache had returned. He pressed the heel of his hand to his temple.

"I'm so sorry I don't have better news for you," Emma said, and they began walking again.

"It's not your fault." Oliver was fully aware that he was the one to blame for all this.

They continued in silence for a long while until Emma spoke her thoughts openly—as she often seemed to do, without reserve.

"I can guess where we're going," she said. "This must be why you were up at the crack of dawn. You want to see your ship?"

"I do," Oliver replied. "But I'm usually an early riser, regardless."

"I'm the same." Emma's gaze slid to meet his. "As soon as I hear the birds chirping, I want to get moving."

The rules of proper etiquette were pushing Oliver to respond in a polite manner, but his honest self was bucking violently. His head was pounding, and there was a bitter bile in his stomach because he hated himself for what occurred here twenty-four hours ago, and he wanted to be alone.

"I don't feel much like talking," he said brusquely, under the assumption that she would understand and return to Main Station.

But Emma stopped. Her horse stopped as well. Oliver continued for a few more strides before he finally paused, squeezed his eyes shut, and wished he had not encountered her at all.

Reluctantly, he turned around.

"I should probably head back," she said awkwardly, her cheeks flushing with color. "There's quite a lot to do. Breakfast for the men in the staff house and . . ."

Good God. She was hurt.

Oh, bloody hell, when had he become such an ornery old man? He took a tentative step toward her. "I apologize again, Emma. That was rude of me. I'm not myself."

She regarded him with a look of genuine empathy, which surprised him. "Please, Captain Harris. Don't apologize. It's perfectly understandable. I shouldn't have intruded upon your walk."

"You didn't intrude."

"Yes, I did," she argued. "I saw you walking, and I galloped faster to catch up with you, and then I invited myself along. My father would scold me for having the manners of a walrus." Emma started walking again. "I think I've been living on this island too long. I don't know how to interact with new people. It's a skill I need to learn."

"Clearly, a shipwreck was just what the doctor ordered." It was a grim attempt at humor, and he regretted it immediately.

Emma nodded at him knowingly and continued walking.

A short while later, she said, "I have binoculars in my saddlebag, if you'd like to use them to see your ship. And if you have any questions about the rescue effort, I'm happy to answer. I was there for all of it."

Despite Oliver's throbbing head and his melancholic wish to be alone, he was grateful for the offer. "Thank you. I appreciate that."

She glanced over her shoulder. "This is Willow, by the way."

He glanced over his shoulder as well. "Hello, Willow. I'm Oliver Harris. New to the area."

The mare tossed her head as if she understood every word, and Emma laughed.

"She's very smart."

"I can see that."

They continued along the beach, walking briskly toward the tip of the island.

~

Abigail McKenna woke with a start, sat up, and remembered the dream—a recurring dream where she was sinking into quicksand and a band of wild horses stood in a circle all around her, heads down, watching her struggle. She begged them for help, but they galloped off to frolic in freshwater ponds. A beautiful black stallion neighed and nickered, bucked and clawed at the air with his powerful hooves, his long mane blowing in the wind. Meanwhile, Abigail sank deeper and deeper into the quicksand, up to her nose.

She woke drenched in sweat, panting. It was morning, and she was alone in the bed. What time was it? Past seven. Abigail cursed herself for sleeping late and prayed the captain wasn't up and moving about in the kitchen, riffling through her cupboards for coffee.

She quickly dressed and flew down the stairs but found both the kitchen and sickroom empty. Philip's jacket was gone from the hook on the wall, which was not unusual. He was probably outside, launching another ridiculous weather balloon. Perhaps the captain had gone with him to watch.

She pulled on her rubber boots, walked out the back door, and marched to the hut where Philip was alone, bent over a table, recording data.

"Where's the captain?" she asked, looking around in disbelief.

"I beg your pardon?"

"The captain!" she shouted. "He's not in the sickroom. Did you see him this morning?"

"No," Philip replied vacuously.

"You didn't check on him?"

"No."

She swung around and stalked back to the house, but there was no point going inside because the captain wasn't there. Perhaps he'd gone to John Clarkson's house, because everyone seemed to think the superintendent's residence was the center of the universe.

Abigail was out of breath by the time she pounded on John's door. While she waited, she looked down at herself and became conscious of her unsightly appearance. She hadn't brushed her teeth or her hair, or washed her face. Squeezing her eyes shut, she willed herself to appear composed, but no one came to the door.

Finally, she stomped down the steps and looked around the station yard for signs of activity. Her gaze finally settled on the large Quonset hut where the staff men lived.

Abigail strode furiously toward it, working through what she would say when she knocked. But before she had a chance to resolve that question, the door flew open. She leaped back as four crewmen from the *Belvedere* burst out and sprinted toward the boat shed.

Joseph and his crew darted out, one by one, chasing after them. "Stop! Hold on there!"

Abigail backed out of the way. John Clarkson was last to exit the hut, and he moved slower than the younger, fitter men under his supervision.

Abigail followed and fell into a jog beside him. "What's happening?"

"Don't ask."

The *Belvedere* crew reached the shed and attempted to open the door, but it was locked. The others caught up with them, and a scuffle broke out.

Abigail stood motionless, shocked by the anarchy before her. A shot rang out. The sailors scuttled away from each other and held up their hands while John aimed a pistol at each one in turn.

"Settle down," he ordered. "No one's going anywhere. You'll wait patiently for the supply ship to arrive."

"I told you, I ain't stayin' a whole week!" one man shouted. "This ain't nothin' but a sandbar!"

"This island has been here for centuries," John replied. "We're all perfectly safe."

"What about the skulls?" another man asked, pointing at the shed. "What sort of people keep a shrine like that?"

Abigail shook her head. She'd always rued that ghoulish collection of bones and never understood why John allowed it.

"It's not a shrine," he explained. "It's a record of lost souls, and a reminder of why we're here. To provide safe sanctuary."

"Feels more like purgatory to me," the largest man snarled through a clenched jaw.

In that moment, a shout from the distance caused a hush among the men. Abigail turned and caught sight of Captain Harris on horseback, like a phantom hero galloping out of the mist.

Her heart nearly burst out of her chest as he reached the station yard and reined the horse to a halt. Only then did she realize that young Emma Clarkson was on the back of the horse. Abigail's gut squeezed like a fist.

They both dismounted.

The captain strode toward the ruckus. "What's going on?"

None of his crewmen responded.

He turned to John. "Lower the weapon please, sir, if you will."

John did as the captain asked. Captain Harris then approached his men and spoke to them privately. Abigail watched with a shortness of breath, mesmerized, not knowing what to expect.

To her surprise, before long, they were all laughing and joking, and the men dispersed and headed back to the staff house. On the way, one of the Sable crewmen patted a *Belvedere* man on the back, as if they were fast friends again.

What magic words has the captain bestowed upon them? Abigail wondered. He certainly had a way with people, herself included, because she couldn't take her eyes off him as he was speaking to John.

But then Emma entered the periphery of her vision. As she led her horse to the barn, she pulled a ribbon from her thick auburn hair and shook it down her back until it blew lightly in the breeze.

What a performance. Abigail could have expelled the entire contents of her stomach. And where had Emma and the captain been that morning, obviously alone? Did no one else wonder this? Did her father not recognize the impropriety of it? His daughter was barely out of school, and the captain was a man of experience. Not to mention the fact that he had a wife. And a concussion. He was in no condition to be galloping around the island with anyone, much less a single young woman.

Turning to march home, Abigail struggled to set her thoughts on making more sandwiches—but damn them all to hell! She couldn't get the striking image of Captain Harris on horseback out of her head. Nor could she forget the sight of Emma's thick, beautiful hair. It wasn't fair. She wanted to spit.

~

It was past noon when the captain finally returned to the McKennas' house. Abigail was in the kitchen, slicing sandwiches. At the sight of him, she dropped her knife onto the worktable, wiped her hands on her apron, and hurried to greet him. "Captain Harris. My word, you look about ready to fall over."

"I might have overdone it this morning," he admitted, wincing with pain as he removed his coat.

"Any dizziness?" she asked.

"No, but the rib's tender."

"Tender?" She reached out and took hold of his arm to escort him toward the sickroom. "That's got to be the understatement of the year. I saw you leaping off that horse earlier. What were you thinking?" she asked scoldingly. "You need to take better care of yourself. You're injured, and you've had a serious concussion. You need to rest." She led him to the bed. "Come and lie down. Yes, that's right. Let me help you." He carefully lowered himself to a sitting position. "Easy now," Abigail uttered as she removed his boots. "Let's get you under the covers, and I'll bring you some hot soup."

At long last, he laid his head on the pillow and let out a breath of exhaustion. "Thank you, Abigail. You're an angel."

She drew back with surprise and stared down at him, then quickly began to straighten the blanket at his feet before drawing it up over his shoulders. "Just doing my job," she replied, feeling a strange tingling in her body and heart. "Get some rest now."

He closed his eyes, and she stood for a while, watching him until he slept deeply. Then she turned and left the room, shutting the door softly behind her.

CHAPTER 5

Emma woke the following morning to more wind and rain. The telephone was ringing in the kitchen, so she rose from bed, pulled on her robe, and moved to the top of the stairs to listen as her father answered it.

"When?" he asked. "Have you notified the mainland? What about Captain Harris? Does he know yet?" Her father paused and listened. "Thank you, Joseph."

As soon as he hung up the phone, Emma quickly descended the stairs. "What's happening?"

Her father faced her with an expression of outrage. "Two of the *Belvedere* men snuck out last night and stole the lifeboat."

"For what purpose?" she asked, stunned.

"We can only assume they made a run for the mainland," he explained. "One of them was superstitious and thought this place was cursed. Evidently, he'd had some whiskey."

"Dear Lord." Emma sank onto a chair at the table. "They'll never make it. Besides that, the other lifeboat was lost in the rescue, so they've left us with nothing. We can't even go after them."

"It was selfish of them," he said. "And foolish. Now we have two men out there on the ocean thinking they can row two hundred miles, and the coast guard has to get involved."

"More lives in danger."

Her father picked up the phone. "I'll call Captain Harris and let him know."

Emma raked her fingers through her sleep-tousled hair. "Just what he needs. More stress, after everything he's been through."

"Don't start with that, Emma," her father warned. "He's a grown man and more than capable of handling the responsibilities of his profession."

~

Emma spent the day indoors baking bread, but after the phone call about the missing crewmen, the captain remained in her thoughts constantly. Hours later, when all the loaves were out of the oven, cooling on the counter, and the low-lying clouds had finally parted, she couldn't resist the burning desire to call Abigail and check in on him. Thankfully, Philip answered the phone and was more forthcoming than Abigail would have been. He revealed that Captain Harris had just left the house to go for a walk on the beach.

Within minutes, Emma was climbing the high dune for a first-class view of North Beach, where she spotted him about a quarter mile away, at the water's edge, facing the angry ocean. Impetuously, she made her way down the sandy slope, where the crashing thunder of the waves stirred her heart and soul.

It wasn't long before the captain saw her from the distance. He began walking, to meet her halfway.

"Emma," he said.

"Good afternoon," she replied.

He raised an eyebrow. "That's up for debate."

She looked down at her feet. "Indeed. Are you surviving all this chaos?"

"I've had better days."

"Haven't we all?"

They turned and stood side by side, facing the stormy horizon. Emma tasted the salty spray on her lips.

"Has there been any news of my men?" Captain Harris asked.

"Not yet."

He shook his head mournfully.

"All we can do is pray," Emma suggested. "And try not to lose hope. Sometimes luck is everything."

"But luck can swing one way or the other. A single unexpected swell from the wrong direction could capsize them." He gestured with a hand. "Look at that wild ocean out there."

Emma agreed wholeheartedly. The odds were most certainly against those unfortunate men.

"If that happens," she said, "I hope you won't blame yourself. We all tried to stop them."

"But they were under my command." A seagull soared in front of them, then hovered low, floating on the wind. Captain Harris kept his eyes fixed on the bird. "They were my responsibility."

"That's the second time you've said that." Emma faced him. "But how can you take the blame for reckless decisions of foolish men? They disobeyed your orders, and it wasn't your fault they drank too much whiskey. It was our crew in the staff house who gave it to them."

"But they should have known better," he insisted.

"Yes, they all should have, which, again"—she paused and put extra emphasis on her next words—"is not your fault."

He considered her fiery speech while watching the seagull fly over their heads toward the dunes behind them. Then he turned to her. "You know a lot for someone so young."

Something fluttered inside her, and she fumbled for words. "I don't know about that."

"It's true. You're wise beyond your years. Mindful and rational."

Her cheeks reddened at the compliment, and she kicked at the sand with the toe of her boot. "I'm not used to receiving such high praise."

He smiled warmly at her. "I doubt that."

Emma's blush deepened because she was aware of the nickname the staff men used behind her back. They called her "the Sable Beauty." She dismissed it because there were so few young women on the island, and she was the only unmarried lady. That, she believed, was why they had singled her out.

"I don't have relationships here, you know," she said, not sure why she felt compelled to tell him this. Perhaps she didn't want him to think she welcomed attention or was a flirt or a tease. "I mostly keep to myself."

He gazed out at the swirling gray ocean. "That's probably wise."

They stood for a while, occasionally stepping back from the constant procession of waves as the tide rolled in, until Emma decided the captain needed to look at something new. She needed the same.

"Come with me," she said.

Without hesitation, he followed, and they walked westward until they reached a break in the dune.

"Where are we going?" he asked.

"To the old, abandoned main station. It's a bit of a walk, but there's a lovely rose garden there."

"Roses? Imported, I assume."

"No, they're native. You'd be amazed at what grows here. We have cranberries and blueberries. As for the rose garden, the story goes that one of the previous superintendents planted it for his daughter who was in a wheelchair."

They walked at a brisk pace, their footsteps in perfect sync as they tramped across the complex network of sandy horse trails through the dense heath.

"What is that?" the captain asked, stopping and staring.

Emma stopped as well. "That's the old superintendent's residence. This is where the community lived at the turn of the century."

"But it's half-buried."

She took in the abandoned house with weathered gray clapboards. It was slowly being swallowed up by enormous drifts of sand that now reached the second-story windows in the front. Only then did she realize what an incredible sight it must be for someone who came from far away.

"Yes," she replied. "That's why the station was moved farther east—because the dunes are constantly shifting. Nothing ever stays the same around here. We can go inside if you like. An old calendar still hangs on the wall. It was left as a historical record, I suppose, to mark the day when they finally gave up trying to fight Mother Nature."

She led him to the back of the house, where the level of the encroaching dune was less aggressive. Drifts of sand covered the steps, but Emma and the captain were able to enter through the back door.

"Clearly it needs a good sweeping," Emma said facetiously.

"It might be a bit late for that." The captain wandered around the main floor and spotted the calendar. "I can imagine archaeologists coming here, centuries from now, with their shovels and whisks, uncovering all this."

"We don't have to wait centuries," Emma said. "We find things constantly. A few months ago, we found a ship's wheel. I don't know what vessel it came from, but we guessed it dated back to the 1700s."

The captain faced her. "Do you still have it?"

"No, we sent it to a museum in Halifax. It's still there if you want to see it."

"I might." He turned and wandered deeper into another room, where the wallpaper was peeling. "This entire place feels like a museum."

"Yes," Emma replied. "Or a tomb. Some of the men say there are ghosts here, but I don't think so. I find it quite peaceful, sheltered from the noise of the ocean. Lately I've been coming here to write in my journal." She pointed. "I sit in that chair."

He turned to her with interest. "What do you write about?"

A flush of heat reached her cheeks. "Oh, just silly things. My dreams and goals for the future."

49

"That's not silly," he replied, and she was caught by the low timbre of his voice and the blue of his eyes, which were so exceptionally unique. He listened to her attentively and didn't seem to think her childish at all.

Suddenly, Emma worried that he could sense how fast her heart was beating and how her emotions were skittering out of control. There was something quite thrilling about this man, something different from anything she'd ever experienced before. Heat coursed through her body, and she reveled in the sensation. It made her feel happy and reckless.

She forced herself to speak calmly. "Why don't we go and see the rose garden?"

He gestured gallantly toward the door. "Lead the way and I'll follow."

She smiled and walked out the door of the abandoned house.

A short while later, after strolling down meandering paths through low-lying junipers and bayberry bushes, and talking the whole way, they reached the rose garden.

"Here we are." Emma led Captain Harris into the vast circular garden where dense bushes climbed up the surrounding slopes and towered over them. The perfume was overpowering.

"I've always thought of this as an oasis," she said. "My very own private English garden."

The captain was quiet as he strolled about. She watched him curiously and wondered what he was thinking.

"Though I've never been to England," she added. "So, I have no idea if that label is appropriate."

"It's perfect," he said. "It smells like home. My wife planted a hedge of roses in our back garden the year we were married, but it hasn't had time to grow this tall."

Emma felt a pang of disappointment, which made no sense because she had no claim on the captain, romantic or otherwise, and the fact that he had a wife should not come as a surprise. Of course he was married. He was at least ten years older than she, a man of the world. Any sort of crush on her part was pointless and inane.

"Do you have children?" she asked, making conversation, sensibly.

"I have two. A girl and a boy. Lydia and Arthur."

What lovely names, she thought. How lucky he was.

"You must miss them when you're at sea."

"I miss them all the time," he replied. "Even when I'm home, because I don't see them very much."

Emma's eyebrows pulled together questioningly. "Why not?"

He circled the round garden while she stood in the center of it, quietly watching him and feeling desperate to know everything about him—his past experiences, his thoughts, and his feelings.

"A long time ago," he explained, "I put my life at sea above everything else." He glanced briefly at her. "This isn't something I normally share, but . . . well, my wife found another man, and we've been living separate lives ever since."

This was not a subject Emma had ever discussed with anyone before, but it wasn't awkward. To the contrary, it felt good to speak of intimate matters with the captain. "I'm sorry to hear that."

He nodded, and she yearned to know more—to understand how a wife could not forgive her husband for his professional commitments.

"Was it because of the war?" she asked. "Is that why you were gone so much?"

"Yes," he replied. "But it was a bit more complicated than that." He fingered a few green leaves on the bushes and seemed reluctant to continue.

"Forgive me," Emma said, lowering her gaze to the ground. "It's none of my business. I've overstepped."

"No need to apologize." He faced her. "You're inquisitive. That's why you know so much for someone so young."

"I'm not so young," she disagreed openly. "I'm twenty-one, and I plan to go to university on the mainland in the fall. I've already been accepted to study psychology."

His eyebrows lifted. "Well, well. Congratulations. Obviously, you've chosen the right path for yourself. You seem to have a keen interest in people's thoughts and feelings."

"Yes." How good it felt to have someone recognize this and not treat her as if she were reaching too high or too far. "I do."

"Hence all the questions," he added.

She laughed and looked down at her feet. "My father's afraid I might be treating you like a guinea pig."

Captain Harris threw his head back and laughed. Then he pressed the heel of his hand to his temple.

"Oh dear," Emma said, moving a little closer. "I've made your head pound."

He squinted a little. "Yes, but at least you've distracted me from my demons for the past hour. That's worth a small headache, in my opinion."

"Demons?"

"You've never met anyone with demons before?" he asked, still squinting. "If you enter the psychology profession, you'll meet your fair share."

Emma stood back. "I've just never heard that term before. It's why I need to get off this island and start talking to people."

He nodded. "Isn't it something, how life is constantly an education?"

She felt a sudden compulsion to ask him a thousand questions about all the things he had learned as a young man, as a sailor, a husband, and a father. She thought of all the nautical miles he must have crossed, the places he'd seen, the people he'd met, his experiences, good and bad, during the war. What a wealth of knowledge he must possess.

But Emma resisted the urge to probe him like the subject of an experiment. She remained quiet in the tranquility of the rose garden, because she sensed, deep down in her soul, that what the captain needed today was peace.

Eventually, they left the garden and walked together back to Main Station. Instead of walking on the beach, they stuck to the horse trails on the heath, walking single file and talking the entire time. When they reached the station, they stood on the high dune and gazed out at the raging ocean.

Captain Harris asked Emma many questions about life on Sable Island, and she answered all of them with pleasure and honesty while she marveled at the extraordinary power of the sea, of fate, and of life.

CHAPTER 6

It was not easy to keep the *Belvedere* crew in good spirits while they waited for news about the crewmen who had rowed recklessly into the dark ocean at night. Emma felt certain it was the trauma of the shipwreck that had infected their minds with terror and an irrational fear that the island was cursed. The whiskey certainly hadn't helped.

Over the next few days, she kept busy cooking and cleaning for the extra guests on their remote little island.

With his concussion on the mend, and a desire to maintain discipline, Captain Harris assigned daily duties to his crewmen. Some were directed to assist Sable's lifeboat crew in patrolling the beaches in search of the missing engineer, whose body might have washed ashore somewhere. Others were sent to assist Philip at the weather station, with an objective to learn about meteorological studies and the collection of scientific data. Those who possessed experience with horses spent time at the corral and helped break a few mares for work at Main Station.

On day four, there was still no news about the men who had attempted to row to the mainland, nor any sign of the drowned seaman. But a group on beach patrol recovered the second lifeboat, which had capsized during the rescue, not far from old Station Number Two. The retrieval of the invaluable craft kept both crews busy and working together for hours. For those men, the sense of accomplishment was a welcome respite from feelings of despondency when they had nothing to do but wait for the supply ship to arrive and to recall the horror of the shipwreck.

On day five, Emma finished her early-morning chores, saddled Willow, and went for a fast, exhilarating ride along the beach, splashing through frothy incoming waves. Her thoughts, as usual, drifted to Captain Harris. There was so much about him she yearned to know—how his childhood and upbringing had led him to a career in the navy, and why he'd taken a wife when perhaps, in his heart, he'd already been wedded to the sea? What could have happened between him and this woman to cause a rift so deep that she could fall in love with another man and deprive her husband of a place in his children's lives?

Feeling breathless, Emma slowed Willow to a walk. Heaven help her. There was no question in her mind that she was becoming infatuated with the captain. Or perhaps it was something more. Was this what it felt like to fall in love? A complete loss of emotional control? The more she thought about it, the more she suspected it was akin to what had driven those two men to steal a boat in the night and row into the dark and turbulent sea.

As Emma wheeled Willow around and galloped back to Main Station, she decided to never tell anyone what she'd been feeling. Especially her father. He'd drop dead if he knew what she was dreaming about when she switched off the lamp in her bedroom each night.

~

Emma could have jumped for joy when she walked through the front door of her house.

"We're having a dinner party," her father announced, with no notion whatsoever that he was throwing fuel onto the desires she'd been hiding from him.

"Who's coming?" she casually asked, which took some effort to conceal her explosion of excitement.

"Captain Harris and Philip. But not Abigail."

"Why not Abigail?" Emma asked, laboring to sound nonchalant.

"I suspect she's tired," her father replied. "The captain has been her houseguest and patient for almost a week. That's why I thought it right to invite him here. To give her a night off."

"That's kind of you." Emma moved to the fruit bowl on the kitchen table, grabbed an apple, and bit into it. "Have you thought about what you'd like to serve for dinner? I could roast a chicken with carrots and potatoes, but I'd have to get started on it right away."

Her father moved toward her and held her face in his hands. "That sounds perfect, sweetheart. What would I ever do without you?"

Despite the thrill of a dinner party with Captain Harris in attendance, Emma found herself bristling at the reminder that her father still didn't want to let her go.

~

That evening, Philip walked in with a bottle of brandy he must have been saving for a special occasion, because her father made a great fuss about it. Captain Harris entered behind him, shook her father's hand, and directed his attention to Emma. He held out a book—one of the titles she'd lent him on the day of the wreck, about the wild horses of Sable.

"I thought I'd return this to you," he said. "I finished it this afternoon."

"And?"

"It was excellent. I appreciate the loan."

She stood there feeling a wave of happiness for their shared interest in horses, but mostly for being near him again. "I'm glad it helped pass the time."

Her father examined the label on the brandy bottle. "Shall we have a drink to start the evening on a high note?"

"I'll pour," Emma offered, reaching for the bottle.

While the gentlemen gathered in the great room to discuss the weather and the latest wireless communications from the mainland, Emma moved into the kitchen. A moment later, she returned with a tray of four brandies in fine crystal snifters and settled in to join the men.

They were about to toast to good weather at last when a knock sounded at the door. Emma rose to answer it.

Outside on the steps stood Frank O'Reilly, the chief wireless operator.

"Hello, Frank," she said.

He swiped his hat off his head and crumpled it in his hands. "Good evening, Emma. You look pretty tonight."

"Thank you." She stepped back. "Come in."

He entered the foyer. "I have important news for your father."

Without delay, she led him into the great room.

"I apologize for the interruption," Frank said to the men.

"No need," her father replied. "We're about to devour a roast-chicken dinner. There must be enough for an extra plate, Emma?"

She smiled at Frank. "Of course. Will you join us?"

"I wouldn't want to impose." He studied her intently, searching for some additional form of encouragement, which she was not prepared to give.

"It's no imposition," her father insisted. "Have a seat, and Emma will fetch you a brandy."

She took Frank's hat and coat, hung them up, and went to the kitchen, but continued to listen to the men's conversation in the great room.

"This must be important news," her father said, "if you've come to deliver it in person. Did they find the crewmen?"

"Not yet," Frank replied. "But the *Argyle* will be here the day after tomorrow to transfer everyone from the *Belvedere* to the mainland. Weather permitting, of course."

Emma nearly lost her grip on the crystal snifter as the news jetted through her mind. She didn't want to think about the captain leaving so soon.

Her father spoke warmly. "There. You see? I knew it would be no time at all before help arrived. We always take care of our guests at Sable. Cheers to that."

Emma poured a glass of brandy for Frank, returned to the great room, and handed it to him.

He looked up at her with unabashed adoration. "Thank you, Emma."

Emma couldn't meet his gaze, or anyone else's, especially after the news he'd brought. When she returned to her place on the sofa, she picked up her brandy and took a deep swig that burned her throat. Then she locked eyes with the captain. His eyebrows lifted a fraction, as if to communicate that he recognized Frank's crush on her, and he remembered what she'd said about not wanting to encourage any of the young men on the island. He looked faintly amused.

Emma grinned, then had to look away before anyone took notice of this familiarity between them—and the fact that she felt drunk from something that had nothing to do with the brandy.

Conversations about the *Argyle* resumed, but Emma couldn't escape her physical awareness of the captain, which brought a glut of unhappy thoughts about him leaving. *Stop, Emma. He's a married man.*

"Emma?"

Her father's voice ripped through her emotions. "Yes?"

"What do you think of that?"

"Of what?"

"A musical evening here tomorrow night. A party. For everyone."

"That sounds wonderful," she replied, reclaiming her composure. "A proper send-off."

"Exactly."

On the bright side, a special gathering meant another opportunity to spend time with the captain. On the downside, he would leave the very next morning, and she would probably never see him again. How in the world would she manage her emotions when that moment arrived?

~

After dinner, Emma cleared the table and washed dishes while the men talked politics and worked their way through the bottle of brandy in the great room. She was just dipping her hands into the warm soapy water and swirling the wet dishcloth around on a plate when she heard the floorboards creak behind her. All her senses came alive with excitement because, somehow, she knew who it was. She felt it in all her nerve endings.

The captain approached the counter beside her, so close that his elbow touched hers.

"You're hard at work." He set down his empty glass.

"I like to keep busy. I hope you enjoyed dinner."

"Everything was delicious."

He lingered a moment, and as she placed another clean plate on the dish rack, she felt yearnings she didn't know how to manage. The rapid beat of her heart made it difficult to think of what to say, but she didn't want him to return to the men in the great room just yet.

Why was this so excruciating?

At last, he spoke. "Since I'll be leaving the island soon, I wonder if you might have time tomorrow to show me the famous wild horses you keep telling me about."

Something gave way inside her—a great cascading flood of relief. A rising euphoria.

She turned to him and dried her hands on a towel. "I'd love to, but we'll have to go early because of the party. Why don't we meet at the barn at six thirty? I'll saddle two horses."

"Wonderful," he said. "Cheers, Emma. I'll look forward to it."

The sound of her name on his lips stoked a fire in her belly, and as she watched him walk away, she wondered if he had any notion of his effect on her.

She suspected that he did.

~

"Ready for a run?" she asked Willow the following morning as she stroked her nose. Willow pawed at the hay-strewn floor, so Emma set to work getting her saddled along with Mrs. Miniver, a strong gray mare.

Emma led both horses outside and spotted Captain Harris jogging energetically toward her. He wore denims and a black wool jacket he must have borrowed from Philip or one of the staff men. "Am I late?" he asked, slowing to a walk. "I'd planned to help you saddle the horses."

"Not at all. I couldn't sleep, so I came early."

"I couldn't sleep either." He turned his attention to Mrs. Miniver. "Who is this enchanting creature?"

Emma laughed. "This is Mrs. Miniver."

"From the Hollywood film?" His eyebrows lifted.

"That's right." Emma mounted Willow, then watched him stroke Mrs. Miniver's neck as he became acquainted with her. He tested the tension on the saddle cinches and assured himself that all was in order before he mounted as well. Together, they trotted out of the station yard with the radiant sunrise warming their faces.

"What are the chances we won't encounter any herds?" the captain asked a short while later as they crossed the green heath, making their way through the network of horse paths.

"Very low. I know most of their home ranges and where they roam at different times of the day. I'll take you to the spot where I usually see Willow's family in the mornings."

"Willow was taken from a herd?"

"Yes." Emma inclined her head. "I know that sounds cruel, but we need horses to survive here, and I feel better about taking them into our care than watching them get shipped off to the mainland for sale. That's painful to see, because I've given names to all of them—which my father tells me not to do, but I can't help myself. Lately, I've been sending letters to people in government to try and stop the shipments from happening. Maybe one of these days they'll pass a law or something to protect the horses here."

"That sounds like a noble cause," he said.

Emma brought Willow to a halt and looked around. "This is where they usually make an appearance, over by that pond. It's strange they're not here today." She gathered up the reins and dismounted. "Let's take a walk."

Captain Harris dismounted as well. "Do you ever worry that Willow will run off and try to rejoin her family?"

"Never," Emma replied. "She loves me too much, and she's spoiled by her life of luxury at Main Station. She gets an apple every morning and a carrot each night."

"You'll miss her when you leave for school," he mentioned perceptively.

Emma turned to Captain Harris, so handsome in the morning light, which turned his hair to auburn at the tips. Looking at him, she felt the same exhilaration she felt on the beach whenever she galloped with Willow.

"I'll miss her very much."

She gave Willow a friendly tap on the rear flank and watched her and Mrs. Miniver trot jauntily toward the pond for a drink.

"Shall we walk this way?"

Emma led the captain through narrow, winding paths among hardy cranberry bushes and wondered what he thought of this place. And what he thought of her.

~

Oliver followed Emma in silence for quite some time. They tramped through sandy meandering pathways. Occasionally, he paused to scan the horizon for a glimpse of a wild herd, but for some reason, the horses stayed away.

Emma raised a hand to shade her eyes from the sun. "I don't understand. They always come here in the mornings."

"Maybe it's my fault," he said. "They can smell a foreigner at fifty paces."

Emma laughed. "I'm glad you can keep a sense of humor after everything."

Oliver immediately thought of his ship, lying on her side, stuck on the sandbar with waves pounding against her hull. He felt Emma's eyes on him and had the distinct impression that she was guessing, correctly, at his thoughts.

It always seemed to be that way between them. Whenever they spoke privately during their walks and rides, there was a natural understanding, an agreement about most things they both considered important, and he felt no need to hold anything back. He'd shared a great deal of his inner self with Emma and had revealed things he'd never revealed to anyone.

But today, he didn't want to go down that road and talk about loss and failure. It was their last day together. He wanted to be positive.

"I've learned to soldier on," he said.

She regarded him knowingly, with compassion, and strolled toward another pond.

Oliver decided to saunter in the opposite direction because this strange emotional connection to Emma had the potential to become problematic. He was feeling too good on this island, too buoyant and optimistic, but it wasn't the real world. It was fantasy. What he needed was a moment to remember his true reality: His unhappy marriage. His failures as a father. The wreck of his ship. These were important issues he would need to confront after he left this place. He couldn't continue to avoid them, because day by day, inch by inch, they were digging deeper holes into his heart and mind.

This was a fact he now understood. His brief descent into madness—when he'd wanted to go down with his ship—had been a distress signal.

Because he didn't want to die. He wanted to live. He wanted to do better for his children.

Oliver stopped on the path and turned to look back at Emma. *Bloody hell.* What was it about her that made him so introspective? Whenever he spent time with her, he talked and talked. Then he listened and ended up reflecting on his past and future and wondered how he'd ended up here—a disgraced captain and a failure as a husband and father.

Pondering all this deeply, Oliver veered off the path into a clearing of clean white sand. In that moment, just ahead, a dark mass on the ground brought him to a halt. The breeze shifted, and he was struck by a fetid stench.

It was a dead horse. He raised his forearm to his nose and breathed through his sleeve.

Emma must have detected it as well, because she came running. "Oh no." She stood beside him, staring. Then she untied the patterned scarf from around her neck, held it to her nose, and approached.

Oliver followed. The ocean breeze blew strands of the horse's mane and tail, while buzzing flies made Oliver's skin prickle.

Standing upwind, Emma lowered her scarf. "This is Willow's mother," she said, her voice breaking.

Oliver turned to her and frowned. "You're sure?"

"Yes. I know her well, and she knew who I was to Willow. Sometimes I fed her apples." Emma raised the scarf to her face again. "I wonder what happened to her. Old age, I guess."

The waves on the beach reverberated gently in the distance, and Oliver found himself sinking deeper into the rhythms of the island, the essence of life and death, so very different from what he'd known during the war. Violence had played no part in this.

While the breezes off the ocean hissed through the marram grass on the high dune, Oliver looked around at the rolling landscape. "Maybe this is why we haven't seen the herd this morning, because they want to leave her in peace."

Emma strolled back to where he stood. "I was just thinking the same thing. But who knows? It's springtime, and they often go looking for sandwort at the west end of the island."

The wind shifted, so they retraced their steps to the pond where Willow and Mrs. Miniver were grazing at the water's edge.

"I apologize," Emma said. "I don't think I'll be good company for the rest of the tour. I'm a bit heartbroken."

She bowed her head, and Oliver wished he could take her into his arms and comfort her, but that would cross a line.

With a slender, graceful hand, she pushed a lock of hair behind her ear and looked up at him with wet eyes. He stared back at her, and that was the moment he knew mere feelings of friendship with this woman were impossible. He was entranced and enamored, and fighting desire.

A tear spilled onto her cheek, and Emma wiped it away. "I don't know what's wrong with me. This is so embarrassing."

He was embarrassed himself because he was awestruck and speechless. He'd never known anyone like this woman. His heart was cracked open.

"Maybe this has something to do with the fact that I never knew my own mother," she suddenly confessed in a flood of emotion, her breath shuddering, more tears streaming. "She died when I was born, which maybe was my fault . . . I don't know exactly what happened that day. My father doesn't like to talk about it. And I've always felt guilty that Willow was separated from her mother as well. And now her mother is dead, and there's no future for them, no chance to be together someday. No more hope for that. It's the end."

Oliver observed Emma's deep self-awareness, which was remarkable for one so young. He was equally surprised by her openness and candor. What a rare person she was.

"I'm sorry you lost your mother," he said, because it was the proper thing to say, and he was grateful for social conventions. Without them, he would be lost.

Or would he? He stared at Emma, their eyes fixed on each other's, and felt a surprising calm wash over him. He was glad to be there for her, simply to listen. That was all she needed.

"I wish you weren't leaving so soon," she said. "I've enjoyed getting to know you."

"I've enjoyed getting to know you as well."

"I wish we could talk more."

"I wish the same."

And there it was—the admission, and the surrender to the impulses of his heart, an organ that had become sadly unresponsive in recent years.

"But we still have time, don't we?" he added. "We can keep talking. Would you like to walk back to the station rather than ride?"

He waited while Emma considered his suggestion. She glanced toward the clearing where they'd found the remains of Willow's mother. Then she took a deep breath and let it out. "No. I promised you wild horses. Let's ride to the beach."

As far as Oliver was concerned, it didn't matter what they did. He wanted whatever she wanted.

"All right," he replied.

Oliver strode to Mrs. Miniver and swung himself up into the saddle.

"This is your last day here," Emma said as she tapped her heels to urge Willow into a trot. "I want you to remember Sable Island for its beauty, not as a place of shipwrecks and death and my foolish crying just now."

Oliver felt a jolt. He knew he was looking at someone very important—someone who would have a profound effect on his life. He didn't know what that effect might be, but he knew he would never forget Emma Clarkson.

"I promise I'll remember nothing but beauty," he told her.

Emma steered Willow toward the high dune and launched into a gallop. He kept pace with her as they climbed to the breezy top, and there, down on the beach, beneath the blue sky and cottony clouds, with the vast, rolling ocean behind them, was a family of horses.

There were striking against the white sand, walking leisurely ahead of a magnificent black stallion. They moved in perfect harmony with each other.

"You've kept your promise," Oliver said, feeling dazzled by the smile Emma gave him.

Together, they watched from the high dune until the herd began to gallop and soon grew distant.

"Should we follow?" he asked, wanting to be wild and reckless.

"I wish we could," Emma replied, "but I'm expected back at the house to prepare for the party."

Oh yes, the party. He'd forgotten about that. It was a disturbing reminder that this was his last night on the island. Tomorrow, he and his crew would board a ship and return to civilization, where he would face questions about the loss of the *Belvedere* and her cargo. It could mean the end of his career and livelihood.

But there was another reason for his reluctance to sail away from Sable Island. Something had cast a spell on him, and he wasn't sure he truly understood it. Maybe it was his attraction to the young woman at his side. Or maybe it was something more. He didn't know what to call it exactly, except a soulful experience, a connection to peace and serenity.

All his adult life, he'd been surrounded by chaos. War. Explosions. Terror. Before that, a rush to get married. And always, the unpredictability of the ocean from a place of command where lives were at stake—and where he held each of those precious lives in his imperfect hands.

Oliver realized his entire existence had become one of hypervigilance. He had never paused to simply be quiet, to reflect and look inward. He still didn't know what he was looking at, but at least he felt alive, and he was grateful to be so.

~

By the time Emma and Captain Harris returned to Main Station, the sun had retreated behind a misty veil. It was lovely in its own way—a soft and gentle light upon the island.

Emma led Willow to the barn doors. She was conscious of Captain Harris dismounting behind her—the sound of the leather straps creaking, his boots landing on the ground. She forced herself not to look back as she entered the barn. Instead, she listened to the rhythm of Mrs. Miniver's hooves on the plank floor as the captain walked her to her stall.

Bobby, one of the staff men, was filling a bucket with water. "I'll take care of these two," he said to Emma. "You should get home. Your father's been looking for you."

She handed Willow's reins to him. "He wasn't angry, I hope." She hadn't told her father she was going riding that morning, and he expected her to be setting up for the party.

"You'll have to ask him," Bobby said, leading the horses away.

Emma and the captain walked out of the barn. As soon as she inhaled the fresh air off the water, she touched the captain's arm. "I want to apologize again for my emotions this morning."

"Please . . ." He stopped and raised a hand.

"No, I need to say this because I don't want you to think that I feel sorry for myself, or that I was a poor orphan girl with no mother. I was quite lucky, actually, to have a mother figure on the island during my childhood."

The captain inclined his head curiously. "Abigail?"

Emma laughed softly and lowered her gaze. "No, not Abigail. She and Philip came here a few years ago to replace the former meteorologist and his wife, Ruth. They were here for fourteen years, and Ruth took care of me when I was young. She was a wonderful teacher of life, and she loved me, truly. Sometimes I wonder if my mother sent her here to be my guardian angel."

"You must miss that woman," the captain said.

"I do."

"I can't imagine that Abigail has been able to fill those shoes," he added with a knowing look.

Emma tucked a stray lock of hair behind her ear. "No, but I'm not a child anymore and I don't need babysitting."

"I understand that," he replied. "But still, I saw how she treated you when you brought the books to me. She's not . . . How can I say this without sounding ungrateful? Because I do appreciate her care over the past week. But she's not a very pleasant person, is she?"

"No," Emma replied matter-of-factly. "But I can't fault her for that because I heard that her family abandoned her and she grew up in an orphanage, never adopted. My childhood was heaven compared to that. Which is why I can't be too critical of her."

His blue eyes connected intimately with hers. "You're a very forgiving person."

Emma's whole being flushed with contentment. "I just think everyone has their own struggles," she explained. "No one's life is perfect, even if it appears that way on the surface."

He let out a sigh, which, to Emma, felt like admiration. "More wise words that I won't forget."

They started walking slowly across the station yard, still talking, and finally said goodbye to each other at Emma's front door. The captain walked on toward the McKennas' house, and Emma watched him go, dreading the thought of his departure from the island the following day.

At least she would see him again at the party. If she could have her druthers, she'd spend every single minute with him, talking all night, until dawn.

CHAPTER 7

At the sight of Abigail sitting on a chair outside her house, knitting furiously in the sunshine, Oliver stopped in his tracks.

He had not revealed the whole story to Emma when they'd spoken about Abigail earlier. He'd refrained from describing Abigail's troubling possessiveness, and that she was either fawning over him—caring for him like mother cares for beloved sick child—or she was cross with him for getting out of bed or, heaven forbid, leaving the house. Over the past week, Oliver had grown all too familiar with the many shades of her temperament, both light and dark. Her husband, Philip, seemed only to experience the spiteful version of his embittered wife. She was openly critical of Philip at the dinner table, often asking why he didn't do something he was supposed to do, or complaining about the way in which he did it. She never let anything go. It was embarrassing for Philip and equally awkward for Oliver as their dinner guest.

He took a deep breath to prepare himself, because he had the uneasy feeling that she'd been waiting for him all morning and he was about to get an earful of her disapproval.

Crossing the sandy yard toward her, he kept his eyes on the ground. When he drew near, Abigail lowered her knitting needles and, without a word, glared up at him.

"Good morning," he said, fully aware that she was in a huff and wanted him to know it.

"You were up early," she said with a lift of her chin, waiting for him to explain himself.

"I went riding with Emma," he told her bluntly. "She wanted to show me the wild horses before I left."

"How nice for you." Abigail's tone was vindictive. It was clear she wanted to punish him.

Suddenly he felt fatigued, weary of her constant need to know his whereabouts, as if she owned some part of him or as if he owed her something for her care of him—tending to his injuries, cooking for him, anticipating his every need. He hadn't asked for such devoted attention, but now it seemed she expected some form of fidelity in return.

He fought to conceal his annoyance because he'd appreciated her nursing skills and hospitality. Truly, he did. "I hope I didn't keep you waiting at breakfast."

"No, I saw that you'd gone out," she replied, "so I cooked only enough for myself. But I suppose you're hungry now." There it was again—the spite and malice, as if she wanted to pick a fight and she was waiting for him to punch back.

"No need to trouble yourself," he replied courteously. "I'll just make a cup of tea."

His politeness knocked her down a notch, and she rose from her chair and followed him into the house, hovering. "Don't be silly. I'll get it for you, and maybe there's some porridge left over on the stove."

They entered the kitchen, and she set the kettle to boil while Oliver served himself some cold porridge from the pot. When the tea was adequately steeped, Abigail poured a cup for each of them and sat across from him at the table.

"You're leaving tomorrow," she said.

"Yes."

When he offered nothing more, she cleared her throat. "I can't believe how fast the time went."

"I agree." He thought of the night of the wreck. The terror, the deadly threat of the violent breakers, the loss of a member of his crew, which still pained him. "Life on the *Belvedere* is still very fresh in my mind."

"Are you worried about what will happen when you reach the mainland?" she asked. "That you'll be blamed for it?"

"That's quite likely."

Abigail leaned back in her chair. "As far as I'm concerned, you were a hero that night. You refused to abandon your ship, which was the honorable thing to do."

He stared at her, dumbfounded. "There was nothing honorable about it. Because of me, your crew was forced to make a second trip out to fetch me. Others could have died."

She studied him with what appeared to be enthrallment. "Why *did* you stay behind?"

Oliver's brow furrowed. There was something malicious in the set of her jaw, the dark glimmer in her eyes. It struck him as a hunger for confessions of misery and lost hope, perhaps even self-destruction, but not because she wanted to relieve his suffering. To the contrary, she wanted to bask in it. To share in it. Witness it for herself.

"Does it have something to do with your shame?" she asked, pressing further.

"Shame over what?" Oliver was growing increasingly infuriated.

"Over abandoning your wife and children," she replied.

She might as well have hit him in the head with a steel mallet. She was taking far too much pleasure in this. It was perverse, and he could no longer tolerate it.

"Abigail," he firmly said. "This isn't something I wish to discuss with you."

"Why not? Wait, let me guess. You've already discussed it with Emma when she asked you the same question."

He refused to answer. He merely sipped his tea.

Abigail scoffed. "Everyone's talking about it, you know. The time you've been spending with her. It's disgusting, if you ask me. You're a married man, and she's far too young for you. You're making a fool of yourself, Captain Harris, and you'll spoil her chances for a decent future if you've already ruined her."

He set his teacup onto the saucer with a noisy clatter. "What do you mean, ruined her?"

Abigail sat forward, looking like a hissing cat. "Oh please. No one believes you're just friends. And her father—God help that idiotic man if he thinks he can keep her in a cage. She's wild, but he can't see it. He's blind as a bat."

Oliver slid the teacup and saucer away from him and stood. "That's enough, Abigail."

"Should we place bets on how many crew members she's been with?" Abigail stood and followed him to the back door, pecking at him with her words. "I can't wait to watch you at the party tonight. She'll be all over you, and you won't be able to resist her because she's young and beautiful. And you'll leave here telling yourself that you can forget what happened here, because this place is another planet to you. But you'll remember, and your crew will remember. So will I and everyone else here. The dishonor will follow you. And *her*. Mark my words!"

Oliver pushed the door open and walked out. "Thanks for the tea."

She shouted after him mockingly. "You have no soul, Captain Harris! You only want pretty things!"

Oliver thought of what he'd learned about Abigail that morning, and strove to be as forgiving as Emma, but he couldn't bring himself to see Abigail as anything other than a jealous and vengeful woman.

～

As hostess of the party, Emma could barely find a moment to sit down. She'd set drinks and snacks on the kitchen table so that everyone could help themselves, but there was always something that someone needed or wanted—a straw, a towel to sop up a spilled drink, or a safety pin for one thing or another.

When Captain Harris finally arrived, almost an hour late, she was at the sink, filling a pitcher of water for a fresh batch of orange juice from canned concentrate. At the sound of his voice in the foyer, her heart exploded with excitement and anticipation. He soon took a seat in the great room next to her father, and they became engaged in a spirited conversation about fishing rights on the Grand Banks.

When at last Emma escaped her duties in the kitchen—and the rowdy kitchen crowd—she moved into the great room. The captain was so absorbed in his conversation with her father that he didn't even look up or say hello to her.

Emma sat down on the sofa next to June Shaw, wife of the lighthouse keeper at East Station. It was not often that they saw each other, so they had much to catch up on.

Then Frank O'Reilly joined them. Emma spoke to him for a while, grateful for an excuse to remain in the great room, but she was distracted by the captain and hurt by his aloofness. He kept his back to her the entire evening, and not once did he make eye contact.

Much later, when the kitchen cleared out, June offered to help Emma wash the dishes and put away the food. When the dishes were done and all the young men had left to play cards at the staff house, Emma returned to the great room.

It was empty except for her father. "Where's the captain?"

"He went off to the staff house with the men," her father replied casually, as if it were nothing.

Emma blinked a few times, stunned. Then the news fell like broken glass into her heart. She sank onto the sofa.

Why had Captain Harris avoided her all night? Perhaps she'd revealed too much of herself that morning and he'd recognized her infatuation and didn't wish to lead her on. Had she behaved foolishly, like a childish girl, crying over a dead horse? Clearly lovesick and besotted by an older man of the world?

June entered the room and sat down to wait for her husband to return from the card game. Emma spent the next hour listening to her father advise June about her husband's Sable Island contract and how to set goals for the future.

Emma listened to all this with polite interest, but inside, her mind was screaming. She was restless and agitated, itching to dash out the door, run to the staff house, and join the card game.

When June's husband returned and announced it was time to head home to East Station, she and her father walked them to the door and waved as they drove away in their horse-drawn cart. Then her father turned to Emma.

"You were an excellent hostess tonight. The party was a resounding success, don't you think?"

"Yes."

He kissed the top of her head. "Now I'm off to dreamland. Big day tomorrow. Good night."

Emma watched him go upstairs. Then, discreetly, after waiting for him to close the door to his bedroom, she slipped out of the house and walked briskly across the station yard. Laughter and hooting from inside the staff house told her that the card games were still in full swing. She could barely contain the fervor in her heart. A clock was ticking in her mind. There were so few hours left before the supply ship would arrive and take the captain away.

She knocked on the door and entered.

Frank, who sat at the far end of the table, looked up from his hand. "Emma! Come in!" He rose from his chair. "Can I get you a root beer?"

She glanced around the table, searching for the captain, but he was not among the players, nor was he in the common area with the others.

"No, thank you," she replied. "I only came to say good night and wish you all the best for tomorrow."

"But you'll come to the beach and see us off, won't you?" one of the *Belvedere* men asked.

It was difficult to speak with good cheer when she was drowning in disappointment, but she gave it her best. "Of course. I wouldn't dream of not being there." After a brief pause, she added, "Is the captain around?"

"He's gone to bed," someone told her. "He's not much a cardplayer. He likes his books too much."

A few of the other men nudged each other, so Emma backed toward the door and gave them a friendly salute. "Good night, then, gentlemen. Don't stay up too late. You won't want to miss the boat tomorrow."

"Don't even say it!" someone shouted, and the others laughed and moaned about that appalling scenario.

Emma walked out, shut the door behind her, and glanced around the dark station yard. It was a clear night. The stars were shining. The distant crash of the waves on the beach called out to her, and she wondered if the captain was there, standing in the moonlight, waiting for her to come to him. They'd made no such arrangement, but she clung to the hope that he might wish to share another hour with her, privately, before he departed.

Her pulse thrummed, and she hastened across the station yard to the high dune, her body fueled by anticipation as she climbed to the top. Out of breath, she stood beneath the star-speckled sky and scanned the beach below, but there was nothing but sand and ocean, the white-capped waves in constant motion beneath the gravitational power of the moon.

Disheartened, she sat down on the cool sand, among the tall marram grass, and hugged her knees to her chest. Below, foaming waves rolled onto the beach, one after the other, in a never-ending rhythm. She looked up at the clear night sky—a sure sign that the rescue ship would not be detained by weather. Philip had promised that tomorrow would be a good day for the landing.

Emma should have been happy for the shipwrecked crew of the *Belvedere* and their captain, but all she felt was sorrow, as bottomless and unfathomable as the ocean that constantly reshaped this lonely island—every second, every moment, every day, month, and year. Nothing was ever predictable. Nor did anything in life, for better or worse, remain the same.

~

The following day, the sky was a dense blue and cloudless, the sun blinding. The *Argyle* laid anchor about a mile off North Beach. All residents of the island gathered for the unscheduled Boat Day, which included the delivery of supplies—an efficient use of drained government resources after the long war in Europe.

Emma stood on the breezy beach with the others, waiting by the horse-drawn carts for barrels of salt and flour and giant sacks of potatoes. The staff men, despite their late-night card playing, were full of energy and eager to deliver the *Belvedere* crew to their rescue ship.

Emma shared none of their excitement. Her heart was an anchor plunging into the deep. Where was Captain Harris? Why was he not here?

Her father moved about, greeting everyone personally in his typical friendly fashion. Again, he complimented Emma on the success of the party the night before.

Joseph, the chief staff man, approached. Feigning a casual curiosity, she turned to her father. "I haven't seen Captain Harris yet. We can't let the ship leave without him."

Her father laughed. "Goodness, no! I'm sure he'll be here soon." He leaned toward Joseph. "Unless Abigail has him strapped to the staircase railing."

Joseph laughed, and Emma wondered if people were making jokes like that about *her*.

A small surfboat from the *Argyle* motored onto the beach, and the men set to work in the sunshine, unloading crates and barrels. Once that was done, five men from the *Belvedere* stepped aboard, and off they went, bounding over the blue swells and waving their hats in goodbye as they grew distant.

Emma turned and looked around for Captain Harris. Finally, she spotted him, walking up the beach from the direction of the *Belvedere*. Even from a quarter mile away, she recognized his masculine gait.

If she were not so heartsick, she would have waited on the beach with the others, but her emotions were running wild. She couldn't bear the thought of saying goodbye to him forever. How could she waste precious minutes, simply standing there with a sick feeling in her belly, while he crossed the long distance? She yearned to be near him, touch him, talk to him, and perhaps even arrange to see him again, somehow. Perhaps she could travel to England one day. Or if she lived on the mainland, attending university, he might dock in Halifax.

The alternative—never seeing him again—was unthinkable. It sent her mind into a fighting frenzy. She began to panic, so she excused herself from the others and trudged fast through the deep sand to meet him halfway.

The long walk was torturous.

"Hello, Emma," he said, apprehensively, as he finally drew near.

The sound of his voice and the striking sight of him in the morning light made her realize there was so much of the world—so much of *life*—that she had not yet experienced. An entire universe of the unknown presented itself in the man before her, who aroused her passions in ways she'd never imagined.

Out of breath, Emma stopped. "I didn't get a chance to talk to you last night," she said in a rush of words. "You left without saying goodbye, or even looking at me. Why did you do that?"

Anxious and desperate, she waited for him to explain. Perhaps he was as confused as she by what was happening between them. Or maybe she was living in a fantasy world, and he'd avoided her because he'd realized she'd developed a childish and inappropriate crush on him.

"I'm sorry about that," he said. "But it seemed best not to socialize. I think people were starting to notice."

"Notice what?"

"That we . . ." He paused. "That we'd grown fond of each other."

The words were a balm to her aching heart, and it took a moment for her to settle down and start again, less desperate now. "Yes," she said. "I *am* fond of you. So much more than I expected to be."

It felt lovely to say it, to speak the truth at last.

Exhaling heavily, the captain faced the water. "I understand, and I do feel an affection for you, but I'm leaving today, so you need to put that aside."

Her hopes took a sudden dive, like the surfboats cresting a frothy white wave, then descending down the other side of the mountain. "Why?"

He spoke sharply. "Because I'm a married man, too old for you, and—"

"You're not too old," she argued, "and your wife chose a life with someone else. Doesn't that give you the freedom to—"

He turned on her. "*I'm* the one to blame for that." For a few shuddering seconds, his expression was almost frightening, his eyes full of torment. "Either way, it doesn't give me the freedom to . . ."

He stopped and faced the ocean again. The steady breeze lifted his dark hair, and the morning sunshine, from the east, illuminated his profile.

"To what?" she pressed.

"To do what I want."

She closed her eyes and felt her body slump in defeat. "That makes no sense."

"I don't know how else to say it, Emma."

She struggled to decipher what he was truly feeling. "Is it because you don't believe you deserve happiness?"

He shook his head and met her gaze. "You're overanalyzing this, when it's perfectly simple. I'm a married man, and you're a young single woman, and it's not right."

"But—"

"I can't give you what you want."

She fought to bring her breathing under control. "And what do you think that is?"

He took his time to consider how best to answer the question. "Commitment," he finally said. "Companionship. A proper future. I'm not that man, and you know it."

Her heart slammed against her rib cage, and she wanted to cry out mournfully. "I don't believe you."

Dear God! This was probably the last conversation she would ever have with him, and she couldn't let him leave without making him see how desperately she loved him. He needed to understand how happy they could be together. But heaven help her, she was paralyzed. There wasn't enough time. She couldn't find the words.

"I'm sorry," he said. "I have to go." He started walking toward the other people, the horses and wagons and supplies coming off the surfboats.

"Please, wait!" Emma hurried to keep up with his long, purposeful strides. "I feel things for you I've never felt before, and I don't know what to make of it or what I'll do with myself after you're gone."

"There's nothing for you to do," he replied, "except forget about me and live your life."

"But I'll miss you," she told him, slogging through the deep sand. "I won't be able to stand it." She knew she was begging, and she sounded pathetic, but she couldn't help herself. There was no more time to be subtle.

Captain Harris strode faster, seeming determined to escape the awkwardness and discomfort of this conversation. "Focus on your future, Emma. You'll do well at school. I have no doubt about that."

She couldn't take it anymore. She caught his sleeve in a tight fist, tugged at it, and forced him to stop and turn. "Please, tell me. Do you have feelings for me beyond fondness? Or am I just dreaming? Am I a child to you?"

She needed to know what he felt. She needed truth.

His blue eyes settled on her face. He grimaced slightly, and Emma felt a heavy pressure on her chest, a sensation that was emotionally crushing.

"Emma," he said. "You have so much growing up to do."

The look of compassion in his eyes was the ultimate humiliation. She stood motionless and embarrassed. *Oh, God . . .* all those foolish fantasies . . .

"I'm sorry if I made you think there was anything more than friendship between us," he added.

She closed her eyes briefly, squared her shoulders, and groped for whatever was left of her shredded dignity. "Please don't apologize. It's not your fault. I just . . . I misunderstood things."

He said nothing more, but he didn't walk away.

Suddenly, her pride bucked and roared. Emma lifted her chin. "You should go. You don't want to miss that boat."

He turned his gaze toward the others on the beach.

"Go on," she said fiercely. "I'm fine here. I understand everything you've said to me, and I appreciate your honesty. I needed to hear that. Now I just want to be alone for a few minutes."

"You're sure?"

"Yes."

He continued to hesitate until it became unbearable.

"Please go," she implored, clinging to her pride.

"All right." He held out his hand. "Goodbye, Emma. It was a pleasure to know you."

Swallowing hard, she accepted the hand he offered and shook it. "Likewise."

His hand was strong and warm, and she made every effort to remember how it felt, to imprint it on her mind forever. Then she forced herself to pull away from him because she wanted the rest of this parting to be swift. She couldn't bear it any other way—the slow, agonizing ravaging of her heart.

The captain finally turned and left her standing alone on the beach with the cruel ocean wind whipping at her hair. She watched him walk away, and although she tried, she still could not accept that she would never see him again. Everything in her heart and soul cried otherwise—that this was not over, and somehow the connection they'd shared would continue to exist, even from afar.

As she began to walk in the other direction, the terns darted and screeched incessantly over their colony on the dune. They always seemed so riled up. So incensed. That morning, Emma felt completely in tune with them.

CHAPTER 8

Following the departure of the *Belvedere* crew, life on Sable Island returned to its rhythmic ebb and flow, day to day, week to week. The wild herds came back from their springtime feast of sandwort on the west end of the island, and the staff men resumed their scheduled beach patrols, morning, noon, and night, searching for signs of shipwrecks.

During the war, the Sable Island community had been on high alert for German U-boats, but since the invention of radar, and now during peacetime, the odds of a ship running aground at Sable had diminished. Some said the wreck of the *Belvedere* might be the last of its kind and the Humane Establishment might become a thing of the past.

Although Emma had loved growing up on Sable, she now saw no future for herself there. Something had changed since her experience with Captain Harris. Perhaps it was an awakening of some sort, physical and emotional. Suddenly her goal to receive a proper education on the mainland had become vital, her own personal lifeboat. It gave her a sense of purpose and helped her to remain hopeful and optimistic whenever her thoughts drifted to the captain and the horrible agony of his departure.

There were times when it all felt like a dream—the bliss of those hours they'd spent alone together, walking or riding—but it was a dream that had not ended happily. It had, in fact, become rather nightmarish. Captain Harris was gone, but her longings persisted. Sometimes they weighed her down like an anchor, and it became difficult to focus on the simplest task when she was gazing off into space, dreaming about the sound of his voice and imagining his touch, his kiss, and so much more.

But oh, how those desires grated on her. They were constantly eclipsed by the hurtful things he'd said to her that final morning on the beach. Whenever she replayed that scene in her mind, the humiliation returned, usually accompanied by exasperation and anger.

She was not accustomed to falling apart emotionally. It was not something she was enjoying, so she struggled to soldier on—as the captain of her dreams had once put it so eloquently.

~

Early one foggy morning when the mist was so thick it left a cold wet film on her cheeks, Emma walked westward across the heath. She was still melancholy about the captain but continued to promise herself that all she needed was change—a new life on the mainland with scholarly pursuits to keep her mind occupied, new friends and places to explore. All she had to do was survive the summer on Sable Island and try not to think of him so often.

Suddenly, out of the fog, came a shadow. But no . . . it was not a shadow but a person, walking toward her on the same narrow horse trail. They met in a dense cluster of fragrant bayberries.

"Good morning," Frank said, smiling. "I didn't expect to see anyone else out so early."

"Neither did I," Emma replied, feeling none of the awkwardness she usually felt around Frank. There was something about his smile that morning. For once, it didn't seem to prey on her.

"I needed some exercise after a long overnight shift," he said. "I'm just heading back now."

"I should turn back as well." Emma glanced over her shoulder, toward Main Station. "I didn't realize how far I'd walked."

"Let's walk together?" he asked.

"Why not? But let's take the beach."

"North or south?"

"You choose."

Frank didn't need to think about it. He led Emma to a break in the dune on the north side of the island.

"Have you gone to look at the *Belvedere* lately?" he asked.

"Not lately," she replied. She'd been resisting the urge because she knew it would only take her backward.

"She's more than half-buried," Frank told her. "It must have been that nor'easter on Wednesday. Soon she'll be gone, sucked into the sand with all the others. Like she was never here."

Emma swallowed uneasily. There were more than three hundred shipwrecks buried around her island home. More evidence to confirm that it was time to leave this place and start fresh somewhere else, with new memories and fewer ghosts.

She and Frank emerged onto North Beach, where the fog was thick and milky. The temperature dropped, and Emma fastened the top button of her coat.

"Are you cold?" Frank asked.

She felt his eyes on her and sensed he was evaluating her mood, which proved to be correct, because he spoke cautiously.

"Emma. I don't mean to pry, but you haven't been yourself lately. Not since Captain Harris left. Are you all right?"

It was a direct question—painfully direct—and Emma couldn't think of how to respond.

Frank gently continued to probe. "I understand . . . because I know how it feels to love someone and not have your feelings reciprocated."

Emma had never doubted that Frank was a decent young man, but unfortunately, her feelings for him had never gone beyond friendship. Only now was she beginning to see how she'd hurt him over the past few months. In her defense, it hadn't occurred to her while it was happening, especially recently when she'd been so caught up in her blind passion for Captain Harris. But she understood the world better these days.

"It's not easy," she confessed.

They walked in silence, looking down at the path before them.

"Does your father know?" Frank asked.

"Good heavens, no. I'd be mortified."

"You can always talk to me about it if you want to. I just want to be your friend, Emma." He spoke in a low voice, his eyes downcast. "If I can't be anything else."

Emma felt an ache of regret for the pain she'd caused him—and was *still* causing him—but she was afraid of where this conversation might lead if she surrendered too deeply to her sympathies. So she stayed mute as they walked.

"Did you ever tell the captain how you felt?" Frank asked after a time.

"Yes," she replied. "On the last day, just before he left."

"What did he say?"

She sighed dejectedly. "He told me to forget him because he's a married man and too old for me."

Frank slid his hands into his coat pockets. "I can't say I disagree. At least he was honest with you."

Emma knew that Frank was right, but she still couldn't seem to let it go. "But his wife is with someone else. And he's not *that* old."

Frank stopped walking and faced her. "He's still married, Emma, and he's deserted two children. He's lived an entire life that you know nothing about, so I'm pretty sure you don't know him as well as you think you do."

She felt as if she'd been struck across the back with a wood plank. She couldn't argue, and Frank knew it, so he pushed on.

"If you want my advice," he said, "you should forget about Captain Harris. Otherwise, you'll make yourself miserable dreaming about something you can never have."

Emma pressed her lips together and shivered in the chill of the damp fog. "What do you know about him that I don't?" she asked, craving information. "You spent time with his crew. Did you hear things?"

Because of their intimate conversations, she'd thought she knew the captain better than anyone on the island. But maybe that wasn't the case.

Frank shook his head with frustration and started off again. "I haven't heard any gossip, if that's what you mean. But those are the facts that everyone knows. He's been to war, he has two children he never sees, and he ran his ship aground. He'll be professionally disgraced by that. Honestly, you could do better, Emma."

With someone like you?

If she had listened to her father and given Frank O'Reilly a chance at the outset, maybe she wouldn't be wallowing in grief right now.

She hurried to catch up to Frank, and all her feelings came spilling out. "I know I have to accept that there's no future there, but I just can't get him out of my head. It's like an obsession. The love won't let go of me."

"It wasn't love," Frank said irritably. "You only knew him for a week." He stopped walking, raked his fingers through his hair, and shook his head with remorse. "I'm sorry. That was mean. I understand what you're going through. I really do."

Emma stared at him for a moment, wishing she could feel more than friendship for him, but her relationship with Frank couldn't hold a candle to what she'd felt for the captain.

Linking her arm through Frank's, she invited him to walk on beside her.

"Please don't apologize. It's fine. You're a good friend to me." It was important to her that she made her feelings clear.

"You're a good friend to me as well," he replied.

They continued along the foggy beach, arm in arm, listening to the constant low thunder of the ocean, feeling the cool mist on their cheeks. Thankfully, Frank let the sensitive subject of their friendship go, and they spoke instead about what her living arrangements would be in September when she began classes at university.

Emma could hardly wait for Boat Day at the end of August, when she would finally board the ship, steam off to the mainland, and begin a new chapter in her life—because she wanted very much to turn the page on this one.

CHAPTER 9

"I don't understand why you're packing so many outfits," Emma's father said grudgingly from the open doorway of her bedroom.

She sat back on her heels next to her trunk, where she'd been folding sweaters happily. But now she felt the weight of his disapproval roll into the room like a thundercloud.

She wished she was leaving in three hours instead of three days, because lately he'd become disparaging about everything.

"I need clothes for two seasons," she explained, "because I won't be back until Christmas."

Her father moved into the room and sat on the chair by the window. He watched her fold a tweed jacket and place it in the trunk. "It's so far away, Emma."

She let out a breath of fatigue. "It's not that far. And we've been through this a hundred times. You know how much this means to me. Please don't make me feel guilty. I don't want to worry that you're angry with me—or worse, that you're lonely or depressed."

Her father was a proud man, and under normal circumstances, he'd be offended by the mere insinuation of emotional weakness. But today he stared at the floor and spoke woefully. "I don't know what I'm going to do without you, Emma. It won't be the same."

In that instant, something caught in her chest, and she regretted their recent hostilities, the fact that they'd been at war. She loved her father with all her heart, and she didn't want to leave him like this.

"You'll get along fine, Papa," she said gently, with compassion. "And I'm going to miss you too. I'll miss you *terribly*."

His eyes lifted. "That's the first time I've heard you say it."

She realized it was true, and she wished things could have been different between them these last months. "I guess I've been on the defensive," she explained.

Wanting to fix things, Emma stood up and held out her hand. "Let's go for a walk. Like old times."

He rose from the chair.

An hour later, they were laughing as they skidded down the steep side of the high dune toward North Beach, where the sun beat hotly onto the bright sand. The wind in Emma's face thrilled her—along with the fear that she was sliding too fast and might tumble and roll down the slope. It carried her back to her happy childhood, when her father had taken her on grand adventures to every corner of the island to run and play, and to frolic in the waves. He'd taught her about the horses and vegetation, and the unique geography of their special island home, surrounded by swirling ocean currents. He told jokes and let her drive the horse-drawn carts when she was barely big enough to grip the reins. He picked her up and swung her high in the air before depositing her into her bed each night to read her a story.

"What a perfect day," he said, sounding jovial for the first time in ages as he walked briskly ahead of Emma on the wide beach, jogging toward the crashing waves.

At the water's edge, the sand, dampened from the outgoing tide, was packed tight. Dozens of gray seals basked in the sun, lolling about lazily, but her father's approach sent the herd into a frenzy. They bounced laboriously on their bellies, galumphing into the noisy surf.

Emma watched her father crouch down to touch the water and test the temperature. Another wave rolled in, so he flicked his hand dry and backed away to avoid getting his shoes soaked.

"How is it?" Emma called out.

He rubbed his hands together and strolled back to where she stood. "As cold as midwinter."

"Gosh darn Labrador current," she lightly replied.

Two seagulls screeched in the air above them, and Emma looked up. Then she and her father turned to stroll eastward, with the wind at their backs. She moved close to him and wrapped her arms around his waist, rested her head on his shoulder. "Thank you for letting me go away to school. And I promise, I *will* miss you, and I'll write as often as I can."

He wrapped his arm around her shoulders. "I wish the *Argyle* could come more often than once a month. It's a long time to wait for a letter."

"Yes, but on the bright side," she replied, "you'll have a whole sack of them arrive all at once, which will keep you busy reading for weeks."

He laughed at that. "I'll read them all in a single day."

"I'll do the same. I just hope they don't get delivered when I have a test or exam, or I'll fail miserably."

"You'll fail at nothing," he said, "because you're brilliant."

She smiled up at him. "I'll try not to let that go to my head."

They came upon a large piece of driftwood and separated to walk around it, then walked for a while in silence, ten feet apart, each of them enjoying the sensation of vigorous exercise in the fresh air and blood flowing robustly through their veins.

After a time, her father moved closer and walked beside Emma. "Maybe it was the wreck of the *Belvedere*," he suggested, looking up at the cottony clouds in the sky, "that's made this more difficult. It reminded me about loss, and ever since then, I've been thinking about your mother, about what she would have wanted for you."

"What would that have been?" Emma asked, eager to know.

"She would have wanted you to follow your dreams. She was always keen for an adventure and believed we should all make the most of life while we're fortunate enough to be alive and healthy. She would have hated for me to hold you back. She wouldn't have stood for it."

"I wish I could have known her," Emma said.

"I wish that too. But here we are, and these were the cards we were dealt."

Just then, an enormous gray seal, shrieking and barking, launched itself out of the waves and onto the beach.

"Watch yourself!" her father shouted.

Emma scurried away, and her father followed, keeping himself between Emma and the seal, which nipped at his heels. They ran and didn't stop until they reached a safe distance and the seal retreated.

"Are you all right?" her father asked, out of breath.

"Yes. What about you?"

He bent to rub his ankle. "She snapped at me, but I'm fine."

"Are you sure? Let me see." Emma lifted the cuff of her father's trousers and discovered a small gash above his Achilles tendon. "It's not bad," she said. "But we should put a bandage on it." She lowered the trouser cuff and straightened.

"We should be getting back anyway," he said, unfazed. "You still have some packing to do."

They decided to walk through the interior on the return journey and avoid any further confrontations with overly aggressive seals on the beach.

~

The following morning, Emma stretched her arms over her head and said aloud, "Forty-eight hours until Boat Day."

She rose from bed, dressed and washed, and ventured downstairs to the kitchen to cook a pot of oatmeal. Expecting to see her father at his desk with a cup of coffee as usual, she passed by his den, but his chair was empty. She walked into the room and opened the curtains to see if he was out in the station yard. There were no signs of anyone, but it was still early, barely past the first glimmer of dawn.

Emma returned to the kitchen, filled a pot of water at the sink, and carried it to the stove. While she stood over the pot, waiting for it to boil, a memory surfaced, and she was carried back to the day she and Captain Harris had found Willow's mother, dead in the sand. He had listened to everything she'd needed to say about the loss of her own mother. It was a moment that continued to echo in her mind—the sound of his voice in her ear, the touch of his hands, and the awakening in her body and soul.

She had hoped that by now, after an entire summer, the memories would come less often, but it still wasn't the case, and she was losing patience with herself.

The water began to boil. With intention, she wrenched herself out of the past, measured a cup of dry oats, and dumped them into the pot. Giving it a stir, she listened for sounds of her father moving about upstairs. He was usually awake by this time, so she went hesitantly to the bottom of the stairs, listened more carefully, and still heard nothing.

Something felt not quite right.

Emma called up to him. "Papa? Are you awake?"

No answer.

She waited a few seconds, then climbed the stairs and knocked on his door. "Papa?"

Again, no answer, so she opened the door a crack, peered in, and saw him lying in bed, sleeping. The window was open. The curtains were billowing on gentle gusts of fresh air coming in off the water. A fly buzzed and bounced against the glass, looking for a way to escape.

Hesitantly, she approached, and abruptly began to perspire as she imagined her father not sleeping but dead, just like Willow's mother lying in the sand. Emma's pulse quickened. Her stomach lurched with sudden nausea, but she fought to ignore it and told herself that she was being foolish.

Using the back of her hand, she touched his forehead.

To her great relief, he was warm and still breathing. "Papa, wake up." She shook him, but he remained unresponsive.

"Papa!"

Still nothing.

Feeling as if she'd been physically struck, Emma turned and ran. She barreled down the stairs to the telephone in the kitchen and called Abigail.

~

"I don't know what's wrong!" Abigail snapped after trying everything to rouse Emma's father, including pinching and shaking him. "Has he been sick lately? Complaining of a headache or anything else?"

"Nothing," Emma said. "He was fine when he went to bed last night." She imagined the worst. "Do you think he's had a stroke or a heart attack?"

"I don't know."

"Wait . . . ," Emma said, thinking. "He was bitten by a seal yesterday. Could that have something to do with it?"

"Where?"

"North Beach."

"No! I mean where on his *body*!" she barked. "Show me."

Emma pulled the covers back and raised the hem of her father's pajama bottoms. "Right here. *Oh, God!*"

The flesh around the small wound was dark red and swollen, and an ugly rash was traveling up the length of his calf.

"It's infected," Emma said.

Abigail examined the area. "It's worse than that. I'm not even sure what this is."

Emma stared at the red blotches, and her breath came short. This wasn't happening. She shook her father again, more violently this time. "Papa, wake up!"

In a fit of anxiety, Abigail squeezed her hair in her fists. "I don't know what's wrong with him!"

Panic was getting them nowhere, so Emma held up a hand and fought for calm. "Let's think this through. If it's an infection, does he need penicillin?"

A medical professional Emma was not. She had no idea if that was an appropriate treatment, but she needed Abigail to focus on a solution, not the problem, because the problem was terrifying.

Abigail stared at the unsightly rash. "It could be a putrid ulcer. Or galloping gangrene. He might have sepsis."

"I don't know what any of that means," Emma said with frustration.

Abigail locked eyes with her. "It means he needs to get to a hospital."

This, at least, was something Emma could attack. She hurried toward the stairs. "I'll call Frank."

As chief wireless operator, Frank would contact the mainland, and if the weather cooperated and the beach was stable enough to use as a runway, an airplane might come.

PART TWO

WILD HORSES

CHAPTER 10

October 10, 1946

Dear Captain Harris,

It's been many months since you left Sable Island, but because you and my father established a close friendship during the short time you were a guest here, I felt it was important to deliver some unfortunate news. I'm not sure if you recall, but I had planned to leave Sable at the end of August to attend Dalhousie University. A few days before I was supposed to board the ship for the mainland, my father and I went strolling on the beach, where he was bitten by a large gray seal. He considered it "only a small nip," and we went home thinking nothing of it. The next morning, however, I couldn't wake him, so I called Abigail, and we discovered that the wound had become infected.

My father was taken by air to the Victoria General Hospital in Halifax where it was determined that he had contracted a bacterial infection that was spreading quickly up his leg. To prevent further spreading of the bacteria, the decision was made to amputate. Thankfully, the surgery was a success, and for that I am grateful.

I'm not sure why I felt compelled to write to you about this, but since you had come to know all of us so well while you were stranded at Sable, I thought you might want to know.

The good news is that, after a lengthy recovery in the hospital, my father is now home with us and has resumed his duties as superintendent. He can't get around as quickly as he used to because he has a prosthetic leg, and I'm sure you can imagine how challenging it is for him to walk on the dunes or even in the station yard where the sand is shifty. But he always loved working at his desk, so that is unchanged.

Thankfully, the Canadian Government has been excellent, and they sent supplies for the construction of concrete walkways between all the buildings at Main Station. Everyone loves our modern "sidewalks" and I'm sure the nesting beetles in the sand appreciate it as well because, when we all keep to the concrete, it prevents them from getting stomped on.

As for the rest of us, we are doing well. The weather has been mild lately (shockingly fog-free!) and the staff men are busy with some seasonal repairs at Station Number Two. Philip McKenna is still launching weather balloons every day, and Abigail has been knitting non-stop. She gave my father a lovely afghan for the parlor sofa to celebrate his return from the hospital.

Unfortunately, I must report that there has still been no word about your crewmen who rowed into the storm on that dreadful night, nor has there been any sign of the boat they sequestered. It has therefore been concluded that they were lost to the sea. I'm very sorry.

As for my own situation, sadly, I had to postpone my studies, but the university was understanding of my circumstances, and they expect me next fall. Hope springs eternal!

In all seriousness, despite these setbacks, I am not discouraged, and I am enormously content to be here with my father, helping him navigate this new existence with so many unique challenges. (I think, after the long war, we've all learned how to be patient and wait for the things we want, am I right? Nothing is ever instant or predictable. Occasionally, a grenade is dropped into our best laid plans, and we must leap out of the way and adapt to a changed environment. Oh, dear me. Now I've become philosophical.)

In more practical terms, I remind myself that one day I might have patients with physical disabilities who will need care regarding their mental health, so in a way, I consider this a valuable prologue to my education, because Papa certainly has his struggles.

So that is all the news from Sable Island. I hope this letter finds you well and that things were not too difficult for you with your employer after what happened during that deadly spring storm that brought you to our shores.

Best wishes,
Emma Clarkson

CHAPTER 11

Christmas on Sable Island required much planning. Preparations began in the fall with the arrival of the Eaton's catalog, and Santa's much anticipated arrival depended entirely on the Christmas boat, which laid anchor mid-December. Spruce trees were shipped from Nova Scotia, and each family enjoyed their own traditions. Some waited until Christmas Eve to decorate their trees, while Emma had grown up with an early celebration of stringing lights and hanging tinsel the same day the tree came ashore.

The Christmas following "the Great Seal Attack" (as that horrendous event came to be known), Emma took charge of dragging the spruce tree into the great room and setting it up vertically in the stand, which she had, that morning, pilfered out of deep storage. Luckily for her, Frank knocked on the door just as she was wrestling with the tree in an epic battle to stand it upright.

Frank helped string the lights while her father sat in his leather chair, supervising the placement of the ornaments and sipping sherry in an exquisite crystal glass that was reserved specially for the holiday season. It had been a gift from him to Emma's mother the first year of their marriage.

Frank and Emma took some sherry as well, and it was a lovely day. Snow began to fall shortly after sunset, and Emma felt blessed to see her father in a state of good physical health and cheerful optimism—a rare thing since the accident. She looked forward to ringing in the new year and hoped that 1947 would be better than '46.

~

"What's this?" Emma asked on Christmas morning as she reached for a large but unfamiliar package under the tree. It was wrapped in plain brown paper and tucked against the back wall.

"You'll have to take that up with Santa Claus," her father replied as he sipped his hot chocolate.

Emma raised a curious eyebrow and carried the box, which was quite heavy, to the sofa. "There's no tag." She sat down and held it on her lap. "Who's it from?"

"Open it and find out."

Emma tore at the paper and unearthed a decorative box with brass fittings and images of peacocks. When she raised the lid, she found an antique sextant and three books inside. She withdrew each one and read the titles aloud to her father.

"*A General Introduction to Psychoanalysis*, by Sigmund Freud. How wonderful." She examined the second one and opened to the first page. "*Black Beauty*. Oh, my goodness, this is a first edition." She moved on to the third. "*Modern Man in Search of a Soul*, by Carl Jung, also a first edition. Good heavens."

Her heart fluttered with cautious hope as she began to suspect who had sent the gift. She dug into the box, hoping to find a tag or a card, and there, beneath the white tissue paper at the bottom, was a sealed letter with her name written upon it.

"It's from Captain Harris," she said, feeling breathless and slightly dazed. "The sextant must be for you. How nice of him to remember that you collected them."

"The package arrived on the Christmas boat," her father explained, "with a return address from England, so I hid it away until this morning. I thought you'd enjoy the surprise."

She smiled across at him. "Thank you, Papa. And thank you for being so cheerful this morning."

He sipped his hot chocolate. "I can't guarantee I'll be cheerful tomorrow, but it's Christmas Day, so I'll do my best not to be an old grouch." He set his cup on the side table and rubbed his hands together. "Well then? Don't keep me in suspense. What does the letter say?"

She reached into the box and discovered a second sealed envelope beneath the first. "There appears to be two of them—one for each of us."

Emma stood and delivered her father's letter to him, then returned to the sofa and ran the pad of her finger across her name, written elegantly in black ink. She turned the envelope over, and with great care not to rip the paper, she broke the seal.

November 12, 1946

Dear Emma,

Thank you for sending news about your father's accident and—thankfully and mercifully—his recovery, though I am very sorry to hear about the loss of his leg. How difficult that must have been for you both to manage the shock of that diagnosis. Allow me to convey my deepest sympathies.

I must have read your letter at least five times until I finally decided I must reply and send gifts for Christmas. I have no idea if the package will arrive in time, but if not, please consider it a gift for the new year instead.

In your letter, you asked about the situation regarding my employer following the wreck of the Belvedere. *An investigation is still ongoing, but each member of the crew has provided information about the storm and the events that led to our misfortune on the sandbar. My solicitor made good use of the letter your father sent (I am greatly* indebted to him), and a respected weather expert from London has insisted that no ship could have remained on course under the force of such high winds and the enormity of the swells.

So, as it stands today, I am still gainfully employed, and the shipping company is rather pleased to be collecting funds from an insurance policy. I set sail for another transatlantic crossing in the new year, on a recently refurbished steamer, this time heading to North Virginia. Wish me luck and no monster storms like the last one.

But enough about the weather. I am disappointed to hear that your studies had to be postponed, but I hope you can take that leap again next fall when your father has had a chance, God willing, to become accustomed to his new circumstances. I'm sure that, over the coming year, he will have no shortage of help and support from the community at Sable, which I will remember forever with great fondness and affection. Such a generous and charitable group of individuals you all were. Especially you, Emma.

I'm not sure if you realize it, but you helped me through a difficult time. Your father is a lucky man to have you at his side during these enormous physical and emotional trials. One of the things I admired most about you was your ability to see a glass as half full, not half empty. It is clear to me that you are displaying that quality yet again in the way you've accepted the postponement of your studies. Your positive outlook will take you far in life, and I have no doubt that you will be a tremendous success, whatever path you choose.

So that is that. I hope you and your father enjoy the gifts, and more importantly, I hope you know how deeply

I will always treasure the memory of our conversations,
not to mention the appearance of the wild horses.
  Sincerely,
  Oliver Harris

Emma lowered the letter to her lap and realized there were tears streaming down her face. She supposed she shouldn't be surprised by the overflowing of her emotions. Since the captain left her on the beach that terrible final day, she'd been burying her feelings in an attempt to mend her broken heart. But suddenly, those feelings of loss and longing were exploding out of her soul with a vengeance, and she felt crushed all over again.

Emma sucked in a breath and fought to compose herself. She wiped the tears away and glanced across at her father.

"Bad news?" he asked with a frown.

"Not at all." She laughed ridiculously through her tears. "Goodness. I don't know what's wrong with me."

"I think I know," her father said with a note of concern.

Emma shook her head. "No, Papa, you can't possibly know. And please don't try to guess. I'm fine."

"I may have lost a leg," he said, "but I'm not blind. I saw how you looked at the captain when he was here, especially that last night when he ignored you, which I'm glad he did because it was obvious that you were infatuated. At least to me. And ever since he left the island, you've been broken down and miserable. You've tried to maintain a stiff upper lip for my benefit—which I appreciate—but I know you too well, and I can't bear to see you broken."

"I'm not broken," Emma argued, clinging to her dignity and wishing she could convince herself of her recovery as much as her father. "I'm fine."

He sat back and relented, to some extent. "I'll trust that you're telling me the truth. As long as you can promise me . . ."

She waited impatiently for him to finish the thought. "Promise what?"

"That you've accepted there's no future in that dream," he said. "Captain Harris isn't the one for you. I hope you know that."

The words struck her like a door slamming shut in her face. "Of course I know it." Her voice trembled as she wiped another tear from under her eye. She wanted to catch it before it reached her cheek. "Why do you think I'm crying?"

At the sight of her tears, he lowered his gaze and softened his tone. "We've all been through hard times lately, but we're looking at a new year. Let's try to move forward and put the past, and futile dreams, behind us. Can we both do that?"

Emma understood that he was referring to the loss of his leg and his own impossible wish that he could be the man he once was, physically. But what happened in the hospital could never be reversed, and time would march on. His only choice was to accept his disability and learn how to live with it. Emma understood this.

"Yes," she said. "I want to move on." She wanted to be happy and satisfied, free of her painful yearnings.

"You'll go to university next fall," he declared, having come to accept that choice as well. "Focus on that goal, and my advice is to not write back to the captain. Nothing good can come of it. It'll only ignite your feelings again. I'll send him a thank-you letter for the gifts myself, from both of us, and that will be the end of it. Agreed? It's not likely you'll ever see him again anyway."

Emma nodded morosely and slid the letter back into the envelope. She placed it in the bottom of the box and covered it up with the crumpled white tissue paper.

CHAPTER 12

In April, daily temperatures were on the rise, and the speed of the winter winds died down. The spring migration of shorebirds began, and sandpipers, sanderlings, and willets congregated around the freshwater ponds. But the marram grass was still brown.

Emma had been kept busy that winter caring for her father, doing more for him than ever before. It was the little things that took up most of her time. He often asked her to fetch small items for him—a glass of water from the kitchen or a book on the top shelf in his den when he was seated at his desk—simply because it was faster and more efficient for her to do it, rather than for him to rise laboriously, reach for his cane, and cross the room.

She'd ordered a book about depression due to chronic pain after an injury, and it arrived on the March supply ship. She found it immensely helpful, especially regarding her own enabling behaviors, which allowed her father to continue to feel sorry for himself. As time went on, she used many of the suggested techniques to motivate him to do things for himself and also to cope with the grief and anger over his reduced mobility. Some days, the techniques worked. Other days, they did not.

~

The phone rang in the kitchen, and Emma hurried from the great room to answer it. "Hello? Frank, I thought you'd never call. What's the status?"

"The ship's anchored, and the surfboats are on their way."

"Wonderful. We'll head down to the beach now. Papa wants to be there to greet the new man and see what he's made of."

The Sable Island lifesaving crew was a tight-knit lot. It was essential to morale that a new member was the right fit.

"He should come ashore within the hour," Frank replied. "I'll see you down there."

"Right then." Emma hung up the phone and grabbed the keys to the Jeep.

~

Emma drove the open-topped Jeep onto the beach so her father could supervise the unloading from the passenger seat. When the first surfboat finally came bounding over the frothy waves and slid onto the sand, four staff men ran to unburden the small craft of boxes and barrels. Emma got out of the Jeep to stretch her legs and chat with their neighbors, who gathered around.

It was not until the fourth boat arrived that the new employee, a man named Logan Baxter, stepped onto the beach. He brought a dark-red duffel bag, which he slung over his left shoulder, and shook hands with one of the staff men who pointed toward the Jeep.

"That must be him," Emma said to her father, curious to get a closer look at him as she leaned against the passenger-side door, shading her eyes in the blinding sunshine.

As Mr. Baxter trudged through the deep sand toward them, she took in his appearance. He wore a gray wool jacket, black trousers, and a blue plaid cap, but it was his coloring that struck Emma the most. He had blond hair, blue eyes, and suntanned, freckled skin, which was different from the men on Sable, who all had brown or black hair with beards or mustaches. This man was clean shaven. He looked almost Nordic.

He stopped in front of the vehicle. "Are you John Clarkson?"

"I am," her father replied in that deep, commanding voice that never failed to earn people's respect in an instant. "You must be Logan Baxter. Welcome to Sable. This is my daughter, Emma."

Logan dropped his duffel bag on the sand and moved to shake her hand, then her father's. "It's a pleasure to meet you."

His eyes twinkled with friendly appeal, and she felt her cheeks flush with color. *Oh dear.* This one was a heartbreaker for sure. She turned away and resolved to be on her guard. No more blushing permitted.

She spoke with aloofness. "It's nice to meet you as well. Grab your bag and hop in the back, and we'll take you to Main Station." She circled around the front of the Jeep to the driver's seat and got behind the wheel.

While Logan hustled to retrieve his bag, her father leaned close to Emma and spoke quietly. "Do you think he'll last?"

It never took long for new people to grow weary of the isolation.

"Only time will tell," she replied, and turned the key in the ignition.

~

"This place isn't at all what I expected," Logan said as he followed Emma's father into his den to fill out some papers.

"What were you expecting?" Emma asked as she entered behind them.

"For it to feel smaller. I've read a lot about Sable Island, and I imagined a sandbar. But now that I'm here, it feels so much bigger. Like a real island."

"Bigger?" Her father chuckled cynically as he sat down behind his desk and rested his cane up against it. "It's barely a mile wide from one beach to the other."

"True," Logan said, "but looking out your windows, everything's so green, like a big meadow. You can't even see the ocean from here."

"But you can always hear it," Emma assured him.

After an awkward pause, he set his duffel bag on the floor and riffled through it. "I have papers here. The office told me to give them to you as soon as I arrived."

"Let's have a look, then," her father said.

Logan withdrew a large envelope and handed it to Emma. She felt his eyes on her as she carried it around the desk and passed it to her father, who laid it out on the tidy leather blotter.

He donned his reading glasses and read over the first page. Peering up at Logan over the rims of his glasses, he asked, "You're a veterinarian?"

Emma leaned over her father's shoulder to look at the file.

"I mostly treated horses and cows," Logan explained.

"That'll be an asset here," her father replied. "And you're from Saskatchewan?"

"Correct."

Her father removed his glasses and dropped them onto the blotter. "What in the world brought you all the way to Nova Scotia? And even farther, to Sable Island?"

Logan removed his wool cap. He squeezed it, almost mangled it, in front of him. "I'm here because I don't want to work on farms for the rest of my life. I'd like to teach."

Suddenly curious, Emma inclined her head. "Teach what?"

He shifted his weight nervously. "I'm not sure yet. But I came here to study the wild horses, maybe even do a research project—in my spare time, of course. I thought that might help me get my foot in the door at a university."

Emma's father glanced over his shoulder at her. "Are you listening to this?"

"I am." She clasped her hands loosely behind her back. "What would be the focus of your research project, specifically?"

"Well . . ." Seeming nervous, Logan continued to wring his cap in his hands. "I'm curious about natural herd behavior, how the stallions behave as alpha males, whether the herds take on any family dynamics, and, if so, if the families stay together for life."

Her father wagged a finger at Logan. "My daughter will be a great help to you. She's been studying the herds since she was ten years old. It's her passion."

Logan's eyebrows lifted. When he spoke, his voice was animated. "No kidding. I'd love to talk to you about it sometime, if you're willing to share what you've learned."

She opened her mouth to respond, but her father spoke first. "She already has pages of written notes. You wouldn't believe it. A whole box full of scribblers in her bedroom. Do you know where they are, Emma?"

"Yes, but . . ."

Her father continued presumptuously. "You can read over what's she's already jotted down. But don't forget that you have a job to do here. That'll always take priority. Understood?"

"Absolutely," Logan replied. "That goes without saying."

Her father picked up his pen and leaned forward over the desk. "Good. Now let's fill out some forms. Then Emma can take you to the staff house and introduce you to your supervisor, Joseph. After the supplies are dealt with, you'll start your training with lifesaving techniques. I hope you're a good swimmer in rough currents, because if we have any more shipwrecks like we had last spring, you'll be up to your ears in salt water."

Emma met Logan's apprehensive gaze and considered the fact that he'd grown up on the prairies. Had he ever experienced the full force of the ocean in a storm? Did he have any idea what he'd gotten himself into?

Since it was too late for him to back out now, she endeavored to ease his fears. Emma shook her head and crinkled her nose because there was no point inducing unnecessary anxiety—and potentially a sleepless night—when the poor man hadn't even set foot in the boat shed yet.

She hoped he wouldn't be too put off by the skull collection.

~

"I never saw so many brazen birds in one spot," Logan said as Emma steered the Jeep through a colony of terns. They flitted about and screeched constantly. One landed on the road, directly in front of her left tire, so she hit the brakes.

"This is their territory," she explained, "so they have the right of way."

"Is that a Sable Island bylaw?" he asked.

"Not exactly," she replied, "but it's an Emma Clarkson law, and everyone on the island respects it."

Logan leaned over the side of the open vehicle to keep watch on the sandy path. "Slow down—there's a stubborn one just ahead of your right tire."

Emma touched the brakes and waited for an all clear.

"There he goes. Out of harm's way now." Logan sat back. "Carry on, soldier."

Emma gently hit the gas and drove slowly.

"How long have you been living here?" he asked, looking up at the noisy birds teeming about.

"All my life. I was born here."

"I didn't think anyone lived here permanently," he replied. "I thought it was always a one- or two-year posting."

"There aren't many of us who have been here this long. Most come and go. After they've been here awhile, they find the isolation more difficult than they expect."

"But not you?"

She shrugged. "It's all I've ever known."

The road opened to the wide sandy beach, and Emma shifted into a higher gear.

~

"How did he get along at the staff house?" Emma's father asked when she returned and hung the keys to the Jeep on the hook by the door.

"He hasn't met the men yet," she explained. "They're still unloading supplies. I took him to drop off his bag at the staff house and returned him to the beach. He's Joseph's problem now."

"I suspect he put him straight to work."

"He did," Emma replied.

"Good." Her father leaned on his cane as he limped from the kitchen to the great room. With a groan of annoyance, he sank onto his chair. "I wish I could be out there."

Emma remembered how he loved to roll up his sleeves and help with the deliveries. She squeezed his shoulder as she moved to the sofa. "Is there anything you'd like me to do on your behalf? I could go back out."

"I'm sure Joseph has it all under control," he replied. Then a shadow moved across his expression, and he frowned at the window. "Let's face it. They don't need me anymore."

Emma sensed an oncoming wave of depression, and wished she knew how to head it off at the pass. Some days it was easy to redirect his thoughts. Other days, his mood spiraled fast and there was no way to prevent him from falling into a dark and distressing melancholy.

"That's not true," she swore to him. "They look to you for leadership."

He dismissed her comment, and they sat in silence for a moment or two.

"That new man isn't like the other staff men," her father said. "I hope he can survive."

"I think he will. He seems intelligent."

Her father nodded. "That's what makes him so different. Half the men who come here don't even have a high school diploma, and he's talking about a university-level research project."

"He's ambitious." Emma scratched the back of her head. "How old is he?"

"Twenty-eight. Single. Never been married."

She gave him a look. "Don't start, Papa."

He reclined in his chair and sighed dejectedly. "Oh, you can't blame me for trying. Anything to help you forget you-know-who."

Emma pressed both hands to her heart. "I give you my solemn word, I'm over that. Because you were right. It was a childish pipe dream. All I want now is to get through the summer and start my program in the fall."

"Good," her father said. "Because the last thing I want is for you to spend the rest of your days being my nursemaid. Your mother would come back to haunt me."

The return of his wit and humor came as a relief to Emma. "You don't need a nursemaid," she assured him. "You've come leaps and bounds since the surgery, and you continue to improve every day."

"From your lips to God's ears." He reached for his book and opened it.

Emma rose from the sofa and kissed the top of his head.

CHAPTER 13

In June, with the welcome arrival of warmer temperatures, Emma covered more distance during her morning rides on the beaches with Willow. These were the special moments when she took time to think about her future and reflect upon the present. Since her father's accident, the house had become a place of dark moods and occasional bursts of temper, followed by tears and apologies. But he was slowly recovering and becoming more accustomed to his mobility challenges. Emma did her best to boost his spirits and only wished she knew more about applied psychological therapies.

Earlier in the spring, she'd felt as if she were sitting on a blank page between two chapters in her life: the happy times before the accident and whatever might come next. Maybe another dramatic event from out of the blue would carry her away, somewhere unexpected. The wreck of the *Belvedere* had swept her into a whirlwind of emotions and, more recently, onto a path of new wisdom regarding her feelings and desires for the future.

This became apparent to her one morning mid-June, when she felt hopeful for the first time in a long while. She and Willow galloped all the way to Station Number Two, working up a sweat until Emma finally leaned back in the saddle and said, "Whoa!"

Willow slowed, and Emma patted her neck. "Good girl. What a run!"

She wheeled Willow around to walk home at a more leisurely pace.

Before long, Emma spotted another rider in the distance, probably one of the staff men on beach patrol. When he drew near, he removed his cap and waved it in the air. "Good morning!"

It was Logan, the new man. Emma pulled Willow to a gentle halt as they came together in the shade of an eroded dune.

"I see they've put you on the early-morning shift," Emma said.

Logan's cheeks were red from exertion, his body full of restrained energy in the saddle. Even his bay horse was restless, stomping about.

"I wouldn't call it a graveyard shift," he said, "but none of the others seemed eager to take it."

"I hope they're not giving you last choice for *every* chore," Emma replied.

He shrugged cheerfully. "It wouldn't matter. I'm grateful to be here, and I enjoy everything. Even cleaning the toilets. Well, maybe not that. But I'm a morning person by nature, so this early patrol on horseback sets me up for a first-rate day. I mean . . . What could be better than this?" He waved his arm about and gestured toward the sea and sky.

Emma laughed. "You're a jolly person, aren't you."

His eyebrows flew up in mock surprise. "Are you making fun of me, Miss Clarkson?"

She laughed again. "Not at all. It's refreshing, actually. And I agree, what could be better than this?"

They fell into step beside each other as he turned his horse around to walk back to Main Station.

As they trotted past a herd of gray seals sunning themselves on the beach, Logan asked, "Are you afraid of the seals after what happened to your father?"

"I've always been cautious around them," she told him.

"But you must feel some animosity."

Emma considered that carefully. "How could I? As far as I'm concerned, Sable belongs to the wild. We're just guests here."

"Or intruders," he suggested, studying her profile.

Surprised, she turned in the saddle to meet his gaze. "That's probably the most accurate term I've heard. Although it depends on how we behave while we're here. We don't always do the right thing."

"How do you mean?"

Sometimes Emma felt like a broken record, going on about the situation with the wild horses, but it was an important cause that mattered to her. "Sometimes we capture horses and ship them to the mainland for sale. I've been trying to put a stop to that for years."

Logan took a moment to digest this. "How does your father feel about it? He's superintendent here. He must have some say in the matter."

"Yes," Emma replied. "Deep down, he doesn't like it, but he's hesitant to ruffle feathers because of how much we depend on the government for our survival." She steered Willow around a large section of driftwood and returned to Logan on the other side. "So, he doesn't stop me from protesting with regular letters, and I live in hope that eventually we'll have the right sort of politician in charge who understands the cruelty of it. Until then, I'll keep writing and protesting."

They paused to let their horses nibble on some salty peat. Emma and Logan gazed out at the ocean and listened to the waves breaking on the shore.

After a moment, Logan crossed his wrists over the saddle horn. "Do you remember our first conversation in your father's den, the day I arrived?"

"Yes."

"He mentioned you had notebooks."

"About the herds." Emma kicked her heels to get Willow moving again. "Yes, I remember, and my father offered them to you freely, without my permission."

Logan followed. "I understand what you're saying. I wouldn't have liked it much if I were in your shoes—to have my life's work handed over to someone else, who might take all the credit and glory."

Emma glanced over her shoulder and chuckled. "I wasn't thinking in those terms exactly. But yes, I felt a certain degree of . . . let's just say I'm a bit territorial."

"Understood." Logan removed his cap, scratched the top of his head, and replaced it. "But it hardly matters, because I haven't had time to be the least bit scholarly. Joseph keeps me too busy."

Emma glanced across at him. "I've seen you practicing drills on the beach."

"And in the station yard," he said, "and during the patrols, and inside the staff house . . . it never ends. But I do believe I'm ready for the worst shipwreck of the century, and I'll know exactly what to do. But do they even happen anymore? With radar and sonar and all that?"

Emma shook her head. "Hardly ever. So it's lucky that you came here to see this place when you did. I'm waiting for the government to render us all obsolete. Then no one would live here."

They approached the break in the high dune that took them back to Main Station.

Logan locked eyes with her. "Any chance we could make a date to talk about your research? I'd love to see your notebooks and learn what you know about herd behavior. And I promise, if I ever publish, I'd cite you as a source and give you full credit for any material you share with me."

She pulled Willow to a halt. "I shouldn't admit this to you, but I don't know the first thing about citations or how to write university-level papers."

His eyes sparkled, and his voice brimmed with excitement. "I can teach you about that. But it's not exactly a fair trade, depending on how much of your research I end up using. Maybe we should be coauthors."

Coauthors? Emma sat back in the saddle and considered the long summer ahead. A project like this might be the perfect diversion from the challenges of her day-to-day life, baking bread, helping to cook for the staff, and waiting for her future to begin.

"That sounds intriguing," she said.

He smiled. "Wonderful. When can we meet?"

"How about tonight after supper? Come to the house, and I'll dust off my notebooks."

Logan's excitement seemed to rouse his young horse, who spun in a circle, raring to bolt. "I owe you the world!"

Emma laughed. "That's a lofty price tag. I'll be satisfied with an author credit on your paper if we produce something worthwhile."

Logan held out his hand. "It's a deal."

They shook on it.

Emma grinned and urged Willow into a fast trot. With the fresh sea breeze in her hair, she felt a pleasant rush of anticipation. It was just the sort of visceral sensation she'd never expected to feel again.

~

Logan arrived after supper, and Emma served biscuits and tea in the great room. Her father was present, of course, reading a book in his leather easy chair, glancing up frequently with interest while they pored over Emma's notes, which were spread out on the coffee table before them.

It had been years since Emma had read the journals she'd kept as a young girl. Most of the entries were childishly written, but interesting facts emerged about the horses and other wildlife on the island, including encounters with beetles and insects. Thankfully she'd never written about movie stars—or worse, any handsome young staff men.

When the hour grew late, Emma's father began to yawn—a not-so-subtle signal that it was time for Logan to leave—so they packed up their books and papers, and Emma escorted him to the door.

"I can't thank you enough," he said as he shrugged into his wool coat. "I hope we can do this again. It feels like we barely scratched the surface."

"I agree. Are you free tomorrow evening at the same time?"

He spoke heartily. "I'll make sure of it. Maybe getting up at the crack of dawn for those early patrols will pay off if it means I can have free time after dinner."

"The early bird gets the worm," she replied. "Good night. Sleep well." Emma closed the door behind him.

When she returned to the great room, her father reached for his cane. "It sounded like a productive evening."

"It was," she replied. "And it's so strange. I'd forgotten about some of the things I wrote. In a way, it was a trip down memory lane."

Her father rose from his chair and limped to the kitchen. "For me too, listening to the passages you read aloud." He seemed in good spirits as he set his teacup and saucer on the counter. "It was good to have company tonight. It was a nice change."

It was, indeed, Emma thought as she watched him walk to the stairs. "Good night, Papa."

"Good night, sweetheart."

Emma let out a sigh of contentment. How wonderful that he could now manage the stairs on his own.

~

Over the next several days, Emma went for her regular morning ride on North Beach and met Logan consistently, at the end of his patrol. They became accustomed to the "coincidence" of bumping into each other and established a habit of riding back to Main Station together. Conversation was never strained as they discussed research methods, naturalist philosophies, and what Emma might expect from her teachers and fellow students when she began her formal education in the fall.

With each passing day, she felt more inspired and confident about her future at university. It was Logan who made it so. He assured her that most high school graduates were not nearly as educated as she.

They also discussed their personal histories. Logan described his upbringing on a large commercial farm on the Saskatchewan prairies, where the land stretched from one horizon to the other, as far as the eye could see. It was incredible for Emma to imagine such vast stretches of land, having grown up on a narrow strip of sand in the open Atlantic, barely a mile wide.

As for Logan, the way of life on Sable Island was equally astounding. He never failed to be amazed by how fast the fog could roll in off the water and make everything disappear.

~

"I think you should start a petition," Logan suggested one evening as they discussed the inhumane treatment of the horses when they were removed from the island and shipped to the mainland.

"And get thirty-five signatures?" she asked, referring to the population of Sable. "That's if I'm lucky. Not all the men would sign it." Her blood began to boil, and she scribbled furiously on the page in front of her. "Some take a disgusting pleasure in rounding up the horses."

Logan leaned close and lowered his voice in front of Emma's father, who was reading in his chair. "I think I know the ones you're referring to," he whispered.

She looked at him and nodded, and they said nothing more about it as they flipped through another journal.

"You could gather names when you start classes at Dalhousie," Logan suggested, circling back to the idea of a petition. "By the end of the first week, you might have enough to make a difference with the politicians."

"That's brilliant," she replied. "I'm going to do that."

Sitting close to Logan on the sofa, Emma was aware of their elbows and thighs touching. He nudged her playfully with his shoulder, and they grinned at each other, then glanced cautiously at her father, who was starting to nod off in his chair.

"I should probably go," Logan whispered.

"Yes, I think it's time to call it a night."

Emma stood and walked him to the door, where he donned his jacket, buttoned it, and then looked at her surreptitiously.

"Will you come outside with me?" he asked, still whispering. "Just for a minute."

There was a thrilling intimacy in his eyes, and she couldn't resist.

"All right." Emma strove to be quiet as she opened the door and followed Logan down the porch steps.

Outside, the moon was full. The sky was dusted with stars. Waves crashed thunderously onto the beach beyond the high dune.

Emma tipped her head back, closed her eyes, and inhaled the fresh, salty fragrance of the Atlantic. "Summer is so brief here. I want to soak up every moment."

When she opened her eyes, Logan was standing before her, his gaze level with hers. "Emma . . . I think you're the most beautiful woman I've ever seen."

Her cheeks flushed with heat, and she remembered her first impression of him on the beach when she'd judged him as a heartbreaker. Now that she knew him better, she was letting down her guard, and so far, she had no regrets about that. The past week had been wonderful, like a dream.

"I don't know what to do with myself when I'm around you," he added.

She laughed nervously. "What do you mean?"

"I don't know. I feel like I'm going to trip over my own feet. You're all I think about every minute of the day. I can barely sleep when I know I might see you on the beach the next morning. I'm always so glad when you're there, galloping toward me. I don't know what I'd do if you didn't show up. I'd probably wither away and die."

Emma frowned. "Don't joke about that."

"I'll hate it when you leave for school. It won't be the same after you're gone," he replied. He took hold of her hand, opened her palm, and Emma gasped when he kissed it. He held his lips there a moment, and she felt his breath become trapped against her flesh. Shivers of delight rippled through her.

"Logan . . ." She wasn't sure if she was warning him to stop or pleading with him to continue.

"Can I kiss you good night?" he asked.

Before she had a chance to think too hard about it, she nodded.

He moved a little closer, cupped her face in both his hands . . . looked deeply into her eyes, and then kissed her tenderly on the mouth. His lips were soft and warm, and the kiss sent tremors through her body.

Gracefully, he drew the kiss to a smooth finish, stepped back, and looked at her with wonder. "I didn't expect to meet someone like you when I came here. I just wanted to disappear for a while. And work on that project."

"We *are* working on it," she reminded him, while her heart raced.

He grinned. "Is that what we're doing?"

Emma brushed a lock of hair behind her ear. "I'm not sure." She felt suddenly shy, along with a need to be cautious. She'd fallen too hard once before and didn't want to get hurt like that again.

Logan must have sensed her hesitation because he took another step back. "Thank you for the tea. Everything about tonight was wonderful."

He turned and walked toward the staff house. Emma remained on the bottom step, watching him grow distant in the misty glow of the outdoor lights until he stopped and looked back.

"Will you be riding tomorrow morning, as usual?" he shouted across the yard.

"Of course!" she answered. "Unless it's raining cats and dogs."

"Then I'll pray for sun!"

As he was backing up, he stumbled over the uneven ground and nearly fell, but was cheerful and undaunted, making Emma laugh as he turned and began to jog. Seconds later, he reached the large Quonset hut and went inside.

For a moment, Emma stood and looked up at the stars. It was all so astonishingly beautiful: The night sky. The constant roar of the ocean. *Life.* Eventually, she climbed the porch steps and smiled when she reached the door. There was so much joy in her heart. Where had it come from? The night sky? Or the kiss? Or both?

Inside the great room, her father was snoring in his chair. She went to him with love and shook him gently. "Papa, it's time to go to bed."

He woke with a start. "Already? Is Logan gone?"

"Yes, he left a few minutes ago."

Her father reached for his cane. "He's a nice young man. I like him."

"Me too."

"Shame I didn't get to say good night."

Emma held his elbow to support him as he rose from the chair.

"I can't complain, though," he added, "because I was dreaming about your mother just now."

"Was it a good dream?" Emma asked.

"Oh yes. She walked in from the kitchen and told me that I should go to bed. She said she couldn't fall asleep without me. It was like having a little visit from her."

Emma walked with him to the bottom of the stairs and couldn't help but feel sadness and sympathy for her father, who had slept alone for the past twenty years, missing the only woman he'd ever loved.

She supposed that his loneliness for her mother, like an inheritance, was buried deep inside her bones.

CHAPTER 14

Emma met Logan every morning for the next six weeks, sometimes in secret not far from abandoned Station Number Two. There was a deep hollow in the heath—cozy like a candy bowl surrounded by bayberry bushes. Each time Emma and Logan rode up to it, dismounted, and skidded down the steep slope to the bottom of the sandy basin, they felt the temperature rise a few degrees. The sun's warmth in their private sanctuary felt luxurious on their skin after the chill of an early-morning ride on the breezy beach where fog lingered.

Regarding the regular nightly meetings in Emma's great room after supper, always with her father present, Emma learned about thesis sentences, footnotes, and formal conclusions. She came to appreciate the importance of paragraph structure and how grammar and punctuation could affect clarity.

But it was not only Logan who taught her these things. Her father made many contributions as a first reader and editor. As an added benefit, the project gradually pulled him out of his doldrums, and he was finally back behind the wheel of the Jeep and making his way confidently along the concrete sidewalks at Main Station.

Most importantly, at the end of those six weeks, she and Logan were in possession of a thirty-two-page academic paper, written in longhand, waiting to be typed—and Emma was happy again. Her heart had become full of passion, and she no longer pined for Captain Harris. In fact, she barely thought of him. Or if she did, she was able to shrug it off and take pride in her accomplishments and the thrills and joys of new experiences.

Like kissing. How delicious it was . . . to be kissed. Dizzyingly wonderful. Furthermore, it was addictive.

But somewhere on that addictive path, Emma had lost the discipline to resist what came next . . . when the kissing wasn't quite enough. And like the meandering horse trails through the heath on foggy mornings, the kissing had taken her to unexpected destinations.

$\sim$

In mid-August, Emma woke to the song of the Ipswich sparrows chirping outside her bedroom window. Normally, the sound of their music inspired her to rise from bed, don her riding clothes, and venture to the barn to present Willow with her morning apple. But on that day, Emma fought a flood of tears, rolled to her side, squeezed her pillow in her arms, and buried her face into it so snugly that she nearly smothered herself.

$\sim$

An hour later, distressed and desperate to talk to Logan, Emma rode Willow along North Beach, homebound. At long last, he appeared in the distance, galloping toward her. She let out a breath of relief and battled another outpouring of tears.

They reached each other, and Logan pulled his horse to a halt. "I'm happy to see you," he said. "What happened last night? I was worried."

At the last minute, Emma had called and left a message at the staff house to cancel their regular meeting.

"I'm sorry," she explained, feeling fragile, "but I couldn't see you. I needed some time to myself."

Logan's eyebrows pulled together with concern. "What's wrong?"

She spoke confidentially. "We need to talk."

"All right."

They dismounted and led the horses toward the water.

"You're so quiet," Logan said. "You're scaring me."

"I'm sorry. I don't mean to. I just don't know how to do this."

"Do what?" he asked. "You're not breaking up with me, are you?"

Emma's stomach pitched and rolled. She worried she might throw up. Swallowing heavily, she stopped and faced him. "I'm late."

Logan shook his head. "What do you mean?"

"I mean my monthly hasn't come," she explained. "It should have started two weeks ago, and I don't know what to do." Her voice broke on the last word, and she couldn't keep the tears at bay.

Logan immediately pulled her into his arms. He held her close and rubbed her back. "My God, Emma. Are you sure? Maybe you mixed up the dates."

"I'm positive." She buried her face in his shoulder. "I've been anxious for days, waiting for it to come, but it never does, and this morning I felt sick. I'm still feeling sick right now."

"Shh," he whispered, cupping the back of her head. "Everything's going to be all right."

She stepped back and wiped under her nose. "Is it? I'm supposed to leave for university soon. How can I tell my father that I'm pregnant?"

Logan took hold of her hand. "Let's sit down."

Together, they dropped to their knees on the sand and sat back on their heels.

"I don't want you to worry," he said. "We're a team, you and me. I've never been as happy as I've been since I came here."

"I've been happy too," she replied, fighting more tears.

"I can't imagine my life without you," he continued. "And I understand that you're anxious, but maybe this isn't such a bad thing. You know how I feel about you. I'm not sure if I've said it, but I love you. So, if this is what holds us together, then I'm glad it's happening."

Emma looked at him through the blur of tear-drenched lashes. "What are you saying?"

He pulled her close and held her tight. "That I don't want to lose you. Ever. As far as I'm concerned, this is fate, and it means we should get married."

She sat back again and spoke shakily. "Really?"

"Yes," he said with a smile.

"Are you sure?"

"Of course I'm sure. Please, Emma . . ." He cupped her chin in his hand and locked her in his gaze. "Marry me and make me the happiest man in the world."

She began to laugh through her tears. "Oh, my gosh. Yes!"

Logan's eyes lit up, and he kissed her quickly on the lips. "This is the best day of my life."

Emma wiped fresh tears of joy from her cheeks. She laughed jubilantly and hugged him. *Thank you, God. Thank you. Thank you!* Relief surged vigorously into her heart. Everything was going to be all right now. It wouldn't matter that she was expecting a baby out of wedlock. There would be no shame in it because she'd be married. She was engaged!

Wanting to savor this moment and the relief she felt, Emma lay down on the sand and invited Logan to lay next to her, where they held hands and gazed up at the sky. There were no clouds. Nothing but blue.

What will come next? she wondered.

Announcing the news to her father, who would, no doubt, be over the moon. His smile would split his face in half. She couldn't wait to tell him.

A wedding. Sooner rather than later would be best.

Beyond that? The baby's arrival, obviously . . .

Emma's brain became a waterspout of thoughts and plans. The dress. A nursery. Pink, blue, or yellow?

And what would happen after the next nine months? In the years beyond?

A white cloud sailed in from the west, and Emma watched it float slowly across the sky. Her pulse calmed, and the hot rushing of blood in her veins relaxed. The waves rolled onto shore, in a relaxed and steady rhythm.

It was then that Emma realized she had questions.

"What about me going to university?" she asked, turning her face toward Logan's.

He looked at her and grimaced, and she wasn't sure what she saw in his eyes. Was it sympathy?

"I'm sorry, Emma," he said. "You'll have to withdraw, because you'll be a married woman. You can't possibly look after a baby and get a degree at the same time."

"But why not?" Emma asked, genuinely confused, because she'd never been held back by obstacles before. At least not in her own mind.

"But you'd be there to help," she argued, in a last feeble appeal, unsettled by the sound of defeat in her voice, when they'd only just begun to discuss it.

Logan looked at her as if she'd sprouted horns. "But I'd be working. Besides that, we'd need to move to Halifax. I'd have to find a new job and an apartment for us." He regarded her with a frown. "Emma . . . you do understand that it's not possible right now?"

She stared at him blankly. He was right. Of course he was. She was speaking nonsense.

But another side of her couldn't bear to accept the permanent annihilation of her dream, the forfeit of her passion.

When Emma said nothing, Logan squeezed her hand. "I'm so sorry. I know you were looking forward to all that, but believe me, college isn't all it's cracked up to be. And I'm sure that after the baby comes, you won't even think about sitting in a classroom because you'll love being a wife and mother."

She forced herself to have an open mind and listened respectfully to him, but for Emma, it wasn't simply about sitting in a classroom. She wanted to be a psychologist. Even now, she was analyzing Logan's mental and emotional responses to her disappointment. He was a man, and she was a woman. He had his own set of core values and social expectations. He had no idea what it felt like to have only one path to choose. And he wanted what he wanted, which was her love, forever, and this baby.

But she, too, had her own set of expectations, which stemmed from having been raised on a remote island with a sense of autonomy that was not common elsewhere. Logan, on the other hand, had grown up in the real world. A world she knew nothing about.

It took a moment for this new reality to sink in. Perhaps this was what it meant to be a woman. She reminded herself that most women who became mothers lost interest in a career. It wasn't something they cared about—or so she'd been told. Was it true?

She supposed she wouldn't know until she experienced it for herself.

Emma sat up, hugged her knees to her chest, and looked out at the ocean. At the very least, she would need to put off her education for another year. But she was young. She had time. And she'd certainly learned how to adapt to the postponement of a dream, even the death of one. She'd learned that she could recover and survive.

"You're probably right," she said to Logan, surrendering. At least for the time being.

She watched Willow nibble contentedly on some salty peat a short distance away and reminded herself to appreciate the good in this. Lately, she'd found happiness again after a terribly dark phase. And now, she wouldn't have to leave all the things and people she loved. There would be no sad goodbyes. Nothing to dread in that way.

"When should we tell your father?" Logan asked, sitting up beside her.

"The sooner the better, I suppose. We could tell him today." She shot a fast glance at Logan. "But don't tell him I'm expecting. Only that we're getting married. One thing at a time."

Logan regarded her uncertainly. "He'll be happy, I hope?"

"Oh, I *know* he'll be happy," she replied, linking her arm through his and resting her head on his shoulder. "He never wanted me to go to university in the first place. He always wanted me to stay here and get married to one of the staff men. This is his dream come true."

Logan nodded, and she sensed a renewed confidence in him. "Then I'll say it again. It's fate. We were meant to find each other, Emma. I'll keep my job here and support us, till death do us part."

Emma tensed slightly. She had no doubts about speaking those vows, but if there was one thing she'd learned on Sable Island, it was that nothing ever stayed the same.

"You won't want to return to Saskatchewan one day and apply to teach somewhere?" she asked. The possibility filled her with hope. If they lived in a university town, she could perhaps apply to a different psychology program. Part time, of course. Eventually.

"Not anytime soon," Logan replied. "I signed a one-year contract for this job, and with a baby on the way, I think we should hang on to that paycheck. Then we'll see how things look at the end of it."

Emma agreed and believed her father would support that plan as well. It was sensible.

She felt another welcome wave of relief as her private fears from the past few days dissipated. Logan loved her, and they were going to raise this baby together as man and wife. The rest of it they'd figure out as they went along.

With a newfound rush of happiness, Emma tackled Logan on the sand and planted a dozen kisses on his cheeks while he laughed, and the waves rolled onto the shore, and the horses nickered nearby.

~

Emma and Logan were married a month later, on Boat Day, when a Protestant minister came ashore for the afternoon to perform the ceremony. All residents of Sable Island crowded into the superintendent's great room to watch Emma walk down the stairs. She wore her mother's white silk chiffon wedding dress, which her father had kept in his wardrobe for many years. Only a few alterations were required to fix the lace on the asymmetrical hem, and she carried a bouquet of pink Sable Island roses she'd collected that morning.

As for the rings, her father provided that for Emma as well. On the day she and Logan revealed their intention to marry, he'd presented them with the diamond engagement ring and wedding band her mother had worn until the day she was laid in the ground. Logan's wedding ring came on the supply ship with the minister, just in time for the ceremony.

Shortly after they said "I do," Philip McKenna helped them pose for a formal wedding portrait on the stairs.

～

That evening, after the supply ship departed, Emma said good night to her father, who took the Jeep to the McKennas' for dinner and to sleep in Abigail's sickroom, which would give Emma and Logan privacy on their wedding night. Emma had cooked a roast-chicken dinner for her new husband. After dark, as a thick, briny fog enveloped the island, they drank bubbly wine, wound up the gramophone, and waltzed to "Louise" in the great room. Then they went to bed with hearts and bodies filled with desire.

Shortly after midnight, they were interrupted by a noisy ruckus in the yard. Emma slipped out of bed, pulled on her white silk robe—specially ordered for her wedding night—went to the window, and pulled the curtain aside.

Outside, the lifesaving crew was gathered, each man wearing his Sunday best. Frank was among them.

"What are you all doing down there?" Emma shouted with amusement as she opened the window, leaned out, and rested her elbows on the sill.

Joseph strummed his guitar. "We've come to serenade the newly-weds! Ready, boys? Five, six, seven, eight . . ."

The men launched into a harmonized version of "The Way You Look Tonight," one of Emma's favorite tunes. Her eyes found Frank's, because he knew this about her. He gave her a friendly, affectionate salute.

Logan joined her at the window. By the end of the song, she was weeping with laughter and joy, blowing kisses at the men as they waved goodbye and departed, slowly disappearing into the fog.

After she closed and latched the window, she and Logan returned to her warm bed, snuggled together under the covers, and felt amorous again—for the third time that night.

CHAPTER 15

The month of October brought cooler temperatures and a shift in hues from lush green to golden brown as plant life fell into dormancy for the long winter ahead. The Eaton's Christmas catalog arrived, and the following month, extensive orders were placed for the Christmas Boat in December.

As the holidays approached—and Emma's condition as a newly-wed continued to deliver all sorts of new pleasures, day and night—she found it surprisingly easy to forget about her old dream of a university education. With each day that passed, her interest in psychology retreated one step further toward the back of her mind while marital bliss and the anticipation of motherhood advanced to the front.

And of course, Emma was pleased that her father was delighted to see her settled at last. Thanks to Logan, her departure from the island had been postponed, perhaps indefinitely, and for that reason, in her father's eyes, his new son-in-law could do no wrong.

During that first Christmas of 1947, Emma adored being a wife, had never been happier, and saw no reason why anything should ever change.

∼

It was not until early January that Emma began to show. It was only a small bulge at first, but by that time, Logan knew every curve and contour of her body. One night, he kissed her belly and looked up at her lovingly. "I want to raise our child here on Sable. There's nowhere better than this, don't you think? It's like the world's best-kept secret."

Emma laughed and ran her fingers through his wavy golden hair. "You're a special man to feel that way. Most men can't bear to be so far from civilization. Did I tell you about the two men from the *Belvedere* who stole a lifeboat and rowed into a storm to escape?"

"You did." He crawled over her on all fours, kissed her on the mouth, and then toppled onto the mattress beside her like a felled tree. "Clearly, they were mad if they were willing to leave the famous Sable Beauty behind."

Emma laughed and turned her head on the pillow to look at him. "Where did you hear about that?"

"In the staff house, my very first day. When the others saw you drop me off on the beach, they couldn't wait to tell me your nickname."

"What else did they say?" she asked uneasily.

"Nothing you need to worry about. It was all good, I swear."

They lay beside each other, flat on their backs, gazing up at the ceiling.

Emma shook her head. "I don't know whoever came up with that. As far as I know, no one has ever admitted to it."

"Good thing," Logan replied, "or I'd have to have a word with him, because you're mine now. I don't want anyone else coveting you."

Emma rolled to face him in the dim moonlight that filtered through the window. "I like that you're jealous."

Logan faced her as well and stroked a lock of her hair away from her forehead. "I was serious about raising our child here. How would you feel about that? Would you be willing to stay? We could continue our work with the horses and do other types of research here."

"Like what?"

He shrugged. "Anything. The seals, the sparrows, the stuff that washes up on the beach. Or how the grass and plants keep this giant sand dune from washing away."

"You have the mind of an academic," she told him, feeling intrigued and fortunate, but also saddened that he might not reach his full potential on Sable. He'd once dreamed of being a college professor.

"I suppose," he replied and rolled onto his back. For a long while, he lay there thinking, and she wondered if he had any regrets.

"I never imagined I'd end up in a place like this," he said, "so remote and secluded. I want to make the best of it." He glanced at her. "I mean the *most* of it. So few people have been here, and it's such a unique place. It needs to be documented."

Yes. She felt the same.

As for regrets . . . that night, she had none.

He rolled to face her again and kissed her softly on the mouth. Her body tingled all over.

"I think you were right that day when we got engaged. It was fate that you came here when you did."

Suddenly, Emma thought of Captain Harris and wondered if she would still be pining away for him if Logan hadn't landed on the beach the previous spring. Not that there weren't still moments when the captain entered her thoughts, but the image of him floated away whenever Logan walked into the room. Every time he kissed her, she thanked the heavens that he'd rescued her from that lonely and hopeless abyss she'd fallen into. Along with her father's accident, it would always remain a low point in her life, and sometimes she wished she could erase it fully from her memory.

～

In February, when Emma's condition became obvious to everyone on the island and she began to let out the seams on a few outfits, her father decided that the time had come for a delicate conversation.

"I've been waiting for the right time to talk to you about something," he said one morning at the breakfast table when Logan was out on patrol.

"All right . . . ," she replied hesitantly.

Her father rubbed the back of his neck. "I'm not sure how to begin, exactly. I've never talked to you about this before." His obvious struggle to find the right words persisted until he finally sat back and folded his arms. "We need to discuss what happened to your mother when you were born."

Emma's stomach dropped, and the air in the room became thick, almost difficult to breathe. She'd always wondered about the events of the day her mother died. How long had the labor lasted? Did she pass quickly, or was it a slow, painful death, hours later? Or days? And was it Emma's fault? Was it something she'd done in the womb that had caused trouble? Would her mother have survived with a different child—a boy who was more fearless and ready to be birthed faster?

Now that Emma was expecting a child of her own, she wasn't sure she wanted to hear *any* of that. There was a temptation to cover her ears.

Her father met her gaze, and she felt exposed and defenseless, as if she were staring down the long barrel of a gun. Outside it was snowing—not the pretty, fat snowflakes that fall gracefully on a windless day and make the world feel like a snow globe. These were the small icy pellets that stung your face in a bitter gale. They sounded gritty against the window. She thought of Logan out there, riding on the beach, and braced herself for a different kind of sting.

"I might as well dispense with modesty," her father finally said, "and be frank about it. What I'm about to tell you won't be pleasant to hear, but I need you to be informed so that you can make the right decisions for yourself."

Emma wrapped her hands around her coffee cup. "I'm listening."

"Everything was fine during your mother's pregnancy," he explained. "She was young and healthy, and we were confident in the woman who lived at Station Number Two, who had delivered babies before. Her name was Jane, and she came to the house when your mother went into labor. But you were in the wrong position, and the labor seemed to go on forever. She was in the bedroom with your mother for ten hours."

"I was breech?" Emma asked, having witnessed enough horses birthing foals on the island to know such things. More importantly, it didn't help her feel any less guilty about her mother's death.

Her father went pale, and he spoke shakily in a quiet voice, as if talking about it might send him back physically to the horror of that day. "I wasn't in the room, but I was told that your leg came out first, and Jane had to work hard to deliver you. She did, thank goodness, but it was a long and complicated process, and afterward, your mother . . ." He paused and swallowed over the rising of his grief. "I was told that her womb didn't contract like it should have. When I was finally allowed into the room, there was so much blood . . ." He stopped and looked away.

"Take your time," Emma gently said.

He nodded but charged ahead, speaking fast, to be done with it. "We only had a moment or two together, and she knew she was dying. She told me to take good care of you and that she loved me . . ." His voice broke, and he squeezed his eyes shut.

"Go on, please," Emma said, desperate to hear the rest of it.

He met her gaze. "What I'm trying to tell you is that childbirth doesn't always go smoothly. Sometimes there are complications, and I'd like you to consider going to Halifax to give birth in the hospital, where there are doctors who can perform a cesarean delivery—or do whatever else needs to be done if something goes wrong." He grabbed hold of her hand across the table. "I don't want to lose you."

Snow had accumulated on the windowsill, and Emma stared at it pensively. She found herself pondering all the forces necessary to place it there—the drop in temperature, the cloud vapor in the sky turning to ice crystals, and gravity pulling those snowflakes to the surface of the earth. Nature was a mysterious power that she didn't fully understand, and over which she had no control. Living on Sable Island had taught her that at a very young age.

She sat back, laid both hands on her belly, and rubbed in a wide circle. "It was always such a mystery to me," she said, "how she died, exactly. I don't know what I imagined . . . it was always something very vague."

"I'm sorry to tell you about it. I don't want to scare you, but I felt you should know. And I don't know if it's a hereditary thing . . . or just bad luck."

Emma thought of the *Belvedere* suddenly, getting caught in a storm in the worst possible place, and a man dying. What was that, if not bad luck?

"Where would I stay?" she asked. "Do you think Ruth would take me in?"

"I'm sure she'd love to have you," her father replied, "and she lives near the hospital. There isn't anyone I would trust more."

Emma considered it. "But what about Logan? I don't want to leave here without him. I could be there for a month or more. Could he come with me?"

Her father pushed his spectacles up his nose. "It's possible for me to amend his contract to allow for it. I'd suggest going on the next boat in March, a few weeks before your due date, just to be safe."

Emma nodded. "Thank you for telling me all this."

~

That night at the supper table, she and her father, together, explained everything to Logan and outlined the plan for her to give birth on the mainland. Emma assured her husband that they would both be welcome at Ruth Montgomery's home in Halifax. They would stay until the baby came, then board the next available supply ship back to Sable Island, where they would return to the life they loved and raise their child in this paradise they called home.

Logan agreed that it was the right thing to do, but he was quiet after supper. That night, he stayed up late in the great room. He did not come upstairs to bed until after 3:00 a.m.

~

A few nights later, after Emma's father went to bed and left her and Logan alone in the great room, she looked up from the book she was reading. "Have I said something wrong? Or done something? You've been quiet lately."

Sleet pelted the windows like a spray of pebbles, and the rooftop creaked and groaned in the wind.

"Everything's fine," he replied.

"You're sure?"

"Yes. I'm just tired," he explained, and went back to his reading. Within seconds, he looked up again and spoke irritably. "Honestly, Emma, I don't know how much longer I can keep up these early-morning shifts. They're hell in this weather."

"Yes, I can only imagine." Hoping to lift his spirits with a reminder of their passionate summer together, she grinned flirtatiously. "But there was a time when you enjoyed them. Remember?"

"That was different." His snappish tone caused her hackles to rise.

Emma cleared her throat and dispensed with any romantic inclinations. "Why? Because you were happy then? Are you not happy now? Because you've hardly spoken to me the past few days. What's going on?"

Logan shut the magazine and huffed. "I'm happy," he said, "but in case you haven't noticed, it's the middle of the goddamned winter, and like I said, those beaches are pure hell, frozen over. I don't see *you* riding Willow at dawn, like you used to."

Emma closed her book also and gave him her full attention. "You're right. I don't ride in the mornings, but do I need to remind you that I'm seven months pregnant?"

He waved a hand dismissively through the air, as if it were nothing of importance, which rubbed her the wrong way, because her nerves were already raw with anxiety about her approaching labor and delivery.

"How can we fix this?" she asked, focusing, as always, on a solution, not the problem, because she didn't want to argue. "Is there a way you can get a later shift? Could you talk to Joseph?"

Logan responded petulantly. "I'm at the bottom rung when it comes to seniority."

"Yes," she replied, "but the night shifts are shared equally among the senior men. They all take turns. Maybe Joseph would consider that. It wouldn't hurt to ask. Or I could talk to my father . . ."

"No!" He slapped his magazine down on the coffee table. "For Pete's sake, Emma. I don't want any special treatment because you're my wife. I'd rather drown myself."

Having grown up on an island surrounded by shipwrecks, words like those didn't sit well with Emma. "Please don't say things like that."

He stared at her with a fraught expression, then picked up his magazine and went back to reading.

In the hopes that some affection might help Logan express himself better, Emma slid closer on the sofa and rubbed his back. "I only want to help, darling. If there's something that's making you unhappy . . ."

"Stop it." He slapped her arm away. "There's nothing wrong. I'm just tired of this godforsaken island. There's nowhere to go. Nothing to do. We're all trapped here."

His response was like a slap in the face, and Emma was confused, because he'd been so keen and determined, initially, to raise their child on Sable.

But then Emma strove to remember that he was not the first person to experience the adverse effects of isolation, especially during the long, cold winter, when it became necessary to remain indoors most of the time. Others struggled as well, and not just during the winter. She thought again of those men from the *Belvedere* who had stolen the lifeboat. And Abigail often showed signs of depression and anger. She became resentful in bad weather and didn't always behave rationally.

As Emma slid away from Logan, she wondered if her experiences watching others come and go from the island was the catalyst that had sparked her interest in psychological therapies.

Not that it mattered now. There wasn't much point thinking about it, because a university education was not in the cards for her—not currently, at any rate. What mattered today was her husband's happiness and well-being, and his future ability to be a good father to their child. She only wished there was something more she could do to help him.

~

As Boat Day approached, Emma saw no improvement in Logan's mood. Though he'd been granted a generous leave of absence from his posting and was bound for Halifax—a city of restaurants, theaters, and new people to meet—he grew increasingly quiet and distant in the days leading up to it. Emma wished she could better understand the source of his depression. Whenever she suggested they talk about it, he withdrew further and implied that she was henpecking.

~

Finally, Boat Day arrived. Two full weeks before Emma's due date, she and Logan boarded the *Argyle* and settled into their cabin. Having learned to tread lightly with her husband, she avoided saying anything that might upset him and instead fell into the habit of overcompensating with light and cheerful conversation, always with a wish to lift his spirits.

"Isn't it wonderful," she said, "that we'll get to spend a few weeks in Halifax? I'd love to walk through Public Gardens at some point, but I'm not sure if they're open this early in the spring."

Logan had packed a rubber ball for some reason. He lounged back on the bottom bunk, threw his feet up onto Emma's suitcase, and tossed the ball repeatedly against the bulkhead.

Emma moved into the small bathroom and unpacked her toiletries. "Ruth lives in the South End," she said, "only a few blocks from the hospital, and she's quite close to the Gardens."

Logan offered no reply.

"She's a wonderful cook," Emma added, putting on fresh lipstick in the mirror, then dabbing her nose with some powder from her compact.

Emma wondered wearily how many times she would use the word *wonderful* before the day was out.

The ball continued to hit the wall, and Emma worried that someone in the next cabin might complain to the porter. But she said nothing about it. God willing, when they reached the mainland and Logan stepped onto the wharf in the big city—and he heard honking car horns and the wail of police sirens—the psychological effects of his isolation would recede, and his mood would improve.

CHAPTER 16

Ruth Montgomery lived in a two-story Victorian town house on Inglis Street. The front of the house was painted Wedgwood blue with red trim and a bright-red door. Colorful pink and white geraniums spilled from flower boxes at each of the front windows, upstairs and down.

Emma stepped out of the cab and waited on the sidewalk while Logan took care of the bags and paid the driver. The cab was just pulling away from the curb when the front door of the house opened, and Ruth appeared.

It had been four years since Emma had seen Ruth in the flesh, and she was overcome by a staggering wave of love, along with a shock of surprise at how Ruth had changed. Her hair had gone almost completely gray, and the laugh lines around her eyes were more pronounced. She'd aged, to be sure, but she still looked lovely to Emma. It was the warmth of her smile that kept her so devastatingly beautiful.

"There you are at last." She trotted down the steps, grasped Emma's hands, and held her at arm's length to look her up and down from head to foot. "You're all grown up. I can't believe it. And absolutely glowing."

Ruth pulled Emma into a tight embrace. Emma laughed openly, overjoyed to be in the arms of her old friend and beloved mother figure.

"It's so good to see you," Emma cried. "I've missed you so much."

"I've missed you too, but you're here now, and finally we can catch up on everything in person. I'll put the kettle on. It'll be so much better than letters." Ruth turned to Logan. "And this must be your husband." She held out her hand. "I'm Ruth. It's nice to meet you."

"It's nice to meet you too," Logan replied courteously with a handsome smile—looking like his old self as he shook Ruth's hand. Emma exhaled with relief and pride. "Thank you for having us," he added.

"I'm happy you're here." Ruth turned. "Now, come inside, both of you. I know I said I'd put the kettle on, but maybe we'll have a sip of brandy to celebrate."

Ruth led them up the steps to the front door, and Emma reached for Logan's hand. As she squeezed it, she gave him an appreciative smile because she was pleased that he'd made a good first impression. The last thing she'd wanted was for Ruth to worry about the choice Emma had made in a husband. She wanted Ruth to be proud of the woman she had become.

~

That evening, in Ruth's formal dining room, Emma and Logan gorged themselves on a hearty chicken casserole with warm buttered rolls and rich chocolate cake for dessert. Emma told the story of her father's encounter with the angry seal, and Ruth spoke about the death of her husband and how, since becoming a widow, she'd returned to teaching young children at kindergarten.

Logan shared stories about his childhood growing up on a farm in Saskatchewan and his work as a veterinarian, and Emma was delighted to see him continuing to act like his old self. He was pleasant and good humored, and it was the best night she could remember since they'd made the decision to travel to the mainland for her delivery. For the first time in ages, she went to bed feeling good about her marriage, and she was pleased when her husband was receptive to her affections.

~

The following day, Emma wondered if it was just the brandy. Logan had begun sipping it the moment they'd arrived at Ruth's house and had continued throughout the evening. He'd been affable all night long, but at breakfast the next morning, he retreated into his shell of silence and gloom.

At times, Emma was tempted to offer her husband more brandy to lift his spirits, but she was wise enough to know that liquor was not the solution to the problem—whatever it was. Most likely, over time, it would only make things worse.

~

On their fourth day in Halifax, the sun shone brightly from a blue sky, and the scent of spring filled the air. The snow had begun to melt, so Emma decided it would be a good day to drag her husband out of bed for a leisurely walk around the neighborhood.

As soon as they stepped onto the damp sidewalk, she looped her arm through his. "Thank you for coming out with me. They say walking is a good form of exercise for late pregnancy, and it can sometimes bring on the labor."

Logan laid his hand over hers. "Should I be ready to carry you to the hospital?"

His tone was disappointingly lackluster, but Emma managed to laugh it off. "I hope that won't be necessary. I'm as big as a barn. You'd put your back out."

He offered no reply.

They made their way toward the end of the street, while shiny silver icicles dripped from the eaves on the houses and cars splashed through slushy puddles.

After a while, Emma spoke delicately, as she often did lately, with her husband. "Is everything all right with you?"

"Not really," Logan flatly replied.

She gazed at him with surprise, because getting him to express his feelings of dissatisfaction or irritability—or whatever was dragging him down—was often like getting blood from a stone.

"Please, Logan . . . tell me what's wrong," she pleaded with genuine love and compassion for whatever ailed him. "I only want to help."

He scoffed, bitterly. "Of course you do—because you want a new guinea pig to replace the last one."

The words shocked her and stole her breath. Emma halted on the sidewalk. "What are you talking about?"

Logan continued for a few tense seconds before he finally stopped and turned around. "I heard you and Ruth in the kitchen last night. I came down for a drink, and the two of you were sitting at the table gossiping, so I listened for a while."

Emma's heart began to race and throb. What she'd discussed with Ruth was the farthest thing from gossip. It was the most personal and intimate confession of her soul. But Logan had heard what she'd said? *Oh, God.* She remembered all too well the main points of their conversation. Emma had confided in Ruth about Logan's recent feelings of depression, and she'd opened up about her relationship with Captain Harris and her terrible heartbreak after he'd left.

"You were eavesdropping," she said, feeling violated.

Logan stared at her piercingly. "Don't try and turn this on me. You know what you said."

"I'm not sure that I—"

"Oh, stop it, Emma," he barked. "All you did was complain about me, so obviously I'm a disappointment to you. But just tell me this." A muscle flicked at his jaw. "Are you still in love with him?"

All the breath sailed out of Emma's lungs. Logan might as well have hit her across the back with a two-by-four.

He looked up at the sky and scoffed. "I should have known. You were in such a hurry to get married. Is the baby even mine?"

Emma's shock spun into anger, and it was her turn to speak with ire. "Of course it's yours! I was a virgin when I met you. You know that!

You were the one who always pushed things to the limit and told me how beautiful I was, and how badly you needed me. Those hands of yours—always coaxing and persuading! Your hands could have talked me into anything! But I believed you loved me, and that's why I married you. So don't make a ridiculous accusation like this, Logan, even if you're not happy that we're stuck with each other now—because it's not *my* fault I got pregnant. It's yours. You were the one who couldn't wait."

Logan strode toward her, so fast that she took a few steps back. "Stuck with each other. There it is. The truth at last! You never would have married me if you weren't forced into it—because you're still dreaming about that captain . . . whatever his name is."

"I'm not dreaming of him," she insisted. "I'm over that."

He bowed his head, rested his hands on his hips, and turned toward the street. "Tell me another one, Emma, because after what I heard last night, it's obvious I was just a distraction last summer. A way for you to forget about him."

"No." She took hold of Logan's arm. "I loved you. I *still* love you."

A woman pushing a pram down the sidewalk crossed the street, obviously giving them a wide berth. Emma was mortified that they were causing a scene. She linked her arm through Logan's and began walking again, slowly, willing herself to calm down.

"You and I had an incredible summer together," she reminded him. "I loved working on the paper with you and . . ."

"Maybe you were more interested in writing the paper than you were in me." Logan quickened their pace, and, in her condition, Emma could barely keep up. "You only liked me because I gave you what you couldn't get on the island—an educated man."

She pulled him to a halt again. "That's not true! There are plenty of educated men on the island." She thought of Frank. He'd gone to college before he began his training as a wireless operator. "But you're right," Emma conceded. "I admired you because you were intelligent, and we shared the same interests. My father liked you for the same reasons. What's wrong with that?"

"Don't bring your father into this," Logan said. "He's half the reason you wanted to marry me—because you couldn't bear to leave him on his own. How convenient that I arrived and provided you with an excuse to stay."

Suddenly, Emma's blood began to burn with fury in her veins, but she couldn't think of how to respond because it was partly true. She'd been conflicted about abandoning her father, who had still been struggling with difficult physical challenges, not to mention his grief over his lost limb.

She forced herself to be honest. "I admit . . . staying on the island felt easier in some ways. But that doesn't mean I wasn't happy to be your wife. Don't you remember how in love we were on our wedding night? I thought all my past heartaches were over." She wiped hot, stinging tears from her cheeks. "But you've become so distant lately. It's like you don't love me anymore."

At a standoff on the sidewalk, she and Logan stared intensely at each other. Eventually, his shoulders relaxed. He dropped his gaze and offered his arm, and they resumed walking, but at a slower pace.

Cars sped by, too fast, swishing through slushy, dirty puddles. Water splashed onto the sidewalk, and Logan pulled Emma back a few steps to avoid the deluge.

When they reached an intersection, Emma tugged at Logan's sleeve and forced him to stop. "Please. We're about to have a child together. I just want us to be happy."

He glanced up and down the street, avoiding her gaze. "I want that too."

Regret, like a cold and terrible ground swell, washed over Emma. She never should have spoken to Ruth about Captain Harris. That had been terribly disloyal. Besides, it was in the past, and Emma had made her choice. She'd chosen Logan, the father of her child, and she didn't want to lose him.

Emma stepped forward, wrapped her arms around his waist, and pressed her tearstained cheek against the scratchy wool of his winter coat. She squeezed her eyes shut and let out a breath of relief when his hand cupped the back of her head.

"I'm so sorry," she said. "Please forgive me. I love you, and I don't want anyone but you."

He hugged her and gave her time to collect herself before he stepped back. "Let's go home. I don't want to fight anymore."

"I don't want to fight either."

Logan took her face in his gloved hands and kissed her lightly on the forehead.

Relieved, Emma linked her arm through his and walked with him back to Ruth's house in silence.

~

That night in bed, still distressed by her argument with Logan, Emma lay awake with her hands on her belly, staring up at the ceiling.

It was no wonder he was upset. She'd spilled out her heart to Ruth about how deeply she'd fallen in love with Captain Harris and how heartbroken she'd been for months after his departure.

Logan didn't deserve to hear that. She should have been more careful, more focused on the present and what was ailing her husband. But there was no changing it now. She only wished Logan was more open to discussing it further and fixing whatever was wrong. If only he could allow her to assure him that she loved him and wanted their marriage to succeed.

But sadly, again, when they slipped into bed that night, he rolled over, faced the wall, and went straight to sleep. Emma felt completely shut out of his heart, his soul, and his mind.

It made her wonder if perhaps *she* was the one with the problem. Having grown up in a small, isolated community with only books and a few dozen square miles of sand and grass to explore, maybe she was too analytical. She hadn't known many people in her life. Most came and went, remaining only briefly, providing a mere snapshot of who they were during that one specific year of their life.

And only a certain type of person agreed to spend a year in a place like Sable Island.

During her adolescence, Emma had read about Sigmund Freud and had become stimulated—intellectually—by the mysteries of the unconscious mind. She'd thrown all her fiery young passions into the study of psychology and human behavior, but it was all just words on a page. What did she really know about life and relationships and the real trauma that people endured in other places in the world? Maybe she knew far less about the human psyche than she believed.

Turning her head on the pillow, she looked at Logan, who was still facing the wall and snoring loudly.

He was her husband. She wanted desperately to understand him. At the same time, she didn't want him to feel as if he were a research project.

In that moment, her baby kicked. Emma laid her hand on her belly, pressing here and there. It was obvious that the baby's feet were low; it was not the head that was engaged toward the pelvis.

Emma squeezed her eyes shut and felt a burst of anxiety in all her nerve endings. Or perhaps *terror* was a better word.

Please, God. Help my baby turn in the coming days.

Emma didn't want to die young like her mother. She wanted to live. There was so much of the world she had yet to experience. She wanted to know life beyond Sable Island, not death. She wanted to hold her baby in her arms, raise her child from infancy, and watch him or her grow through childhood and adolescence, long into adulthood. She wanted to know her grandchildren.

But again, she was dreaming and wanting . . .

Today, Emma still didn't know who she was supposed to be. She wanted so much out of life, but everything always felt so out of reach and so unfinished.

~

At dawn, Emma rolled to her side in bed to face Logan, who was still facing the wall and snoring. A deep cramp squeezed in her belly, and she hugged both arms around herself, waiting for the discomfort to pass. When it did, she settled down and tried to go back to sleep.

It wasn't long before another cramp squeezed at her innards. Recognizing that this was quite likely a contraction in her womb, Emma strove to remain calm. She fingered the locket she wore around her neck, thought of her mother, and couldn't fend off the dark, cold nightmare that twisted like a snake in her mind.

Not yet. I'm not ready.

A gush of water poured out of her—a clear message that she had no control over what was to come. There was no stopping it now. It was time to go to the hospital, where she would be forced to push her baby out.

What if it was a breech delivery? Would they cut her open? What if she didn't survive?

Her mind screamed in terror at the unknown. Would Logan be a good father to their motherless child? Would he return to Sable Island? Or would her baby, all its life, never set foot there, never know its beauty?

Emma groaned as another contraction put pressure on her abdomen. Slowly, she swung her legs to the floor.

"Logan, wake up. It's time."

"What?" He sat up groggily.

Her heart was on fire, beating fast and uncontrollably. "I need to go to the hospital. Go and wake Ruth. Ask her to start the car."

For a split second, he stared at Emma in a daze. Then he tossed the covers aside, leaped out of bed in his pajamas, and scrambled from the room.

~

Fourteen excruciating hours later, a doctor shouted at a nurse. Exhausted, Emma was barely conscious under the medications, but she was still aware of people flying into a panic around her bed, like the terns darting about, protecting their colonies on the dunes . . .

Minutes later, she moaned feebly with a mixture of terror and despair as she was wheeled on her bed by a team of nurses and orderlies, through white hospital corridors, under the passing glare of florescent lights. A woman bent over her and spoke reassuringly. "Everything's going to be fine. You're in good hands."

"Please . . . save my baby," Emma mumbled, gazing imploringly into the woman's concerned eyes before a plastic oxygen mask was placed over her mouth and nose, and she surrendered to exhaustion.

Some time after that, she stood on North Beach, facing the wind and wild whitecaps on a stormy gray ocean. She listened to its thunderous roar and realized suddenly, with surprise, that she was a bird. She spread her wings, began to run, and took off to soar high above the frothy white surf as it crashed and rolled onto the beach. Gray seals frolicked in the sea below.

She flew higher and higher until the crescent-shaped island looked tiny beneath her, barely a sliver of existence. From such a height, the lush interior was a narrow green brushstroke, and the horses were little black dots.

Emma swooped down and flew westward to circle over the sunken *Belvedere*, half-buried in the sandbar. It broke her heart to watch the ship suffer under the cruel battering of the waves. When it became unbearable, she flew upward to the misty clouds, but felt a grave loneliness there.

Oh, how she longed for Sable Island—for that special fragrance of the marram grass, the wild roses and bayberries, and her horse, Willow. Her father. Her books. The faithful, unbroken roar of the sea . . .

Longing desperately to hold her baby in her arms and take him back to her special island home, Emma flew, in a rapid descent, straight down from the clouds.

CHAPTER 17

Five days later, Emma was discharged from the hospital. According to the doctor, her labor had been long and grievous, alarming at times, but the cesarean section, to everyone's great relief, had gone swimmingly.

"This one just wanted to stay a little longer with his mum," he'd said as he handed the crying newborn to a nurse. He then congratulated Emma and later, in the hospital waiting room, pumped Logan's hand vigorously.

"Would you like some soup?" Logan asked, resting his arm along the back of the sofa in Ruth's living room, watching his son sleep soundly in Emma's arms.

"I'd love some," she whispered. "The hospital food was terrible, and I hardly ate a bite. Ruth's cooking is so much better."

Ruth walked into the room just then. "Did someone say I was a good cook? Not that I'm fishing for compliments, but I can't deny it's nice to have mouths to feed."

Emma smiled at her, then looked down at little Matthew. "I'd like to get up and eat at the table, but I'm afraid I'll wake him."

Ruth moved closer to help. "Hand him to me, and I'll lay him down in the bassinet. I'll watch him so that you and Logan can have supper together."

Emma carefully passed Matthew to Ruth. "Thank you. You're an angel."

Ruth bounced at the knees and carried him to the wicker basket on the floor beneath the window. As soon as he was settled, she carried the basket to the kitchen. "You both need to eat and get some rest when you can, because babies like to keep you up at night."

"Duly noted," Logan replied, with genuine appreciation for the advice, as he pulled Emma's chair out for her.

She sat down with care because she was still sore in certain places. But oh, how grateful she was for Ruth's kindness as she served hot chicken soup to each of them in heavy crockery bowls, then took a loaf of fresh bread out of the oven. Ruth cut a few thick slices and placed them on a small wooden platter, which she set on the table with a stick of salted butter.

Emma glanced down at Matthew, sleeping peacefully in the wicker bassinet at Ruth's feet. Never had she felt more fulfilled. Motherhood was something entirely new: a wonder she'd never imagined. The depths of her love and the heights of her joy were completely unexpected and astonishing.

Perhaps this was it—her true calling. Perhaps this kind of love was all anyone could ever need.

~

Two days later, Logan walked into the bedroom where Emma was pacing about, patting Matthew gently on the back, trying to get him to burp. He was fussing, and she wanted to put him down for the night.

"I don't know why we have to wait so long to get on the supply ship," Logan grumbled. "No offense to Ruth, she's been very kind, but I'm tired of being a guest here. I want to get back to Sable."

"I want to go home too," Emma replied, "but the *Argyle* only goes once a month, and we're at the mercy of the weather."

Logan sat down on the foot of the bed. "Can't we just hire a private plane to take us? I've seen planes land on the beach before."

"That would cost a fortune," she replied, "and we don't have that kind of money."

Matthew let out a gurgled burp, and Emma exclaimed with delight. "Oh! What a good boy. That feels better, doesn't it?" Smiling down at his sweet, pudgy face, she cradled him in her arms.

Logan flopped onto his back on the bed and squeezed great clumps of hair in his fists. "I don't want to be here anymore."

Recognizing that her husband was at his wit's end, Emma moved to lay Matthew down in the bassinet. "I find it odd," she said impatiently, "that a few months ago you used the word *trapped* to describe how you felt about living on Sable. But now you can't stand to be in Halifax. I'm starting to worry that you won't be happy anywhere."

"That's ridiculous," he replied, scowling at the ceiling.

Emma tucked the blanket around Matthew and made sure he was settled. "Are you sure? Because you left Saskatchewan too, which was your home province. Or maybe it's *me* you want to get away from. Or any sort of long-term commitment." She turned and faced him.

Logan sat up and looked at her with combative eyes. "You're always questioning my intentions, making mountains out of molehills. Maybe I don't know why I want to move from one place to the next. Maybe I just like to go with the flow. Why does everything have to be so complicated with you? You never just take things at face value."

Emma hadn't slept much over the past few days because of night feedings, and she lacked her usual compassion for her husband's moodiness. "What a lovely thought," she said with obvious sarcasm, "to just go with the flow, take off whenever you want, on a whim. How nice to be a man."

His eyes narrowed. "Are you trying to pick a fight?"

Emma's blood had already reached the boiling point in her veins. She stared at her husband for a few seconds, wanting fanatically to throw all her recent frustrations at him—and maybe throw a lamp as well. But she didn't want to fight in front of the baby, so she took a few deep, slow breaths to calm herself.

The oxygen to her brain helped her remember that neither of them had slept much over the past few days. They were both short tempered.

Emma moved to the bed and sat down beside her husband. "I just want you to be happy."

But the words felt hollow in her mouth. She was so tired and discouraged, and heaven help her, there were all sorts of other things she would have preferred to say to him. But none of them were very nice, and they would undoubtedly lead to more fighting, and she didn't have the energy for that. Nor did she want to wake Matthew after she'd finally got him settled.

Logan looked at her with resentment. "You say that a lot."

"Because it's true," she replied, both defensively and contemptuously. She was doing her best, and she was running out of patience.

"Is it?" Logan replied. "Because sometimes I think you just want me to be agreeable. You want me to want the same things you do at any given moment."

"No." She frowned. "I've always cared about your happiness, and I've tried constantly not to upset you. I don't understand. Where is this coming from?"

He flopped down on the bed again. "Forget it. I don't want to talk about it anymore. I just want to get back to Sable."

"That's what I want too." It was the honest-to-God, absolute truth. "I just hope you won't feel trapped like you did before and want to leave again after a few months."

Emma suddenly found herself thinking about Captain Harris and his failed marriage in England because he couldn't resist the lure of the sea and whatever lay beyond the horizon. Did all men have that same wanderlust? Or was Emma only attracted to the ones who craved adventure?

Maybe that's what she wanted deep down as well. For years she'd been dreaming about leaving Sable and going off to university. And there were moments when she'd felt trapped because of her father's needs, which had become substantial over the past year.

"Let's just be patient, all right?" She took hold of Logan's hand. "The supply ship leaves in two weeks. I'm sure the time until then will fly by."

He tugged his hand from hers, stood up, and walked to the door. "I hope so."

He shut the door too hard, and Matthew immediately began to cry. Confused and disillusioned, Emma rose irritably and crossed the room to settle her baby boy back down in the bassinet.

~

The following afternoon, Emma left the house and pushed Matthew to the Public Gardens in the pram. The park was not yet open for the summer season. The gates were locked, so she walked around the exterior of the wrought iron fence.

She knew the laps around the park were good exercise but felt as if she were going in circles to avoid returning to Ruth's house, where the mood was bleak. It had been a difficult night, with frequent wakings, so Logan had decided to sleep late. But Emma was the one who had gotten up to feed Matthew, so it was hard to feel sorry for her sleep-deprived husband, poor thing.

As she rounded the northwest corner of the park for the third time, she chewed over their heated arguments lately, along with Logan's perpetual discontent, and grew angrier by the second.

A police car sped by, splashing through puddles of melting snow, its siren wailing, so Emma bent over the pram's canopy to check on Matthew. Despite the noise and chaos of the morning traffic, he slept soundly. Emma touched his soft cheek with the back of her finger, then straightened and gripped the pram handle. She gazed intently at the old graveyard across the street from the park and was reminded of the skull collection in the boathouse on Sable Island. She thought of all the shipwreck victims who had perished there, and all the dead horses that had quietly decomposed on the heath. Emma had grown up with an awareness of death, but she suddenly found herself truly and deeply contemplating the brevity of life. With this notion came an acute awareness of her own mortality.

She didn't want to spend her life feeling angry or hateful. This was supposed to be a happy time. Why was her husband so miserable?

Another police car sped by on the street, heading in the same direction, and Matthew began to cry.

Emma felt a strange vibration in her chest, followed by a sudden sense of dread. She broke into a run and pushed the pram all the way back to Ruth's house.

~

At first, she thought the two police cars had surrounded the neighbors' house. She stopped on the street corner to catch her breath and examine the scene—flashing lights and bystanders on the sidewalk, a crowd gathering to watch some sort of drama unfold. A third paddy wagon sped past her and squealed to a halt in front of Ruth's door. Ruth had left for work at the kindergarten early that morning, so it was only Logan at home.

Emma stood motionless, watching three uniformed officers get out of a car, climb Ruth's front steps with weapons drawn, and pound on the door.

Keeping her distance in case of danger, Emma approached an older woman on the street. "What's going on?"

"We're not sure," the woman replied. "They knocked on the door earlier, but no one answered, so it looks like they called for backup."

"Do you know why?"

The woman shrugged.

Two officers approached them. "Step back, please. We need to clear the area."

Emma couldn't make her feet move. "What's happening? That's my aunt's house. My husband's in there."

The taller officer's gaze zeroed in on her. "You're the wife? From Sable Island?"

"Yes."

He guided her toward a police car parked at the corner and addressed another officer. "This is the woman from Sable."

Emma began to shiver in the cold. "I don't understand what's happening."

There was a loud crash, and Emma jumped. She turned quickly and saw four policemen breaking through Ruth's front door. They stormed inside and a short moment later escorted Logan out of the house with his hands cuffed behind his back.

Emma stood paralyzed. It was as if her body had run out of blood and her pulse stopped.

Still gripping the handle of the pram, she shouted, "Logan!"

He glanced in her general direction but said nothing as the officers shoved him roughly into the back seat of the paddy wagon.

Numb with shock, Emma watched the car drive off.

CHAPTER 18

"I'm Sergeant MacIntosh. Mind if I ask you some questions?"

"I don't even know what just happened," Emma replied, dazed and exasperated. "Why did you arrest my husband?"

"Because he's wanted for a wrongful death in Saskatchewan," the officer explained. "He'll be transferred back there to face charges." He watched her carefully while she processed this information.

"Wrongful death? Are you telling me . . . he might have killed someone?"

"He never spoke to you about this?"

"No."

Matthew woke and began to fuss, so Emma bent over the pram, found his soother in the folds of the blanket, and used it to settle him.

The officer's expression softened. "Is this your baby? With Mr. Baxter?"

"Yes."

In that moment, Ruth drove up in her car, pulled over at the curb, and got out. She slammed the door shut behind her and ran to Emma. "I came as fast as I could."

"Did you know about this?"

"Yes," Ruth replied. "They came to the school this morning looking for Logan, so I told them he was staying with me. I had no way to find you." She stared at Emma in dismay. "I'm so sorry."

Emma was floating on waves of shock and denial. "I don't understand what's happening. I don't know what he did."

"I'm going to need a full statement from you," Sergeant MacIntosh said. "You'll have to come to the station for that."

"Should she have a lawyer?" Ruth asked.

"That's up to Mrs. Baxter."

Emma didn't know what to say. She had no experience with this sort of thing, the machinations of the real world. "I had nothing to do with whatever happened in Saskatchewan. I've never even been there, and he never told me anything about anyone's death."

"No? Well, I'll be the one to tell you, then. Your husband is facing a murder charge."

Emma's heart began to beat raggedly in her chest. "No. That can't be right."

It had to be a mistake. Logan wasn't perfect, but Emma could never accept that he would kill someone. Intentionally.

"I need to talk to him," she said. "When can I see him?"

"I'm not sure about that," Sergeant MacIntosh replied. "First, we'll need a full statement from you. Can you come to the station now?"

Confused and rattled, Emma couldn't form words. Her brain wasn't working properly.

Ruth laid a hand on her shoulder. "I'll look after Matthew. You go and do what you need to do."

"All right." Emma bent over the pram and kissed Matthew on the forehead. Still half-dazed, she followed the policeman to his car.

~

The next twenty minutes in the back seat of the paddy wagon was like walking slowly out of a thick fog. It gave Emma the time she needed to comprehend the situation: Logan coming to Sable Island and wanting to stay there forever, hidden from the world; Logan growing depressed and irritable when he knew he had to return to the mainland; Logan impatient to return to the seclusion of Sable.

Like a thunderbolt, Emma realized that for most of the past year, she'd been living in a romantic fantasy with a man who'd come to her home with an agenda. But now a treacherous wave was washing her onto the shores of reality.

She'd wanted so badly to be loved. How could she not have seen or felt that Logan was hiding something momentous from her?

~

Two days later, Emma walked into the city jail. She was taken through a heavy door and down a gray-painted corridor to a cell where Logan was incarcerated.

As soon as he saw her, he stood up from the cot, approached the bars, and fell to his knees, where he rested his forehead on the cement floor and wept inconsolably.

The policeman uneasily backed away and left Emma to look down at her husband, who reached through the cell bars and wrapped his hands around her ankles.

Emma had always been a compassionate soul, but after two days of speculating about what he had done—and what else he might have kept from her—strangely, she felt nothing. Her body was completely numb. Her emotions were dead and flat. All she could do was stand there, waiting for him to gather his composure.

At last, he stopped crying and slowly got to his feet, but with the look of a broken man.

That was the moment Emma was hauled out of the pit of emptiness and felt the first stirrings of heartbreak. And pity. How in the world had Logan come to this? Why hadn't he trusted her enough to tell her?

"I didn't think you'd come," he said, clutching the bars, his nose running, his face wet with tears.

"They wouldn't let me come until now," she explained, "and they told me you're leaving tomorrow."

Emma had lain awake in bed half the night remembering their summer together—meeting at dawn to gallop on the beaches, the excitement and anticipation of every encounter, and the sharing of ideas, knowledge, and theories about the horses. Most importantly, her first sexual experience with a man. Physically, at least.

"But you can't leave without telling me what happened," she said. "Not just in Saskatchewan, but between us. Was any of it real?"

"Of course it was. What do you want to know?" he asked. "I'll tell you everything."

It was not an easy question to answer. Of course she wanted to know his side of the story about the death of a dairy farmer, and other sordid details she'd been told, but she needed to know something else first.

"Did you actually love me? Or was it all just a way to escape this?"

"Of course I loved you," he replied, sounding almost indignant. "And I still love you now. Maybe I was a fool, but after I met you, I thought I had a chance to be happy, that I could start a new life and be a new person. I wanted that more than anything."

"But that's not possible for anyone," she countered. "You can't escape who you are."

Logan dropped his gaze to the cement floor. "Obviously not. I see that now. But I couldn't help wanting it." After a moment, he shook his head. "How did they ever find me?"

It was a rhetorical question, but Emma provided the answer regardless. "There were wanted posters in the police station, and one of the clerks thought he recognized you at a pub on Argyle Street. You were followed back to Ruth's house, and the next morning, she was questioned at the school."

He nodded, accepting the information. Then his bloodshot eyes lifted. His brow was creased with worry. "They're not accusing you of anything, are they? For harboring a fugitive?"

"No," she replied. "Ruth explained how you and I met on Sable Island, and I confirmed that with the police. They understand that I was duped."

He bent his head to rest on the cell bar. "You weren't duped, Emma. I swear to God, I fell in love with you."

For a moment, she felt the tug of seduction—the desire to believe that love and passion could conquer all, and that she could find her way back to the bliss of those early days in his arms, in the warm, sandy hollows of Sable. She had trusted him then, but he was different now. And so was she.

"What happened between you and that man?" she asked. "And please tell me the truth. I can't handle any more lies. Lies would kill this even more dead than it is already."

Logan bowed his head. "Please don't say that."

"Then tell me the truth."

"All right." He moved to the cot against the wall and sank onto the thin mattress. "But I hope you'll give me some credit for honesty if you're going to hate me forever."

"Don't jump to false conclusions," she said. "Just tell me."

He took a deep breath, as if to summon courage. "Fine. Here's the truth. Before I left Saskatchewan, I had an affair with a married woman. It went on for about six months."

The words hit Emma like gun pellets to the chest. Despite everything—how his behavior over the past month had challenged her patience, and how the discovery of his lies now made her doubt their entire relationship—she still loved him. It wasn't that long ago that they were passionate and euphoric on their wedding night. Hearing of another woman felt like a terrible betrayal.

"Did you love her?" Emma asked, hearing a tremor of hurt in her voice.

"I suppose I did." His gaze fell to the floor. "I'm sorry, Emma. You wanted honesty."

"I did," she replied.

But the truth, spoken from his own lips, made her sick to her stomach. Her heart clenched, and she writhed with jealousy, but she was angry too.

She steeled her emotions and pushed on. "Tell me the rest. All of it."

He paused, then spoke in a low monotone, as if he needed to tamp down his shame. "She was the wife of a farmer whose herd I looked after. I guess he figured out what was going on, because he called me one night, late, to come look at one of his cows. He was waiting for me in the barn, and I knew as soon as I saw him that he was fit to be tied. We got into a scuffle, but I managed to pin him down and . . . I . . . I killed him. I didn't mean to. I swear to you. I just . . . I snapped."

With a strange absence of feeling, she simply stared at him. "What do you mean, you snapped?"

"I went into a rage . . . trying to defend myself . . . because I knew he was going to kill me."

Emma swallowed uneasily. "How did you kill him?"

The police had already told her, but she needed to hear it from him honestly and directly.

Logan kept his gaze fixed on the floor. "I strangled him."

As she imagined her husband choking the life out of someone, she fought a rising nausea. "So, you're saying it was self-defense."

His eyes lifted. "Yes, that's what I'm going to tell the court."

"But is it the truth?"

He stared at her with resolve. "Of course it is. I didn't *want* to kill him. I didn't plan it."

"But his wife says that you did," she argued. "She says you wanted her to leave her husband and run away with you."

Logan covered his face with both hands. "I'm not going to lie. I did suggest it once, but I didn't mean it for real. It was just romantic babble when we were caught up in . . . you know . . ."

"Caught up in what?" Emma demanded to know. "Go ahead and say it."

He sighed dejectedly. "The excitement of the affair." He lowered his hands to his lap. "But that doesn't mean I actually plotted to murder her husband. He's the one who called *me* that night."

"Why would she say it, then?"

Logan shrugged and spoke helplessly. "I don't know. She's probably mad because I took off that night and left her. That was a mistake. I should have told her what happened and called the police."

Emma rubbed the back of her neck.

"Do you believe me?" Logan asked.

"I don't know." Her nausea was still on the rise. "You've been lying to me since we met, so it's not easy to trust you."

He stood and slowly approached the bars. Emma took a full step back. She didn't want him to think he could simply reach out, touch her, and have her love and trust return.

"Please don't give up on me," he said. "I swear I wanted to tell you, and I figured I would, eventually, but I was so afraid you'd cut me off. And I'm sorry for being so surly lately, but I was afraid of leaving Sable and getting caught—because I knew if that happened, I'd lose you. If it weren't for the baby, everything would have been fine. We wouldn't be here right now."

She shook her head in disbelief. "Are you suggesting that our son spoiled everything? Or that my need to go to a hospital was what caused all this trouble?"

He bowed his head and shook it. "No, I'm sorry. That came out wrong."

"It's not my fault you're in jail," she said. "I'm not the one who killed a man."

Thankfully, Logan had the sense not to argue. But he reached through the bars, held out his hands, and urged her to take hold. "Please, Emma . . . all I ask is that you stand by me. You could come to Saskatchewan and stay with my sister. Or at least wait for me, because I'd come back to you, I swear."

She looked down at his outstretched hands—at the familiar lines on his palms that she'd often traced with her fingertips and thought she could read. But in that moment, she felt numb. Her heart was cold and empty, as if it had been gouged out by disappointment after disappointment, and there was nothing left inside. No love, no sorrow, not even any compassion. What had happened to the person she once was?

Oh, she knew exactly what had happened—she'd wanted so badly to feel passion and desire, to love and be loved in return, that she'd let herself fall into a fantasy. Logan wasn't the man she'd believed he was or wanted him to be. He'd been keeping secrets from the beginning. And if he could hide something as horrendous as manslaughter or murder, what else had he hidden from her? What had she not seen?

This man before her, locked up in jail and holding his hands out to her, was a stranger. She'd been utterly blind.

"Emma?" he asked.

Wrenched from her thoughts, she froze. She did not take hold of his hands.

"I don't know what my feelings are," she explained. "Except for confusion and uncertainty. I can't promise I'll wait for you. I can't promise anything. But I'm not going to Saskatchewan. That much I know."

He slowly withdrew his hands back inside the cell and let his arms fall to his sides.

"I have to go now," she said.

Logan darted forward. "No, please don't go . . ."

She started walking.

"Can I write to you?" he asked.

She stopped and turned. "Of course. You're Matthew's father. You can write to me on Sable Island, because that's where I'll be. Because I'll be taking the next ship home."

In the end, she walked out of the jail, where a cold rain fell hard and pounded the asphalt in the street. Cars swished through puddles, their windshield wipers whipping back and forth. Emma raised her umbrella and hurried to where Ruth was waiting in the car with Matthew.

As she walked briskly, she tried to imagine what her future might entail. Logan could go to jail for life, or he might be acquitted—but either way, Emma could never regret their relationship, even though it was built on lies. Nor could she hate him. Because how could she possibly hate the man who had given her Matthew?

PART THREE

THE CAPTAIN

CHAPTER 19

Autumn 1953

It was just as he remembered it. Windswept and wild.

Perched on the transom seat of the motorboat, skipping fast over rollicking swells, Oliver adjusted the rudder to steer westward toward a convenient passage between two high dunes. Main Station wasn't visible from the water, but he knew its location like the back of his hand. He also recalled the precise position where the *Belvedere* had run aground, though the wreck was gone now, buried beneath the ocean floor.

As for the island itself, the dunes were unrecognizable, altered, no doubt, by the continual hammering of storms over the past seven years.

Oliver approached the beach and drove his boat fast and aggressively onto the sand, where he waited briefly for a wave to retreat before he leaped out and dragged the vessel to dry ground.

Out of breath from exertion, he bent forward and rested his hands on his knees, then straightened and looked all around. He'd half expected a small crowd to come running at the sight of a visitor, but he was alone on the beach. Where were the patrols on lookout for signs of shipwrecks? Not that he fell into that category. His steamer was anchored comfortably a mile out, manned by a capable crew, and it was a clear, sunny day. But where was everyone? The island felt deserted.

Oliver glanced back at his motorboat to ensure it was safe from the incoming tide, then trudged up the sandy incline toward the dunes.

"Hey, there!"

The sound of a voice, shrill like the call of a bird, arrested him on the spot. He gazed in all directions until he spotted a small boy sliding fast down the slope of a dune to the east. The boy reached the bottom and ran toward Oliver, who paused, feeling slightly like an enemy invader.

When the boy reached him, he was panting, and he dropped to his knees. "Who are you?"

"I'm Oliver Harris," he replied, turning to point toward the ocean. "I'm captain of that ship out there. I came ashore to visit some friends. May I ask who you are?"

"I'm Matthew," the boy replied, shading his eyes against the blinding sun behind Oliver. "But today isn't Boat Day."

Oliver laughed. "You're right about that. I'm not with the supply ship. I'm just passing through. I was hoping to visit John Clarkson, the superintendent. Have I come to the right place?"

The boy's eyes lit up. They were deep blue, like the ocean. "That's my grandfather!" He swung around to point inland. "We live just over there."

As Oliver comprehended the boy's identity, he felt the familiar stirrings of those old feelings—not forgotten, just withdrawn. John had written years ago with the news that Emma had married and given birth to a child. At the time, Oliver had done his best to be happy for her—and he was, he truly was—but that lingering sense of regret and the inevitable question "What if?" had never left him.

"I was here once before," Oliver told Matthew. "But it was a long time ago, and everything looks quite different. Could you take me to your grandfather's house?"

"Yes! Come with me." Waving his whole arm for Oliver to follow, Matthew loped clumsily over the shifting sand.

Amused by the boy's enthusiasm and eager to return to Main Station, Oliver plodded up the sloping beach.

~

Main Station was mostly the same, except for the narrow concrete walks between the buildings. What had changed was the level of activity. There was no one about to notice the arrival of a stranger.

"Where is everyone?" Oliver asked with curiosity as he followed Matthew to the Clarkson home.

"They're at East Light, doing repairs. Everyone's gone except for me and my mom."

Oliver's thoughts drifted back to the day Emma had walked with a sack full of books into Abigail McKenna's sickroom, where he lay convalescing.

"She stayed behind?" he asked.

"Yes, it's bread day," Matthew replied, "so she's in the kitchen."

Matthew led Oliver up the steps to the front door and walked in. "Mom! Someone's here to see Grampa!"

Oliver kicked the sand off his boots before he entered. He quickly ran a hand over his windswept hair and wished he'd thought to bring a comb.

"Who is it, Matthew?" she called out.

The sound of her voice and the familiar scents of the house stirred more memories for Oliver—mostly of fresh feelings of hope and anticipation when he knew he would spend time with Emma and talk to her about things he'd never spoken about with anyone.

Seven years ago, she'd brought him back to life, and he'd been alive ever since. He'd come a long way since the war and the ordeal of the *Belvedere*.

"It's the captain of a ship!" Matthew shouted as he ran into the kitchen, leaving Oliver to stand and wait uneasily in the entrance hall, where he listened to Emma speak in soft tones to her son.

A full minute must have passed before she finally appeared, wearing faded, baggy blue jeans and a white oversize collared shirt with the sleeves rolled up. Her dark hair, which had grown long, was loose and wavy about her shoulders. The sight of her was like a thunderbolt in Oliver's chest.

"Hello, Emma," he said, doing his best to be friendly and open.

She cleared her throat and tucked a lock of hair behind her ear. "Captain Harris. What a surprise to see you." She took a tentative step forward. "Goodness. What in the world are you doing here? How long has it been?"

All he could do was shake his head at the time it had taken him to finally come back here. "Too long. How are you?"

"I'm well. But . . ." She glanced in the direction of the sea. "How did you get here?"

"I came on my ship," he explained. "The *Overton*. We're bound for New York, but we're ahead of schedule, so I thought I'd stop by." An awkwardness overcame him, and he waved his hand about. "I took a small tender boat on my own and left it on the beach."

"I see."

They gazed at each other in silence for a few seconds.

To Oliver, Emma seemed taller somehow. Her figure was more womanly, but of course it would be. She was a married woman now, and she'd had a child.

Suddenly he felt the distance between them, deep as a canyon. The last time they'd spoken, she'd confessed a passionate love for him, and he had rejected her quite cruelly, which had, of course, been a necessity. Months later, her letter about her father's accident had suggested she bore no ill will toward him, which had come as a tremendous relief. But Oliver never heard from Emma again after that. It was her father who kept in touch over the years.

Matthew darted out of the kitchen, slammed into her legs, and wrapped his arms around her waist.

Emma laughed. "This is my son, Matthew." She looked down at her boy and pushed his blond hair back from his forehead.

The mood grew lighter, and Oliver was glad.

"We met on the beach," he said cheerfully. "Matthew was kind enough to show me the way here."

"Yes, he told me that," Emma replied. "He also said you came to see my father. I'm sorry to tell you that he took the Jeep to East Light this morning and won't be back until suppertime."

Oliver scratched the back of his head. "That's unfortunate. Is your husband here?"

It would be proper to meet him. Oliver wanted that very much.

Emma inclined her head slightly, then spoke to Matthew. "Darling, will you be a gem and go outside to get me some flowers for the table tonight? Roses will do fine."

"Is Captain Harris staying for supper?" Matthew asked.

"I'm not sure," she stammered. "We'll have to talk about that. If he's expected in New York, he might need to be on his way."

Oliver remained silent until after Matthew dashed past him and out the front door, which he shut fast behind him.

"He's a wonderful boy," Oliver said. "You should be proud."

Emma smiled, and it was the first time her expression truly warmed to him. It made him realize that she was no longer the impassioned young woman who thought herself in love with him and couldn't wait to share intimate thoughts and feelings. She must now reserve that part of herself for her husband.

"Would you like a cup of tea?" she asked.

"I don't want to impose if you're busy," Oliver replied. "Matthew said it was bread day."

"It's no imposition. I just put a few loaves in the oven, and the last of the dough is rising. All the hard work is done. Please, come into the kitchen, and I'll put the kettle on."

He followed soberly and entered the room that he remembered so very, very well. His eyes settled on the sink. He recalled escaping the gentlemen's company one evening and speaking to Emma while she washed dishes. He also remembered the window above the sink, with a view of the rolling dunes and waving marram grass.

His gaze swept across the floor, sprinkled with flour. A blue floral apron, also dusted in flour, hung on a hook by the back door.

"Have a seat at the table," Emma suggested, "and we'll get caught up."

While she filled the kettle, Oliver sat down and wondered if coming here had been a mistake. He'd expected her father to greet him on the beach. He'd imagined the animated pumping of hands and manly talk about the conditions of the sea and the might of his new steamer. But it was Emma who had welcomed him, and in that sphere, nothing was entirely comfortable. Oliver's feelings were complicated, and he suspected the same of hers.

Emma carried the kettle to the stove and switched on the burner, then moved to fetch a few tea bags from the cupboard. When at last she faced Oliver, she leaned back against the counter by the sink, her hands curled around the lip of the countertop.

"You asked about my husband," she said, casually but bluntly. "I'm afraid he's not here because . . . well . . . it didn't work out."

More than a little shocked, Oliver shifted uneasily on the chair. "I'm sorry to hear that. I didn't know. Your father never mentioned that in any of his letters."

Emma lowered her gaze, and he sensed a resignation in her, or perhaps shame. "I'm not surprised."

"May I ask what happened?" Oliver carefully asked.

Emma moved to the table and sat down across from him. "It's quite embarrassing, to be honest—not something I'm particularly proud of, because . . ." She paused. "I suppose I was a bit naive."

Sympathy rose up in him, and while he waited for her to continue, she couldn't manage to look at him. When her eyes finally lifted, they held a touch of animosity.

"I might as well just come out with it," she said. "The man I married came to Sable Island to hide from the law."

"Oh dear," Oliver replied. "What did he do?"

"He killed someone."

Oliver nearly lost his breath. "My God. Really."

She sat back and nodded. "Imagine *my* shock when I found out. Obviously, he never revealed that to me when he came courting. I only found out after Matthew was born."

Still reeling from shock, Oliver asked, "How did you find out?" He craved every detail.

"The police finally tracked him down and arrested him in Halifax. And he's been in prison ever since, for the past six years, halfway across the country, in Saskatchewan, which was where he'd come from."

Oliver shook his head. "I can't believe it." They sat in silence for a few seconds. "I'm so sorry, Emma."

Her eyes were downcast again, and she spoke, surprisingly, with indifference. "Thank you, but it's been six years, and I'm over it. I've been fine here on my own. I'm grateful to have Matthew. He's my whole world now."

Something inside Oliver broke, for this was not the spirited young woman he'd once known. The woman before him had experienced betrayal. She'd learned that the world was not always a kind or safe place, and not everyone could be trusted.

He wanted to reach across the table and take hold of her hand, to show her some sympathy and understanding—because God knew he understood—but the kettle began to whistle, so he sat back as Emma stood and poured the steaming water into the teapot.

A moment later, she was seated again, and they were sipping their tea.

"Does Matthew know?" Oliver carefully asked.

"Yes," she replied. "He started asking questions about his father last year when a new wireless station chief came here with his wife and children. They often play together, and the oldest asked Matthew where his father was. Matthew didn't know the answer, so he asked me." She paused and sipped her tea. "I'd never intended to keep it secret from him, because I've come to learn that secrets never stay hidden. I knew that if I kept the truth from him, he'd find out eventually and resent me for not telling him."

"That's true. He probably would have."

She nodded. "So, after I told him, I dug out all the letters his father had written to him from prison, which I'd been stuffing into a box. I read a few of them to him, and I've been using them to help him learn how to read."

"You're a good person, Emma. Not every mother would be so honest or levelheaded about it."

She laughed. "I didn't say I wasn't tempted to burn each one to a crisp whenever they arrived on the supply ship."

Oliver chuckled also. "In any case, you did the right thing."

She took another sip of her tea. "I hope so, because it's confusing for Matthew. More than once, he's asked if his father is a bad man. All I can do is try and help him understand that sometimes adults make mistakes."

"That's true." Oliver had made his own share of them.

For a moment, he gazed pensively toward the window, then returned his attention to Emma. "But killing someone is a rather gargantuan mistake. What were the circumstances, may I ask?"

"He claimed self-defense," she explained, "but the court didn't agree. Some people thought it was murder because there was a clear motive. He'd been having an affair with the man's wife." Emma paused. "In the end, he was found guilty of manslaughter, but I'll never know for sure if that was the right verdict, because it's obvious that I didn't know the first thing about the man I married." She finished her tea and set the cup in the saucer.

Oliver gave her a moment. "How long will he be in prison?"

"The sentence was twelve years," she explained, "but you never know. He could get an early release." She ran the pad of her finger around the rim of her teacup. "But that's enough about me. I'd rather hear about the shipping business. How is it?"

"Going well," he replied. "Better than I could have imagined."

"That's wonderful, because I remember your concern after what happened to the *Belvedere*."

He nodded. "It took a while to sort through all that, but I'm pleased to say that I'm now captain of my own ship, and I own two others."

Emma's eyebrows lifted. "Goodness! Congratulations. How did that come about?"

He wondered how much he should reveal, and in the end decided to bare all because she had just done so, and for some reason she still had that same old effect on him. With Emma Clarkson, he couldn't seem to keep anything to himself.

"I have a patron," he explained, "who wanted to keep me at sea and . . . let's just say reward me for certain loyalties."

She tilted her head to the side. "Such as?"

"Discretion regarding my wife," he candidly explained.

Oliver studied the expression in Emma's eyes. She was interested, curious, engrossed, so he continued.

"My father-in-law has friends in high places, as it were, and he wanted to avoid the scandal of a divorce—which I wanted. So, he introduced me to an investor who made me an offer I couldn't refuse. We're partners now, and in return for the favor of the introduction, I've agreed to turn a blind eye to my wife's affair."

"But what about your children?" Emma asked with sympathy.

Oliver swallowed heavily. "That's the fly in the ointment, so to speak. But I was able to make sure that my presence in their lives was part of the arrangement. I see them every time I return to England, and we usually go on a holiday, just the three of us. But I'm away a lot, so it isn't easy. Sometimes I feel as if I've sold my soul to the devil, in a way."

The front door opened, and Matthew ran into the kitchen with a fist full of flowers. "I found some!"

Emma stood and took them from him. "Well done. These are beautiful. I'll put them in water."

While she retrieved an empty vase from a shelf and filled it at the sink, Matthew sat down on the chair she'd been occupying, rested his chin on his small hands at the table, and stared at Oliver. "Are you staying for supper?"

Oliver wasn't expected back at the ship until dusk, but he would never dare to presume that Emma wished to extend an invitation.

She returned to the table with the flowers and set them down. "The captain is welcome to stay if his schedule allows. What do you think, Captain Harris? Would you like to join us? I know my father would be disappointed if he missed you."

Oliver's gaze rested on Emma's face, and he could barely comprehend the heights of his elation. "I'd be delighted. And we're old friends, Emma. I think it's time you called me Oliver."

Matthew looked up at his mother and grimaced. "He talks funny."

Emma gave him a stern look. "That's not a polite thing to say, darling. Please say you're sorry."

"I'm sorry," Matthew said sheepishly to Oliver.

"Apology accepted," he easily replied. "But you're quite correct. I do speak differently, because I'm from England, and I have what they call a British accent. And you have a Canadian accent."

Matthew looked up at Emma again. "Is that true, Mom?"

"Yes, it's true."

When she smiled at Matthew and rubbed the top of his head, Oliver saw a joyful light in her eyes and recognized that old spark in her. He was relieved to see that it had not gone out completely, and something in his heart took to the air.

~

"Do my eyes defy me?" Emma's father asked jovially as he walked through the door with his cane and spotted Oliver rising from the sofa in the great room. "Captain Oliver Harris! I saw a ship anchored offshore and wondered if it was you." He set his cane against the wall and limped toward Oliver to shake his hand.

"It's good to see you, John." Oliver patted him on the back. "You look well."

"As well as can be expected." He turned to Emma. "What a surprise, eh? You must have fainted with shock."

"Not quite," she replied with a chuckle as she helped John remove his coat. "But it was definitely a surprise."

"How long can you stay?" he asked Oliver.

"I told the crew I'd be back before dark."

Her father checked his watch. "Well then. We've got a few hours. You've been invited for dinner, I assume?"

"I have."

"Then let's not waste time. We should have some brandy. Emma, will you join us?"

"I need to finish making dinner first," she replied. "But I'll bring you the drinks tray."

"Wonderful." Her father limped to his chair in the great room. "Just like old times, eh?"

"Old times and good times," Oliver replied. "With the exception of the sinking of the *Belvedere*, of course."

Emma's father slapped his thigh. "Good God. Let's not mention that. Ah! Here comes the brandy. We'll drink to better days ahead."

~

A short while later, they all sat down in the kitchen to dine on duck stew and fresh bread for dipping. Matthew finished his entire bowl and remembered all his table manners, and the conversation was relaxed and friendly.

"Are Abigail and Philip still here?" Oliver asked, reaching for another slice of bread.

As Emma dabbed the corner of her mouth with her napkin, she exchanged a look with her father. He scratched behind his ear—a gesture that was his habit when he needed time to formulate an appropriate response to an awkward question.

"They left the island for greener pastures," he said. "When was it, Emma?"

"April of '49," she helpfully replied.

Oliver turned to her. "Where are they now?"

"Back in Halifax," she told him. "Philip has family there, and he still works for the federal government, studying and reporting on the weather."

"And Abigail? Is she working as a nurse?"

"She's retired," her father quickly put in.

"Knitting her fingers to bone, I suspect," Oliver said, with good humor.

Emma looked down at her bowl. "Most likely."

Matthew fidgeted with his spoon and shifted restlessly in his chair. "May I be excused, Mom?"

"Of course, darling. Go upstairs and brush your teeth and get ready for bed. I'll come up to say good night. But before you go, say goodbye to Captain Harris, because he'll be leaving us soon."

Matthew rose from his chair, walked around the table, and held out his hand like a little gentleman. "It was nice to meet you, Captain Harris. I hope we'll see you again."

Oliver shook his small hand. "I hope so too, Matthew. Good night."

Matthew turned and hugged his grandfather. "Good night, Grampa." Then he left the kitchen and ran to the stairs.

A quietness settled upon the room. Emma stood up to clear the table. "Would you like coffee or tea?" she asked as she carried the bowls to the sink.

Oliver glanced at the window, where the sun was setting in glowing streaks of pink. "I'd love some, but I really should be going."

"Yes, you must," her father replied. "Otherwise, your men will think you've been captured by the locals."

Oliver smiled at the jest. "Indeed." He folded his napkin and made a move to rise. "But to be imprisoned on paradise. There could be far worse fates."

Emma was flattered by the compliment to her island home. Or perhaps part of the compliment was directed at her?

Heaven help her. She'd been fighting all afternoon against an undercurrent of her old feelings for this man, but they were irrepressible. Once she and the captain had begun talking—and he'd asked her to call him Oliver—it all came rushing back. It was as if not a single day had passed since the week that followed the shipwreck. Emma wanted to keep talking to him, to share so much about her life these past seven years, and to learn more about his.

And it could not be overlooked that she was still wildly attracted to him. There was no one more handsome, more striking, or manlier than Oliver Harris. And she was a woman of experience now. She understood what was possible between them, as a man and a woman, in private.

At the same time, she was determined not to let herself go down that road again. He was leaving, and who knew if he would ever return?

Her father turned to her then, and she quickly hauled herself out of the depressing depths of that reality.

"Emma, we can't just send him out alone when it's getting dark. Take the flashlight and walk him to his boat."

With the sudden, fast beating of her heart, her body felt energized. "Of course." She fetched the light from the drawer in the hall table, and after her father said goodbye to Oliver, she led him out the door.

～

The small bulb from the flashlight illuminated a narrow sandy path through the tall marram grass. Emma stepped carefully in front of Oliver, who followed as they walked in silence, in single file.

Soon, the noise from the ocean grew louder as they approached, and Emma felt an increasing tightness in her belly. She didn't know what to say, yet she wanted to say everything—to lift the lid on her feelings and let them all come flying out.

When they reached the passage to North Beach, the narrow trail widened to a small field of sand, and Oliver moved to walk beside Emma.

"I hope you won't mind," he said, "if I ask a question."

"Not at all." Despite everything, she was pleased by the return of their natural intimacy.

"At dinner," he said, "I sensed you weren't telling me everything about Abigail and Philip. Maybe it's none of my business, but did something happen?"

Emma sighed. "Yes, I'm afraid so. It wasn't a good situation when they left us. The isolation finally caught up with Abigail, and she had a . . . let's just call it a nervous breakdown."

"Dear God."

"She'd kept to herself all winter," Emma continued, "and wouldn't come to any of our social gatherings, not even to the beach on Boat Day. Then one evening, she ran to the water and tried to wade into the surf, but Philip chased after her and dragged her back in. That's when we all realized she needed help, so she was taken ashore, and they have no plans to return." Emma shook her head at the memory of that harrowing night. "I wish there was something I could have done to help her, but even with all the reading I've done about the workings of the mind, it was beyond my level of understanding."

"Is she better now?" Oliver asked, genuinely concerned.

"In some ways, yes. She was released from the hospital, and Philip writes every few months to keep us updated."

By now, the sun had dipped below the horizon, and the sky was a dark shade of purple. Bright stars began to flicker and shine.

Emma gazed out at Oliver's ship, a stark black figure on the edge of the world, and she resented it for taking him away. Side by side, they trudged down the beach until the tender became visible in the fading light. When they reached it, they turned to each other.

This was it. The painful parting. But this was Emma's life. It was the way things were on Sable Island, and she'd accepted long ago that there was nothing she could do to stop the world from turning.

Oliver hesitated, looked toward the high dunes, then back out at his ship. "I wish we could talk more."

"I wish the same thing."

"What about the work on the East Light?" he asked. "Do you think your father could use some help?"

Her blood began to race at what he might be suggesting. "I'm sure he could."

Oliver pondered it for a moment and scratched the back of his head. "What if I bring some crewmen ashore in the morning and provide a few extra hands?"

Her body was now on fire with excitement at the prospect. "But don't you have to be in New York soon?"

"I'm days ahead of schedule," he told her.

He turned toward the ocean and stared at the horizon, and Emma admired his profile in the colors of twilight, and how the breeze lifted his thick dark hair. How pensive he looked.

"Who knows," he said. "Maybe I planned it this way, so that I'd have an excuse to come here."

The hostility she'd felt on the beach seven years ago, when he'd called her a child and told her to forget him, became hazy. All that mattered was the prospect of seeing him again the next morning.

"If you can delay your departure," she said, "and lend a hand at East Light, I'm sure my father would be thrilled."

Oliver faced her, and a faint light twinkled in his eyes. Or perhaps it was just the moon's reflection as it began its slow rise over the ocean.

"I'll bring three men with me," he said. "What time does the work usually begin?"

"They start at nine."

"Very good," he said. "Tell your father we'll meet him there."

As he turned and dragged the small boat in a circle to face the waves, then dug his boots into the sand, hauling it to the water, happiness charged through Emma's heart.

"No need to cook us breakfast!" Oliver shouted as he strode into the waves. The water splashed above his knees before he leaped into the boat. "We'll eat on the ship and bring our own lunches!"

Emma watched him start the motor and pick up speed. The boat bounced over the breaking waves. When it reached the heavy swells beyond, he looked back at her and waved. She waved in return, her body alight with anticipation for the morning.

Moments later, Oliver's figure grew distant. As he faded into the darkness, she was jolted by the image of Logan's face in her mind. She saw herself with him—working on their paper night after night, galloping on the beaches at dawn, sneaking away to private hollows in the dunes to be alone together and drown each other in sensation.

God . . . Emma had fallen too fast with him, without the slightest hesitation. She'd been swallowed up by the pleasure of her desires after the frustrations of her unrequited love for the captain.

She stood on the beach for another moment, then turned to walk home, shivering the whole way in the chilly north wind.

CHAPTER 20

The noisy ringing of the circular saw cut through the air as Emma drove the Jeep into the East Station yard. She pulled to a halt, shifted into park, and turned to her father in the passenger seat.

"I promise we won't get in the way." She glanced over her shoulder at Matthew in the back seat. "Right?"

"Right!" he replied. It wasn't every day a new frame was built for the East Light, not to mention a crew of workers arriving from a passing ship.

They all got out of the Jeep, and her father leaned heavily on his cane to make his way toward Kevin, the chief staff man in charge of the repairs. Three other men stood around, waiting for direction.

"Stay with me, Matthew," Emma said when he made a move toward the table saw. "Let the men talk for a bit. Then we'll see the equipment."

While the men discussed what had to be accomplished that day, Emma turned toward the ocean.

"Look, Matthew," she said excitedly for his benefit, pointing. "Here comes the tender." The small boat was motoring fast, halfway between the ship and the shore.

"Is it the captain?" Matthew asked.

"Yes, and some of his crew. Would you like to go down to the beach and meet them?"

"Yes, come on! Let's go!" He ran ahead.

~

The tender skimmed onto the sand on a powerful breaker. Two men jumped out to drag the craft out of the water, and then Oliver leaped out as well and strode toward Emma. "Good morning!"

Matthew was running back and forth, jumping up and down in front of the tender boat.

"I wasn't sure if you'd be here," Oliver said.

"We couldn't possibly miss the excitement," she replied, laughing at Matthew.

Oliver's gaze remained fixed on Emma, and his mood was cheerful and energetic. "I'm so glad." The members of his crew reached into the boat for a few sacks of supplies and toolboxes. "We came ready to work," Oliver added. "Allow me to introduce you to the men."

The crew members approached, and Oliver made the introductions. Then Matthew ran ahead, thrilled to lead the way to the station yard.

~

"Captain Harris! Do you want to see a dead seal?"

It was lunchtime, and the men were spread out, seated on the back of the horse cart, on overturned crates, or in extra chairs that had been brought out from the station house.

"Truth be told, Matthew, I would," he replied. "But you'd better ask your mother first. And be sure to invite her along."

Matthew ran into the station house, where Emma was wiping the kitchen table. "Mom! The captain wants to see the dead seal, and he wants you to come."

Emma balled the wet cloth in her hand. "Right now?"

"Yes. Can we go? Please?"

Mrs. Jordan pulled the plug from the sink and let the water drain out. "That sounds like fun. Go ahead, Emma. I'll take care of things here."

Emma placed the damp cloth next to the sink and followed Matthew outside.

~

After viewing the smelly carcass down by the water, Emma and Oliver walked together leisurely, a short distance behind Matthew, who was playing tag with the incoming waves.

"Tell me," Oliver said, "whatever happened to the young wireless operator who was enamored with you when I was here last? His name was Frank, I believe."

"Yes. Frank O'Reilly. He turned out to be a good friend to me in the end. But that's the thing about living on Sable Island. Most people only stay for a year or two. So many friends come and go from your life." Emma sighed and slid her hands into her pockets. "He left shortly after I married Logan."

"All hope was gone for him, I suppose," Oliver replied, giving her a meaningful look.

She turned her face toward the wind. "Maybe so. I've thought about Frank many times since then. He was a decent person, and I probably would have been better off with him than the man I chose, but then I wouldn't have Matthew."

"Everything happens the way it's meant to." Oliver bent down and picked up a colorful shell, which he slipped into his pocket. They walked on.

"You know," he said after a time, "the real reason I wanted to come back here was to see you."

Emma shot him a look. "Me?"

"Yes. I enjoyed our conversations back then, but I didn't realize how much until after I left. So, for a long time . . ." He paused. "For a long time, I've regretted some of the things I said on the day I left. And I've also wanted to thank you."

Two seagulls darted sharply overhead, and he looked up at them.

"Thank me for what, exactly?" Emma asked.

"Well . . ." He hesitated. "After the wreck, and from talking to you, I started to think more about life and what a gift it is. Even after the war I never really understood that, but when I left here, I realized that I needed to find meaning somehow. And contentment. So, I decided to stop punishing myself over every little mistake I'd ever made, or things I had no control over, like my wife's wishes and feelings. I was fully prepared to set her free, with no hard feelings, to pursue her own happiness. But then her father wanted to set the terms of our separation, so I let him. I decided to stop swimming against the current and just enjoy what I could out of my life, even though it's far from perfect."

Emma was fascinated by this. "So, you feel less burdened by the choices you've made in the past?"

If only she could feel that way too.

"That's exactly it," he replied. "But it's funny—I'd looked death in the eye many times during the war, but it wasn't until I spent time here with you that I truly appreciated the miracle of being alive. Do you remember our morning ride, the day before I left?"

"Yes."

"Every moment of that day with you is etched on my brain," he said. "Especially seeing the wild horses. Nothing was quite the same after that."

Emma watched Matthew dash into a group of seagulls roosting on the beach. They took off frantically.

"I wish you'd told me all this when you left," Emma said. "All these years I felt like such a fool for imagining that you found me at all interesting. Eventually I came to the conclusion that you were just being kind, humoring me the whole time."

"Humoring you? Emma, I was amazed by you. Was that not obvious?"

Amazed?

"But you ignored me that night at the party," she reminded him, having never forgotten the hurt. "I thought I'd done something wrong, or that I'd insulted you somehow. Then you left me feeling mortified the next morning because of the things I said to you."

He looked down at his shoes as he walked. "I hope you can accept my apology. I should have handled that better."

Emma thought about everything. "I suppose you were right, in a way. You told me I was a child, and I was. I had no experience in the real world."

He glanced down at her. "But you have it now."

"Oh yes," she said, with a bitter laugh. "More than I ever wanted. I have firsthand knowledge of lies and betrayal and criminal court, and now I understand why some people become so bitter and jaded." She started walking again. "So maybe it was a good lesson for me, because I won't get into trouble like that again. I'm much more cautious. Far less trusting."

He regarded her intently. "It makes me sad to hear that."

"It shouldn't. Clearly, I had a lot to learn. I was so preachy before, giving people advice, thinking I knew everything. I was arrogant to imagine that I could sit in a classroom, get a degree, and counsel people about how to cope with their traumas, when I'd never experienced anything remotely traumatic in my own life."

"You lost your mother on the day you were born."

"Yes, but I have no memory of that—at least no conscious memory— and I had a wonderful childhood, relatively speaking."

"Because of your friend Ruth," he said.

Emma was surprised that he remembered Ruth's name after so many years. He wasn't lying about everything being etched on his brain.

"Are you still in touch with her?" he asked.

"Yes, we write to each other, and I take Matthew for a visit every summer. Ruth was with me in Halifax when Logan was arrested. We were staying at her house because I went to the hospital to deliver Matthew. Speak of the devil . . ."

Her son came running toward them. "Can we go back now? I'm hungry."

"You just had lunch," Emma said.

"Can I have a snack?"

She laughed and rubbed the top of his head. "I think I saw a cookie jar in Mrs. Jordan's kitchen. Maybe if you ask nicely . . ."

"I'm always nice, Mom." Matthew took off toward East Station.

"Oh, to have that energy," Oliver said wistfully, with amusement.

"Tell me about it. Shall we head back as well?"

They turned to retrace their steps back to East Light.

~

At the end of the day, when all the gear was packed up, Oliver's dread felt like a vise grip in his gut. He didn't want to leave. He wanted to spend more time with Emma. There were so many things he wanted to talk with her about. He wanted to hear more about her marriage, her father's long recovery, what Matthew had been like as a baby.

He sent his crewmen down to the tender boat but held back to say goodbye to Emma and her father. Anything to stall the inevitable.

"We made good progress today," John said, "thanks to you and your men."

"They enjoyed every minute of it," Oliver replied.

Emma, her father, and Matthew got into the Jeep, and Oliver shut the passenger-side door for John. He stood at the open window for a moment, looking at Emma behind the wheel. He still wasn't ready to say goodbye.

She turned the key in the ignition, and the engine sputtered to life.

"Hop in," John said. "We'll give you a ride down to the beach."

A reprieve! Oliver smiled and got into the back seat beside Matthew.

~

It was a bumpy ride in the back of the Jeep, and Oliver held the grip overhead as he bounced on the seat. Emma drove slowly through a narrow passage of thick bayberry bushes while swallows chirped and darted above them. When they reached the open beach, she shifted into a higher gear and sped up on a direct path toward the tender boat, where his men were standing around, waiting.

She pulled to a halt, shut off the engine, and got out. She thanked Oliver's crewmen and shook their hands while her father remained seated in the Jeep. Then she turned to Oliver.

"Well . . . thank you again. It's too bad you couldn't stay longer. I would have loved to show you the rose garden. It's grown up quite a bit. You wouldn't recognize it."

Oliver contemplated how badly he wanted to go with her to the rose garden, and that's when he knew: the feelings he'd wrestled with years ago had never died. They were as strong as ever, perhaps even more so after certain life experiences and deeper self-reflection.

It had taken Oliver seven years to return. Seven years to think about their week together and drum up the courage to see her again and face what could have been if he'd been brave enough to love her when he'd had the chance.

And there it was—the truth of it all. He'd always regretted walking away from something that could have been beautiful. At the time, he couldn't fully comprehend how important it was to grab hold of happiness while you could, and hang on to it. But he understood it so much better now. He'd been through a war and a shipwreck. He knew how fragile life could be. Perhaps a part of him hadn't believed he deserved happiness. He'd lost so many people who mattered to him. Sometimes he still felt guilty for being alive when others were not.

But he was not without hope. Getting to know Emma, and leaving her behind, had taught him something about a life squandered. And he'd squandered enough. Seven years' worth.

Oliver checked his watch. "I still have some time."

"Are you sure?" Emma replied. "You don't have to stick to your schedule?"

"We do, but we don't have to raise the anchor until sunset." He strode to his crewmen, who stood around the boat. "Change of plans, gentlemen. Take the supplies to the ship, unload, then come back for me in an hour, down at the west end."

The men cheerfully agreed. They dragged the boat to the water's edge and hopped in, and Oliver pushed them farther out until they floated. Then he ran back in, splashing through a shallow incoming wave.

"Let's go," he said to Emma with enthusiasm, and got back into the Jeep.

A short while later, back at Main Station, he said goodbye to John and Matthew. Then Oliver got into the front seat beside Emma. She told Matthew she'd be back in an hour, shifted into first gear, and steered toward the beach and the rose garden to the west.

CHAPTER 21

It was like walking into an explosion of fragrance.

Oliver followed Emma into the circular garden, where the bushes had flourished and grown more densely together. The pale-pink roses were in full bloom.

"You were right," he said. "It's barely recognizable."

Emma walked backward, facing him. "I didn't come here for years after you left. Life was so busy, looking after Matthew when he was a baby. I only returned for the first time a few months ago, so I had the same reaction you're having now."

They strolled in silence, apart, smelling the soft petals and admiring the astonishing array of blooms.

"It's amazing how nature can endure like this," Oliver said. "In the open Atlantic. Completely out of sight." He glanced over his shoulder at her. "I have to ask . . . Have you ever thought about trying again to go to university?"

Emma laughed. "Not in years."

"Why not?"

"Because I'm busy. I have Matthew."

He nodded and sauntered around the garden. "I'm sorry. I shouldn't have brought it up."

"But you did," she said. "Why?"

He regarded her in the dappled shadows of the evening light, and the way her hips swayed when she turned away from him.

"You wanted it so badly before," he said, "and you'd be good at it. Being a psychologist, I mean."

Emma fingered the tiniest twiglike branches of a younger shrub, low to the ground. "It's a nice thought, but I'm a mother now."

"Maybe you could be both."

Something flirtatious sparked in her eyes as she gave him a sidelong look of warning. "You're going to have to stop doing that."

"Doing what?"

"Stirring up old hopes and dreams."

Good God, he was completely enraptured. "Why?"

"Because it's pointless," she replied. "I'm not that person anymore."

She spoke willfully, but Oliver didn't believe her. Not for one single second.

"And I don't want to pine for the road not taken," she added. "Or feel as if I gave up on something, or quit like a coward. This is the life I *chose*, Oliver, and I told you I have no regrets."

She sat down on the old weatherworn bench and looked up at him with an expression that beckoned, and Oliver sat down beside her.

∽

Emma squeezed her hands together on her lap. *Damn this man. Damn Captain Oliver Harris.*

She'd thought all this was behind her. Her life had certainly taken some unexpected turns that she might not have chosen at the time, but she was happy with where she'd ended up—back on Sable Island with her father and a son who meant everything to her.

Why did Oliver have to come back and upend everything? Make her doubt her choices and long for the paths not taken?

Turning her head, she looked at him sharply. "Why did you come back here?"

"I told you," he replied. "Because I wanted to see you."

"But *why*? You thought I was married, but you came anyway. Didn't it occur to you that it might be awkward, considering our last conversation on the beach when you left?"

For a few seconds, he seemed lost for words, but soon managed to form a reply. "I'd hoped enough time had passed."

"For *you*, maybe. But what happened that week left me absolutely wrecked. It crushed all my confidence, and when Logan came along, I wanted so badly to forget you that I practically dove into his arms."

"Emma . . ."

Her pulse was racing. All the pent-up hurt and anger that she'd repressed over the past seven years came surging out of her, and she wanted to lash out at him, to express everything.

She stood and strode to the other side of the garden. "Please don't try and tell me that you didn't mean to hurt me, or that everything happens the way it's meant to. I told you I'll never regret anything because I have Matthew now, and I wouldn't change that for the world. But that doesn't mean I want to be friends with you, which seems to be the reason you came here. So that we could all be best pals."

He looked away, toward the ocean.

"Well, that can't happen," she insisted fiercely. "Because I don't want to get caught up in that whirlwind again."

"What whirlwind?"

"Where I start to dream about you!" She swung her arm about. "Last night, I couldn't wait to wake up and drive to East Light and see you this morning. I hardly slept a wink. I tossed and turned, trying not to think about you, but it was impossible. And today, I forced myself to stay away from you, but you had to send Matthew into the house and invite me on that damn walk to see the stupid seal!"

She stared at him heatedly and fought to quiet her fury, then wished she had the discipline to keep her feelings to herself. But clearly, her emotional floodgates had broken completely open. He probably thought her mad for ranting like a hysteric.

"Emma, you're mistaken if you think you were the only one tossing and turning last night."

She drew back slightly as he stood up.

"And I can't believe," he continued, "that you have no idea how badly I wanted you back then. That you didn't recognize that it was torture for me to pretend otherwise. But I had to because I was a married man, years older than you, and it was completely inappropriate. I said the things I did because I wanted you to move on."

Emma frowned with confusion, not entirely sure she could believe or accept this. Everything in her mind was telling her to reject it. "You were expecting me to read between the lines?"

"I suppose I was, yes. And when I asked my wife for a divorce," he continued, "it was because I thought that . . . maybe eventually . . . I could come back here, see you again, and things would be different. But then your father wrote and told me about your marriage, so I accepted my father-in-law's offer in Manchester and did my best to move on."

Emma was still in a daze of denial, and now she was fighting tears. "Then why did you come back yesterday if you thought I was married? What was the point in that?"

He lowered his head in defeat. "I don't know. God knows I tried to resist coming here. I *did* resist it—for *years*—which wasn't easy every time I steamed past this island on my way to America." He looked up and waved his hand through the air, as if he were conducting an orchestra, grasping for an explanation. "Maybe I thought coming here would put an end to that stubborn little dream in the back of my head. Maybe if I saw you happily married to another man, I'd stop romanticizing what happened between us that week and accept reality."

The mention of reality left Emma in a state of incomprehension, not entirely sure if this was actually happening. She strolled to the garden entrance and looked out at the rolling dunes. The marram grass blew, but inside the circle of roses, the world was sheltered, and still its own special little world.

"You kept in touch with my father," she said with her back to Oliver. "Why didn't he tell you what happened with my husband? We've been apart for seven years."

"I don't know. That's a question you'll have to ask him. I'd like to know the answer myself."

Emma gazed up at the misty clouds and the rapidly changing light across the sky. It had been nearly an hour since the captain had sent his men away with the supplies. They would be back for him soon. A dreadful heaviness settled into her heart.

"Your tender is probably on its way."

"My men can wait," he replied and strode closer until he stood beside her in the garden entrance.

Emma kept her eyes down and struggled to control her breathing.

"Look at me," Oliver said.

Reluctantly, she turned to him.

"When you told me that your husband wasn't here, and that he was no longer in the picture, I was overjoyed."

Emma should have been thrilled by this confession, but she could only gaze up at Oliver with wariness—because he could do it again. He could leave in a few minutes and never come back.

That thought sent her pride bucking.

"You were glad? Why? What did you imagine would happen? That I'd become infatuated with you again and all would be forgotten?"

He slowly shook his head. "No, I could see that you'd changed, and there was a wall between us. It's still there now."

She looked away. "I don't know why you're telling me all this."

"Because I want you to know the truth. I want honesty between us."

"For what purpose?"

"That depends on you."

"Me?"

"Yes," he said. "We're both married, but not happily. I've never been able to forget you, and I'd like the chance to be with you, Emma."

A battle was still raging inside her, and it made her feel cold and antagonistic. "What are you suggesting? That I become your mistress? Isn't that what they call it in your country?"

"No. That's not what I want." He paused and took a breath. "Ever since I left you on that beach, I've imagined all sorts of scenarios. I've imagined what I would do if I found out your husband had died. I pictured myself giving you the proper amount of time you'd need to grieve. Then I would somehow win you back. Then we would marry, and I'd retire from the sea."

She stared at him with brows drawn together in disbelief. "You imagined that?"

"Yes. Every possible logistic."

Emma couldn't lie. Over the years, she'd imagined similar things and worked out, in her head, every obstacle. "I don't know what to say." She couldn't think straight. "Your men are probably out there by now, waiting for you," she reminded him.

Oliver gazed toward the Atlantic, thunderous in the distance, and a muscle twitched at his jaw. He took Emma's face in his hands. "Please, just tell me there's hope."

But Emma was afraid to hope. More than once, hope had only sent her plummeting from the clouds to the earth and had caused her dreadful pain.

"I'm married," she said. "And so are you."

"But do you love him?"

Her answer came all too easily. "No. I thought I did at first. Maybe I did, because he helped me forget you for a while. But he's not a part of my life anymore."

"Neither is my wife."

"But your children . . ."

"I'll always be their father, and they know it. They're old enough to understand that now." His voice was steady, and his eyes were clear.

Emma felt a wave of panic charging suddenly toward her. He was suggesting the kind of relationship she'd wanted in the beginning, and she would have walked through fire to hear him say these things seven years ago. But nothing was the same as it was. She wasn't the same person. She'd been here before and done this before.

"I'll be broken after you go," she said. "Just like last time."

He pulled her into his arms and spoke close in her ear. "No, you won't, because I'll promise to come back."

"But when?"

"As soon as I can." His breath was hot and moist in her ear. "If you tell me there's hope, at Christmas, I'll bring a ring for you. I'll get down on one knee and propose properly."

Trembling, Emma stepped back. A part of her was still afraid to believe this was truly happening.

He laid his hand on her cheek and looked into her eyes. "I'll do whatever it takes to never say goodbye to you again."

"How?"

"I'll file for divorce. I'll come back here a free man—or a soon-to-be free man. Then we can make plans."

"But I won't be free," she reminded him. "I'll still be married."

"Do you want to stay married?" he asked.

It was another question that was easy to answer. "Not to Logan."

A smile spread across Oliver's face, and he laughed. His joy was contagious, and she found herself laughing too.

He cupped her face in his hands again. "Emma. Please. Can I kiss you?"

"Yes."

His lips found hers, and the pressure of his mouth sent her heart into a frenzy. She grasped blindly for his face and slid her hands around the back of his neck to pull him closer, to deepen the kiss—a kiss she'd dreamed about for what felt like an eternity.

Their bodies melded together in the fading light. Oliver led her deeper into the heart of the garden, and Emma followed willingly. He got down on his knees and held out a hand. Emma knelt too. Then she lay back and reached her arms out to him. He covered her body with his, kissed her deeply, and laid light kisses across her cheek and down the side of her neck.

A soft breeze whispered through the greenery, and the perfume of the roses was like a fine wine sliding into Emma's soul. It was the most welcome, exquisite intoxication, which made it easy to ignore the vague and distant voice in her head that was warning her to be careful and protect her heart. She was still afraid of losing this man, but she'd wanted him for too long. She couldn't possibly deny herself this pleasure, the fulfillment of a dream. Whatever happened between them, even if she never saw him again, she knew she could never regret this. She would cherish the memory for the rest of her life.

In the magic that followed, Emma pushed aside any fears about the future. All that mattered was this gift of rapture as they made love. It was like floating inside a dream.

~

Afterward, Oliver held Emma in his arms. "I promise I'll be back by Christmas. But for now, take this." He removed his gold signet ring and handed it to her.

She slid it onto her index finger, but it was too big. "I'll wear it on the chain with my mother's locket."

She was almost delirious with happiness.

For a long while, they clung to each other, skin against skin in the shelter of the garden, their foreheads touching, while the ocean roared in the distance, beyond the high dune.

"We should go," she finally said, still breathless but thinking of his crew in the tender boat, waiting on the shoreline.

"You don't like to be late, do you." His voice was husky and low, touched with amusement, and he brushed his nose against hers. "We're the same, you and me. God, I don't want to leave you."

"I don't want you to leave either," she replied. "I hate this."

He took hold of her hand, raised it to his lips, and kissed it. "Walk me to the beach. And I swear, this time, goodbye won't be forever."

They helped each other to rise and dress and attend to the fastenings of their clothes. Then they left the privacy of the garden and began the journey back to the beach.

Outside in the open, where the wind blew steadily and the sand shifted beneath Emma's feet, the dream slowly began to recede, and the dread of his departure gained traction.

"I'll return soon," Oliver promised, as if he could read her thoughts. "After that, I'll do whatever you want. I'll stay here if you like. Or I'll take you to England, or the mainland. You could go to university if you still want that. Or if you don't, that's fine too. I'm done with my own ambitions, Emma. I've seen enough of life without you. I only want to be with you and make you happy."

"I'll be happy no matter where we are," she replied. But as she spoke the words, she felt as if she were playacting, fighting to hold on to the dream, to believe in it, even though it still felt distant and out of reach. What could she do but pray? Pray for everything to work out as he promised it would.

Soon, they came to the beach. Oliver stopped and took Emma into his arms again. He held her close, and she prepared herself for the painful agony of goodbye.

"When I come back," he said, "I'll speak to your father. And I don't care what it takes. Whatever we need to do to be together, we'll do it."

The tender boat was waiting on the sand, its solid hull weathering the steady stroke of the waves. The men sitting in the boat were quiet, their gazes averted.

Oliver kissed Emma goodbye, then finally tore himself away and jogged to the boat. He grabbed hold of the stern and leaned into a heavy thrust to launch it. As soon as it lifted off the sand and floated, he leaped into it with impressive agility and sat on a bench facing Emma, who stood on the beach.

The boat rose and fell over the wild surf, and their gazes held. They watched each other raptly.

Emma clasped her hands together over her heart, and remained on the beach for more than an hour until the *Overton*'s anchor was raised. With dark smoke billowing from her twin stacks, she steamed onward, and Emma watched until eventually she disappeared around the western tip of the island.

CHAPTER 22

September 19, 1953

Dear Ruth,

If you could only know how eager I've been to sit down and write to you. I wish I could deliver this news in person because it might remove some of the sting from that horrible day when Logan was arrested at your house. I was quite downtrodden then, and you were so worried about my emotional wellbeing. But I survived, didn't I? (Now I wonder if it was all some sort of test to teach me about patience. All good things come to those who wait. Isn't that what they say? It certainly applies to me today!)

But that's enough philosophizing. I won't keep you in suspense. Do you remember Captain Oliver Harris and all the times I poured out my broken heart to you about him? (I can't thank you enough for all your letters of advice, sympathy, and encouragement over the years.)

I'm not even sure where to begin, except to tell you that the captain paid us a visit this week. (!) At first, I wasn't happy to see him because, as you know, I grew to resent him after he left in such a cruel way. And rightly or wrongly, I've always blamed him for my weakness with

Logan. So, when he showed up at our door this week, I was guarded, maybe even a bit rude (I'm not sure). But as always, we got to talking, and I couldn't help but fall back into those old feelings of love, which weren't gone, just dormant.

He stayed an extra day to help with some repairs at East Light, and when it came time for him to leave, he proposed to me and promised to return with a ring at Christmas.

I wish I could see your face as you're reading this! I hope you haven't fallen out of your chair. I'm still pinching myself, and though I'm happy, I'm also terrified that for some reason he won't come back. I've been disappointed before, so it's hard to trust that everything will work out. Obviously, I'm jaded. That's no secret. So, the next few months will be a challenge while I wait. I'm not even sure if I should tell Matthew in case something goes wrong. What do you suggest about that?

Also, if you don't mind, I'd like to ask your advice about something else. Should I come to Halifax now and start divorce proceedings? That's what Oliver plans to do when he goes back to England. Or maybe I should wait until I'm more certain about the future?

That's all for now. I will send this letter on the next boat in a few days. Papa says hello.

Much love,

Emma

P.S. I forgot to mention that Oliver had no idea that Logan was in prison and that we were no longer together. Papa wrote to him many times but never mentioned it, so that's why Oliver stayed away.

As you can imagine, Papa had a lot to answer for and we had a heated discussion about it. His excuse was that he had no idea that Oliver had feelings for me, and if he'd known, he would have encouraged a visit. He said he was just trying to protect me from further heartbreak.

In all honesty, I'm not entirely sure I believe him. It wouldn't be the first time he's arranged things to keep me at his side. (But not the seal attack. I'm 100% confident that he didn't arrange for that to happen!) At any rate, he said he was sorry, and he was quite remorseful.

Hugs and kisses,
Emma

~

September 26, 1953

Dear Emma,
I almost did fall out of my chair when I read your letter!

I'm so happy for you! It was always crystal clear to me that you loved Captain Harris deeply, and it wasn't just a schoolgirl crush, as you often suggested. There was something special between you. And I also suspected that he said what he did on that last day to allow you to move on and go to university as you'd planned. He didn't want to hold you back.

I'd very much like to meet him. Based on your descriptions, I'm sure he's an impressive man. He must be intelligent, too, if he recognized how special you are. But I'm sorry you've both had to wait so long. So many lost years . . .

I crossed that out because nothing good can come from regretting the past or wallowing in what can't be changed. Don't let yourself fall into that trap. Nothing can be done about what happened, so go forward with gusto and dive headfirst into the future.

I'd like to imagine that you're smiling right now. I hope you're happier than ever.

To answer your questions about telling Matthew or starting divorce proceedings, my only advice is to follow your heart and do what you feel is right. Perhaps you'll prefer to wait until you have a ring on your finger before you divorce Matthew's father. (But that sounds like advice, doesn't it? I apologize. You're a grown woman and I have faith in your good judgement. It's just food for thought, tossed into the air. And maybe I'm a little jaded, too. Or maybe "careful" is a better word.)

Say hello to your father for me, and please forgive him for his missteps. He's a good man and he loves you dearly and only wants to protect you. Maybe you can relate to that better now that you're a mother. It's so difficult to let our children go into the big, bad, dangerous world. Worrying about them is unavoidable. It comes with the territory.

Much love,
Ruth

CHAPTER 23

On New Year's Eve, the great room was alive with laughter and singing as the staff men gathered around the piano, where Emma's father played a continuous parade of popular tunes from the '30s and '40s. One of the crewmen had visited earlier in the day to hang streamers from the ceiling and drop off a basket of noisemakers.

But Emma was in no mood for singing or blowing horns. She'd been feeling down since Christmas Day because Oliver had not yet returned, nor had she received a letter from him. She tried to remind herself that letters often went astray en route to Sable, and it certainly wasn't easy for anyone to arrive exactly on schedule. Sometimes, if the weather was foul, the supply ship could be detained for a week or more. And no doubt, Oliver had much to do in England to arrange his affairs before his return.

So she did her best to remain optimistic, which wasn't easy under the circumstances, because she'd been feeling sick in the mornings for quite some time, and her monthly was long overdue.

There was no point sticking her head in the sand. Clearly, she was expecting, but what could she do about her anxieties except to wait for Oliver to arrive?

$\sim$

Shortly before midnight, the wireless station chief popped the cork on a bottle of bubbly and poured drinks for everyone in white paper cups. The clock struck twelve. Her father played "Auld Lang Syne," and with arms about shoulders, swaying from side to side, everyone sang along.

Emma remained in the kitchen, watching from afar. She'd been so tired lately, sapped of energy, always wanting to nap in the afternoons. The fatigue made it difficult to stay awake and share in everyone's high spirits.

Turning away from the party, she grabbed her wool coat from the hook at the back door and ventured outside, down the wooden steps.

It was a mild winter night. The fog was thick with the salty fragrance of the sea. There was not a single breath of wind, but the damp chill caused Emma to gather her coat collar tighter about her neck as she left the noise of the party and crossed the station yard to head toward the high dune over North Beach. She climbed to the top and paused, slightly out of breath, and looked out at the ocean. The fog was thick, and the night was dark. She could barely see the waves. She could only hear them.

Emma's heart squeezed painfully in her chest. *Why hasn't he come?*

With bone-deep despair, she sank to the ground, sat back on her heels, and clasped her hands together in prayer. *Please, God, keep him safe and send him home to me. Oliver, hurry if you can. I couldn't bear to be disappointed again. Not with our baby on the way.*

The sand was cold, and her knees grew numb. Emma rose to her feet, faced the ocean, and listened to the surf breaking on the beach below. A chill rippled down the length of her spine, so she turned away and walked down the steep slope to return to the warmth of home.

By the time she arrived, the party was over, and everyone was saying goodbye in the station yard, wishing each other a happy new year. She joined them and pretended to be jovial.

~

A week later, the January supply ship arrived.

There was no letter from Oliver.

In early February, the temperatures plummeted. Sable became a landscape of sparkling silver and a symphony of crackling ice as the frozen marram grass faced the harsh North Atlantic winds on the high dune.

No mail arrived for Emma in February either, and still, Oliver did not come.

The bitter cold days were spent indoors with Matthew, teaching him arithmetic and the science of the clouds and universe and assigning him household chores and good books to read. Emma did her best to hide her anguish from him, but each night, when she slipped into bed, she burrowed deeper into her old den of mistrust.

She began to believe that Oliver had changed his mind. Or perhaps he never had any intention of returning. Maybe she was the most gullible woman on the planet and he was a Casanova with a woman at every port.

Night after night it was the same—until on one occasion, Emma tossed the covers aside and sat up on the edge of her bed. Restless and alert while others in the house were sleeping, she chewed at her thumbnail.

What a fool she'd been in the rose garden. So easily seduced. Had she learned nothing from what happened with Logan?

Laying a hand over her long-suffering heart, she tried to settle her anxieties—which were always at their worst at night—and quietly rose to her feet. She tiptoed across the braided rug to where Matthew slept in his small bed soundly, beneath a heavy blue-and-white-checkered quilt. His face was like an angel's—sweet, round, and peaceful. The sight of him spread a blanket of calm over her soul.

Thank God she had Matthew. If not for him, she might have stopped believing in the kind of love that lasts forever.

As for the child she carried in her womb, she knew she would love it too, just as much as she loved Matthew.

Emma tucked the quilt around him to keep him warm, then tiptoed back to her own bed. As she slid beneath the covers and stared up at the ceiling, she wondered if perhaps this had always been her fate: to enjoy the love of her children but to be denied the love of a man.

If this was the way it was meant to be, she decided that she could survive on her own. She'd been doing it for years, without Oliver or Logan, with only the love she shared with Matthew and her father. It had been enough—more than enough—and another child would only bring greater love into her world.

Emma considered that for a profound moment, then rolled to her side, rested her cheek on her hands on the pillow, and watched Matthew sleep. The love she felt for him was infinite like the cosmos and the constant, traveling waves on the ocean. The steady sound of his breathing finally lulled her into a peaceful slumber.

~

The following morning, Emma woke at dawn. Her bedroom windows were cloaked in ice. Sleet pelted the glass. Matthew still slept, so she rolled to her side and faced the wall, curled up in a fetal position, and tugged the covers over her ears to stay warm.

As she lay with her hand on her belly, she knew she couldn't go on like this much longer, hiding her secret. Keeping it from her father was tearing her apart, and now she was beginning to show. Very soon, she would have no choice but to tell him the truth.

Or perhaps the time for truth and honesty had already come.

~

"Now you have me worried," her father said from his chair in the great room that evening.

Emma had just settled Matthew into bed for the night. She'd come downstairs, taken a seat on the sofa, and told her father point blank that she had something important to discuss with him.

"I wish I could tell you not to worry," she said, "but I don't think you're going to like this."

He removed his glasses and set them on the open book on his lap. "Continue."

With her earlier bravado long gone, she forced the words out. "I've been keeping something from you, Papa. Something that relates to Oliver Harris."

He frowned. "What is it? Nothing bad, I hope. Is he all right?"

"I have no idea," she replied, "because I haven't heard a word from him since he left in September."

Her father spoke with sympathy. "I understand how that must make you feel, but, sweetheart . . ."

"How could he just disappear like that and not even write?" She covered her face with her hands.

Her father reached for his cane and rose from his chair. He limped around the coffee table and sat down beside her on the sofa, where he took her into his arms and rubbed her back. "You know what the mail is like here. Sometimes we get letters six months old. And Oliver is trying to arrange a divorce, which can't be an easy thing, especially if his father-in-law wants to avoid a scandal. It might take time."

Her father was right, but time was not on Emma's side. She had very little of it to spare when her baby was growing bigger in her belly every day.

"But it's been months," she said. "We should have heard something by now."

"Yes," her father replied. "I've been wondering about it too, but we can't lose hope. Oliver is a good man." He wiped a tear from under her eye. "No matter what happens, just remember that you have Matthew and me and a home here, where you're loved. It's a good life, and it's all yours."

She wondered miserably if it might be time to wake up and face reality. "You think he's not coming back?"

"That's not what I said."

Emma wiped a tear from her cheek and fought to pull herself together. "I hope I'll still have a home here after I tell you what's been happening, because you're not going to like it."

Her father's expression darkened with concern. "I'll always support you, sweetheart, no matter what. But you need to tell me what's wrong."

Despite her tears and apprehensions about how her father might react, it would be a tremendous release to confess the truth. So she let it all out. "I love Captain Harris. I've loved him since the day I met him, and when he came back here and proposed to me, I thought all my dreams were coming true." She paused briefly and wiped her runny nose. "And we . . . we were intimate."

Her father drew back slightly. "What are you saying?"

She kept her eyes downcast, until at long last, she managed to get the words out. "I'm pregnant."

The world stopped spinning. Her father didn't speak. He looked away, then stood and returned to his chair.

"Please say something," Emma pleaded.

He blinked a few times. "I don't know what to say." He rested his forehead on his knuckles. "Is this why you married Logan? For the same reason? I always wondered about that."

Emma couldn't form a response.

"And is this why Captain Harris offered to marry you as well?"

"No!" Emma shouted, resenting the implication that she had tried to trap both men. "He proposed to me before anything like that happened. I thought we were going to be together, and I loved him. Please don't hate me, Papa, or him either. He still has no idea I'm pregnant."

But that was a lie. Emma had written several letters to Oliver and shared the news of her condition. She'd pledged her undying love and admitted that she was desperate for him to hurry back. Why in the world was she defending his honor when it was quite possible that he'd already abandoned her?

Emma shut her eyes and reminded herself that, since Logan, she had trouble trusting people. Maybe it was possible that Oliver was simply delayed, along with his letters, and she needed to continue to give him the benefit of the doubt.

Or maybe something terrible had happened.

In the end, she supposed she defended Oliver to her father because she didn't want him to think her a fool. Nor did she want to think it of herself.

CHAPTER 24

March 1954

Sable Island during the winter was a good place to hide—and a very good place to hide a pregnancy. Most days, the residents remained indoors or scurried from one building to the next, ducking their heads in the frigid North Atlantic winds. On milder, rainy days, the dampness sent a stubborn chill into everyone's bones that was not easy to expel. It nestled deep into the marrow and gave winter a bad name.

Contrarily for Emma, those months of hibernation provided a welcome element of disguise. A heavy wool coat could hide a multitude of sins—though not necessarily at home.

"Mommy, you're getting fat!" Matthew chortled one evening in the great room as he nuzzled his face into her belly, where she lay on the sofa, reading a magazine.

Emma tensed, and her father slapped his hand on the armrest of his chair. "Matthew! Never say that to a lady, much less to your mother."

Taken aback by the reprimand, Matthew sank to sit on the floor beside Emma. "Sorry, Grandad."

Emma rubbed the top of his head. "It's all right, sweetheart. You didn't know. But Grandad's right. That's not a nice thing to say to someone."

He spoke sulkily. "Can I go upstairs?"

"Yes, it's time for bed anyway. Go brush your teeth, and I'll be up in a minute to say good night."

He dashed up the stairs.

Emma sat forward and tossed her magazine on the coffee table. "You didn't need to be so harsh with him."

"I don't want him saying things like that," her father staunchly replied.

"Are you trying to teach him manners? Or are you worried he'll say something that might start rumors?"

"Both."

It had been a long week, and Emma hadn't slept well. She always seemed to wake up with lower back pain that persisted all day. It was difficult not to be irritable, and she huffed with displeasure. "At least you're honest about it."

"I might as well be," he replied, equally irritable, "because people are going to find out eventually." His eyes darkened, and he thumped his fist on the armrest. "I wish Oliver Harris would come back here so I could give him a piece of my mind. And it would be ugly, I can tell you that."

"That's something I'd like to see," Emma replied. "In fact, I'd pay money for it." She rested a hand on her bulging belly. "All jokes aside, Papa, we should talk about this, because you're right. Everyone on the island will figure things out soon enough, and the gossip will be . . ." She paused. "It's a good thing we don't have a local newspaper. I can see the headline now. 'Sable Beauty Disgraced.'"

Her father spoke with cool authority. "Whatever happens, we'll weather it."

"But it'll be confusing for Matthew," she argued. "I don't want the other children to say cruel things."

"When the time comes, we'll talk to him about that, and school him on how to defend you."

Emma let out a weary sigh. "But I don't want that to become our world. Not here."

He nodded and ruminated for a moment. "Maybe we both need to consider other options."

"Like what?"

He leaned forward. "I hope you'll want to deliver in the hospital again, just to be safe."

"Absolutely. And I'd like to take Matthew with me, to the mainland. If nothing else, it'll be an adventure for him."

"Ruth will be happy to have you come and stay with her. Every time she writes, she mentions it, and I thank God for her every day. Which is why I think you should consider reapplying to university this fall."

The suggestion came at Emma like a bullet, and she nearly fell off the sofa. "Are you mad? I'm about to have a baby."

"Yes," he replied, "but Matthew could enroll in school in Halifax, and Ruth would love to help you take care of the baby. She's the one who suggested that you consider part-time classes. All you'd need is a few hours a day, and that would give you something else to . . ." He paused. "It would give you something new to focus on."

"Besides my hostility?" Emma asked, with a raised eyebrow. "Or my self-pity? Or the thickness of my ankles?"

"All of the above," he replied with gentle understanding. Then he sat back and spoke wistfully. "Sometimes I wonder where you'd be right now if I'd supported your dream in the first place, when you came to me years ago. Why didn't I just encourage you in that direction?"

Emma shook her head. "It's not your fault that I didn't go to university like I'd planned. It's the fault of that crazy seal, and maybe it was fate, because if that hadn't happened, I wouldn't have Matthew."

Her father sat quietly, pondering the past while the clock ticked steadily on the wall. Then he met Emma's gaze. "You should do it. Apply again."

She studied his expression. "Are you just trying to avoid a scandal here?"

"Maybe. But mostly I just want you to be happy."

Fingering her mother's locket and Oliver's ring around her neck, Emma mulled it over. It had always been in her nature to look for clever ways over and through obstacles. But this pregnancy—and the emotions that surrounded it—had taken all the stuffing out of her. She'd lost her confidence and drive to push through shifting sands.

"It's hard enough to raise a child on my own," she said, hating that she sounded like a defeatist. "But then to add classroom attendance and homework on top of it . . ."

Her father held up a hand. "Pipe down, kiddo. You're barking up the wrong tree. I've had more than my share of challenges lately, but you were always there, pushing me to carry on. You got me back on my feet. So, if I could do it, so can you. Where there's a will, there's a way. You can go to school part time if you need to, and it doesn't matter how long it takes. Don't let that stop you—because the months and years are going to go by anyway." He gestured toward her belly. "You could have a degree by the time this child has finished kindergarten."

Emma considered the next five years and ran her fingertips over the magazine on the coffee table, where a woman was modeling the latest spring fashions.

Oh, horsefeathers!

Emma couldn't care less about new clothes, nor was she the least bit enthused by the best way to keep pillowcases smelling fresh. When she'd tossed the magazine aside earlier, she'd been overcome by boredom.

Yet something inside her continued to resist her father's encouragement.

"I'll think about it," she finally said, supposing that if she embraced this fresh start and accepted it as a new dream, that would mean she'd finally given up on another.

She wasn't entirely sure she was ready for that. It would depend on whether Oliver arrived before the spring thaw.

PART FOUR
THE MAINLAND

CHAPTER 25

Spring 1954

For young Matthew, the crossing on the *Argyle* was a grand adventure. All he knew of the world was his sturdy little island home of sand and grass, but the ship was anything but sturdy. It rose and fell under his small feet, traveling fast, slicing through the salty ocean, generating its own waves that rolled off the steel hull. The big city that lay on the far side of the sea was a mystery to him, and he was restless with anticipation.

When at last they steamed into Halifax Harbour under a gray sky, Emma—seven months pregnant and showing it—stood at the rail with Matthew and took in the city, as if for the first time, through his innocent eyes. She pointed at the white clock tower on Citadel Hill and explained that it had been built in 1803 as a gift from Prince Edward, Duke of Kent, who'd been commander of the British forces in North America. But Matthew was far more drawn to the fleet of Canadian naval warships docked in the harbor—frigates and destroyers with gun turrets and missile launchers.

"Did Captain Harris work on those boats?" he asked, surprising Emma with the question.

She laid her hand on her belly. "No. Those are Canadian ships. He served in the British Royal Navy during the war, before you were born. The ships would have been similar, though."

Emma paused the rest of her narration because the question had awakened her heartache. Where was Oliver at that moment? In Boston or New York? Back in Manchester with his family? Or somewhere else, in the middle of the Atlantic Ocean, fighting a squall on his way back to her?

Clearly, she still clung to old hopes and dreams. Maybe she always would.

Curses on him for not coming back! Or for not at least writing to tell her that he'd changed his mind or couldn't get a divorce. Whatever the reason, she deserved to know.

It was the *not* knowing that made it unbearable.

~

The *Argyle* docked on the Dartmouth side of the harbor, where Ruth stood on the wharf, waving exuberantly at Emma and Matthew as they descended the gangplank steps, their hands gripped tightly on the handrail. When they reached solid ground, Emma took hold of Matthew's hand and walked briskly toward Ruth.

"It's so good to see you!" Ruth cried, wrapping her arms around Emma. "I couldn't wait for this day to come."

They drew apart, and Ruth bent forward, hands on knees, to greet Matthew at eye level. "The last time I saw you, you were barely a month old. I can't believe how much you've grown."

Suddenly shy, he sidled close to Emma's hip. She bent to speak softly in his ear. "Hold out your hand and say hello to Aunt Ruth."

He did as she asked and spoke politely. "It's nice to meet you."

"It's nice to meet you too," Ruth replied and shook his hand with a warm smile. "Now, let's go to the car. I tipped a porter handsomely to deliver your baggage."

"Of course you did," Emma replied, feeling blessedly restored as she took Matthew by the hand and followed Ruth across the dockyard.

∼

Ruth's blue Victorian town house was unchanged. Flower boxes underscored every window, each one spilling over with pine boughs left over from the winter season. The front door was a delightful burst of color. It gleamed gorgeously with a fresh coat of glossy red paint.

Emma stepped out of Ruth's car and stood on the sidewalk, looking up at the house.

Suddenly, with unexpected angst, she found herself recalling the moment when she'd pushed Matthew's stroller around the corner at the end of the street and had seen police cars parked outside the house.

The memory of that day was a jolt to her heart: Logan in handcuffs. Shock and terror. Later, a wave of betrayal and fury, neither of which had drained from her spirit.

Holding tight to Matthew's hand, Emma fought to expel that day from her mind, and she quickly climbed the front steps.

∼

"Tell me something," Ruth said that evening after Emma had settled Matthew into bed and returned to sit by the fire. "Are you all right?"

Emma's mouth fell open slightly. "In what sense?"

"You seem different. I know you're trying to be cheerful, but I can see something's wrong." She inclined her head. "Emma, darling. You're hurt, and it's obvious. Do you want to talk about it?"

"There's not much to say, really. Except that being back here makes me remember what happened with Logan and how awful that was." Feeling suddenly frustrated, she raised her hands in mock surrender. "What is wrong with me that I keep falling in love with men who lie to me? How can one woman be so unlucky?" She shook her head wearily.

"Or maybe it's not bad luck, but stupidity. I still can't believe it about Oliver. I know I should take his ring off this chain around my neck, but I can't. I'm still hoping he'll show up at the door." She pulled it out from under her blouse and showed it to Ruth.

"What if he comes back at some point with a reasonable explanation?"

Emma tucked the chain back under her blouse. "I suppose it would depend on the explanation. But I don't want to spend the next ten years of my life checking a mailbox every day, waiting for a letter. I've done enough of that. And even if he did come back today and grovel and beg for my forgiveness, I think I'd find it difficult to ever trust him again." She pressed her fingertips to the space between her eyebrows. "How could I have been so wrong about him?"

"Like I said," Ruth replied, "maybe there's a reasonable explanation."

Skeptically, Emma raised an eyebrow. "You mean . . . maybe he got hit by a bus or got shipwrecked . . . *again*?" She scoffed. "Maybe he washed up on a different beach and fell in love with some other local girl from heaven knows where, younger than me and without children. She'd be a much cleaner slate."

Ruth regarded Emma in silence, with sympathy and concern.

"Sometimes I want to hate him," Emma continued, "but I try not to because he's the father of my baby. It's funny how history likes to repeat itself." She felt her muscles begin to burn. "Every time I think of the hours we spent together—when I thought he was wonderful—I want to scream my head off. Or kick myself in the pants, all the way down to South America."

Ruth squeezed her hand. "It's never a mistake to love someone. And I'm sure things will be different when the baby comes. You'll be so busy and happy that you'll think less of Oliver."

"I couldn't possibly think any less of him," Emma replied, leaping on that convenient slip of the tongue. "But I'd prefer not to think about him at all. He doesn't deserve it. What he deserves is to be forgotten."

That night in bed, Emma couldn't quiet her mind. Her thoughts were like electric sparks, exploding in her brain, sending her into a state of blind fury. She tossed and turned for hours as she dwelled on Oliver's abandonment and all the mistakes that she'd made—believing him and trusting him.

Sometime before dawn, she felt herself land at the bottom of a deep crater of anger and lost hope. Emotionally and mentally exhausted, she got out of bed, finally removed his ring from the necklace she wore, and locked it away in her jewelry box. Only then, when she slid back under the covers, did sleep come at last.

CHAPTER 26

It was remarkable how—even on the mainland—Emma's life was still profoundly affected by the monthly comings and goings of the Sable Island supply ship.

By mid-April, she'd finally begun to settle in at Ruth's house and had reapplied to Dalhousie University for the fall session. Her pregnancy was progressing well, and she had a new female doctor, which at first made Emma uncomfortable and uncertain, but after a few visits, she realized that Dr. Frizzell possessed an uncanny knowledge of women's health issues. She'd given birth to two children herself, and Emma had never felt more heard or understood. She began to hope that Dr. Frizzell could remain her physician for the rest of her life.

Matthew, too, was adapting to city life in surprising new ways. He'd made friends with some children in the neighborhood, and they rode bicycles to the park, played baseball and ball hockey in the street. Each of those activities led him to declare one night at dinner that he loved asphalt and couldn't imagine his life without it. He described its physical qualities and deemed it a "great wonder of the world." Emma threw her head back and laughed, and clapped her hands together. How wonderful it was to smile and laugh again after so many sorrow-filled days and nights.

But then the supply ship arrived. It docked on the Dartmouth side of the harbor, and two days later, a letter was delivered to the mailbox at Ruth's front door.

~

Emma was relaxing on the sofa, reading a book about early childhood development, when Ruth walked into the living room, gray as a ghost.

With a wave of apprehension, Emma sat up heavily and propped herself up with her arm. "What's wrong? You look upset."

"A letter came," Ruth replied. "It's from your father. I just finished reading it."

Emma frowned. "Is he all right?"

"He's fine." Ruth held the letter at her side and moved woodenly to sit on the sofa beside Emma. "It concerns Oliver. Your father asked me to prepare you for some bad news." She paused. "I'm afraid it's . . . it's *very* bad."

Emma's blood went cold in her veins. "Tell me." She couldn't sit in suspense. She couldn't bear the not knowing. "Please, just say it."

Ruth bowed her head. "I'm so sorry, but not long after Oliver left you on Sable Island last September, on his return trip to England, his ship hit a mine in the ocean. There was an explosion, and they sent an SOS, but it took too long for a rescue ship to reach them."

The news floated around Emma's ears, not quite sinking in. She could only seem to process it as an account about a distant, nameless ship somewhere on the globe, far away.

Then it hit her, full force. The sound of the explosion. The fire. Oliver on a burning ship, fighting to save it, fighting to save his crew. The ship filling with water and slowly going down. Oliver holding his breath, then sucking in water, drowning in the cold, empty darkness. His body slowly sinking.

The shock was like a bullet in the heart. Nausea spurted through her. If she tried to speak, she might choke.

With concern, Ruth laid a hand on her shoulder. "Are you all right?"

"No. I think I might be sick."

In a flash of movement, Ruth reached for the vase of flowers on the side table, dumped the flowers and water onto the floor, and handed the empty vase to Emma. She retched into it violently, her body continuing to gag and heave even when there was nothing left to come up.

Eventually, she set the vase on the coffee table and wiped her mouth with the back of her hand. Tears stung her eyes. Her nose was running. She began to shake uncontrollably.

Ruth went to the kitchen and returned with a warm, wet cloth and a glass of water. She sat down beside Emma and handed her the cloth. Emma pressed it to her mouth, her cheeks, her neck, and took a sip of water.

"There's a letter here from Oliver's wife in England," Ruth explained, looking down at the envelope on the table.

Emma couldn't keep the hurt from her voice. "His wife?"

"Yes. Would you like me to read it to you?"

Emma stared at it for a moment. "No. I think I should read it myself."

With hands that shook, Emma reached for it, removed it from the envelope, and unfolded it.

Dear Mrs. Baxter,

I'm not sure how to begin this letter, except by introducing myself. I'm Mary Harris, wife of Oliver Harris, captain of the Overton. *I found your letters at his flat in Manchester, which is why I'm writing to you. I'm afraid I have some sad news. Oliver has died. His ship went down after colliding with a mine off the coast of Africa as he was making his way back to England from America with a shipment of cargo bound for Tangier. From what I've been told, the radio operator sent an SOS and reported that they were going down fast and intended to abandon ship. The nearest steamer was sixty miles away, so it took too long to reach them. An air search followed, but there was no sign of the ship or any survivors in lifeboats. A search went on for six days, and some wreckage and cargo were eventually found floating in the ocean, but nothing more than that.*

I'm sorry to be the one to deliver this news to you, but I couldn't let you continue to write, asking when he might return. I also understand and sympathize with your sense of urgency, as I read all your letters. I was the one who cleaned out Oliver's flat after the news of his death, and that's where I found them, unopened on the floor in the front hall where they were slipped through the mail slot.

I wanted you to know this because I can only imagine what you must think of him after receiving no replies to your letters. Allow me to assure you that he was a decent, honorable man, and I'm sure he would have returned to you if not for the accident. In fact, he was a changed man in recent years, which has left me with many regrets since his death.

Sincerely,
Mary Harris

Feeling sick and dizzy, Emma lowered the letter to her lap and began sobbing. Tears streamed down her face and neck, all the way to her collarbone. She was vaguely aware of Ruth wrapping a blanket around her shoulders, resting a hand on her back, sitting down beside her.

At long last, Emma turned on the sofa cushion and looked blankly into Ruth's eyes, then buried her wet face into her shoulder.

"I was so wrong to hate him," Emma cried, the words gushing out of her. "He didn't abandon me. I can't bear to think about what might have happened on the ship when they were sinking. It must have been terrifying—like the wreck at Sable, only worse, because they were in the middle of the ocean with no one to rescue them."

Ruth rubbed Emma's back. "I'm so sorry."

"How could I have let myself believe that he'd abandoned me? I never wanted to believe it. Everything in my heart told me it couldn't be true, but I let myself assume the worst. What does that say about me, Ruth? How could I have been so quick to hate him?"

"You didn't hate him," Ruth said. "You didn't know. How could you know?"

"But I should have! I should have felt it in my heart!" She pressed a tight fist to her chest. "My soul! I should have felt *something* when he was drowning. Why didn't I *feel* it?"

Ruth hugged her fiercely. "He was far away."

"Oh, God, Ruth! I hate the ocean! I'll never go back to Sable Island. It's a graveyard there. A widow-maker! It lures ships and sucks them into the sand. Think of all the dead people . . . the skulls in the boat shed!"

Emma's thoughts were frantic, her emotions out of control. She feared she might lose her mind. Thank God Matthew was outside with his friends, peddling around the neighborhood. She didn't know how she could ever explain her hysteria to him. Or her wrath. Or the dark and immeasurable depths of her grief.

CHAPTER 27

On the morning of June 19, Emma sat up in bed and wished it wasn't time yet to face the day. It had been more than a month since she'd learned of Oliver's passing, and her raw feelings of loss had not healed over. If anything, the wounds had grown deeper and become more open as she approached her due date and imagined the beauty of what could have been.

Since that dreadful day when she'd read his wife's letter, Emma had put his ring back on the chain she wore around her neck with her mother's locket. She'd also spent time reflecting upon her lack of trust in him and her harsh, unfair judgments. Soon, she came to realize that it had been easier to hate Oliver in ignorance than it was to grieve for his death. Easier to tell herself that she was better off without him.

Sliding her bare feet out of bed, to the floor, she tried—as she tried every morning—to be grateful for the brief time they'd had together. What was it they said about such things? *It's better to have loved and lost than never to have loved at all.*

Maybe she'd believe it if she could feel happy again—about anything—but the euphoria she'd experienced in the rose garden seemed a million miles away, and unimaginable.

Suddenly, Emma found herself thinking about Abigail McKenna. Perhaps one day Emma would relate better to that poor woman's moodiness and resentments after a lifetime spent with the lasting anguish of abandonment.

Fighting that dire thought, Emma rose from the edge of the bed, took two steps across the floor, and felt a great gush of water leave her body. Stunned, she stared vacantly at the puddle on the floor. Then she gathered her senses and called out to Ruth, who woke Matthew, got him dressed, and drove them all to the hospital.

By the time they arrived, Emma's labor pains had progressed to two minutes apart, and all she could think about was Matthew's grueling birth, and the hours of terror and exhaustion. She couldn't do it again—she couldn't!—yet all she wanted to do was push.

After that, everything was a blur, and by 9:22 a.m., she had given birth to a healthy baby girl, eight pounds, nine ounces.

When the nurse placed the sleeping infant in Emma's waiting arms, she gazed down at her daughter's sweet, angelic face and marveled at the vastness of love that flooded into her heart. Its beauty was immense, extraordinary, comparable only to what it must be like to enter heaven.

Hugging her baby close, Emma wept with equal parts joy and sorrow, and cried for at least an hour, until she was dry of tears.

"You're so beautiful," she blubbered as she kissed her daughter's soft, warm forehead. "I'm going to call you Rose."

Her darling baby Rose had a full head of soft black hair, just like Oliver's. Blue eyes too, like his.

"And I'm going to love you forever," she whispered tenderly in Rose's ear, and Rose rooted toward her breast.

~

Ruth turned out to be correct. Rose had entered the world and brought a whole new bottomless batch of love with her. Though Emma still grieved for Oliver, she also felt reborn, jubilant, and enormously infatuated. She spent each day tending joyfully to Rose's needs—changing her, feeding her, singing to her.

In addition, having read widely about early childhood development, Emma knew the importance of not neglecting Matthew. She fostered his interactions with his baby sister and praised him for his attentiveness. Most of all, she encouraged him to be protective. She told him that Rose would always need her older brother.

There was one thing, however, that surprised Emma. Her love for Rose felt different from the love she'd felt for Matthew when he was born. It wasn't any better or worse, just different. Perhaps because Rose was a girl? Or maybe there was something truly miraculous about her birth—as if God had known in advance what would happen to Oliver, and Rose had been a gift from heaven—a little piece of Oliver's soul to remain with Emma forever and help reduce the potency of her grief.

CHAPTER 28

In late June, the Halifax Public Gardens were in full bloom. Giant rhododendrons flowered colorfully, fragrant rosebushes abounded, and crowds gathered for live music around the Victorian bandstand. While couples danced on the freshly mowed grass, swans and ducks swam in the murky ponds, in the shade of ancient oaks and gigantic maples.

Early one Saturday afternoon, Emma pushed the pram around the winding paths and marveled at how the onset of summer could inspire new hope. She'd finally received a reply from Dalhousie University with an offer to attend classes in September. Emma had accepted the offer, paid the deposit, and selected her courses with an excitement she hadn't felt in years—not since she'd first applied, before her father had been attacked by the seal.

She'd been young and innocent then. Ambitious and optimistic. She'd lost that spirit for a while, but it was slowly coming back to her. She loved her children and wanted to give them a good life. She had no husband, but by God, she had a good head for academics, and she wanted to understand the human psyche. Now was the time. She had support from Ruth, who was ecstatic to have children back in her empty house. Ruth and Emma may not have been related by blood, but Ruth was as good as any devoted grandmother could be.

Isn't it remarkable? Emma thought as she pushed the pram through the wrought iron gate and exited the park onto Spring Garden

Road—how life could pitch and roll like a ship on a stormy sea, then suddenly, the sun would come out? Perhaps there might be smooth sailing ahead, in Emma's future. She'd weathered enough storms.

Walking quickly home from Public Gardens, along the flat concrete sidewalks, she delighted in her increased pulse rate and felt rejuvenated by the fresh summer air. She was out of breath and famished. Thankfully, it was almost time for dinner. Ruth had promised a pot of hearty chicken soup with split peas and potatoes.

Before long, the blue house with the red door was in sight, and Rose was stirring in the pram. She would be ready for a diaper change and a bottle as soon as Emma kicked off her shoes. Then Rose would welcome a retreat to her cozy crib. She was a wonderful sleeper. She'd been sleeping through the night since the second week, unlike Matthew, who had cried and woken Emma for a feeding every two hours from dusk until dawn.

Emma wheeled the pram to the bottom of the steps, set the brake, and bent to gather Rose into her arms and carry her up the steps. She'd just settled Rose comfortably over her shoulder when the front door of the house opened.

Emma looked up, and her heart dropped. She stood on the sidewalk, immobile, staring up at Logan.

"Hi, there," he said, recognizing her shock.

His blond hair was cut short. He was clean shaven and wore a smart-looking blue-checkered shirt tucked into gray trousers, a dark-blue sports jacket with a zipped front, and a fedora. When her gaze lifted to his face, she saw age lines at the outer corners of his eyes and down the center of his forehead. He looked quite a bit older. Thinner also.

But he was supposed to be in prison.

Emma struggled to find her voice. "My goodness." She felt completely breathless. "Logan. What are you doing here?"

She'd known nothing about his release. She hoped he *had* been released. The alternative didn't bear thinking about.

"I got out on good behavior," he explained. "I was out on probation for a while and was finally allowed to leave the province. So I thought I'd surprise you and Matthew."

Emma nodded, but resented the fact that he hadn't asked if it was all right to come. Perhaps he'd feared she'd say no. "When did you arrive?"

Ruth appeared in the doorway just then. "Emma. You're back. Look. We have a visitor."

Seeing the apology in Ruth's eyes, Emma took a few seconds to gather enough composure to climb the steps with Rose in her arms, over her shoulder. Logan backed into the foyer to allow her space to enter. She wiped her shoes on the mat, and they regarded each other awkwardly until he leaned forward and kissed her on the cheek. It shocked her, and she recoiled slightly.

"It's good to see you," Logan said.

An uncomfortable silence ensued.

He strained to fill it. "This must be Rose?"

"Yes." Emma shifted Rose into a cradled position and allowed Logan a proper view of her face.

"She's beautiful," he said.

Emma's stomach tightened into a clumsy knot. She didn't know what to say or do.

"Ruth told me about Rose and what happened to her father . . . the explosion at sea," Logan explained, strangely calm about the fact that his wife had been with another man—not to mention a man they'd once argued about heatedly in the street. He couldn't have forgotten, could he?

"I had no idea about any of that," he added. "Why didn't you mention it in a letter?"

Emma found it odd that there was no accusation in his voice, only curiosity.

"I didn't know how to," she replied. "Everything was always so uncertain with Oliver, and then . . . when I found out what happened to him . . . I didn't really want to talk about it. Or write about it."

Rose began to squirm and fuss, and Emma was grateful for the timely reprieve because this was not a conversation she was prepared for.

"I'm sorry," Emma said, frazzled. "I need to change and feed her. Will you excuse me?"

"I'll bring you a bottle," Ruth offered, and made for the kitchen.

Emma started up the stairs. "I'll be back down shortly. Um . . . please, have a seat in the living room."

"Take your time," Logan easily replied as he watched Emma dash up the steps to the second floor.

~

Ruth walked into Emma's bedroom and closed the door behind her. In a quiet voice, she said, "I swear I had no idea he was coming. He just showed up at the door, out of the blue."

Emma finished pinning Rose's diaper. "Where's Matthew?"

"Off somewhere on his bicycle. I told him to be home in time for dinner."

Emma began to dress Rose in a clean flannel sleeper. "What are we going to tell him when he comes home? 'Hi, Matthew. Say hello to your father. Now go wash your hands for supper.'"

Ruth sat down on the edge of the bed. "Should we ask him to leave and come back tomorrow?"

"Where's he staying?" Emma asked.

"At a hotel in Dartmouth. He took the ferry across and walked here."

"How long has he been in town?"

"Since yesterday, he claims."

Emma fastened the last snap on Rose's sleeper, carried her to the rocking chair, and sat down. Ruth handed her the bottle.

"Thank you." She placed the rubber nipple into Rose's mouth and watched her suck hungrily. It was a welcome moment for Emma to collect her thoughts and think about what was best for her son.

She looked up at Ruth. "I need time to prepare Matthew for this. Will you go downstairs and tell Logan that? Ask him to leave and come back tomorrow morning. And find out what hotel he's staying at, in case we need to call. Hopefully, he'll understand."

Ruth nodded and left Emma alone with Rose, rocking her to sleep in the chair.

~

Twenty minutes later, Rose was down for her afternoon nap, and Logan had left. Emma went downstairs and found Ruth in the kitchen, stirring a pot of cabbage soup. "Thanks for sending him away. I was so caught off guard, I didn't know what to say to him, and I don't want that to happen to Matthew. I want to arrange a proper meeting between them so that he can be prepared."

"It was a good decision," Ruth said. "Definitely talk to Matthew first."

A short while later, as Emma was setting the table, the front door opened and Matthew walked in.

"Welcome home!" she called out from the kitchen.

He kicked off his shoes. "What's for supper?"

"What, no hello?"

"Hi," he said, as he entered the kitchen.

Emma laid a cloth napkin beside each plate. "How was your day? Where did you go?"

"We rode our bikes all around the park."

"You must be tired."

"Kinda." He took a seat in his usual spot at the table.

Emma rubbed the top of his head, which only added to the chaos of his windblown hair. Then she turned to Ruth. "When will supper be ready?"

Ruth bent over the pot, inhaled, and gave the soup a gentle stir. "I'd say it needs another five or ten minutes."

Taking that as a cue to start a conversation, Emma sat down across from Matthew. "Well, since we have some time . . . before we eat . . ." She nervously cleared her throat. "I have something important to tell you."

He stared at her with sleepy eyes.

"We had a visitor today. It was unexpected and . . ." Emma swallowed uneasily. "I have to admit, I was caught off guard because I hadn't seen him in a long time and . . ."

Matthew propped his elbow on the table, rested his chin on a hand. "I'm hungry."

Emma reached for the bread basket. "Help yourself to a slice. There's some butter right there." She pointed at the butter dish.

While Matthew buttered a slice of bread, Emma waited patiently for him to take a bite, chew, and swallow.

"I might as well come right out with it," she finally said. "The visitor today was . . . it was your father."

Matthew stopped chewing and spoke with his mouth full. "What? My dad was here?"

Emma nodded.

"When?"

"This afternoon," she replied. "He left about a half hour ago."

Matthew stared at her with wide eyes, then threw his bread onto the plate, shoved his chair back, and stood. "Why didn't you get him to stay?"

Emma's heart began to beat with a ruckus. She'd hadn't expected this from Matthew. "Because I didn't want you to be shocked when you got home. I wanted to prepare you first."

"Where is he?" Matthew asked, with rising panic. "Can you get him back?"

"Uh . . ."

Ruth approached the table. "Don't worry, Matthew. We asked him to come back tomorrow."

"No!" Matthew cried. "What if he changes his mind and leaves? I want to see him! I need to see him now!"

Emma stood up. "He won't change his mind. I promise."

"How do you know? You don't know everything!"

"Matthew . . ."

"Get him back!" he sobbed. *"Please, Mommy!"*

Emma turned to Ruth, who checked her watch. "He was walking to the ferry terminal. If I take the car now, he'll probably still be there."

"Yes. Please do that," Emma implored. "I'll set out an extra plate for dinner."

Ruth hurried to the door. "I'll try my best to catch him."

~

Matthew refused to speak. He was perched on his knees on the sofa, his chin resting on his arms on the back cushions, looking out the front window.

Emma joined him and peered up and down the street. "Ruth should be back soon. Unless she drove to Dartmouth to meet him on the other side."

"You shouldn't have let him go," Matthew grumbled, still cross with her.

"I'm sorry, but I was surprised to see him. I needed time to consider how to handle the situation."

"You think too much," he replied.

Just then, Ruth's car appeared from around the corner and pulled up in front of the house. Matthew's eyes grew wide as saucers.

The passenger-side door opened, and Logan stepped out. Emma sat up straighter on her knees, instantly alert. She was reminded of the day he'd jumped out of the surfboat and landed, for the first time, on the beach on Sable Island. She'd been quite curious that day.

"Is that him?" Matthew asked.

"Yes."

Within seconds, her heart settled, and she sat back on her heels.

Emma and Matthew watched in silence as Ruth walked with Logan up the steps, and they entered through the front door. Matthew leaped off the sofa and ran to the foyer, where he stood up straight, staring. Logan stared back at him. Emma felt frozen in space and time.

"Are you Matthew?" Logan finally asked.

Matthew nodded.

Logan held out his hand and stepped forward. "It's nice to meet you. Do you know who I am?"

Matthew nodded again.

"Good. But I need to say it anyway. I'm your dad, which is probably a lot to sort out in your mind."

"I've been sorting it out for years," Matthew replied. "Ever since Mom told me about you. She read me all your letters."

Logan met Emma's gaze. "I'm happy to hear that." Then he returned his attention to Matthew. "But why didn't you ever write back?"

"I didn't know I could." Matthew shot Emma a heated glare, filled with accusation.

Feeling instantly guilty and defensive, she quickly explained. "I wrote letters on your behalf."

Logan watched their exchange, then squatted to speak to Matthew at eye level. "Your mom sent me pictures of you, and I kept every single one. But now I'm here in person, so I want to know all about you. Do you miss living on Sable Island?"

Matthew's face lit up. "No! I never had a bike there, and you can't play ball hockey."

"But you must miss the horses and the beach."

"A little." Matthew thought about it. "I miss Georgie."

"Who's that?"

Emma slowly approached. "Willow's offspring. Matthew was two years old when Georgie was born."

"Is Georgie a boy or a girl?" Logan asked Matthew.

"A girl," Matthew replied with a chuckle. "But we don't call her a girl. She's a mare."

Logan rose to his full height. "It's good to use the correct terminology. Do you ride her?"

"I used to," Matthew replied. "Until we left. I hope she's okay. Grandad promised to take good care of her."

"I'm sure he will," Logan said. "You must miss your grandad as well."

"I do. We want him to come here and live with us."

Logan turned to Emma. "You don't plan to return to Sable?"

Before she had a chance to respond, Matthew answered the question for her. "We're not going back because I'm going to school here in the fall. So is Mom."

Logan's head tilted to the side as he regarded her. "You are?"

She waved it off dismissively. "Only part time. Ruth will help take care of Matthew and Rose."

Logan slowly nodded. "I always knew you'd become an academic one day. I would have put money on it."

Emma was flattered by the compliment, but that was the extent of it. Her husband's looks and charm no longer had any effect on her. She certainly had no interest in any romantic entanglements, with him or anyone else.

She supposed she wasn't the same impressionable young woman she'd been when they'd first met. After everything that had gone wrong in their marriage, and since the news of Oliver's death, Emma felt as if some of her emotions had gone numb. Or perhaps they'd died with Oliver.

Ruth gestured toward the kitchen. "Are you hungry, Logan? I have a pot of soup on the stove."

"If that's a dinner invitation, I accept."

They all made their way to the kitchen, where conversation around the table was, on the surface, light and full of laughter. Matthew giggled constantly at Logan's funny faces and his amusing tales of veterinary medicine on the farms of Saskatchewan. The easiness of it all came as a relief to Emma because she hadn't known what to expect from their first meeting. She was pleased to see Matthew so happy and engaged.

After dessert, when it was long past Matthew's bedtime, Emma gave him a look. "I think it's time to go upstairs, young man."

Logan slid his chair back. "Your mother's right. I've kept you up too late. I assume you brush your teeth before bed?"

"Yes," Matthew replied.

"Then off you go."

"Now you sound like my mom!" he chortled.

Logan saluted him. "I'll take that as a compliment, sir."

Emma watched their exchange like a mother hawk, protective and on her guard.

"Will you come back tomorrow?" Matthew asked.

"I'll talk to your mother about that," Logan replied.

Matthew rose from his chair, hugged Emma tightly, and looked up at her with pleading eyes. "Can you let him come? Please?"

She kissed the top of his head and—for his sake—forced herself to remain friendly and open. "He's welcome to visit if he wants to."

Matthew smiled again. "Okay. Good night." He left the kitchen and ran up the stairs.

Emma and Logan stood for a few seconds in silence, gazing at each other from opposite sides of the table. She found herself observing the fact that even though he was older and thinner, his eyes were still the same.

"Could we take a walk?" Logan asked, catching Emma by surprise.

His request hit the wall she'd recently erected around her heart, which only filled her with regret. So many of her feelings, good and bad, were out of reach. She wished suddenly that she could go back to that day in the rose garden with Oliver, after they'd made love, when they'd walked to his boat and her heart had felt fully open and vulnerable—and joyfully so. She'd never felt more passionate and alive.

Thank God she hadn't known what the future would bring. Otherwise, she might have put walls up that day as well, like she was doing now, and she wouldn't have that beautiful memory to remind her that she'd once truly lived and loved.

Ruth stood up and began to clear the table. "Go ahead, Emma. I'll take care of this and make sure Matthew gets to bed."

With caution still in her heart, Emma went to fetch her sweater from the front hall closet.

~

"Thanks for not saying no to a visit tomorrow," Logan said as he stopped on the bottom step to light a cigarette. He took a deep drag and savored it as he slowly exhaled.

"I couldn't say no to Matthew," Emma replied. "He's been curious about you for a long time."

"And I've been curious about him."

They began walking down the dark street, past other houses that cast light from their windows onto the sidewalk.

"When did you start smoking?" she asked.

"First week in prison. Not much else to look forward to, except for your letters, of course. I can't tell you how much I appreciated them, and the pictures you sent of Matthew. It's obvious that he had a good upbringing on Sable, and I'm sure he'll look back on it someday with amazement. I feel that way too, when I think about the year I spent there. With you."

Emma wanted to be positive and agreeable, but she couldn't keep her cynicism at bay. "You weren't so happy at the end of it," she reminded him. "You didn't enjoy the winter."

"Only because I knew I had to leave, and I was afraid you were going to find out what I'd done. Which you did." He took another drag of his cigarette. "That was the worst hell for me, you know—fearing the truth coming out and seeing your disappointment."

"Worse than going to prison?" she asked with skepticism.

"Ten times worse."

Though he spoke decisively, she found it hard to believe him.

"What about the research paper we wrote?" he asked, changing the subject. "You never mentioned that you did anything with it."

"It's in a box at my father's house," she replied. "After what happened, I couldn't look at it. It felt like a sham."

Logan grew quiet. "I'm sorry. I spoiled a lot of things, didn't I?" He tapped his cigarette ashes onto the sidewalk. "But I wonder what you'd think of our paper if you looked at it now. We certainly worked hard on it."

Emma chuckled. "Who knows? I might think it the worst piece of drivel ever written. What did I know about the world back then? I was a girl with her head in the clouds."

"That's not true," he said, gazing up at the sky. "I'd bet you'd be pleasantly surprised by what you wrote. Now that you're going to school in the fall, you might meet the kind of people who could help you do something with it."

Emma considered it. "Sometimes I do wonder . . . maybe I just need a bit of a nudge to force me to dig it out of the box."

Logan nudged her with his elbow, and Emma chuckled.

"Point taken. I'll write to Papa and ask him to send it on the next boat. Then I'll read it with a critical eye."

"But not too critical," Logan said with a sidelong grin.

They rounded a corner and emerged onto Young Avenue, where grand stone mansions were lit up in the night. Point Pleasant Park, with miles of winding walking paths, lay ahead in the darkness.

"Matthew mentioned he wanted his grandfather to come and live with you," Logan said. "Is that a possibility?"

"I'm not sure," Emma replied. "Papa's been superintendent for so long. It's in his blood now. Even the loss of his leg couldn't keep him from doing his job."

"But it'll be different for him now, living there without you. And Ruth told me he hasn't met Rose yet."

"That's right. He hasn't."

They walked awhile, saying nothing while crickets chirped on the tidy, clipped lawns. An occasional car drove past, headlights beaming.

"Ruth also told me about what happened to Rose's father, the captain," Logan said. "You haven't said much about him."

"No, I haven't."

When she offered nothing more, Logan pressed on. "It must have been devastating."

"It was."

They walked to the next intersection, crossed the street, and continued toward the park. Logan finished his cigarette and flicked it onto the street.

"I'm not surprised you were with him again," he said. "You had feelings for him before, and I suppose I was as good as dead to you."

"That's not true," Emma replied. "You're Matthew's father, and it's clear that he wants you to be a part of his life. I'd never deny him that."

They continued in silence, taking in the fresh evening air scented with lilacs, until Logan stopped. "Can I ask you something?"

Emma stopped as well and faced him.

"I'm curious," he said. "Did you always love Oliver, even when you married me?"

Emma glanced toward the darkness in the park ahead. She couldn't seem to form a response, because Oliver continued to live in a place in her heart where Logan had never been permitted to enter.

"I can't pretend I'm not jealous," he added. "But I have to remind myself that you were alone for a long time, and I can't blame you for giving up on us."

"I wasn't alone," she told him. "I had Matthew and my father."

Logan nodded, but he seemed unable to let go of the subject. "But you still haven't answered my question. I want to know about your relationship with Harris. You had his child. Were you going to ask me for a divorce?"

Emma stopped and stood under the glare of a streetlamp. To her surprise, she felt no reluctance about delivering the cold, hard truth to Logan, which was not like her at all. In the past, she'd always tried to be gentle with her words and protect people's feelings, which sometimes required white lies. But tonight, all she wanted was candor. She wanted to spit everything out, onto the street.

"Yes," she confessed. "I wanted to marry him. He promised that he'd come back with a ring at Christmas, and if he had, I would have accepted his proposal and asked you for a divorce."

Logan grunted, as if she'd punched him in the stomach. She felt a small twinge of regret but knew it was nothing that wouldn't soon recede, and she weathered it with defiance. Perhaps this was a settling of scores for Logan's betrayal and the pain he'd caused her. He was, after all, the one who'd abandoned her and left her to raise their son on her own. For seven years she did that. Until Oliver came ashore.

"I'm sorry if that's not what you wanted to hear," she said bluntly, "but it's the truth. And now that he's dead, I suppose he's become martyred, in a way, and I'm always going to consider him the great love of my life."

It was a cruel addition to everything she'd already said to him. Emma was beginning to worry about herself. Had she lost all sense of compassion? Was she dead inside? Or worse, vindictive? Like Abigail? Was this how it had started for her?

Logan kicked at the moss between the cracks in the sidewalk, then started walking slowly. "Well, then. I appreciate your honesty."

They reached the entrance to Point Pleasant Park, but it was too dark to enter, so they turned back. Emma tried to resume conversation by changing the subject. She asked Logan about his life in prison. Then they shifted to postwar politics.

When they rounded the corner at the end of Ruth's street, Logan touched Emma's arm. "Please. Before we go back . . ."

She stopped and looked up at him.

"I don't expect anything from you," he said. "I'd even understand if you hated me forever for what happened. But I'd like to be part of Matthew's life. That's what kept me going in prison, especially on the bad days, and there were plenty of those." He paused. "But I wanted to make it to the end of my sentence so that I could meet him and be some sort of father figure to him—and somehow make up for lost time. And for all my mistakes."

With parted lips, Emma pondered his words and the tone of his voice and her own private resentments. She'd spent the past seven years distancing herself from thoughts of her husband's suffering. She hadn't wanted to think about him in prison, so she didn't think about him at all. It was easier that way—to simply detach.

But now that he stood before her, she felt a light tug.

He was Matthew's father. He'd once loved her passionately, and she'd loved him equally in return—though it was years ago. Today, nothing was the same. Emma was not the optimistic young woman she'd once been, and Logan was not the man she first fell in love with. But still . . . their shared past could never be erased.

"Matthew wants to get to know you," she said. "And I can't deny him that."

Logan squeezed his eyes shut, in obvious relief.

Emma cupped his elbow in her hand. "Come back tomorrow. We can all take a walk around Public Gardens, feed the ducks, and get some ice cream."

"Thank you, Emma."

She simply nodded and walked on.

CHAPTER 29

Sable Island

July 16, 1954

Hello Papa,
I hope you are well. All is well with us, but I have some news to share. I hope you're sitting down.

Last month, I arrived home from an afternoon walk with Rose and was greeted at the door by Logan. He'd paid a visit without notice, and Ruth was as shocked to see him as I was. He explained that he's been out of prison for some time and was finally permitted to leave Saskatchewan.

As you know, Matthew has always been curious about his father, and he was excited to finally meet him in person. In a way, it's been a good thing. Sometimes the mystery of something creates a certain ideal—good or bad—that doesn't exist in real life. And you know what they say . . . what is forbidden is coveted. So, I didn't want to stand between them in any way.

At any rate, Matthew has been enjoying the time he's been spending with Logan, playing ball and going fishing in a boat they borrowed from a friend of Logan's from St. Margaret's Bay. Maybe I shouldn't have allowed it, but Ruth was willing to lend her car to Logan for the day, so I relented. Matthew came home with a bucket of fresh fish on ice, and he was as happy as I'd ever seen him. The pictures I've enclosed were taken in Ruth's backyard after we all helped to clean the fish. Quite an adventure, I admit.

Darling Papa—I know how you feel about Logan. What we went through was unpleasant, to say the least, but since his return, I don't feel it would be right to cut him out of Matthew's life. I'm sure Matthew would never forgive me for it. So, I think we will have to find a way to be a family in some form or another.

~

John lowered the letter to his lap and felt a grave gnawing in his gut. He was seated in the open Jeep, watching the unloading of supplies on the beach. He was supposed to be supervising, but with the sudden increased blood flow to his extremities, his vision became clouded.

Emma . . . What were you thinking, allowing a killer back into your life? Near your children? He strangled a man to death!

Stomach burning, John raised the letter to continue reading Emma's letter . . .

Which brings me to my next question, which you've been avoiding for many months now. Will you leave Sable Island once and for all, and come to Halifax? Ruth has an extra bedroom which you are welcome to use, or if you prefer to find a place of your own, there are plenty of options in the city.

I know how much you love Sable Island, and I won't lie—I'm asking you to come for selfish reasons because I miss you, and so does Matthew, and I would love for Rose to know her grandfather. I'll be busy over the next year with my studies, and Matthew will be settled into school, so a visit to Sable Island will be unlikely any time soon.

I know it's a lot to ask because you've given your life to the Humane Establishment, but perhaps the government could find another dedicated person to take over the position? You could retire with great pride, having saved many lives during your impressive career.

Food for thought, Papa! Selfish of me, for sure. But I miss you and I want you close by.

With love,

Emma

With a sudden jolt, John remembered that Emma had mentioned some photographs. He quickly dug back into the envelope and withdrew them.

Oh, Emma! So beautiful. And Ruth, smiling . . .

John flipped to the next black-and-white photograph.

Darling Matthew—holding a fish.

John had to squint to view the details. He lowered his glasses to the tip of his nose and peered over the metal rims. The last picture showed Emma with Rose in her arms, Matthew, and Logan. They stood together, arm in arm, behind a bucket of fish in Ruth's backyard. They looked like the happy family they might have been if Logan hadn't turned out to be such a rotter.

John sat back in the Jeep and rubbed his forefinger repeatedly over his eyebrow.

Roger Smith, the new weather station chief, came trudging through the deep sand with one last crate in his arms. Roger was twenty-four years old with no wife or children. Keen for adventure, he'd come to Sable for a one-year contract. His goal in life was to travel the world before he settled down somewhere, anywhere.

"That's it for us," Roger said jauntily as he set the crate in the back of the Jeep and came around to the driver's seat. He got in and slammed the door shut.

They sat for a moment, watching the last surfboat rise and fall over the waves as the crew rowed back to the *Argyle*. Staff men on the beach finished loading a few more barrels onto the horse-drawn wagons, but John was distracted.

"What do you have there?" Roger asked, looking down at the pictures in John's hand.

He handed them over. "That's my daughter, Emma."

Roger looked closely at each one. "She's very beautiful."

"Yes." John was suddenly overcome with sorrow and longing. "They used to call her the Sable Beauty. I raised her here since she was a baby, and we had a wonderful life."

What he wouldn't give to return to those days—reading bedtime stories, exploring the ponds, and teaching his little girl to ride a horse.

What he wouldn't give to live his whole life again.

"That's her son, Matthew," John said, "and her new baby."

"I assume that's her husband?" Roger asked, examining the last photograph.

John's stomach clenched tight with agitation. What the devil was happening on the mainland? It had been weeks since Emma had posted the letter. Was Logan still there?

"Yes. That's him," he replied. "They were married for less than a year before he was sent to prison for killing a man."

Roger's mouth fell open, and he gaped at John. "No kidding." He examined the photograph more closely. "He doesn't look like a killer." He passed the photos back to John, who slipped them into the envelope.

"He claims it was self-defense, but the courts called it manslaughter. I still have my doubts."

"And your daughter waited for him?"

"I wouldn't say *waited*," John replied. "But she never divorced him. Now he's out of jail and back in her life again."

Roger started the engine, pressed his foot to the gas pedal, and steered the Jeep toward Main Station. As they picked up speed on the beach, John gazed out at the gloomy gray ocean and thought about what Emma had written in her letter.

He turned to Roger, behind the wheel. "For months, my daughter's been trying to convince me to leave Sable and join her in Halifax to be close to my grandchildren."

Roger glanced briefly at John. "Does she know they're shutting us down?"

John rubbed his palm on his pant leg. "Not yet, but I wrote to her about it yesterday. The letter went out with the ship today. She'll be shocked when she reads it—and sad—because it's the end of an era."

Roger agreed. "All these newfangled ships, eh? With radar and sonar and who knows what else?"

John spotted a few horses grazing on the high dune. They raised their heads at the roar of the Jeep, then galloped away in perfect unison and disappeared over the rise.

"You're too young to remember," John said, "but there was a time when shipwrecks were a regular occurrence here. We were busy, taking care of survivors and salvaging cargo. Now the lifesaving crew just trots up and down the empty beaches, day after day, carrying out pointless patrols. You've seen them. It's hard to keep up morale when the work seems so futile. I'm not surprised they've cut our funding."

In all honesty, John was glad. It was time to go.

"I guess you can't fight progress," Roger said as he shifted into a higher gear and increased speed on the beach.

"I suppose not," John replied, and looked down at the envelope that contained photographs of his daughter, his grandchildren, and his son-in-law, Logan. "But sometimes we have to try. Take me to the wireless station, will you? I need to contact the ship right away, before she leaves."

"Why?"

"Because I'm getting off this island today."

John had an itch to scratch—a hankering to grab Logan by the throat and remind him what would happen to him if he ever hurt Emma again. If the man had any sense, he'd never put another foot wrong for the rest of his days.

PART FIVE

PROGRESS

CHAPTER 30

Summer 1995

There were few things Joanna Griffin liked better than an open road, especially after leaving the congestion of the city. Gridlocked traffic, obnoxious car horns, and sickening exhaust fumes had no place in the stifling humidity of a hot summer day. It didn't help that earlier, when she'd made her way from the veterinary clinic to her car, a teenager had bumped into her and knocked her fruit basket out of her arms. Mangoes, oranges, and plums flew everywhere, bouncing and rolling across the pavement. By the time Joanna finished picking everything up, she was drenched in sweat, and the kid hadn't even glanced back to apologize, let alone give her a helping hand. What was the world coming to, when people forgot how to be polite? When they stopped caring about each other?

At least now she was free of stoplights and traffic jams, driving past sprawling green fields and forests on the way north, to her grandfather's house. It was a special day—an anniversary of sorts—because one year ago, Joanna's grandmother had passed away after a long and agonizing battle with thyroid cancer. Now her grandfather lived alone in the country house they'd shared for more than fifty years, and every time Joanna walked through the door and saw their large gilt-framed wedding portrait on the wall, her heart frayed a little at the seams.

The house was so quiet these days, like a church with only one person sitting alone, praying in the pews. The absence of aromas from the kitchen, which had always been her grandmother's domain, made the house feel lonely and abandoned.

A few fat raindrops splattered against Joanna's windshield, which wrenched her from her thoughts. Leaning over the steering wheel, she peered up at the sky. Angry thunderclouds loomed overhead, and within seconds, a raging downpour began. Joanna touched her foot lightly to the brake pedal and switched her wipers to full speed. They batted back and forth while she gripped the steering wheel and focused all her attention on the road ahead.

~

Joanna's grandfather lived in a two-story, centuries-old stone house at the base of a small forested mountain. Out front, an ancient limestone wall with a wooden gate surrounded a well-tended English garden.

When at last she turned onto the gravel drive, the storm was still raging, as if it had singled her out on the highway and followed her like a stalker. Joanna pulled to a halt and shut off the engine, tipped her head back on the seat, and let out a breath of relief to have arrived without having skidded off the motorway.

A sudden, rapid knocking at her window caused her to jump.

It was Grandad peering in at her. He stood outside the car with a red polka-dot umbrella over his head.

She grabbed her purse and the fruit basket and opened the driver's-side door. "Who ordered this weather?"

"I don't know, but it's perfect for the weekend, don't you think? Couldn't be more fitting."

She nodded morosely in agreement and got out of the car. Together, under the umbrella, they dashed to the front door and swept into the foyer like a couple of autumn leaves on a swirling gust of wind. Joanna shut the door behind her and lowered the hood of her trench coat. A fire blazed in the hearth, and the kitchen smelled of cinnamon rolls.

"You've been baking," she said with surprise before turning her eyes to the wedding portrait.

"I couldn't help myself. It felt like the day needed a marker of some sort, and flowers seemed too easy."

"Good choice." Her grandmother's mouthwatering cinnamon rolls were always just coming out of the oven whenever Joanna had come to visit, ever since she was a young girl.

Her grandad set the open umbrella on the plank floor to drip dry—something Nana would never have permitted, because she positively *lived* for domestic chores. She was always doing dishes, scrubbing counters and floors, organizing cupboards, or baking bread. As far as Joanna knew, keeping the house clean and orderly was her greatest passion.

"Let me take that for you," her grandad said, reaching for the fruit basket in her arms. While Joanna removed her coat, he carried the basket to the kitchen and set it on the worktable. "How was your week?"

"Pretty good," Joanna replied, changing from her shoes into her slippers, which she'd stuffed into her tote bag that morning. "We delivered a foal yesterday."

"That must have been exciting."

"It was," she replied, joining him in the kitchen. "And it was extra special because that baby horse starts a sixth generation in the stables—in a direct line from a horse that was born at the end of the war, on VE Day. They named her Victoria, so this foal is kind of like royalty."

"Amazing." Her grandfather gave her shoulder a squeeze. Then he inspected the contents of the fruit basket.

"We'll need to wash those," she said. "They fell on the ground."

He picked up a plum. "This one looks badly bruised, but I'm sure it'll still taste great."

"Forever the optimist," she replied with a grin and turned to watch the rain streaming down the windowpane.

Her grandad clapped his hands and rubbed them together. "Well, it's past five o'clock. How about we brighten things up with an anniversary cocktail?"

Joanna spotted Nana's sterling-silver drinks tray on the sideboard in the lounge, already set out with a bowl of fresh lemons and an ice bucket. "Gin and tonic, I presume?"

"Her favorite."

~

Joanna sat forward on the sofa and raised her tumbler in the air. "To Nana. May we never forget her loving arms and her sweet cinnamon rolls."

"Cheers to that."

They clinked glasses and took the first sip.

"Delicious." Joanna licked her lips, set her glass down on the coffee table, and leaned back against the sofa cushions. "I can't believe it's been a whole year, but sometimes it seems longer than that. It feels like forever since she stood in that kitchen."

"Nana was sick for a long time," he replied in agreement.

Joanna recalled the years of chemo and radiation therapy, remissions, and relapses. "The last few months were especially rough," she said, "but this past week I've really tried to focus on what we should be grateful for. At least you and Nana got to spend your whole lives together. I hope someday I'll be as lucky as you and find the great love of my life and grow old with that person. Even if it means saying goodbye at the end. If you think about it, it was a blessing that you were spared this kind of loss until now."

He took a deep swig of his cocktail and set it down. "I haven't always been lucky, Joanna. Life is never perfect."

She realized her gaffe and covered her forehead with the back of her hand. "I'm so sorry. Of course you've had losses. You lived through a war."

"It's not that," he replied, meeting her gaze.

Joanna regarded him steadily. "Are you going to tell me or leave me guessing?"

He let out a heavy sigh, then reached for her hand and held on to it. "Sweetheart, you say you want to find the great love of your life, but sometimes I worry that you're waiting for a lightning bolt to strike. Or that you're too concerned with . . . What do you call it? Red flags."

She shook her head and raised a hand. "No, Grandad. First of all, in my defense, the last few guys I dated were total imbeciles. You'd think so too, if you'd met them. Other than that, I've been focused on my career. You know that. You're the one who encouraged me and supported me through vet school."

"I understand," he replied, nodding, "and I'm proud of you. I always wanted you to pursue your passion, whatever it was. But when it comes to love, I sometimes worry that you have unreasonable expectations. Your grandmother and I were . . . ." He paused. "We had a good life together, but it wasn't a fairy tale, especially in the beginning."

Joanna drew back, bewildered. "What are you trying to say?"

He looked down at their hands, still clasped together. "I just want you to understand the reality surrounding our relationship. I've known my share of losses, and I've certainly made mistakes. Stupid ones."

"With Nana?"

"No. With someone else."

Joanna felt her eyes widen. "There was someone else? Someone before Nana?"

"Not exactly before . . ."

Joanna thought suddenly of her grandparents' wedding portrait in the hall, hung prominently with a beautiful gilt frame, and felt her stomach churn, along with a need to look at it again with fresh eyes. To examine every detail of their wedding day—because what was he hinting at?

"Grandad . . . Did you have an affair? Did Nana know?"

Appearing more frustrated than ashamed, he pinched the bridge of his nose. "It was complicated." Then he stood up and gestured toward Joanna's empty glass. "Would you like another?"

"Definitely." She handed her glass to him, then rested her arm along the back of the sofa and watched him move to the drinks tray, unscrew the cap from the gin bottle. "You can't say something like that to me," she said, "and leave me hanging. Who was the woman? What happened?"

He dropped a few ice cubes into both glasses and faced her. "How about we cook dinner?"

"Are you joking?"

"No," he replied. "I'm hungry."

She shook her head at him. "Only if you promise to tell me more."

"I will."

While he finished mixing their drinks, Joanna stood up and wondered how he'd managed to keep this part of his life secret all these years. No one had ever mentioned anything about an affair. She wondered if her own parents knew.

"What was the woman's name?" she asked.

"Emma."

"How did you meet her?"

He handed the fresh drink to Joanna and led the way into the kitchen. "My ship ran aground on an island off the coast of Nova Scotia, and she was part of the rescue brigade. It was 1946."

Joanna's lips parted. All her thoughts were in a jumble. "And you fell in love with this woman?"

"Yes," he replied. "Very deeply." For a moment, he stared at the window, as if he were gazing into the past. "We formed a connection that was . . . I can't really explain it, except that it was very deep over a short period of time. Not exactly love at first sight, but damn close. But it wasn't meant to be."

He switched on the oven, then went to the refrigerator and took out a marinated pork tenderloin. Joanna sat down at the table with her drink and waited eagerly to hear more.

CHAPTER 31

By the time the pork came out of the oven and they sat down to eat, Joanna had learned about the wreck of the *Belvedere* and the week her grandfather had spent on Sable Island, a place that sounded make-believe, like something out of a children's story. How was it possible that a community had grown on a sand dune, hundreds of miles from the edge of the North American continent? And how in the world had wild horses become the natives?

"I'm in shock," she said, watching her grandfather open a bottle of wine at the table. "You spent a week with this woman, and you wanted to marry her?"

"Not at that point," he replied. "When I left, I didn't expect to ever see her again, which I thought was best."

"Because you were already married to Nana," Joanna said.

"Yes, and I was too old for her. It seemed ridiculous to imagine us being together."

"You weren't that much older. Twelve years isn't so bad."

He shrugged as he popped the cork. "She was only twenty-one, and it was a small community. I didn't want to cause talk. Times were different then."

"I understand," Joanna replied. "But you said Nana was already with another man, so *she* was the one having the affair. That must have been so difficult for you. Does my mum know?"

Her grandad poured wine for each of them. "Yes. When she turned twenty, she asked me about a man she remembered from her childhood as Uncle George, who spent a lot of time with Nana when I was away during the war. I knew your mum was suspicious about that, and I couldn't lie to her, so I told her the truth—that her mother needed company because I couldn't love her the way she needed to be loved. I'm not sure if your mother understood, but she never asked me about it again. Whether or not she confronted Nana, I have no idea. She and I never spoke about that."

"It sounds like you both swept a lot of things under the carpet," Joanna said.

"We did." He sat down. "But our relationship was like that . . . we didn't talk about intimate things. It was very . . . superficial."

Still reeling, Joanna sliced into her pork and swirled it around in the gravy. "I guess I shouldn't be surprised that Mum never told me about this. It happened so long ago, and it's not exactly something that needed to be known." She met her grandfather's gaze across the table. "But if you intended to marry Emma, you would have had to divorce Nana. Were you prepared to do that?"

Joanna found it difficult to imagine because they'd always seemed so content. She'd never once seen them argue.

"That was my plan," he replied. "But remember, our marriage wasn't on solid ground. She was in love with someone else, and I thought she'd be glad to be rid of me."

"But that's not what happened," Joanna said. "Obviously, you changed your mind about marrying Emma, and you forgave Nana, and you reconciled. But how did you work things out? What brought you back together?"

Her grandad reached for his wine. "I didn't change my mind about Emma. I loved her and I wanted to be with her, but the universe had other plans."

Joanna set down her fork. "What happened?"

The stark fluorescent light over the table flickered, and Joanna glanced up at it. Suddenly it went out and left them sitting in the dim golden lamplight that spilled into the kitchen from the front hall.

"What was that?" Joanna asked, her heart fluttering in her chest. "Please don't tell me it's Nana trying to stop you from spilling the beans. I'll never get a wink of sleep."

"It's that bulb," he replied irritably. "I need to replace it."

Joanna glanced toward the front hall again, where the large wedding portrait hung. She felt an odd twinge of gloom and urged herself to return her attention to her grandfather. "You were saying? About the universe having other plans for you?"

"Yes." He paused a moment to gather his thoughts, then continued at last. "I returned to Sable Island a few years later, and the love was still there, so I promised Emma I'd arrange for a divorce and return in time for Christmas to propose properly. But I wasn't able to keep that promise."

"Why not?"

He picked up his wine again, took another sip, and his eyes clouded over. "This is the part that's difficult to talk about."

Joanna sensed a heightened reluctance in him, a need to leave the past buried in the forgotten caverns of his heart and mind. "Take your time," she said.

He nodded and rubbed hard at the back of his neck. "I took my ship to Boston first for a load of cargo destined for Morocco. Then we crossed the Atlantic and . . ." He paused and cleared his throat. "Somewhere off the coast of Africa, we struck a mine—one of those floating hazards left over from the war." He reached for his wineglass again, slid it toward him, but left it on the table, holding it by the stem. "There was an explosion, and I thought we were done for. We radioed for help, but the ship was going down." He paused for a drawn-out moment, remembering the events of the night, his brows slowly pulling together with a look of both rage and terror. "It was going down fast by the bow. Listing forward. I'll never forget the sound of the water rushing up the deck, the men shouting and screaming." He took a quick sip of his wine and gulped it down. "It was a miracle we all made it into the lifeboat, except for the two men who were killed in the blast."

Joanna covered her lips with her hand. "My God."

His eyes turned glassy, unseeing, as if he were floating again in the ocean, in darkness. Joanna knew that in his mind, he was not sitting in his warm kitchen with his granddaughter, decades later. He was somewhere else. Reliving it. She waited patiently for him to continue.

"We rowed for at least a week," he finally said, "and ran out of food and water. By that time, I'd given up. I tried to make my peace with God, but I was so angry with Him for everything—the explosion, the deaths of those men, and for keeping me from getting back to Emma." His gaze slowly turned toward the window. "I thought about her a lot in that boat when we were adrift. I tried to understand why God refused to let us be together. Why did He hate me so much? Then I thought maybe it was my fault, because I'd abandoned my wife for the honor of serving in the war and I thought nothing of it at the time. I was more devoted to the British navy than I was to my marriage. Maybe this was my penance for that, for being selfish, for putting my career first. I started to think that, in a way, that was a form of infidelity." He returned his attention to his wine and swirled it around in the glass.

Joanna watched her grandfather with concern as his face reddened, and his eyes darkened with resentment.

"But then one of the younger men spotted land," he said, "and I found out I still had some fight left in me. I remember thinking that maybe God didn't hate me after all. As weak as we were, we rowed like hell."

He finally raised the glass to his lips and sipped what was left of his wine.

"Where did you end up?" Joanna asked.

"On a small island with a good beach for landing," he replied. "I learned later that it was about four hundred nautical miles from the Canary Islands, due west of the Sahara." He paused to remember and reflect. "I don't know why it took so long for anyone to find us after our SOS, but it was months before a young couple in a sailboat came ashore. They were sailing around the world, exploring uninhabited islands. Pure luck for us. Or maybe it was God who decided that I'd served my penance—because I'd certainly spent enough time on my knees, begging forgiveness for everything I ever did wrong and pleading for another chance."

Joanna's heart was beating convulsively in her chest. She couldn't take her eyes off her grandfather, who was staring down at his plate, looking almost catatonic.

"I can't believe you never told me about this," she said. "What a terrible experience. Thank God you were rescued."

"Yes," he replied, "but not before two more of my men died from infections. And the rest of us were so malnourished it's a wonder we survived, even after we made it back to England."

For a while, all Joanna could do was stare at the wedding ring on her grandfather's hand—the same hand that had gripped an oar on a lifeboat and rowed to save his life and the lives of his crew, probably until his palms were blistered and bloody.

He stared pensively at the floor. Then he looked up again, more alert now, and contemplative. "All my life, I've never understood why I've been given so many second chances. Whenever I thought I was done for and all hope was lost, a hand would reach down and pull me back from the brink." He paused and gazed across the table at Joanna, as if she had all the answers.

"Was it God?" he asked. "The same God I'd cursed in the lifeboat? I don't know. Maybe. Either way, I can't help but wonder why. *Why save me?* Why not others who were just as deserving, or even more so?"

He sat back in his chair and rubbed his forehead, while Joanna sought to answer a question that had no concrete answers, only guesses—and most of them required some kind of belief in God or the power of the universe.

"You told me before," Joanna said, "that the universe had a plan for you. Maybe this was it." She waved her arm about, gesturing around the kitchen. "The years you spent with Nana, the family you raised. I'm so grateful you're my grandad because you fed my passion for horses and helped me find my way in life. You're still helping me now. I'm happy with my career, and I'm a vet because of *you*. I can't imagine where I'd be without you in my life."

Joanna wiped a tear from her cheek and clutched both her grandfather's hands across the table. "So maybe this was your destiny—to touch the lives of your children and grandchildren in incredible ways. But please tell me, Grandad. Have you been happy? I hate to think that you didn't live the life you wanted, or that you sacrificed something or felt that you were repaying a debt. Do you ever still dream about what your life might have been like with Emma?"

Her grandfather slowly drew his hands back and shook his head. "Let's not talk about regrets. I'm an old man. The past is out of my hands, and I can't change it. But Sable Island will be with me forever, because Emma helped me see the glass as half-full, not half-empty, which served me well all my life. She was like that herself, and it rubbed off on me. I learned to be grateful and appreciate what I had. Which was Nana and our children—your mum and your uncle, Arthur. Later, you and your cousins. It's been a good life, more than I could have asked for when I was stuck on that island, praying for another chance just to live."

Joanna sat back and decided that the old adage must be true: with age comes wisdom. Her grandfather was able to look back on his life with a bird's-eye view. He saw the whole picture—the beginning, the middle, and the end. Everything made sense to him now.

Joanna was twenty-eight and couldn't possibly imagine what might be next for her now that she'd achieved her career goals. What might the middle of her life look like? Or the end? And how fortunate she was, in that moment, not to be praying for a second chance to live. She was blessed to be alive, in times of peace, not war, with her whole future ahead of her.

But there was still one question that lingered in her mind.

"Can you at least tell me what happened to Emma? After you were rescued, did you ever see her again?"

Her grandfather took a breath and sighed with resignation. "I knew you were going to ask me that."

"You always said I had a curious mind," she reminded him teasingly, and he nodded in agreement.

"Fine." He rose from his chair. "But let's clear the table first and bring out those cinnamon rolls. Then I'll tell you what happened."

CHAPTER 32

Sable Island, August 1955

Oliver jumped out of the tender boat and landed in the cold frothy salt water of the North Atlantic. A few gray seals lounged on the beach, basking in the warmth and humidity of a cloud-covered summer day. They watched him, but otherwise seemed wholly undisturbed by his arrival.

He dragged his boat up the sandy slope, reached a safe distance away from the incoming waves, and then doubled over in exhaustion, fighting to catch his breath. He was still down twenty pounds since his rescue and return to England, and his appetite had not fully returned. His doctors had advised him not to travel, but here he stood, back on the beach on Sable Island after sending an urgent wireless message to Emma: I'M ALIVE. ON MY WAY TO YOU. OLIVER.

As soon as he recovered from the exertion, he left his boat and trudged across the deep, shifting sands toward the high dune and Main Station beyond. Oliver felt like a starving man, dehydrated, crossing a desert, desperate for water—but it wasn't water he wanted. It was the sight of Emma.

Finally, he made it through the break in the high dune and stopped to catch his breath again and take in the view of Main Station—the familiar cluster of white buildings and Quonset huts. All at once, a flood of emotion erupted inside him. He'd never imagined he'd live to see this place again, but here it was, just as he'd remembered in his dreams. His prayers had been answered.

Overcome with relief and gratitude, and overwhelmed by the incredible gift of his good luck, Oliver fell to his knees on the sand, broke down, and wept rapturously.

When he finally recovered himself, he rose unsteadily to his feet, looked across the station yard at the Clarkson house, and his heart began to race with anticipation. He wanted to run, but he didn't have the strength. All he could do was put one foot in front of the other, unrelenting.

The wind off the ocean blew his hair in all directions, and he continued, trudging toward the superintendent's residence. He was so fixed on the Clarkson house that he failed to notice that there was no one about. Nor did he observe that the door to the staff house was flung open and banging against the outside wall.

Oliver finally reached Emma's door and knocked repeatedly, but no one answered. Still eager and hopeful, assuming they were all off on some errand or gathering on another part of the island, he descended the steps. Only then did he perceive the air of abandonment. Solitude. His gaze moved from the open door at the staff house to the dead blooms in the hanging flowerpot outside Emma's door. The clouds hovered low. The wind blew steadily across the marram grass on the dune, and the vast gray ocean roared.

Where was everyone?

Then he saw a man jogging toward him.

"Greetings! Welcome to Sable Island!"

The young man was a stranger to Oliver. Feeling a bit muddled, his thoughts in disarray, he relied on the dependable rules of social etiquette. "Good morning!" he shouted across the station yard.

They reached each other on one of the concrete sidewalks and held out their hands. "I'm Oliver Harris," he said, "here to pay a visit to Emma Clarkson, or her father, John. I'm an old friend."

"Welcome," the young man replied. "I'm Roger Smith, weather station chief. But I'm afraid you're too late. John left a month ago, and everyone else left just the other day."

Oliver shook his head and frowned. "What do you mean, everyone?"

Roger shoved his hands into his trouser pockets. "You didn't hear? The lifesaving establishment was gutted. The government didn't see much need for it anymore, which makes sense, to be honest. There hasn't been a shipwreck here in almost ten years."

"Nineteen forty-six," Oliver replied with dismay as the news slowly sank in.

Roger shrugged. "Maybe that was it. I don't know, exactly. I've only been here since the spring. But you know what they say: you can't fight progress. So now my job is the only one that seems relevant. Except for the wireless operators, I guess."

Oliver spoke in a rush. "I sent a message a couple of weeks ago. It was meant for Emma. Do you know if she received it?"

Roger made a face. "I don't know about that. There's been some turnover and a lot of confusion since the announcement came. And she hasn't been here for a while. She was long gone when I arrived."

"Do you know where she went?"

"As a matter of fact, I do," Roger cheerfully replied. "John showed me some pictures. Lovely-looking woman. He said they used to call her the Sable Beauty."

"They did," Oliver replied with rising impatience. "But where is she now?"

"With her husband," Roger replied. "Back on the mainland. Did you know he went to prison for killing a man?"

The shock was like shrapnel to the gut. Oliver took a step back, almost staggering. He wasn't sure if he'd heard the man correctly. Or maybe he was just floating in a fog of denial. "She's where?"

"She went back to her husband, and they're living somewhere in Halifax. John said he was released from prison. That must have been quite a scandal when he was arrested. Must have put a strain on their marriage, I would guess, but it sounds like they're making it work."

The news finally hit home, and Oliver felt as if he'd fallen out a high window and smashed into the ground. He took a few more steps backward, wondering if this was another real-life nightmare—like the explosion, his ship going down . . .

Surely this time his heart wouldn't be able to hold out.

"But you know what they say," Roger continued, oblivious to Oliver's distress. "Time heals all wounds. He's out of jail now, and they looked like a happy family in the pictures I saw. But it makes sense, you know? With children in the mix. A boy needs his father. Forgive and forget, that's what I always say."

Oliver turned toward the ocean and listened to its obstinate thunder. He thought of the days in the lifeboat, when he'd cursed God, and the slow, excruciating deaths of the two men on the island—who were his friends—when they'd succumbed to infection.

Maybe he wasn't so lucky after all, because Emma—the only dream that gave him a reason to keep breathing when he was starving to death—was lost to him.

The waves beyond the high dune continued to break onto the shore. It was a relentless reverberation, booming inside his chest, and he felt the same despair he'd felt when he'd given up all hope for a rescue or a way off that wretched island.

"Since you're here," Roger said, "would you like to come to the weather station for a tour? We're working on some new experiments. I could make you a hot lunch at the house."

"No . . . thank you," Oliver replied, walking backward. He was engulfed in grief and rage—aimed at God again. "I need to get going."

He couldn't be sociable. He was in a numb state of shock.

But as he started running toward the tender boat on the shore, his shock turned to defiance. This couldn't be the end. If he rowed quickly back to the sailboat, he could harness the wind, return to Halifax, and find Emma. Tell her he loved her. Beg her to leave Logan. Oliver ran clumsily out of Main Station, fighting for traction in the deep sand, darting through winding horse trails toward the break in the high dune.

But when he emerged onto the beach, the reality of the situation and the consequences of his desires struck him like a stone and shattered him. He stopped dead.

He wanted Emma. Of course he did. But how many times had he broken her heart? God had chosen to spare him from death in the explosion, in the lifeboat, and on the island. For that he was grateful—he truly was—and maybe this was a sign. When he was praying for survival and rescue, Oliver had made countless untold promises. He'd begged forgiveness for his failures as a husband and a father. He'd pleaded for a chance to see his children again and hold them in his arms.

Was this the price for that reward? His children had been at his side in the hospital constantly since his return, and he'd been thanking God ever since. But to go after Emma was to break the promises he'd made to be a better father. Could he abandon his children again? Could he destroy a marriage reunited and steal another man's son from him?

Emma had chosen to abide by her vows and rebuild her family. How could he disrupt another marriage? It would be selfish. Irresponsible. It wasn't right.

Exhausted again and out of breath, Oliver sank onto the cool sand and sat there, staring at the horizon and struggling with his emotions. He still wanted Emma. He wanted her to know that he loved her. But he also wanted to raise his two children, to love and support them through life, and to one day know his grandchildren.

Oliver gazed up at the pale-gray sky. The clouds, thick and dense, rolled sluggishly eastward. For a long while, he watched their graceful movement and felt a gradual settling of his heart.

He was very tired. Tired of fighting for survival, for love, and for the wisdom to do the right thing. He'd been responsible for twelve men on that island off the coast of Africa. There were many deaths over the years, during and after the war, that he had to answer for.

Oliver collapsed wearily onto his back and lay for a long while in the warmth of that overcast August afternoon. Sleepily, he continued to watch the blanket of clouds travel across the sky. Or maybe it was the rotation of the earth he was witnessing.

Eventually, he reached into his jacket pocket and wrapped his hand around the ring he'd bought for Emma. He couldn't bear to think about what might have happened if he'd made it back in time to propose and place it on her finger. What would their lives have looked like?

It was torture to imagine what could never be, so he sat up and stared at the ocean, wondering what to do next.

All he knew was that he had to leave Sable Island and say goodbye to it forever. Though it had wielded a profound power and effect on his soul and had changed him deeply, for the better, it was time to go home.

It was time to go home to his children.

CHAPTER 33

England, 1995

"So, you never saw her again?" Joanna asked. "Ever? That must have been devastating."

Without answering, her grandfather carried the dessert plates to the sink and scraped them clean.

Outside, the rain had stopped. The whole world had gone quiet and still, except for Joanna's heart, which was pounding in her ears. She'd never seen such a look of sorrow in her grandfather's eyes before, except when Nana died. But this was different. Years seemed to have fallen away from his face. He was a younger man again—but a sad one.

He returned to stand behind his chair and gripped the back of it.

"After all that," he said, "when I was walking back to my boat, I saw a small herd of horses grazing on top of a low dune. I couldn't tear my eyes away from them. I stayed there for . . . oh, I don't know, maybe half an hour, just watching, slowly moving closer, but I couldn't get close enough to touch them. Eventually, they broke into a gallop and headed inland, to the heath. My God, they were so beautiful . . ."

He slowly blinked, as if he were continuing to live and breathe in that memory, in the exquisiteness of it all, the good and the bad—because it was *life*, part of the living, breathing world. His children. The war. The shipwrecks. His love for Emma. Even the loss of her. Emma lived only in his memory now—like one of those dreamlike horses he couldn't quite reach, galloping away beyond the dune.

Joanna knew that despite the pain, it was all beautiful, because of where it had taken him—to this moment in this kitchen with his granddaughter, who loved and cherished him and owed him everything for her happiness.

"Oh, Grandad . . ." Joanna's eyes stung with tears until she wiped at both cheeks. "I love you. And I'm so sorry you never got to see her again. I can't even imagine."

Because she'd never loved anyone like that.

Her grandad seemed to wake from a dream and return to the present. "I love you too, sweetheart."

Joanna stood up and hugged him. When she drew back, she still had questions. "So, when you came back to England, is that when you got back together with Nana? For good?"

"Yes," he replied. "While I was gone, her relationship with that other man ended, which I took as another sign from above. She wanted us to try again, and I wanted to be a part of my children's lives, so I moved back home. I've been living in this house ever since."

"So, you did it for your children?" Joanna asked, needing clarity while she thought of her grandfather's shattered heart.

"At first," he replied. "But over time, like I said, I began to see the glass as half-full, and you know the rest."

Yes, Joanna knew how her grandfather had always respected Nana as a mother and a homemaker. Clearly, he'd forgiven her for her infidelity, because he was not without transgressions of his own.

"And here we all are," he said lightly, "still trotting along, on ever-shifting sands."

A sense of profound understanding washed over her. There were no guarantees in this world. Happiness was never constant or unbroken.

Sometimes it fell away, or was ripped away, and it was beyond the range of vision.

But it was still out there, perhaps just over the next rise.

"Thank goodness for second chances," she said, and couldn't help but smile at her grandfather. What a treasure he'd been in her life. How grateful she was for his love—especially now, knowing that he could have chosen another path to an entirely different destination.

~

The following week, Joanna visited the stables regularly to check on Boots, the foal she'd helped deliver, as well as his mother, Ruby. Both were doing well, so a daily checkup was unnecessary, but Joanna went regardless, on her own time, usually at sunset, after she finished work at the clinic.

Each day, she stayed a bit longer than the day before, and spent time in the stalls running a brush over Ruby's thick coat, bringing her fresh water, or interacting with Boots. Often, Joanna simply sat on a stool in the corner of the stall with her elbows on her knees, watching Boots sleep. After a nap, he would rise on unsteady legs, and his mother would nicker gently and nudge him with her nose.

In those moments, as Joanna witnessed the love between mother and child, she found herself enraptured and fully grasping her grandfather's choice to remain with his children. Parenthood was a pure, soulful, and biological love with no comparison. She saw it in horses, and in her family, and she hoped to experience it for herself one day.

She also understood why her grandfather had taught her to ride and care for horses at such a young age. He'd come to appreciate their beauty during his incredible experiences on Sable Island, and perhaps it was his way of returning to that special magic. To feel it in her heart and soul again. In the process, he'd passed that love and connection on to her.

What, she wondered, had become of the wild herds that once lived on the island? Had they survived the past half century? And did the island even exist today if it was nothing but a sand dune in the open Atlantic, constantly reshaped by the wind and storms in the ocean?

Did anyone still live there?

By the end of the week, Joanna couldn't allow those questions to go unanswered. She needed to know more, so she decided it was time to do some research.

CHAPTER 34

Joanna poured herself a cup of coffee and dialed her grandfather's number. He answered after the first ring. "Hello?"

"Hi, Grandad."

"Hey, sweetheart." His deep voice brimmed with affection. "It's nice to hear your voice. How are you doing?"

"Good as gold," she replied. "You won't believe what I've been doing."

"Do tell."

She carried her coffee mug to the kitchen table and sat down among toppling piles of magazines and open books. "I've been researching Sable Island."

For a moment he said nothing, and she worried that she'd overstepped an unspoken boundary.

"Is that okay?" she asked.

He remained quiet until Joanna mentally winced from the silence.

At long last, he responded. "That curious mind of yours . . . Why am I not surprised?"

She sighed with relief, then chuckled into the phone. "I'm so sorry. I couldn't help it. Everything you told me about the horses was so fascinating. I've become a little obsessed, to be honest."

"Obsessed?" He paused. "How?"

She pulled one of the books toward her. "Well . . . at first, I was mostly interested in the horses, but then I stumbled across a book about the history of the island. It covered the Humane Establishment from its beginning to its end in the 1950s. There's a whole section about John Clarkson, because he was the last superintendent, and they mention his daughter, Emma."

Silence dropped into the connection between them. When her grandad finally spoke, his voice was guarded. "You don't say."

Still amazed by what she'd learned, Joanna charged forward. "Grandad, are you aware that your shipwreck was the last one on record before the lifesaving station was shut down? And that the details of the wreck and the rescue are in a book called *Wrecks of Sable Island*? I'm sure you're in other reference books as well."

He pondered that for a few seconds, then asked hesitantly, "Does it say anything about me and Emma? Personally, I mean?"

Joanna paused as she pictured her grandfather alone in the house that he'd shared with his wife for more than fifty years. She imagined him pacing next to the telephone at the mention of the woman he'd once loved and lost.

Joanna turned a page in the book. "No, nothing at all. There's no mention of any connection between the two of you. It only says that you were nursed back to health on the island."

"Well, that's accurate." A half a minute must have passed before he spoke again. "Does it say anything about what happened to Emma in the years after she left the island?"

There it was at last—the curiosity that continued to live and breathe in him. All along, Joanna had suspected it never died.

"No."

She waited patiently for him to react to her flat response. Seconds ticked by conspicuously.

"What else did you learn?" he asked. "You were looking for infor-mation about the horses. Are they still there?"

Joanna picked up her coffee cup. "Yes, they are, and there's a story about that. Remember when you told me about Emma writing letters to the government to try and stop people from capturing them and shipping them off the island to sell them?"

"Yes."

"Well, the government finally listened, and in 1961 they passed a law that doesn't allow anyone to interfere with the horses. You can't even touch or feed them. They're to be left alone and remain wild. They're federally protected."

"Goodness. Isn't that wonderful."

"It is, isn't it? And these days, no one lives there except for the weather station personnel. But here's the best part." Joanna paused a moment—worried again that she was overstepping—but decided to forge ahead nevertheless. "I've looked into it, and it's possible to visit. There's a helicopter pad. Or airplanes can land on the beach."

Joanna forced herself to stop talking. She waited for her grandfather to say something.

"You're chuffed to bits, aren't you," he finally remarked. "I can hear it in your voice."

Joanna set down her coffee cup. "Yes, and I can't lie. I'm buzzin' to go there. I want to see the horses, like you did." She hesitated and chewed on her thumbnail. "I don't suppose you'd come with me?"

He spoke decisively. "No, sweetheart. I'm too old for that."

"Oh, tosh! You're as fit as any sixty-year-old. I was looking at pictures in the books, and most of the people who visit Sable Island these days are older, probably because it's not cheap. But for some people, it's a lifelong dream."

He cleared his throat uneasily, and Joanna sensed his reluctance. It left her feeling deflated. "I really want to go," she told him pleadingly. "It seems like such an incredible place. And the horses . . ."

"I'll never disagree with you about that," he replied. "And you don't need my permission to go."

"I'm not asking for your permission. I'm asking you to come with me. I really wish you would."

"Why?"

She thought long and hard about that. Was it because she didn't want to go alone? Or did she want this for him as much as for herself?

"I don't know," she finally confessed. "Maybe I want to take you back to a place that was special to you, so that you can see it again and enjoy the memory of it and maybe get some closure."

"I don't need closure," he told her. "I got that a long time ago when I went there with a ring."

Joanna looked down at the open book on the table and flipped a few pages. "Forgive me for saying this, Grandad, but I'm not sure I believe you. I saw the look in your eyes when you told me about Emma. I felt your frustration about how things turned out."

Or maybe I'm just a hopeless romantic.

"Either way," he replied, "it doesn't matter. A visit to Sable isn't going to change anything. It's all in the history books now. Emma's not there. She's long gone."

Joanna tapped her finger on one of her travel brochures. "But what if we could find her?"

An electric current seemed to buzz through the telephone lines.

"No, no . . . don't start with that," he said.

"With what?" she asked innocently.

"I know what you're up to. You're trying to play matchmaker."

Joanna chuckled guiltily. "That's ridiculous."

"Don't get shirty with me, you little rascal. I can read you like a book."

Finally, Joanna sat back and groaned. "Okay, fine! But humor me. Wouldn't it be fun to take a walk down memory lane?"

"For what purpose?"

She was usually quick on her feet, but in that moment, she couldn't formulate an answer.

"None of us can go back in time," he told her.

"That's true, obviously," she replied. "But maybe that's not what this is about. Maybe I just want to travel somewhere and see some of that beauty you talked about. I'd love to get a look at those horses. Maybe there's something drawing me there because it might be a game changer for my career."

He paused a moment, then sounded pensive. "If it's beauty you're looking for, Sable Island is the place to find it."

Joanna felt a fresh flush of energy and sat forward. "Then let's go! If nothing else, it'll be an adventure, and something you'd be doing for *me*. I don't know why, but I have a feeling this is where I need to go. Who knows where it might lead me professionally? And you've always been my biggest supporter."

Finally, he exhaled in defeat. "You drive a hard bargain. Fine. Let's go and see where it takes us."

Joanna smiled as she opened the phone book to ring a travel agent.

"Suddenly my life feels full of suspense," she said.

"Mine too," her grandfather replied. "But I still think I'm too old for this."

"Oh, tosh. You'll be grand."

CHAPTER 35

It was a six-hour direct flight from London to Halifax, after which Joanna and her grandfather deplaned, collected their luggage at the carousel, and took a taxi into the city, where she'd made reservations at a luxury hotel on the historic Halifax waterfront. After they checked in, they spent an hour in their separate adjoining rooms to relax and freshen up before dining at the Five Fishermen, a seafood restaurant that came highly recommended by the hotel manager. Then they returned to the hotel and collapsed for the night.

Fortunately, the change in time zones granted them four extra hours, so they woke early, feeling refreshed and energetic. The weather was fine—sunny with a pleasant breeze off the water—and they spent the morning exploring the downtown sector and the Maritime Museum of the Atlantic, where they immersed themselves for three hours in the world of seafaring. They learned about the sinking of the *Titanic* and the Halifax Explosion, but it was the Sable Island displays that captured their interest.

"I can't believe what I'm seeing," Oliver said, walking purposefully toward a wooden white-painted service boat. Joanna hurried to keep up with him.

He climbed steps to a viewing platform. "This is exactly what they used to rescue us," he said, awestruck. "This might even be the very same boat. I can't believe it survived all these years."

Joanna climbed the steps and stood beside him. "It's just like I imagined it."

Later, when they exited the museum, it was time for lunch, so they ate at a pub called The Lower Deck, where they ordered two bowls of seafood chowder with crusty bread, paired with a local craft beer.

Sated and full to bursting from the meal, they boarded a tour boat that took them past the Canadian naval base to the site of the Halifax Explosion, where two ships had collided during the First World War. Then they cruised toward Point Pleasant Park and rounded the point into the Northwest Arm, where they learned about the Atlantic School of Theology and the Royal Nova Scotia Yacht Squadron.

At the end of a full day on the Halifax peninsula, they returned to the hotel for dinner and to pack for their trip to Sable Island the following morning.

That night, Joanna dreamed of wild horses.

~

The following morning at breakfast, Joanna dug in to her fruit-and-yogurt plate. "How are you feeling about this?"

Grandad sipped his coffee. "I'm not sure."

"You were quiet at dinner last night," she said tentatively. "Do you regret coming?"

He poked at his omelet. "The museum yesterday brought back some memories. Not all of them are good. I didn't sleep well."

She reached across the table and covered his hand with hers. "I saw how it affected you, especially the service boat. You must have some PTSD from that, and from hitting the mine. Did you ever get counseling?"

He shook his head. "It wasn't common in those days. Emma was the only person I ever talked to about it. I suppose she was the closest thing I had to a therapist." He leaned back in his chair. "But no, I don't regret coming. I'm looking forward to seeing Sable Island again.

Sometimes it feels like it was just a dream." He sat forward and sliced into his omelet. "I hope we'll see some horses. That would be nice."

Joanna watched him take the first bite and hoped she hadn't pressured him too heavily about accompanying her on this journey.

A short while later, she checked her watch. "We should probably get going. We don't want to be late."

He checked his watch as well. "Good Lord. I'm a navy man. Lateness is not an option."

They stood up and went to the lobby entrance to summon a cab to the airport.

~

At the helicopter terminal, they met some fellow travelers—the Dalrymples, a well-to-do retired couple from the local area, and Jason Abernathy, a professional photographer working on a book about Nova Scotia islands.

As they all became acquainted, Oliver leaned close to whisper in Joanna's ear. "Don't tell anyone who I am. I don't want to talk about the *Belvedere*."

She understood and nodded.

They were scheduled to depart at 9:00 a.m. and arrive back at the terminal by 7:00 p.m. The flight across the water would take approximately an hour and fifteen minutes, which seemed remarkable to Joanna—to reach a place that, in her imagination, seemed like the farthest corner of the world.

~

During the flight across sparkling blue water, Joanna sat beside her grandfather and Jason, and faced their guide, Bill, and the Dalrymples. They all wore headsets to reduce the noise from the engine and propeller, and to speak to each other through a microphone communication system.

When at last they approached Sable Island, the chopper banked left to fly over South Beach. Joanna touched her forehead to the window to peer down at the narrow crescent-shaped island, where she spotted a few horses, like tiny dots, grazing in the green interior. She sucked in a breath of excitement.

As they descended toward the landing pad, she saw more horses lingering around a large pond and couldn't wait to get her feet on the ground and explore the place her grandfather had described with such reverence.

At last, the chopper touched down, the pilots shut off the engines, and the propeller blades slowed. Both pilots, Darren and Denise, got out and opened the doors, and everyone removed their headsets and unbuckled their seat belts. Joanna was first to hop out and was struck instantly by the unfamiliar fragrance of the island. It was like nothing she'd ever smelled before—a singular mixture of the salty ocean, the unique vegetation, and horsehair and manure, all of it floating on the unpolluted breezes of the North Atlantic.

When she turned her head, she saw her grandfather standing tall with his head tilted back, his eyes closed, doing the same thing. Just breathing.

Their eyes met, and he smiled, and she was overcome with happiness, knowing that he was pleased to return to the island that had changed him for the better.

She had come to understand that this was the place where he had discovered his soul.

~

There was no dirt on Sable Island, just sand, which made walking a challenge for their small group as they ventured through the interior toward Main Station. Bill, their guide, warned them to always keep at least twenty meters away from the horses, so when the group encountered their first small band, walking toward them on a narrow path, Bill waved everyone into the low junipers to make way.

Joanna glanced at her grandfather, who stood mesmerized, staring. "Emma and I never got this close," he said to her privately. "We were lucky to see any at all."

"From what I've read," Joanna replied, "the population has grown since they stopped shipping them away for sale. And they're probably more comfortable around humans who never touch or threaten them. It's no wonder they made themselves scarce when you were here last."

"The island felt untouched before," he said, "but clearly it wasn't."

They continued on, trudging along the narrow path.

~

Main Station was a cluster of white buildings used for accommodations, office, and research facilities, as well as communication towers, fuel storage tanks, and a few essential motorized vehicles. Bill gathered everyone to explain how important it was to keep to the concrete sidewalks to avoid tramping on an endangered species of beetle. He then led the group into the big white house in the center of the station yard, where they could use the loo, refill their water bottles, and leave any unnecessary belongings behind for the day.

While Joanna was bent over her backpack, searching for UV protective lip balm, the door opened, and a man walked in. Joanna heard him before she saw him.

"Hi, everyone. Welcome to Sable."

As the group said hello, she straightened and turned.

"I'm Garrett Jones," he said, "the chief meteorologist. It looks like the universe smiled on you today, because the weather couldn't be better. The last group of visitors weren't so lucky—fog rolled in at dawn, and there was a zero-meter visibility. They never even made it here."

Everyone groaned in sympathy. "I guess we're pretty lucky, then," Jason said.

"Maybe we should buy lottery tickets when we get home," Mrs. Dalrymple added, and the others laughed.

Joanna took a good look at Garrett Jones. He wore a black T-shirt, khaki trousers, and well-worn hiking boots. He looked to be the sort of person who knew how to light a fire without matches and could predict the weather simply by sniffing the air.

"I'm Joanna," she said, stepping forward to shake his hand. "This is my grandfather, Oliver." They shook hands as well, which started the ball rolling. Everyone else introduced themselves.

"Will you be coming with us on the tour?" Mrs. Dalrymple asked.

Garrett backed up a few steps. "No, I've got some work to do at the weather station. I just wanted to say hello because we don't get many visitors here."

"Well, hello, then," Mr. Dalrymple said affably.

Bill, their guide, gathered everyone's attention. "Remember what I said about keeping at least twenty meters away from the horses, and don't forget to stay hydrated. We'll be doing a lot of walking. Any questions before we head out?"

With a raised eyebrow, Joanna glanced at her grandfather. He quickly shook his head because he wanted to remain anonymous, so she raised her hand on his behalf. "I've been reading about the history here—that there was a rose garden at the old main station. Does that still exist?"

Bill's eyebrows lifted. "That's the first time I've had that question. And the answer is yes, and no. Sections of the old concrete wall are still there, and there are some roses, but it's quite diminished. Any other questions?"

"What about the old main station in general?" Joanna asked. "I saw pictures of a house buried in sand. Will we see that today?"

"It's westward, I'm afraid, and this tour takes us east. Besides, the structures aren't safe."

"Of course," she replied.

Bill turned to the others. "If that's it, let's get going."

Joanna turned to her grandfather and whispered, "Sorry. I couldn't help myself."

"It was worth a try."

~

Three hours later, after climbing grassy dunes to breezy heights and descending steep slopes into warm, sunbaked hollows in the interior, Joanna knew that she was experiencing something very special, perhaps even miraculous. Sable Island was a place like no other. It owed its existence to the perfect meeting of ocean currents that swirled around the edge of the continental shelf and stirred up the ocean floor. It relied on strong, deep roots of marram grass and vegetation to hold its fragile existence together as it was eroded, then newly sculpted by the wind and water. It seemed impossible that it could even exist, yet here it was—dynamic, durable, and resistant, but malleable enough to change and adapt after every storm. It had been doing so for centuries.

As Joanna stood on the beach looking out at the vast Atlantic Ocean, she began to fully appreciate the wonder of the entire planet— the enduring and renewing of life, in all its forms. Everything about this trip was inspiring her to get out more, to travel more, and to experience as much of this miraculous world as she possibly could.

Joanna turned away from the water and rejoined the group as they made their way toward Bald Dune.

~

Toward the end of the day, rain clouds smothered the horizon and turned the ocean to a foreboding gunmetal gray. The temperature, however, remained comfortable and warm.

Bill led the group onto North Beach, where a herd of gray seals—startled by the sudden appearance of humans—scattered into the foaming surf and dove deep. They surfaced farther out beyond the breakers.

"We have some time before we need to be back at Main Station," Bill said. "So if you want to take your shoes off and dip your feet in the water, feel free."

Joanna met her grandfather's eyes, and they smiled at each other. They removed their hiking boots, rolled their jeans up to their knees, and moseyed down the sloping beach.

"It's so cold!" Joanna laughed as the first wave washed over her feet, halfway up her calves. She took a few seconds to catch her breath, then moved in a little deeper, where she watched a curious young seal swim up close, then cruise back and forth, in front of her.

"I don't know about that sky," her grandfather said with a frown.

She examined the murky horizon. "It looks like rain."

He nodded, barely conscious of the waves dampening his rolled-up jeans.

A short time later, Bill strode to the water's edge. "I hate to break up the party, but we should head back."

Joanna glanced at her grandfather, who was quick to leave the water and reach for his boots.

~

By the time they returned to Main Station, the wind had picked up, and dark clouds were rolling in from the southeast. A few raindrops pelted their faces as they entered the building.

Joanna watched her grandfather walk to the wide bank of windows and observe the sky. Hesitantly, she approached him. "What do you think?"

He shook his head. "If you really want to know, I've seen skies like this before. It doesn't look good."

She studied the angry horizon and felt a shiver of unease. The last thing she wanted was to fly into a raging thunderstorm and risk her life when she'd just begun to fully appreciate it.

All at once, raindrops hit the window like bullets, and the marram grass around Main Station began to whip wildly in high winds that assaulted the island like a fast-moving train.

The door flew open, and Garrett, the meteorologist, walked in. "How's everyone doing? Did you have a good day?"

"It was incredible," Mrs. Dalrymple replied, unfazed by the sudden gale outside the window. Her husband, however, was quiet and solemn.

Garrett slid his hands into his trouser pockets. "I'm glad you enjoyed it. Bill, can I talk to you for a second?"

Joanna and Oliver exchanged a knowing look while Bill and Garrett moved into the sitting room and spoke with the pilots. A few minutes later, they returned.

"I have good news and bad news," Bill said. "Which would you like first?"

There was an overall silence.

"I guess you can start with the good news," Mr. Dalrymple replied.

Bill shifted his weight from one foot to the other, stalling. "All right, then. You're all going to experience something most visitors don't when they come to Sable Island, and you'll get a few free meals out of it too."

His announcement was met with further silence.

"The bad news?" Oliver asked.

"The weather, as you can see," Garrett said to the whole group, "came out of nowhere, so it's not safe to fly back to Halifax. I'm afraid you're all stuck here for the night."

While the others groaned and panicked and scrambled to figure out how to manage this unexpected change in plans, Joanna turned to her grandfather. He simply shrugged and smiled, seeming amused by the swerving vehicle that was the universe.

~

The island visitors were spread out, billeted in two buildings at Main Station. Jason and the Dalrymples were welcomed in the home of a naturalist who had been living on Sable Island, on and off, for more than thirty years, while Joanna, Oliver, and the two pilots took rooms upstairs at the main building for accommodations.

Everyone had only just gotten settled when the storm reached its peak, like a raging beast. The marram grass whipped in near-hurricane-force winds, and the house creaked and groaned as if it were about to be carried off like Dorothy's in *The Wizard of Oz* and spin wildly out to sea.

Thankfully, by dinnertime, the house was still standing when Garrett and Bill served up a spaghetti dinner in the spacious common area.

"Do visitors get stranded often when the weather's dodgy?" Joanna asked Garrett, who sat across from her at the long table.

"Almost never," he replied. "It's more likely that trips get canceled, but no one saw this little flare-up coming until a few hours before."

"Lucky us." Joanna smiled at him as she twirled her spaghetti noodles around her fork. "Seriously, I'm not sorry to be spending the night here."

"I hope the rest of your group feels the same," he said.

In the spirit of making polite conversation, Garrett addressed Oliver, who sat next to Joanna. "You two are from England?"

"What gave us away?" Oliver replied in a friendly manner.

Denise, one of the pilots, laughed. "It's those gorgeous accents. Are you just visiting Canada, or do you live here?"

"Just visiting," Joanna told her.

"And what do you both do?" Denise asked.

Joanna poked at her pasta. "I'm a veterinarian in London."

"She looks after horses at the Royal Mews," Oliver added, not shy about boasting.

Garrett and the pilots swung their gazes to her at once.

"You mean Buckingham Palace?" Denise asked.

"Yes, that's right."

Denise dropped her fork onto her plate. "How in the world did you get *that* job?"

Joanna dabbed her mouth with a napkin. "Your guess is as good as mine, but I've loved horses since I was young, so I always knew that's how I wanted to spend my life, working with them in some way. By the time I was twenty, I had a mountain of volunteer experience, and they just happened to be hiring when I graduated from vet college."

"Sounds like fate," Garrett said.

"Maybe so," Joanna replied.

"And what do you do, Oliver?"

All eyes turned to him, and Joanna was about to intervene protectively when he responded.

"I'm retired," he said flatly.

There was an awkward silence at the table. Then he surprised Joanna by spilling the tea. "I was a lieutenant colonel in the British navy during the war. Then I worked in commercial shipping."

Joanna could have added that he had seen combat in World War II, had survived two shipwrecks in his later career—including one on these very shores—and had gone on to consult for a global shipbuilding enterprise, where he worked with engineers and designers to improve safety features in every aspect of marine travel.

Bill reached for a second roll and buttered it. "I had a feeling you knew something about the clouds," he said. "You knew what was coming."

Oliver was too humble to say yes, so Joanna answered for him. "He did. So I wasn't shocked when you said we couldn't leave tonight."

Denise sat back in her chair. "Mrs. Dalrymple looked like she was going to pass out."

Everyone at the table chuckled.

Joanna took the last bite of her spaghetti, then glanced across the table at Garrett. Their eyes met, and she held his gaze and smiled.

Oliver raised his glass. "Let's make a toast. Thanks to our pilots for putting safety first, and to our hosts, for providing this delicious meal."

"Cheers to that," Denise said.

They all clinked glasses.

"Let's also drink to clear skies in the morning," Darren added. "And hope the universe is listening."

Joanna and her grandfather shared a look of amusement.

CHAPTER 36

Joanna couldn't sleep. Maybe it was the mattress. The springs were digging into her hips. How old was this thing? For all she knew, it could have been the very bed her grandfather slept on in Abigail McKenna's sickroom in 1946.

But Joanna wouldn't dare complain. Here she was, spending an extra day on the island of her grandfather's most profound spiritual experience, or at least she liked to think of it that way. He might have other ideas, having survived a war and two shipwrecks.

She finally gave up tossing and turning, rose from the uncomfortable bed, pulled on her jeans and sweatshirt, and ventured downstairs.

The house was dark, and she shivered a little before she switched on a lamp by the sofa near the brick fireplace. Golden light enveloped the room and reflected off raindrops on the windowpane.

She glanced around and wondered what to do with herself at two o'clock in the morning. If only she'd brought a book to read. Then her attention fell on a deck of cards on the fireplace mantel, so she decided that a game of solitaire would be the perfect diversion on a stormy night on a remote island. All she needed was a cup of tea to help her relax. Perhaps they had some in the kitchen.

She moved to the sink, switched on another light, and riffled through a few cupboards, careful not to slam doors and wake others in the house. She found a box of Red Rose tea. It was not a brand familiar to her, but when in Rome . . .

Joanna spotted an electric kettle, filled it with water, and plugged it in. She had just leaned back against the counter to wait when a gust of wind shook the house and the back door was ripped open. With a fright, Joanna pushed away from the counter and looked hard at the unexpected visitor.

It was Garrett, and she relaxed.

"Is everything okay?" he asked, lowering the hood of his yellow rain slicker. "I saw the light on."

"It's fine," she replied. "I'm so sorry. I didn't mean to wake anyone, but I couldn't sleep."

"Neither could I." He closed the inner door behind him. "This is the worst storm we've had in a while, and I didn't see it coming. We don't usually have guests, so I'm a bit on edge."

"We're all fine," she assured him. "I'd much rather be here than up there, in the sky, getting struck by lightning."

"My thoughts exactly." He unzipped his raincoat. "It's never fun when the coast guard gets involved. Do you mind if I hang out here for a bit?"

"Fill your boots," she replied. "I was just making some tea. Fancy a cuppa?"

"I shouldn't. It would probably keep me up."

"But you're already up," she replied with a grin.

He chuckled as he hung his coat on a hook. "You have me there."

"I was just about to play solitaire," she mentioned, gesturing toward the table. "But now that you're here . . ."

He strolled into the kitchen. "Poker? Crazy Eights? Gin rummy?"

Joanna laughed. "I was going to say we could talk. I'd love to pick your brain about Sable Island."

"Go for it," he replied, sounding invigorated. "I love talking about it. And not to toot my own horn, but I know everything."

She laughed again. "Then I've come to the right place."

The kettle boiled, and Joanna filled a Royal Albert teapot. "This is a beauty. Definitely vintage. I recognize the pattern. It's called Old Country Roses. I wonder how long it's been here."

"Who knows," he replied. "So much of what's here has been kept and reused for decades, maybe even a century."

She leaned on the counter again, waiting for the tea to steep. "I've actually done a lot of research on Sable, and I know about the Humane Establishment."

Garrett inclined his head. "Really? Most people who come here just want to take pictures of the horses."

She didn't want to betray her grandfather's confidence, but she had so many questions about the island and the woman he'd loved all those years ago.

"I shouldn't tell you this," she said, "and if I do, I'm going to need your blood oath. You have to promise you'll keep it private, between us."

"Sounds intriguing. But what exactly do you mean by *blood oath*?" He slanted a look at her.

Playfully, she waved off his concerns. "It won't hurt, I promise. But if you know 'everything' about Sable Island, you probably already know who my grandfather is."

Garrett sat forward. "He has a history here?"

"Yes. He was shipwrecked in 1946."

Garrett's eyebrows lifted. "The *Belvedere*? The one where the captain refused to abandon his ship?"

Joanna slapped her hand against her cheek. "Oh, my word. You do know of it."

"Of course I do. It was the last wreck before the end of the lifesaving station."

His knowledge on the subject sent Joanna's heart leaping, which made her forget about the tea steeping on the counter. Quickly, she moved to sit on the edge of the sofa, closer to Garrett. "That was Grandad. He was the captain."

Garrett sat back in astonishment. "No kidding. Did he tell you much about it?"

"Yes, but only recently," she replied, "which is what made me want to come here and see this place for myself."

Garrett scratched behind his ear. "I haven't told many people about this, but I've been working on a book about Sable Island storms over the centuries. I'd love to interview him, if he'd be willing."

Joanna considered it. "He's a bit shy about sharing. He didn't want anyone on the tour to know who he was because it's not easy for him to talk about it. But you could certainly ask him."

Garrett regarded her intently for a moment. "This morning, you asked Bill about the rose garden and the old main station, and the house buried in sand. Do those places mean something to your grandfather?"

"Yes, but sadly, we couldn't see any of that today."

"But now you're here for *two* days," Garrett reminded her, "thanks to the weather." He paused, thinking. "I could talk to Denise and Darren about delaying the departure tomorrow and giving me some time in the morning to drive you and your grandfather wherever you want to go."

Joanna let out a breath. "Oh, my gosh. That would be amazing. He's been trying to act nonchalant about it, but I know he was disappointed not to see more of the island." Suddenly, she remembered her tea steeping in the pot, and stood up. She went to the kitchen, poured herself a cup, and added a splash of milk.

When she returned to the sofa, Garrett sat forward, elbows on knees. "Can I ask the significance of the rose garden?"

Joanna sipped her tea. "Hmm. I don't feel right sharing his story. Maybe you could ask him tomorrow."

"Sure. I don't mean to pry."

"Not at all. I'm grateful you're willing to drive us around." Joanna ran the pad of her finger around the gold rim of her teacup. "But maybe I could just ask you this *one* question, without betraying his confidence." She lifted her gaze and spoke with purpose. "Do you know anything about Emma Clarkson? She was the daughter of the last superintendent, John Clarkson."

"Yes," Garrett replied. "She was raised here, and she studied the horses. She coauthored an academic paper about them."

"That's right." Joanna's heart did a little dance. "Grandad told me about that, and that she wrote it with the man who became her husband."

Garrett nodded. "The original document is at the Maritime Museum of the Atlantic."

"You're joking." Her shoulders slumped. "We went there yesterday, but we didn't see that."

"It's in the archives. You'd have to make an appointment."

Joanna sighed and sat back. "We'll definitely do that when we return to Halifax." She couldn't help herself. There was another question she was burning to ask. "Do you happen to know what became of Ms. Clarkson after she left Sable for good? Or if she's still alive today?"

Garrett grimaced. "I'm afraid I don't know the answer to that, which I guess makes me a liar, because I told you I knew everything."

Joanna laughed softly. "I'll forgive you, just this once."

As the wind and rain thrashed against the windows and the storm raged over the ocean beyond the dunes, Joanna felt surprisingly safe and sheltered in the cozy common room of the big house at Main Station.

Or perhaps it had more to do with the company. She was intensely aware of Garrett regarding her in the hazy lamplight, and she didn't shy away from staring back at him. She allowed her gaze to roam over his face, down to his neck and shoulders, his strong, masculine hands. How casual and relaxed he looked, sitting back on the sofa in his loose, faded blue jeans and gray cotton sweatshirt.

They were half smiling at each other, and Joanna felt an unspoken communication in it, the open acknowledgment of a mutual attraction.

Garrett's half smile broadened. Seeming almost amused, he checked his watch. "On that note . . ."

What note, exactly? Joanna wondered with a little thrill of pleasure.

"It's almost two thirty," he said. "I should get some sleep if we're going to squeeze in an early tour. How about I meet you here at nine? Be sure to eat a hearty breakfast because we probably won't be back until noon." He stood up to leave.

Joanna stood also. "Thanks so much, Garrett. I can't tell you how much I appreciate this."

"It's my pleasure," he replied, speaking in a captivating way that filled her with excitement.

In that moment, he looked familiar to her, as if she'd known him previously and they'd been close friends for years.

"I'll see you in the morning," he said.

"Sure thing." She watched him walk to the door and don his raincoat. He gave her a wave before he went outside to brave the storm, leaving her standing there in high spirits, keyed up with anticipation for the morning.

~

At 9:00 a.m., the fog was thick as milk. Garrett arrived and escorted Joanna and her grandfather to the Jeep, which was parked next to the carpentry shop. Joanna offered the front seat to her grandad, but he insisted on riding in the back, which gave Joanna a chance, during the drive along the beach, to talk with Garrett about his work.

He told her that the weather station, because of its remote location in the ocean, was a unique and vital component of the national and global weather networks, and he and his crew represented the only year-round presence on the island.

While they talked, her grandfather said nothing from the back seat. He merely gazed out the window at the mist that shrouded everything and made the driving precarious. Garrett had to take it slow.

Eventually, they approached the west end, and Garrett touched his foot to the brake. "This is as close as we're going to get. We'll have to walk from here." He shifted into park, shut off the engine, and turned in the seat to glance over his shoulder. "Ready, Oliver?"

"Yep. Let's crack on."

As soon as they got out of the Jeep and started walking three abreast, Oliver turned to Garrett. "Joanna told me about a book you're working on."

"Yes," Garrett replied. "It's about storms of Sable Island, and there's a section about how they've affected the ships that have run aground here. I'd love to ask you some questions, if you're willing."

Joanna listened while they discussed the wreck of the *Belvedere* and her grandfather's memories of the rescue. They moved through a break in the high dune and reached the hush of the interior. Joanna zipped her jacket tight around her neck to ward off a damp chill as they crossed the fog-shrouded heath.

About ten minutes later, Garrett stopped and looked around. "I'm sorry. It's hard to tell where we are in this fog. I think it's this way."

He started down another sandy path, but Oliver hesitated. "No, it's got to be that way."

Garrett turned back.

"It feels like we're standing inside a cloud," Joanna said.

Aside from the steady roar of the ocean all around them, there was no frame of reference, until the sound of thumping hooves and a few snorts and nickers caused them all to turn in the same direction.

Four horses materialized out of the mist—a bay mare, a young buckskin, a shaggy colt, and an enormous black stallion bringing up the rear.

Garrett spread his arms wide and swept Joanna and Oliver behind him. "Watch out, guys. Back up. Let's clear the path."

They stumbled into a patch of low-lying bayberry bushes to give the horses the right of way, but the band drew to a halt. The mare tossed her head and walked toward them, forcing them to continue backing up.

"I think she wants to say hello," Joanna said, because she was no stranger to horses. She had a good sense of their moods and behaviors.

"Just remember not to touch them," Garrett reminded her.

The young male approached, and Joanna put her hands behind her back. He sniffed her chest, then nuzzled her arm and shoulder and sniffed her ear. His hot breath tickled her neck, and she couldn't help but softly laugh. "Hello, there. It's nice to meet you."

The colt approached and did the same to her other ear, while the stallion seemed unconcerned. He bent his long neck to feed on some beach pea.

"This is something else," Garrett said. "I've never seen this happen before."

"She's always had a way with horses," her grandfather said. "Must be her kind heart. They recognize it."

The young male nuzzled her cheek, and she scrunched up her face, smiling as she squeezed her eyes shut. "You flirt. We hardly know each other."

Then she opened her eyes and looked deeply into his. They each stood calmly, staring at each other on the misty heath.

Joanna found herself awash in a sense of inner calm and a feeling of connection to the earth beneath her feet, the air coursing into her lungs, the blood rushing through her veins, and the continuous pulsing of all her organs. She wanted so badly to touch this particular horse, to stroke his face and neck, to speak soft tones, whisper in his ear. But that would be breaking a law, so she resisted.

The mare nickered and started walking again. The young male hesitated before he finally turned and followed. Within seconds, they all vanished like phantoms into the fog, but Joanna could still hear the soft thumping of their hooves on the sand.

"Blimey," she said, her heart racing. "That was closer than twenty meters."

"I won't tell if you won't," Garrett said, staring at her with fascination. She sensed that his heart was beating fast as well. "That was amazing."

"It sure was. I'm never going to forget it. Not as long as I live."

"Me neither."

They were smiling at each other, and in that moment, Joanna wasn't sure if she was still spellbound by her encounter with the horse or the man before her now. Both, she supposed. It was all part of the same experience, the same special magic.

"Let's follow them," her grandfather suggested, and she had to shake herself back to reality.

Garrett turned to him. "What makes you think they're heading to the rose garden?"

"Nothing," he replied. "But their way is as good as any."

Garrett locked eyes with Joanna, and they shared a look of agreement.

"Works for me," he said.

"Me too," she replied, and felt her attraction to him growing.

They started walking on the same path the horses had chosen, and walked for about five minutes before they came upon a small concrete slab.

"This is it," Garrett said.

Joanna turned to her grandfather, who strode forward with purpose. She followed him a short distance into a vast circular space within a ring of tall tangled rosebushes—alive, but not by any means thriving.

"Yes. This is the place," he said, entranced as he moved toward the concrete bench, where he slowly sat down. He looked around and let his gaze wander.

Joanna—wanting to give him some time alone to reminisce—stood with Garrett outside the garden entrance. Overhead, the sun began to gently penetrate the fog, and Joanna felt its warmth on her face. She closed her eyes and tipped her face upward for a few seconds. When she opened them, she was caught up again in Garrett's steady gaze.

"The sun should burn this fog away by noon," he told her.

"I suppose that's good news," she replied, "that the weather won't keep us here another day."

"I wouldn't mind if it did." Garrett gave her a look.

Joanna allowed the corners of her mouth to curl up in a grin, which was an unambiguous flirtation. "I wouldn't mind if it did either."

Suddenly, her grandfather burst out of the rose garden, his expression drawn with tension. He spoke in a clipped tone. "I need to see the old superintendent's residence."

He strode past them as if he were late for an appointment, without waiting for them to respond.

"Wait, Grandad!" Joanna called after him. "What are you on about?"

Garrett hurried to follow. "That house is off limits to visitors!" he shouted. "It's not safe to go inside, but we can certainly take a look from afar!"

Oliver marched on while she and Garrett scrambled to keep up.

~

"Hold on, Oliver!" Garrett shouted. "You can't go in there! The structure's not sound!"

Joanna halted as she watched her grandfather climb a steep dune toward a rooftop, where three gabled dormer windows poked out of the sand. The shingles were severely weathered and rotting, and the rest of the house was buried in the drift.

"I just need to have a look!" Oliver shouted over his shoulder as he climbed through a window where the glass was blown out.

Fighting panic, Joanna scrambled up the side of the dune. "Grandad! Don't do that!"

"Oliver, stop!" Garrett reached the window ahead of her and peered inside. "Captain Harris!"

Joanna arrived, out of breath, and grabbed hold of Garrett's arm to keep her balance. "Where is he?"

"I don't know. He's not answering." Garrett swung one leg over the windowsill and stepped into what appeared to be a second-story bedroom, where a rusty bed frame remained. He took a penlight out of his jacket pocket and switched it on.

"Stay here, and don't follow me," he said. Then he reached into his other pocket for his keys and handed them to her. "If anything happens—like if the roof collapses—run as fast as you can to the Jeep and get help."

"Are you serious?" she asked, horrified.

"Yes." He moved carefully across the bedroom to an open doorway and shone his light into the hall.

"What do you see?" Joanna asked, leaning in.

"It's dark, but the stairs are clear." Garrett disappeared beyond the door. "Oliver, where are you?"

She heard her grandfather reply. "Down here!"

"I'm coming down the stairs," Garrett told him.

"Please be careful!" Joanna called out as she bent over the window-sill and felt the chill of the interior on her face. It was like a winter cave in there.

She waited anxiously for another update but heard only the muf-fled sounds of Garrett speaking to her grandfather from somewhere inside the subterranean floor. Then she heard a few hard whacks like a hammer.

"What's going on?"

"We're looking for something in the kitchen!" Garrett shouted.

A sudden gust of wind blew grains of sand across Joanna's back, and the house creaked and groaned like an old ship. She quickly drew out of the window and sat back on her heels. Her heart pounded like a bass drum in her chest as she imagined the walls caving in under the weight of all that sand and burying her grandfather and Garrett alive.

"Please hurry up!" she shouted, then waited and listened.

At long last, footsteps tapped up the stairs and her grandfather reentered the bedroom, where the daylight reached him.

"Thank God," she said. "Please come out of there, you numpty!"

She assisted him as he climbed out.

"I'm fine," he grumbled.

"No, you're not. Are you daft? You both could have died!"

Garrett climbed out behind him and flicked sand off his trousers.

"What the devil were you looking for?" Joanna demanded to know.

Oliver held up a small cardboard box. She took it from him, opened it, and found a second, blue velvet box inside. When she opened that one, she nearly fell over onto her backside.

"Sweet Mary, Mother of God." Dazzled by a diamond ring that held more sparkle than the universe, Joanna blinked a few times. Her eyes lifted. "You left this here? What were you thinking?"

"I came here to propose, but when I found out she went back to her husband, I didn't want to bring this home with me. I just wanted to forget about everything. Bury it once and for all. So I put it in a cupboard, thinking this was where it belonged." He waved an arm toward the West Spit. "Just like my ship out there, buried somewhere in the deep."

"They do call this the Graveyard of the Atlantic," Garrett mentioned.

Joanna touched her grandfather's shoulder. "Oh, Grandad. You were grief stricken."

They all stood for a moment in silence, staring down at their feet. Then Oliver asked for the ring back. Joanna gave it to him, and he started skidding down the side of the dune, toward the beach.

"Come on, you lot!" he shouted over his shoulder. "Let's go. We don't want to get stuck here another night!"

Garrett raked his fingers through his hair. "I have no idea what just happened, but he's right. We should get back before the others start cursing us."

He and Joanna jogged to reach a wide sandy path across the heath.

"He was very much in love with Emma Clarkson," she explained to him, "who was separated from her husband at the time. He came back here to propose in '55 but found out that she went back to her husband, so he left. I don't think he ever truly got over her, which is why we're here. He recently became widowed and . . ." She stopped.

"You thought you might be able to find her?"

"Yes, but maybe I'm just a hopeless romantic."

"There are worse things you can be," he replied, and they walked in silence for a while.

"Do you ever go to the mainland?" Joanna asked, not looking forward to saying goodbye to him when they'd only just begun to get to know each other. It wasn't likely she'd ever return to Sable Island. "You must get some vacation time?"

"I do," he replied, "but my Sable Island contract ends next month. Then I'll go back to my old job."

"And what was that?"

"I was a weatherman for a local news station."

Joanna laughed. "Are you having me on? A proper celebrity you must've been. What made you decide to leave all that behind and come here?"

Garrett slid his hands into his pockets. "I'd like to say it was a thirst for adventure, but the truth is my girlfriend dumped me and I was feeling sorry for myself—sitting around doing not much of anything. Then I stumbled across this job posting, which seemed like a good way to avoid bumping into her with her new boyfriend, who just happened to be my boss."

"Oh, blimey . . ."

"Exactly," Garrett replied.

"Any regrets?" Joanna asked. "Because you couldn't have known what you were in for when you took this job."

"I knew nothing," he replied. "But it's been good for me, and now I can barely remember what my girlfriend looks like." He gazed all around and exhaled. "It's incredible here, you have to admit. It kind of wakes you up, you know what I mean? Or maybe that sounds crazy."

"Not crazy at all. I know exactly what you mean. It woke my grandfather up too, all those years ago, and changed his life, even though he didn't end up married to Emma." Still trudging along, Joanna watched her grandad ahead of them as he reached the break in the high dune. "But whether it was Emma and her effect on him," Joanna continued, "or something special about this place that changed him, I'll never know."

"It was probably a bit of both." Garrett led her off the heath, where they had to wade through some marram grass. "I'm certainly going to miss this place when I go. I've been trying to prepare myself mentally for rush hour traffic and crowds in malls. Obnoxious drivers laying on their horns. I might lose my mind."

"It'll be a culture shock, for sure."

They emerged onto the open beach, where seagulls soared and screeched over the booming ocean. Joanna spotted her grandfather standing in the distance, at the water's edge, staring at the horizon.

Garrett slowed his pace. "You know, I was thinking about what you asked me last night—the question I couldn't answer, about whether Emma was still alive or not. Now that I see how determined your grandfather was to find that ring, I'd like to make a few phone calls and see if we can track her down."

Feeling elated, Joanna nearly stumbled over a pile of peat. "Really? That would be so helpful. Thank you. Although . . . Emma might still be married."

"It's possible," Garrett replied. "Or she might be living in Australia, working on her fourth husband."

Joanna laughed, and it felt amazingly good to make light of things.

When they reached the Jeep, she cupped her hands around her mouth and called out to her grandfather. He turned and walked toward them, and she wondered how he was going to feel about a focused and dedicated search for Emma Clarkson.

As they climbed into the vehicle, she decided not to bring it up just yet—in case he resisted the idea and set up roadblocks. Or more importantly, in case there was nothing left to hope for and he only ended up disappointed again.

When the time came to board the helicopter and return to the mainland, Joanna stood on the landing pad and held her hand out to Garrett. "Thank you so much for everything. You really went above and beyond for us."

The sun had come out, and the sky overhead was the color of blue topaz, but shadows were drifting across Joanna's heart. She didn't want to say goodbye.

"It was my pleasure," he replied as he shook her hand. "I wish you could stay a few more days."

"Me too."

Their handshake lasted longer than it should have, and Joanna had trouble tearing her eyes away from his. Eventually, she forced herself to step back and looked down at the ground.

Garrett gave Oliver a casual salute. "Captain Harris. I hope we can speak again soon."

"You have my number," her grandfather replied. "Just remember we're in a different time zone across the pond, and I'm usually early to bed."

"I'll remember," Garrett replied.

Darren called for the passengers to board, so Garrett backed up to the edge of the landing pad and waited until everyone was buckled into their seats with their headsets on. Then he descended the steps and moved along the sandy path toward the beach, where his Jeep was parked.

The chopper's engine rumbled, and the rotor blades began to spin. Joanna looked out the window at the island vegetation whipping in the high winds. The blades spun faster and faster, and soon they rose vertically and hovered for a few seconds over the landing pad before transitioning to forward flight.

Garrett stood on top of the dune, shading his eyes from the sun to look up at them as they flew over. His wavy hair blew in all directions, and as the chopper tilted and banked left to head west over the crescent island, he waved his arm in a wide arc to say goodbye.

Joanna kept her eyes on him until she couldn't see him anymore. Her heart throbbed uncomfortably, and she was surprised by how crest-fallen she felt. She wished they could have stayed longer, for a few more days, exploring. Or not exploring. Just being there. She would have liked to spend more time with Garrett.

Sitting forward and feeling the engine's vibration beneath the soles of her feet, she watched the waves roll over the underwater sandbars that stretched for miles beyond the tip of the island. Though they were plainly visible from the sky, it was easy to see how a ship could run aground on those dangerous hidden shoals.

As the island grew distant, she craned her neck to look back until it was gone completely from view and there was nothing to see but ocean below and sky above. For a while, she watched the sun's reflection on the vast expanse of open water. Then she tipped her head to the side to rest against the cabin wall, closed her eyes, and found herself drifting back to that extraordinary moment in the mist when the horses appeared.

~

Joanna and Oliver returned to their hotel on the Halifax waterfront. As soon as she entered her room, she dropped her backpack on the bed and immediately rang the Maritime Museum of the Atlantic. After requesting an appointment to view Emma's academic paper about the horses of Sable Island, she kept the curator on the phone and asked if he knew anything about the author.

Was she still alive? Did she live in Nova Scotia?

Like Garrett, he couldn't answer the question, but he promised to look into the matter.

~

That night, Joanna made reservations for dinner at The Press Gang, a Halifax restaurant that seemed like a place her grandfather might enjoy. It was known for its historic seafaring atmosphere, its exquisite meat and seafood dishes, a well-stocked oyster bar, and an impressive selection of fine wines and single malt whiskeys.

"Excellent choice," he said as they sat down at a cozy candlelit table beneath a tattered antique British flag behind a glass frame.

They picked up their menus and marveled at the story of the old stones in the walls of the restaurant, which had come from the French Fortress of Louisbourg on the island of Cape Breton. The fort had been dismantled by the British after a siege in 1758, which took place during the Seven Years' War.

Mystified, Joanna ran her fingertips down the gray stones next to their table. Her grandfather did the same. Then they turned their attention to the extensive wine list and selection of entrées on the menu.

"I didn't expect it," she said, "but this trip has turned me into a bit of a history buff."

"It's never too late to embrace a new interest," he replied, then showed her a fine French Bordeaux, which he suggested would pair well with their menu selections of seared duck breast and beef tenderloin.

"On the subject of new interests," Joanna said, setting the menu aside and still feeling a little displaced since their departure from Sable, "I made an appointment for tomorrow morning to read Emma's academic paper about the island horses."

"That's not a new interest," he said. "You're an equine veterinarian. You must have read dozens of papers about horses."

Clearly, he was avoiding the concept of touching pages containing Emma's very own handwritten notes.

"Yes, but this is different, and you know it," Joanna replied. "Emma was someone you cared about. Besides that, I can't stop thinking about that family of horses this morning. They were so friendly. So curious."

He sat back and let out a sigh. "I've been thinking about that too. All of it. It was like a trip back in time. It made it feel like everything happened only yesterday." He looked away, seeming lost in thought. "Life goes by so quickly, Joanna. In the blink of an eye."

She observed and understood his melancholy. He wasn't a young man anymore, but as a result, he was immensely wise. Joanna had learned much from him, and she didn't want to squander a single day by sitting around her flat, watching the telly. She wanted to see new places, try new things, and have experiences that brought her joy—experiences that touched her soul.

She hadn't even known that was possible before her visit to Sable Island, but the world looked new and different to her now. It was filled with a natural beauty that left her enthralled, and she was inspired and uplifted by thoughts of what her future might hold.

~

After dinner, Joanna and her grandfather returned to the hotel, said good night in the hall, and retreated to their separate rooms. Exhausted from the events of the past two days, and sleepy from the Madeira port they'd ordered with dessert, Joanna switched on the light, tossed her room key onto the TV cabinet, and laid her purse on the bed. She rolled her neck, massaged her left shoulder, and couldn't wait to snuggle into the thick duvet and comfortable feather pillows.

She was about to kick off her shoes when she noticed the little red light blinking on the bedside-table telephone. With a spark of curiosity, she moved to pick up the receiver and pressed a few buttons to access the message. It was from Garrett.

Her heart fluttered at the sound of his voice, because he'd been in and out of her thoughts since she'd boarded the helicopter and left Sable Island. Collapsing onto the bed, she listened.

"Hi, Joanna. It's Garrett. I hope you had a good trip back. The island feels a bit empty since you left." He paused for a few seconds, and Joanna thought that might be the end of the message, until he began again. "Yeah, so . . . there's that. I'm not getting much work done around here. I'm kind of playing hooky. But what are they going to do, fire me?" He paused again and cleared his throat. "Anyway . . . I wanted to let you know that I made some phone calls and found out that Emma Clarkson is alive and well and living in Chester. It's a little seaside village on the South Shore of Nova Scotia, about a forty-five-minute drive from Halifax, if you want to pay her a visit."

Joanna sat straight up on the bed.

"I also learned that she's been a psychologist in Halifax for about forty years, and she's somewhat renowned. She's traveled all over the world giving lectures about PTSD and survivor guilt, and she's considered one of the foremost experts in that area. She was a tenured professor at Dalhousie University—she went by Dr. Baxter—but she's retired now." He paused again. "I hope you won't think I overstepped . . . but I asked if she was married. The person I spoke to is a friend of mine who met her at a conference about Sable Island a few years ago, so I felt comfortable asking. Anyway, he said he was pretty sure she didn't have a significant other at the time, but I can't be sure. Who knows what's happened in her life in the past four decades, or past four hours?" Garrett paused. "So, yeah . . . that's all I wanted to tell you, except that I enjoyed meeting you and your grandfather. I'd love to see you both again and catch up on whatever happens next. I hope you'll keep me informed." Another pause. "Now I'm rambling. I should hang up. Take care, and call me back if you want to. I'll be at this number for another month." He left his details and ended the message.

Joanna set the phone down in the cradle and smiled. Her cheeks grew hot, and her insides started to feel like sweet, sticky honey. She flopped onto the bed and stretched her arms out wide.

"I will definitely be calling you back," she said aloud. "But first, I need to call Grandad."

She sat up, picked up the phone, and dialed his room number.

PART SIX

EMMA

CHAPTER 37

Summer 1995

Sometimes Emma wondered if she'd made a terrible mistake when she'd purchased a two-hundred-year-old house. There were dozens of things wrong with it. The plumbing needed updating, and before she'd been able to move in, she'd had to replace the roof. The house inspector had given her a long list of necessary repairs, but nothing could have held her back. She'd fallen madly in love with the house the minute she'd walked through the front door.

Emma hadn't expected to ever live on the water again—not after everything that happened on Sable Island—but something about the little white clapboard house that overlooked Chester's Back Harbour spoke to her. Maybe it was the fresh salty fragrance of the sea or the music of the gulls that took her back to her childhood. Or maybe it was how the floors creaked when she climbed the narrow staircase. It reminded her of her father's footsteps in the early days, when she was young, before he'd lost his leg.

Or it might have been the scent of rosebushes that lined the back path to the water, where an old wooden bench stood under an ancient oak tree.

Whatever the reason, it had felt like home.

~

Since Emma's retirement, she'd learned to take life one day at a time and relax with a cup of tea and a good book. The dishes could wait, and so could the torn wallpaper in the guest bedroom. Her grandchildren were the only ones who slept in that room anyway, every Saturday night when Emma's daughter, Rose, went out on a regular date with her husband. Sometimes Rose felt guilty about leaving her children overnight, to which Emma replied: "Don't be silly. I love having them. And the best thing you can give your children is a happy marriage. So go have fun, and let me enjoy my grandchildren."

This was one such day. Rose was due to arrive within the hour with John and Annette, aged five and seven. In preparation that morning, Emma had driven to the craft store and purchased five tubs of Play-Doh and a colorful plastic mold that squeezed out spaghetti noodles. When they were done with that, she would keep them entertained by playing store in the living room after dark. It was a Saturday-night tradition that began with emptying Emma's kitchen cupboards of canned goods and other nonperishables. Next came the creation of price tags in sticker books and the task of setting out the inventory on imaginary shelves on Emma's coffee table and piano. They all took turns as customer or cashier.

As far as Emma was concerned, for a woman her age who loved both shopping and spending time with her grandchildren, there was no better way to spend a Saturday night. But it was only 3:00 p.m., and Emma still had some pruning to do in the yard before Rose and the children arrived.

After donning her wide-brimmed sun hat, she took the clippers out of the bin, which she would use to trim the rosebushes that were encroaching onto the stone path down to the water. She had just pulled on her garden gloves inside the front porch when she heard a car pull into the gravel driveway. At first, Emma thought it was Rose arriving early, but when she moved to the screen door and stepped outside, she saw it was a blue car she didn't recognize.

An attractive young woman with long dark hair got out and spoke with a British accent. "Good afternoon!" She took a few tentative steps up the driveway and removed her sunglasses. "Are you Emma Clarkson?"

"I used to be," Emma replied, uncertain.

The young woman touched a finger to her temple. "I'm so sorry. Yes, of course. You're Emma Baxter now. You worked in the psychology department at Dalhousie University? Am I in the right place?"

"Yes."

The woman stood speechless in Emma's driveway, staring at her with what appeared to be a mixture of delight and fascination.

"Can I help you with something?" Emma asked. She was still gripping her hedge clippers and was beginning to feel a little impatient, because the clock was ticking and those rosebushes weren't going to prune themselves.

The passenger-side door opened, and a man stepped out. He was an older gentleman, and Emma watched him in the blinding sunlight that reflected off the shiny front bumper of the car. Something about the way he moved was familiar, and it made her body go weak—though consciously she had no idea who he was.

Then he spoke her name. "Emma."

The voice. She knew it. It was like something out of her dreams. Her breath came short, and she dropped the hedge clippers onto the brick steps with a noisy clatter.

"Oliver Harris," he said, introducing himself as he approached. He paused at the bottom of her steps with one hand on the wrought iron railing. "Do you remember me?"

What a ridiculous question. Emma laid her hand over her heart. "Oliver . . ." She could barely speak beyond that one single word. "I thought . . . I thought you were dead."

"Quite a few others thought the same thing," he replied. "But here I am, still alive, which has to be some kind of miracle."

With wide eyes, Emma stared at him, dumbstruck, until the young woman moved to stand beside him.

"It's nice to meet you at last," she said, breaking the spell. "I'm Joanna, Oliver's granddaughter. He's told me a lot about you and Sable Island. We just came from there yesterday."

Emma turned her eyes to Joanna and saw the resemblance. She had the same dark wavy hair and blue eyes. "You visited Sable Island?"

Joanna nodded cheerfully, and Emma's eyes shot to Oliver's. "You went there as well?"

"Yes," he replied in that deep, husky voice that touched something painfully raw in the depths of her soul. At the same time, she was aware of a rise in her body temperature, which she'd learned to recognize in stressful situations. Emma removed her sun hat.

"It's been so many years," Oliver said, sounding slightly dazed. "It feels like another lifetime."

"It does." She wanted to be polite, but inside, her heart was icing over with the realization that the man she'd once loved with every inch of her young heart, body, and soul—the man she'd practically martyred for the past forty years—was alive and standing before her. He hadn't been killed in an explosion on the sea, yet he had never come back for her as he'd promised.

Emma began to descend the steps and spoke cooly to him. "How is this possible?"

They stared at each other for a moment, and her heart trembled. She felt dizzy, like she'd fainted and fallen into the past. Maybe he sensed it, because he stepped forward and took her into his embrace.

Emma went stiff as he hugged her and whispered in her ear. "I'm so sorry. I'm sorry for everything."

Those words—more than forty years too late—caused something to buck and kick inside of her, and she drew back in anger.

"What happened to you?" She recalled all the nights she'd spent crying into her pillow, fearing that he'd abandoned her when she'd needed him most. She'd never felt more alone than in those final days, just before she'd told her father the truth about her pregnancy.

She'd been so angry with Oliver. But then the news of his death had come . . .

"I was told your ship hit a mine and there was an explosion," she said, "and no one survived."

"Most of that is true," he told her. "There was an explosion, and my ship was blown halfway to smithereens. But we got into a lifeboat and made it to dry land, where we were stranded for months."

She stared at him, blinking rapidly, afraid that her knees might give way. "Months?"

"Yes, and by the time I returned to Sable," he continued, "you were gone. You'd reconciled with your husband."

Emma couldn't make sense of this. She shook her head in dismay. "No. Who told you I went back to Logan?"

"The man on the island," Oliver said, as if that explained everything.

"What man?"

"The meteorologist. His name was . . . I'm sorry. It escapes me now."

Emma was still reeling from the appearance of her beloved Captain Harris, alive after all these years, stepping out of a shiny rental car and standing in her driveway. She took a few steps back. "Logan and I divorced after he was released from prison. He stayed a part of Matthew's life, but that was all. And he's been dead for more than fifteen years."

Oliver's face turned red, and his expression slowly darkened to a frown.

His granddaughter, Joanna, cleared her throat, and Emma realized she'd forgotten the young woman was standing there, listening to all this. The whole world, aside from herself and Oliver, seemed to have disappeared in the past three minutes.

"It's quite hot out here," Joanna said. "Why don't you two go inside and talk for a while. I can pop out to the shops and come back later."

Emma was indeed perspiring, and she needed to cool down. Or sit. Or take a few deep breaths and regain her calm. "Yes. We should go into the house."

Joanna touched her grandfather's arm. "I'll be back in an hour or so?"

Oliver met Emma's gaze questioningly, and she nodded in agreement. Everything was a blur after that. Joanna got into the car and backed out of the driveway, and Oliver followed Emma up the front steps, where she picked up the pruners and set them on a chair inside the porch. The next thing she knew, she and Oliver were standing in her kitchen.

"Would you like a cold drink?" she asked out of politeness.

"Yes, thank you."

It was obvious to Emma that Oliver was unsettled by her standoffishness. The whole situation took her back to that day in her kitchen on Sable Island, when she was baking bread and he'd walked through her door, years after breaking her heart. For the *first* time. What did that make this one? Heartbreak number three? Should she be keeping score? Or would that just be cruel self-punishment?

Emma opened the refrigerator door, took out a large unopened bottle of spring water, and set it on the counter. The task gave her a much-needed moment to collect herself as she filled two tumblers with ice from the freezer, picked up the bottle, and poured.

Half-dazed, she handed the glass to Oliver, resisting a brief urge to splash the water in his face.

"Thank you." He accepted it and sipped it thirstily. Then he set it down and rubbed the back of his hand over his forehead.

Their eyes connected.

"I'm in shock," Emma said frostily. "I can't stop looking at you. You're older, but you still look the same."

"So do you. You're just as beautiful as you ever were."

The flattery hit her like a brick, and she felt a fresh rush of bitterness toward him. She resented him for having allowed her to idolize him for the past forty years, for causing her to imagine that their love was something special—that he'd been her soulmate, the great love of her life, tragically ripped away.

"Don't say that to me," she said. "You don't have the right, because you broke your promise."

"I know. I'm sorry, Emma."

"Stop saying you're sorry. You said you'd come back for me, but you never did."

"I *did* come back," he reminded her. "It just took me longer, but I had no control over that. I nearly died on that island, and it took me months to recover. When I finally did make it back, I was told you'd gone back to your husband. That you didn't wait for me. What was I supposed to do?"

She scoffed in disbelief. "How could you even believe that I would take Logan back? I told you I didn't love him. All I wanted was *you*, and I was devastated when I thought you'd died. Now I find out that you were alive the entire time?"

Oliver frowned as he tried to explain. "I thought it would be selfish to disrupt your life again. I thought it best to leave you alone and let you move on."

"With Logan?" She laughed indignantly. "Did you completely forget what happened between us in the rose garden? Or did it not mean that much to you?"

"It meant the world."

"Then why didn't you come after me? Why didn't you at least try to fight for me?"

He stared at her a moment, blinking rapidly, before his gaze dropped to the floor. "I suppose I didn't have any fight left in me, after everything that happened."

An unexpected wave of pity washed over Emma. "Not even for us?"

He still did not look up.

"That's a shame," she said, thinking of the daughter she'd given birth to, a daughter he knew nothing about. "Because you missed out on something wonderful, and not just the life we could have had together."

He finally looked up. "What do you mean?"

She paused because she knew she was about to deliver a heavy blow, but she had to tell him. She couldn't keep it secret. Rose could arrive at any moment.

"When we were together in the rose garden . . ." Her throat closed over a jagged lump, and her voice shook. "The reason I was so desperate for you to come back was because I was pregnant."

He stared vacantly at her while the words floated on a rolling fog between them.

In that moment, Emma realized with a touch of shame that there was a part of her that had enjoyed delivering the news. The psychoanalyst in her questioned if she'd ever truly gotten over the old sting of this man's first rejection of her—when he'd left her humiliated on the beach before boarding the supply ship with no intention of ever returning. Maybe that rejection had been festering inside her for years, even when she'd believed him to be dead. Maybe, deep down, she'd become just as bitter and vengeful as Abigail McKenna, and today, seeing Oliver again, she had morphed into a hissing cat with claws.

Emma felt suddenly humbled. She was supposed to be an expert in her field, but who was she to sit in rooms with broken souls and help them sort through their traumas? She knew every tool available for coping with emotional scars, and for years, she'd handed them out in her office every day.

But here stood Oliver Harris, in her kitchen, embedded like shrapnel into her flesh. She was still wounded, like every one of her patients, and she didn't have the first clue how to use any of the tools at her disposal. All she knew was the timeworn pain of her loss, and a faint recognition of his.

~

Standing in Emma's kitchen, Oliver was aware of the ocean lapping onto the beach beyond her back lawn and the sound of birds chirping in the treetops outside the open window. But he couldn't seem to speak or move. His mind was running riot through the past forty years.

Then it struck him—what Emma had said. They'd had a child. Years had gone by, years that could never be recaptured, a whole life lost to him. There was so little time left, no way to make up for it. He was seventy-seven years old. An old man.

"We have a daughter." Emma's words pulled him out of a strange and cold inertia. "Her name is Rose, and she's coming over soon. She's bringing her two children."

"Grandchildren." His thoughts exploded. He had a daughter he knew nothing about.

Oh, God! What a wretched failure he was as a man! For abandoning the only woman he'd ever truly loved. Why? *Why* hadn't he fought for her? Fought for his own happiness?

"Are you all right?" Emma asked, looking concerned.

He stood a moment, clenching and unclenching his fists, his body tense, his chest aching with all the could-have-beens. "I need to sit down."

"Of course." Emma directed him to the kitchen table, helped him onto a chair, and sat down across from him.

This news had hit him like a death, a loss he would mourn forever. There would be no peace for him after this. No superficial contentment, which had become an adequately comfortable bed for him since he'd reconciled with Mary. But now, there would only be regret.

"What's she like?" he asked. "Our daughter, Rose?"

Emma's expression warmed, which provided some consolation, because at least she was happy in her love for their daughter.

"She's a beautiful person," Emma said. "Smart, kind, generous. She was a schoolteacher until she had her first baby, and she's been a stay-at-home mom ever since. Her husband works in construction, and he's a good man. A good father. They have a cozy home."

"That's good," he replied, empty of breath. "Do you have any pictures?"

"Yes." Emma stood, left the kitchen, and returned with a framed photograph. "This is Rose and her family, last year when they took a trip to Cape Breton. That's David and their two children, John and Annette."

"John. Named after your father?"

"Yes. He passed away in '89. It was standing room only at his funeral."

Oliver looked up at her wearily. "I'm so sorry. What did he do after he left Sable Island?"

Emma sat down at the table again. "First, he retired with a government pension. Then he married Ruth, the woman I once told you about who was like a mother to me. That was a happy occasion. But Papa liked to keep busy, so he went into local politics." Emma stood up again. "Let me get some photo albums. I'll show you more pictures."

Suddenly Oliver was back in Emma's kitchen on Sable Island, with the smell of bread baking in the oven and a deep hope for reconciliation—or of friendship, at least—after a hurtful goodbye in the past. Here they were again, slowly reconnecting. He hoped.

She returned with an armful of photo albums, and Oliver was grateful to spend the next half hour at her table, flipping through plastic-wrapped pages that covered most of the past half century. They included Emma's early life on Sable Island, but Oliver was most interested in the pictures of Rose, from her birth to the present day.

There was only one picture of Matthew with Logan. "Did they see each other much?" Oliver asked.

"Not really," Emma replied. "Logan moved back to Saskatchewan when Matthew was ten, but they wrote letters, and Logan came to visit every few years. But I think the main reason he stayed away was because he was afraid of my father." She gave Oliver a telling look. "Papa was very protective of us."

The sound of a car rolling onto the driveway caused each of them to look up. Oliver realized how warm and humid the afternoon had become. Cicadas were buzzing loudly in the yard, and he was perspiring.

"I wonder if that's Rose." Emma stood to look out the front window. "Yes, it is." She hesitated. "Oh, goodness. Would you mind waiting here while I talk to her first? This is going to be a shock. I'd like to prepare her."

"I understand."

"I'll bring her in afterwards," Emma promised him reassuringly.

He nodded, and she walked out the front door.

Almost immediately, he stood up and moved to the living room to watch from the open window. Outside, two rambunctious children spilled out of a blue minivan and tore across the front lawn to a tire swing in the shade of the trees.

A woman got out of the driver's seat. *Dear God.* This was Rose. His daughter. Strikingly beautiful, with a face like her mother's, and dark hair like his.

"I'm so sorry, Mom," she said. "They've had too much sugar. They'll probably crash early, though."

Oliver stood in a stupor, his body and soul drenched in awe as he watched Emma hug her daughter and whisper something in her ear. He wished overwhelmingly that he could have held Rose as an infant, seen her as a toddler . . . a child . . . a young woman. He'd missed everything—her first words, her wedding day. What had she been like all her life? Had she always been this happy, like she was outside in the yard today? His heart was a bottomless well of questions and wishes.

Emma and Rose stepped apart. Rose looked directly up at Oliver in the window, and his heart throbbed agonizingly. He reached a trembling hand to the back of an upholstered chair to steady himself on this staggering wave of sorrow.

~

"He's been alive all this time?" Rose asked, keeping her voice low.

Emma watched her daughter's expression and knew she had not yet fully comprehended everything this would mean for her—that there was a man with whom she and her children would need to become acquainted, and it might cause confusion, anger, and hurt. But Rose had always been careful to think things through before reacting emotionally.

Emma glanced over her shoulder at Oliver in the window, and he retreated.

"This is unreal," Rose said. "Are you okay, Mom?"

It was just like her daughter to think of others before herself. "Yes," Emma replied. But truthfully, she felt like a leaf floating and spinning on the wind. She took hold of Rose's arm. "Let's take a walk around back."

Together they strolled past the children at the tire swing and reached the sloping lawn that overlooked the water. It was a hot, humid day, and the harbor was flat and still, a perfect mirror that reflected the evergreens on the far shore.

"Mom," Rose said urgently. "You must have fainted when you saw him. And where has he been all this time? Please don't tell me he had amnesia and only just remembered who we are. *My God*. What does this mean? What does he expect is going to happen?"

Clearly the situation had begun to sink in, and for that, Emma was glad. "I don't know, and I'm trying to be sensible. I want to think of you and the children and give you the chance to get to know him, if that's what you want."

They both faced the water and said nothing for a moment while they watched a sailboat in the distance.

"But before we start any of that," Emma finally said, "there's something you need to know."

"What is it?"

Emma faced her daughter. "You're welcome to spend time with him. I would never discourage that, but I might need to set some boundaries."

"In what way?"

Emma felt herself retreating into a state of sensible caution, which she should have employed all those years ago. "I can't do this again," she said. "I don't think I can allow him into my life."

Rose regarded her with concern. "I'm surprised to hear you say that. The way you've always talked about him . . . you said he was the great love of your life and that he was the most handsome man you'd ever seen, and you had a soulful connection that most people could only dream about. Now here he is, back from the dead, and you don't want to see him?"

"No."

Rose shook her head in disbelief. "Then please explain it to me. Was all that made up, so that I'd feel good about who my father was?"

"No, of course not," Emma replied. "It wasn't made up. But I said those things when I thought he had a good excuse for not showing up that Christmas."

"Because he was *dead*? That's a pretty high bar, Mom."

"Don't be facetious," Emma said scoldingly.

"I'm not. But have you talked to him about what happened? Asked him why he didn't come?"

"Of course I talked to him. He told me he went back to Sable Island eventually, but some idiot told him that I'd gotten back together with Logan, which wasn't true. But he believed it and left. Seriously, I don't understand. He knew how much I loved him. I thought it was clear when we said goodbye that final time." She paused a moment and exhaled sharply. "Oh, it doesn't matter now. All that matters is that he turned straight around and went back to his wife in England."

"The one who cheated on him?" Rose asked incredulously.

"Yes." Emma glanced back at the house and wondered if Oliver was watching them from a different window. "The bottom line is . . . oh, I don't know what I'm saying. All I know is that there's been too much water under the bridge for him and me. He's put me through enough hell. I can't do that again." She faced Rose. "But it's different for you and the children. He's your father and their grandfather, and I think it's important that you at least meet him and decide for yourselves if you want him to be a part of your lives." She stood up a little straighter. "As for me, I'm done with that. I just want to be on my own."

The air was windless, thick, and muggy. Rose lifted her long hair off her shoulders and fanned the back of her neck with her hand.

"Really, Mom, you should hear yourself. You said the exact same things about Logan. You told me there was too much water under the bridge, but you understood that he needed to be a part of Matthew's life, but he'd put you through hell. Yada yada yada."

"Rose," Emma said with a note of impatience. "This is more complicated than that."

"Damn right, it's complicated," Rose replied. "So maybe you should go back in there and talk to Oliver some more before you hit the reject button." She waved her arm toward the house. "Who knows what he's been through? Two shipwrecks and a wife who cheated on him. Not to mention the Second World War. You're a therapist, Mom. A PTSD expert. To be honest, I'm a little shocked at how you're so quick to judge him."

"I'm not *judging* him," Emma replied, feeling defensive.

Rose backed off a little. "Maybe not, but you're not trying to understand the situation either."

For a moment, Emma fiddled with her locket and found herself thinking again of that day on the beach when he'd left her humiliated and heartbroken the first time.

Why did she keep going back there in her mind?

Oh, she knew why. Ever since that day, she'd been internalizing the grief from every single loss in her life.

"Fine," she said. "I'll talk to him some more. It's not like I can avoid it anyway. He's standing in my kitchen, waiting for me to introduce the two of you." She turned to Rose. "Are you ready for that?"

"Yes." Rose glanced back at the house. "I want very much to meet him."

CHAPTER 38

Startled by the squeaky hinges on the front screen door as it swung open and slammed shut, Oliver looked up from the kitchen table. He'd been leafing through Emma's photo albums to keep from watching out the windows.

Emma appeared, looking lovely in her faded jeans and oversize white shirt, and he was surprised at how his heart and body calmed at the sight of her as she led their daughter into the room. Their daughter!

"Hello," Rose said warmly. "Captain Harris. I've heard a lot about you."

His anxieties and regrets, like waves, retreated again. In their place came a rush of strong love as he took in the sight of her. "Sadly, I've heard very little about *you*," he replied. "Only what your mother could tell me today, before you arrived. But there wasn't much time." Not nearly enough.

Rose gave him an encouraging nod, and he sensed by her demeanor that she was openhearted and forgiving, without hostility toward him. It came as a relief, because she was a mother—she could just as easily refuse to meet him altogether, to protect her children from developing affections for a stranger who might later walk out on them and never return. That was, after all, the thrust of his history with Emma.

"From what I understand," Rose said, "it's been a day full of surprises. But don't worry. We have plenty of time to get to know each other."

She strode forward, embraced him, and rested her cheek on his shoulder.

Oliver's entire being shuddered with yet more love, and his heart broke wide open painfully. As he held his daughter for the first time, and heard his grandchildren's laughter outside, he wondered how he would ever get on with his life after this. The children were running circles around the tire swing in the shade of a giant maple tree, and as he watched them through the kitchen window and hugged Rose, he felt as if he were floating dizzyingly on a cloud, but at any moment he might fall to earth and land with a punishing blow. His insides flared hotly with panic and a terrible sense of regret about a decision that could never be reversed. The lost years were gone forever. He would never get them back.

"I'm so glad to finally meet you," Rose said, stepping back, and Oliver could have wept. "Honestly, it feels like a miracle."

When he tried to speak, his voice shook. "I can't believe it," he said, wishing overwhelmingly that he had the power to turn back the clock. If only he could return to that day on Sable Island when he'd surrendered to his sorrow. If only he'd been stronger.

All he could do now was apologize. "I'm so sorry I wasn't here for you."

Rose reached for his hand and regarded him with warmth and forgiveness. "You didn't know about me," she said. "But you're here *now*. That's what matters. And I feel blessed."

"Me too."

"I can't wait for you to meet my children," Rose added. "Would you like to come outside and say hello?"

He glanced achingly at Emma, who wiped a tear from her cheek. "Yes. I'd like that very much." Then he stepped forward and followed his daughter out the front door.

~

An hour later, with Rose's wise words still echoing in her mind, Emma walked beside Oliver down the stone path to the beach.

Who knows what he's been through? To be honest, Mom, I'm a little shocked at how you're so quick to judge him.

Again, Emma found herself thinking about poor Abigail McKenna and how she'd not been able to let go of painful things. She'd let them fester and never confided in anyone, or sought help. Emma wished she could go back there, knowing what she knew now, and understand Abigail better, perhaps help her work through her pain. But sadly, there was no going back.

"I'm sorry," Emma finally said.

"For what?" Oliver asked.

"That I was so angry with you when you first arrived."

"You had every right to be," he replied. "I broke my promise."

She glanced up at his profile, still as strikingly handsome as ever. "But you were told something that wasn't true. And you'd been through a terrible ordeal, and probably other ordeals from the war that I know nothing about. So . . . whatever your reasons were for going home to England, I can't judge you. And I certainly don't believe you *deserved* to miss out on the life of your child. That's too great a punishment."

They reached the bottom of the path and paused at the stone steps that led to the rocky beach.

"You should be proud of Rose," Oliver said. "She's an incredible young woman. You raised her well." He descended the three steps, then turned and looked up. "But I'll never be free of my regrets. I shouldn't have given up on us that day."

He offered his hand to her, and when Emma looked down at his open palm—at all the lines and calluses that were so familiar to her, even after all these years—she wanted to cry her eyes out. Why had this happened? What had either of them ever done to deserve so much bad luck and disappointment?

But it wasn't all bad, she supposed, as she placed her hand in his and stepped onto the beach. At least not for her. She'd raised two beautiful children, and their love had always been enough. More than enough. It was Oliver who had been deprived, an ocean away from his daughter. And despite her own perpetual heartbreak, she pitied him deeply.

He let go of her hand and bent to pick up a flat stone, which he rubbed between his thumb and the pads of his fingers. Then he threw it like a spinning disk that skipped six times across the surface of the water.

"Well done," Emma said, impressed.

"That was a perfect skipping stone," he replied.

They walked in silence for a while, and Emma felt like she was back on Sable Island. Today, she was reliving an experience from her youth—the emotional and intellectual exhilaration from her walks on the beaches with Oliver, when it was all so new. It was as if he had stepped out of the past and reminded her of the young girl she used to be.

But it was Rose—older and wiser than her years—who had reminded Emma of who she truly was: A psychologist. A lifelong student of the human condition. Emma had felt that calling long before she'd ever met Oliver Harris on that fateful day, when he was pulled from a deadly shipwreck and dragged onto her shore.

She wished that her younger self could see who she had become: a retired psychoanalyst with a triumphant career behind her, a cozy house on the sea, and grandchildren who kept her busy and entertained. She wished that she could have known, back then, how beautifully her life would turn out. She might have spent less time crying over what she couldn't have.

"You know," Oliver said as they strolled leisurely along, "for years I fantasized about what our lives might have looked like if I hadn't hit that mine."

Emma raised a hand to shade her eyes from the sun. "I did the same thing," she confessed.

They continued walking, and she breathed in the pungent but pleasant aroma of kelp on the rocks at low tide.

"I don't know what *you* imagined," Oliver continued, "but I always liked to think of us getting married and having children and living on Sable Island. I even thought that I might become superintendent one day, when your father retired."

"That would have been a nice life for us," she replied. "I sometimes dreamed about the same thing, but I knew it was just fantasy, because even if you had come back that Christmas, the lifesaving station was doomed."

Oliver bent to pick up another flat stone and skipped it across the water. "We would have survived that," he said. "Because I also imagined supporting you to get the education you'd always wanted. I saw us living in Oxford or Cambridge."

"University of Oxford?" she replied, her eyebrows flying up. "How ambitious of us."

He smiled back at her. "But clearly, in real life, you had all the support you needed right here. I saw the diplomas and awards in your den. Congratulations, Dr. Baxter. You did well."

"Thank you." The compliment filled her with pride.

They reached the west point and stepped carefully from one large beach boulder to another, then stopped on a flat outcropping.

"I suppose it was fate that had other plans for us," Emma said. "We weren't meant to be together back then, for all sorts of reasons. We weren't lucky that way."

He pondered that notion while they watched a fishing boat motor toward open water. "Not many people were lucky after the war. But bad luck touches all of us, even during peacetime."

The sun moved behind a cloud, and the harbor turned gray. The temperature cooled, and ripples appeared on the surface of the water.

Emma touched Oliver's arm. "Maybe we should start over. I've already apologized for being rude when you first arrived. But now I know that we were both told things that weren't true. You thought I went back to Logan, and I thought you were dead. If I'd known you were alive, I would have tried to contact you again. Which makes me wonder . . . Didn't your wife ever tell you about the letters I sent?"

Oliver turned to her, his brow furrowed. "What letters?"

Emma stared at him, processing his response, thinking back to that day in Ruth's living room, when she'd learned of his alleged death.

Slowly, Emma began to grasp the true course of events, the source of their lifelong separation—the rudder that had steered them away from each other.

"I wrote to you about being pregnant," she said. "I sent a number of desperate letters to your flat. That's how I learned about your death, because your wife read them and wrote back to inform me."

He frowned and shook his head with confusion. "You learned about the explosion from Mary?"

"Yes."

"But when I came home, she never mentioned any letters from you. Are you telling me that she knew you were expecting my child?"

Emma was overcome with dismay. "Yes."

Oliver stared at her in shock. "That can't be."

Emma closed her eyes and said nothing. She'd thought she understood everything before, but this was something else. She gave him time to comprehend the facts and accept them, as she was doing.

"In all the years we were together," he said, "she never told me anything about that."

A breeze blew in from the east, and small whitecaps appeared on the harbor.

Oliver bowed his head and grabbed great clumps of his hair in both fists. "Mary, you didn't." His voice was low and gruff with ire.

Over the years, Emma had counseled many patients about how to cope with shock, anger, and the fact that they had been lied to. But now she, too, was a victim of manipulation. She and Oliver, together, had lived separate lives with no knowledge of the truth. And it was his unfaithful wife, Mary, who had misled them both.

All Emma wanted to do in that moment was call Mary directly and rail at her with hateful words and threatening accusations. How could she have kept a father away from his child, even if it was a child born out of wedlock?

"Where is your wife now?" she asked in a threatening tone.

"Dead," Oliver replied numbly.

His response came down on Emma like a hammer. She couldn't form words.

Meanwhile, Oliver's eyes were wild. He was clenching his teeth as he spoke. "She should have told me. It would have changed how our lives turned out. All of us."

"Maybe that's what she was afraid of," Emma replied.

They stared at each other, dumbfounded, while the wind grew stronger and hissed through the evergreens.

"This is all my fault," Oliver said. "I shouldn't have lost faith, and I shouldn't have trusted my wife not to do something like that. She'd betrayed me before. Why didn't I at least try to see you? Why in God's name did I give up?"

Emma shook her head. "I don't know."

"Maybe that's what finally broke me," he said. "Hearing that you'd moved on."

She touched his arm. "But I didn't move on. And it wasn't all your fault, how things turned out. It was a postwar world. We were surrounded by trauma from all directions. You, especially, Oliver. Dear God! What you'd been through and survived! You were right. It's a miracle you're alive today, and I'm amazed."

He cupped his forehead in his hand. "But what does it matter now?"

She grabbed hold of his forearm and shook it. "Oh, Oliver. Don't be foolish. We're still here, aren't we? What good can come from regretting the decisions we made when we were young and didn't know anything? Maybe we need to consider how lucky we've been to have spent our lives with our children, even though you're late to be meeting Rose.

But it's never *too* late. And you didn't abandon Lydia and Arthur. You were a good father to them, present in their lives, and now you have grandchildren. Joanna clearly loves you."

They stared at each other for an emotionally charged moment. Oliver's shoulders rose and fell as he exhaled. Then he closed his eyes. "We can't have it all, can we."

"No," she replied. "Sometimes we have to choose one path over another, and live with that choice, and be happy with it."

Oliver opened his eyes. He looked up at Emma, who stood on a higher slab of stone. He held his hand out to her, and she stepped lightly across the flat rock as he escorted her down to the pebbly beach, where they strolled to the water's edge. For a while, they watched sailboats on the harbor and seagulls in the sky, and listened to the waves that lapped gently onto the shore.

Oliver turned to Emma. "I retrieved something from Sable Island," he said, "and I'd like for you to have it, no strings attached. But it was meant for you."

"What is it?" she asked, curious.

He reached into his jacket pocket, withdrew a small box, and handed it to her. She opened it and gasped at the sight of a large princess-cut diamond ring, set in a gold band. Breathless with shock, Emma covered her mouth with her hand.

"It's the ring I promised you," Oliver said. "When I went back for you, I left it there."

"Where?" she asked. "On Sable Island?"

"Yes. I put it in a cupboard in that old house that was half-buried in sand. Do you remember when you took me there?"

"Of course. I remember everything."

"Well . . . the house is almost gone now," he said. "Only the roof and dormers are still sticking out of the sand. But miraculously, the ring was still there."

"You went inside? Oliver, what were you thinking?"

He waved a dismissive hand. "I know. I shouldn't have."

"Is that why you went back to Sable?" Emma asked. "To retrieve it?"

He shook his head. "No. I'd assumed it was long gone. But when I got there and walked into the rose garden, it felt like everything happened only yesterday. Something came over me, and I had to go and look for it."

Emma admired the ring for a moment, how it sparkled in the sunlight. "My goodness, Oliver. It's stunning. But I can't possibly accept it." She closed the box and held it out to him. "You should give it to one of your children or grandchildren."

"But it was meant for *you*," he replied, sounding baffled by the mere notion of giving it to anyone else.

Emma hesitated, then rubbed her thumb over the top of the velvet box. "Well . . . I suppose I could at least try it on."

She opened the box, withdrew the ring, and slid it onto her finger. It fit perfectly. When she held up her hand to admire it, the diamond sparkled like a thousand exploding stars. Her heart nearly gave out at the beauty of it, and she exclaimed "Oh!" and completely lost her breath.

But it was so much more than just a beautiful ring. Suddenly Emma was twenty-seven again and feeling the long-awaited rapture of her beloved captain's return—just as she'd dreamed about for days, weeks, and years.

She looked up at Oliver, and he smiled at her.

Emma's every emotion, even those she'd thought long dead, rose up and flooded over her walls. She bowed her head, covered her face with her hands, and wept.

Oliver took her into his arms. "I know, I know." He rubbed her back and whispered gentle words of comfort in her ear.

When she finally regained her composure, she stepped back. "I should show you this," she said, then reached into the top of her blouse to withdraw the gold chain she still wore around her neck, with her mother's locket and his signet ring.

"My word. You still have it."

"Yes. I never stopped wearing it. Wait. That's not true. I did take it off for a while when I was angry with you. But then I put it back on."

She reached out, took hold of his hand, turned it over, and studied how their fingers entwined. These were the hands of a ship's captain, strong and sure, but they were also the hands of a gentleman. A husband. A father. An honorable man. These were loving hands, and she'd never forgotten the joy of his touch on that precious day in the rose garden. It had remained forever in her heart, a cherished memory like no other.

Somewhere in the distance, a ship's bell rang. Oliver raised Emma's hand to his lips and kissed the back of it. When her eyes lifted and she met his handsome gaze, the past came rushing forward. It coursed toward her like a fast wave and swept her off her feet.

This time, Emma surrendered to the incoming tide. She simply let herself float.

EPILOGUE

"I can't believe you made it."

Joanna practically skipped across the floor in Gatwick Airport as she made her way to meet Garrett at the baggage claim. At the sight of him, after all this time, she felt a little dizzy. He wore a brown leather jacket and faded blue jeans, and his hair was cut shorter since she'd last seen him—which was from the air when the helicopter blades were blowing his gorgeous wavy locks in all directions.

Seeing him again was like some kind of drug. He was more handsome than she remembered, despite the fact that he'd just come off the red-eye.

Joanna held out her arms, and they embraced like two people who had known each other a lifetime.

"I can't believe it either," he said, burying his face in her neck. "Thank God there were no delays. I didn't sleep a wink on the flight."

"I couldn't sleep either," she replied, still hugging him. "I couldn't wait for you to get here."

Garrett and Joanna had written to each other using webmail every day since her return to London, and they'd spoken on the telephone once a week, usually on Sundays, taking turns with the long-distance charges.

During that time, Joanna had shared everything about herself with Garrett. She'd been as open and honest as anyone could be with another human being, and she felt as if she knew everything about him as well—his favorite bands, favorite foods, and, most importantly, his deepest values and his goodness. He had sent her photographs of his enormous, close-knit family, who lived in various towns all over Nova Scotia, and had made it clear that he wanted her to return someday and meet everyone, because he'd told them all about her.

In the airport that day, there was no point denying their feelings for each other. They'd fallen madly in love from a distance. And for Joanna—seeing him again at last, in the flesh, was better than Christmas.

They stepped apart, and he cupped her face in both his hands. "I can't believe I'm looking at you right now."

"Me neither." Her heart was on fire.

Garrett pulled her into his arms again, held her briefly. He then took hold of her hand and led her to a tall potted tree fern next to a post, where they could hide from the crowds and finally kiss the way they wanted to.

When his lips found hers, the kiss was like heaven. All she wanted was more of it. More of *him*.

An alarm sounded at the baggage carousel, and the conveyor belt began to move. Flight passengers hurried to collect their suitcases, but Joanna and Garrett were not yet done saying hello to each other.

It was not until the carousel slowed to a halt, and most of the passengers had collected their bags and departed, that Garrett and Joanna finally moved away from the potted plant and picked up his suitcase.

"You'll probably need to sleep for a few hours when we get back to my flat," Joanna said. "I wouldn't mind taking a nap myself. Then we can go out for dinner later. I made reservations for us at Rules. It's that restaurant I told you about, in Covent Garden."

"Sounds perfect."

"And I can't wait to show you around London," Joanna said.

"I'd love to see where you work," he replied as he wheeled his suitcase behind him.

"I was planning to take you to the clinic tomorrow. Then we'll visit the horses at the Royal Mews."

He reached for her hand. "I honestly don't care what we do. I'm just happy to be here."

"I'm happy too."

They walked to the train station in the airport, moved through the turnstiles, and rode the escalator down to the platform. The next train was due to arrive in three minutes, so they found a spot to wait near the yellow line.

"How's your grandad?" Garrett asked.

"Good as gold," she replied. "Except that we're still working through what Nana did—keeping that secret from him all their lives. I wish she was still around so that I could ask her about it, but it's not possible."

"She must have really wanted to hold on to him," Garrett said.

"Yes, but it was so incredibly selfish of her, not to tell him. How did she ever sleep at night? And even when she knew she was dying, she still didn't tell him." Joanna huffed in frustration. "I've been driving myself crazy feeling angry about it, but what's the point in that? I have to just lay it to rest because we can't change it, and we'll never know what was going on in her head." She peered up the tracks again, watching for the train. "But enough about that. He still hasn't booked a return flight from Nova Scotia, but he can't stay there forever. There are laws."

"Maybe he and Emma will get married finally," Garrett suggested, "and he'll become a Canadian citizen."

"The way he's been talking lately," she replied, "I wouldn't be surprised. But one day at a time." Garrett wrapped his arm around her waist, and she laid her head on his shoulder. "I sure would miss him."

Garrett kissed the top of her head. "You can visit anytime you like. I have a spare bedroom. Or maybe you could just relocate. There's plenty of work for qualified vets like you."

Joanna looked at him and grinned. "Slow down there, sparky. One day at a time, remember?"

He chuckled. "I'm trying. But life is short, you know?"

"Oh . . . trust me, I do know."

The train approached and slowed to a halt in front of them. As the doors slid open, a voice said, "Mind the gap," and they stepped across. They found seats next to each other and waited for the doors to close.

Joanna linked her arm through Garrett's and rested her head on his shoulder. Then he reached for her hand, raised it to his lips, and kissed the back of it.

Seconds later, the train lurched forward, and they were on their way to an undiscovered future.

AUTHOR'S NOTE

This novel is a work of fiction, but Sable Island does exist in the open Atlantic, just over 290 kilometers (about 180 miles) off the coast of Nova Scotia, Canada. I've been fascinated by its existence since I was a child in elementary school, in the 1970s, where it was part of the curriculum and I did a class project about it.

For many years it was difficult to visit the island, but in 2013 the federal government of Canada took over its management and designated it as a national park reserve. It's still a challenge to get there, but I took a research trip in July 2023. If you'd like to read about that and view some pictures, feel free to visit my website blog at http://www.juliannemaclean.com/research-trip-to-sable-island.

Interestingly, I wrote the first hundred pages of this novel during a turbulent period in my home province of Nova Scotia. In May 2023, we had to evacuate our home due to wildfires (thankfully our house was spared), and in June, we lived through severe flooding after a major storm that dumped three months' worth of rain on us within a twenty-four-hour period (and Nova Scotia gets a lot of rain!). The weather seemed strangely fitting as I was writing about the fictional storm that caused the wreck of the *Belvedere*.

Regarding that element of the story, I drew inspiration from an actual historical event that occurred in 1853. Dorothea Dix—a social activist who was ahead of her time in the area of mental health issues and paved the way for Nova Scotia's first psychiatric hospital—visited

Sable Island to inspect the living conditions. While she was there, she witnessed a shipwreck where the captain refused to abandon his ship. She insisted that the lifesaving crew go back out and remove him by force. She then counseled him afterward and helped him through the ordeal, and that event became the seed from which my entire novel grew. (As always, research plays an important part in my creative process.)

Another aspect of the novel based on fact is the existence of the government-run lifesaving station, otherwise known as the Humane Establishment. It began in 1801 for the purpose of providing rescue and shelter for shipwreck survivors, and to salvage valuable cargo as well. It remained operational until 1958, when it was no longer required due to technological advancements in radar and sonar. Before that, the last major shipwreck had occurred in 1947. (I took some artistic license in the plot of my novel, where John Clarkson leaves the island in 1955, and the fictional wreck of the *Belvedere* occurs in the spring of 1946.)

As for the weather station, it had been delivering daily weather reports to the mainland since the 1800s. Personnel began launching weather balloons in 1944, and this practice continued until very recently. The last weather balloon was launched from the Sable Island station on August 20, 2019. Visit www.sableislandinstitute.org/merlin-macaulay-1955-1956/ to view historic photos of the weather station around the time my novel is set.

And let us not forget the horses. They're still there today, living wild in the natural habitat without any assistance or intervention from man. This is due to a law that was enacted in 1961 by Prime Minister John Diefenbaker, after a public campaign to protest a plan to remove the horses from the island and put them up for sale (which could have resulted in many being slaughtered for dog food). The law's intent was to protect the horses indefinitely.

If you would like to learn more about Sable Island, I recommend the following books, which were instrumental in my research.

Sable Island, by Bruce Armstrong

Sable Island: The Strange Origins and Curious History of a Dune Adrift in the Atlantic, by Marq de Villiers and Sheila Hirtle

Our Sable Island Home, by Sharon O'Hara and Mary O'Hara

Sable Island in Black and White, by Jill Martin Bouteillier

Sable Island: The Ecology and Biodiversity of Sable Island, edited by Bill Freedman

Sable Island: Tales of Tragedy and Survival from the Graveyard of the Atlantic, by Johanna Bertin

There are also some excellent documentaries available. I highly recommend a short black-and-white film produced by the National Film Board of Canada and released in 1956, which is around the time my novel is set. You can see footage of the supply ship as it delivers goods to the beach, a house buried in sand, Quonset huts, and wild horses. The file is available online at www.nfb.ca/film/sable_island/.

Another film worth watching is an episode of *Land & Sea*, "Sable Island," produced by CBC Nova Scotia. It had an original air date of June 2, 2013. You can currently find it on YouTube. Also look for *Geographies of Solitude*, an award-winning Canadian documentary by Jacquelyn Mills, released in 2022. The film follows Zoe Lucas, a naturalist and environmentalist, who has lived on Sable Island for most of her life.

Lastly, here are some websites worth checking out:

Friends of Sable Island Society, at www.sableislandfriends.ca

Sable Island National Park Reserve, at www.parks.canada.ca/pn-np/ns/sable

Sable Island Institute, at www.sableislandinstitute.org

ACKNOWLEDGMENTS

Thank you to my daughter, Laura, for unearthing that little nugget out of history and suggesting it might be good fodder for a novel. You were right! You gave me something that finally set me on the path to Sable Island.

To the incredible team at Lake Union Publishing—you remain this author's dream come true, especially my editor Alicia Clancy, for your incredible instincts and good sense about pacing, character development, and other things I could go on and on about. Every comment you make in the margins is pure gold and spot on. My books are so much better with you backstage, behind the curtain.

Thanks to Fred Stillman with Kattuk Expeditions for the trip to Sable Island in 2023, which allowed me to get my feet on the ground and experience the setting and helicopter ride firsthand. Many unique and special experiences from the day found their way into this book, and your narration about the horses, vegetation, and other topics gave me great material to enhance the atmosphere.

Thanks also to the Maritime Museum of the Atlantic for maintaining your collection of historical photographs and for allowing me into your archives to explore.

On a personal note, thanks always to my agent, Paige Wheeler, for more than twenty-five years of support. I'm grateful to have you in my corner. You've kept me in the game, which has allowed me to have a full-time, lifelong career as a writer.

To Michelle Killen (a.k.a. Michelle McMaster) for being my trusted first reader. And lastly, I'm grateful, Stephen, for your incredible brain. Seriously, your smarts make my books so much better in so many ways, and you make research fun, whether we're traveling, talking, or googling. I love you.

QUESTIONS FOR DISCUSSION

1. At the end of the novel, Emma describes herself as a "life-long student of the human condition." In what ways was this evident in part 1 of the novel?

2. When Logan enters Emma's life, do you believe she was vulnerable to a con artist who was only looking out for himself? Or do you believe that their marriage could have been a success if he had not committed a crime before arriving on Sable Island? Why or why not?

3. Consider Emma's emotions and state of mind in the following passage from chapter 13, after she kisses Logan for the first time: "For a moment, Emma stood and looked up at the stars. It was all so astonishingly beautiful: The night sky. The constant roar of the ocean. *Life.* Eventually, she climbed the porch steps and smiled when she reached the door. There was so much joy in her heart. Where had it come from?" Where do you think it was coming from, for Emma? Discuss sources of joy in your own life.

4. At the time when the novel takes place, PTSD was not commonly understood in general society. How do you think this lack of understanding might have affected Oliver's relationship with his wife, Mary? Consider both their points of view.

5. Discuss how the setting of a novel can be as important to the story as each of the main characters. Consider elements of this novel in your answer.

6. At the end of chapter 32, Oliver makes the following decision: "It was time to go home. Time to go home to his children." Discuss how, in the book, the love of one's children conflicts with the lure of a romantic or soulful love outside of a marriage. Do you believe the characters made the right choices?

7. Horses are a constant presence in the novel. What do you think they symbolize? Which scenes involving horses resonated the most with you as a reader, and why?

8. Do novels inspire you to travel? What places in the world would you like to visit because of a novel you've read, and what was the novel? Have you ever gone somewhere to experience a setting you admired in a novel, movie, or television show?

9. When Logan arrives at Ruth's home and wants to meet his son, Matthew, did you think he and Emma might reconcile? At that point in the story, did you want them to try again?

10. The central love story between Emma and Oliver spans decades. Would you describe it as tragic? Why or why not?

11. Discuss the novel's title, *All Our Beautiful Goodbyes*. Which goodbyes were beautiful? Was there any beauty in those that were painful? Explain.

12. What was your favorite scene in the novel, and why?

ABOUT THE AUTHOR

Photo © 2013 Jenine Panagiotakos, Blue Vine Photography

Julianne MacLean is a *USA Today* bestselling author of more than thirty novels, including the popular Color of Heaven series. Readers have described her books as "breathtaking," "soulful," and "uplifting." MacLean is a four-time Romance Writers of America RITA finalist and has won numerous awards, including the Booksellers' Best Award and a Reviewers' Choice Award from the *Romantic Times*. Her novels have sold millions of copies worldwide and appear in more than a dozen languages.

MacLean studied in Nova Scotia, earning a degree in English literature from the University of King's College in Halifax and a business degree from Acadia University in Wolfville. She loves to travel and has lived in New Zealand, Canada, and England. The author currently resides on the east coast of Canada in a lakeside home with her husband and daughter. Readers can visit her website at www.juliannemaclean. com for more information about her books and writing life and to subscribe to her mailing list for all the latest news.